Murder for Hire: The Peruvian Pigeon

MURDER FOR HIRE

The
Peruvian Pigeon

DANA FREDSTI

YELLOWBACK MYSTERIES
JAMES A. ROCK & COMPANY, PUBLISHERS
ROCKVILLE • MARYLAND

Murder For Hire: The Peruvian Pigeon by Dana Fredsti

is an imprint of JAMES A. ROCK & CO., PUBLISHERS

Murder For Hire: The Peruvian Pigeon copyright ©2007 by Dana Fredsti

Special contents of this edition copyright ©2007
by James A. Rock & Co., Publishers

All Cover Photos ©2007 by Dana Fredsti,
from the archives of MFH Publicity

Address comments and inquiries to:

YELLOWBACK MYSTERIES

James A. Rock & Company, Publishers
9710 Traville Gateway Drive, #305
Rockville, MD 20850

E-mail:
jrock@rockpublishing.com   lrock@rockpublishing.com
Internet URL: www.rockpublishing.com

Paperback ISBN: 978-1-59663-571-5

Library of Congress Control Number: 2007928488

Printed in the United States of America

First Edition: 2007

This book is dedicated
to the cast and crew of
Murder for Hire
(especially Chris 'The Thug' Galante;
Bill 'The Target' Galante;
Mom 'The Judge' Galante;
and Brian 'Flyboy' Thomas'),
but most of all,
to my best friend and
former partner-in-crime,
Maureen 'the Moll' Anderson

Acknowledgments

First I'd like to thank my sister, Lisa, and the rest of the Lurking Novelists (all excellent writers) for their support and critique during the final rewrite of *MFH*, especially Lisa for her constant encouragement of my writing throughout the years. Lisa, I officially forgive you for blackmailing me when we played Monopoly back when we were kids.

A big thanks and a hug to T. Chris 'Cookie' Martindale for your support and continued inspiration since our friendship began. FMOZI forever!

Thank you, Brian, for the years of love and friendship, and for doing what Mo and I asked in the shows even when you thought we were insane. You were the only actor to successfully out-improv Phil, and Mo and I will never forget 'Lumpy' and the lethal chocolate chip cookies.

I'd also like to thank Mom (the Judicial system doesn't know what it's missing), Bill (who took a bullet to the head in the line of duty), Chris (best thug/beat poet ever), for all of the hard work they put into our shows. Huge thanks to Marty and Jan Anderson for putting up with all of our rehearsals at their house! Also Becky, Phil, Teri, Steve, Mark, Greg, Max, Linda, Jim, Marsha, Tony, Dean, George, Peter, and anyone I might be forgetting.

Thanks to Dad for once telling me that I wrote 'like a misogynistic drunken man' (the narrator was a misogynistic zombie detective, so this was a GOOD thing). It made me laugh and try even harder.

Special thanks to Pilar Perez for her help on "A Man's Gotta Eat;" Dave S., Richard and Bess for their generosity and willingness to celebrate my successes; and Dave F. for his love, support, and firm belief in my future success.

Thank you, Joe & Sandy, for EFBC-FCC. Working at the "cathouse" provided much-needed feline therapy when the writing wasn't going so well.

Thanks to Mary at Adlib for the time she put into *MFH*; Dana Wright for her efforts to agent it; Tom Basinski for sharing his marketing knowledge and taking the time to read *MFH*; and Julie Walke for her generous offer to help with publicity. And a very special thanks to James Rock for saying 'yes' to my book, and to Lynne Rock for all of her enthusiasm and help in the production process.

And finally, (drum roll please!) a huge thank you to Brad Linaweaver (please note I spelled your name correctly for once!) for all of your help in getting this puppy published. Your unwavering faith in my writing and your relentless agenting on my behalf made it happen. You read all the drafts, even the bad ones, and I owe you a bottle of Tullamore Dew!

Prologue

The sun was setting as he pulled into his usual spot at the back of the Emerald Cove Library parking lot. He turned off the engine and tried to ignore the shooting pains in his hip and back as he slowly got out of the car. It was an older model Cadillac, the kind of vehicle referred to as a boat, especially by those unlucky enough to get stuck behind it in single lane traffic. He knew he drove too cautiously, but his reflexes seemed to get duller every year and it was either err on the side of caution or give up driving altogether. And he wasn't ready to make that inevitable concession to age quite yet.

Too many pleasures were things of the past because of the heart attack. He was determined to enjoy the things that were still available to him—a few not on his doctor's approved list—as long as he could. Thank God his taste buds were still strong and he could enjoy the fruits of years of wine collecting. He'd once sworn that some of those bottles would never be opened, but if there was one thing a near-death experience had taught him, it was that you really couldn't take it with you.

It was also a blessing that he had always enjoyed swimming because it was the one form of exercise officially sanctioned by his doctor that didn't bore him to death. Of course, the good doctor had no idea that his patient did the prescribed laps in the ocean rather than a heated indoor pool.

Opening the Cadillac's trunk, he detached the ignition key from the ring and tucked it in the little Velcroed pocket of a wristband he'd bought at a surf shop. He secreted the other keys under the spare tire. A gust of chill wind blew through the parking lot as he took out his towel and slammed the trunk shut. Summer had definitely passed the torch on to Autumn and he knew that soon the evening swims would have to be curtailed for a while. He was a strong swimmer, always had been, but he wasn't going to risk hypothermia or pneumonia and the winter currents were harsh and unpredictable.

The side gate of the library was unlocked. The head librarian knew he liked his evening swim and left the beach access open for him, trusting him to lock it after he was finished. He paused to strip down to his bathing trunks, leaving his clothes in a neatly folded pile on the side porch.

He carefully picked his way down the wooden stairs that led to the semi-private beach. He always anticipated the moment after entering the water when the initial cold shock of it wore off, the moment when his aches, pains and daily frustrations were forgotten in the buoyant salt water. The years always dropped away as he dived through the waves like a kid before finally reaching the calm beyond the break.

He paused at the bottom of the stairs for a moment to enjoy the last hint of fire as the sun dipped below the sun. Then without further hesitation, he strode down into the water and plunged in.

When he emerged, exhausted yet rejuvenated a half hour later, the beach was dark. Between that and the water in his eyes, he never saw the blow to his back that dropped him to his knees or the person who delivered it. A second blow sent him sprawling face down in the surf. Salt water filled his mouth and nostrils as a wave curled up and broke over him. He tried to lift his head out of the water, but something sharp pressed down on his neck, grinding his face into the sand until he lost consciousness.

Chapter One

"Hand it over, Club! We know you got it." Scarface Tony's face twisted into a snarl as he pointed his '45 at Carl Club. *"Hold out on us and you'll be leaking tomato sauce all over your nice, shiny floor."*

"Yeah," grunted the other gorilla, towering over Club in a stance meant to intimidate.

"I don't know what you punks are talking about." Unintimidated, Club stared coolly at the two thugs.

"C'mon Club," Scarface barked. *"We want the goods! You know, the loot, the dough, the clams, the hot ice, the moola, the do-re-mi!"*

Club looked at them contemptuously. "I don't got what you scum are looking for. And I ain't no stoolie. And you can tell that to your sauerkraut sucking, Nazi boss."

"Take him, Tiny!" Scarface shouted as the big gorilla lunged, catching Club in a choke hold. "You had your chance, Club. Now you'll be dripping arterial ketchup all over your office ..."

"Oof!"

The seamy world of Carl Club evaporated back into our living room as Brad, aka 'Carl Club' took a real punch to the gut from Chris 'Scarface' Giametti. Everyone immediately broke character as Brad doubled over. Chris stood to one side, looking sheepish.

"Oh, jeez!" I jumped to my feet. "Brad, are you okay?"

Brad wheezed in reply. Further inquiries as to his condition were forestalled by the piercing ring of our phone.

Glancing at my friend and business partner, Daphne Graves, as she watched the action from a comfortable vantage point on the couch, I pointed towards the ringing phone. "I've got to run the fight choreography," I said reasonably. "Besides," I couldn't resist adding, "It's probably Guido." Guido, an Italian sculptor, was current in the long line of neurotics that made up Daphne's boyfriends.

Daphne gave me a dirty look, but hauled herself up from the couch, which had been pushed against the wall to make room for rehearsal. She headed for the extension in the kitchen, muttering, "I need a drink. Something hot, cheap, and strong."

"Make enough for everyone!" I called after her, knowing Daphne's idea of a stiff drink was a few shots of hot chocolate in her gut. She hates the taste of alcohol as much as she loves the hard-boiled prose of Dashiell Hammett and Mickey Spillane. "We're going to need it."

"We're gonna need more than cocoa," muttered Brad, eyeing 'Scarface' with justifiable apprehension.

Shaun, otherwise known as 'Tiny,' nodded in agreement, also giving Chris a rather dubious look.

Chris was a handsome, muscular ex-Marine who bore a slight resemblance to Sly Stallone. Getting him to throw a punch without lethal impact was not without its difficulties. Although Chris had been out of the military for about six months, he still took his combat training very seriously. I take my fighting seriously as well, but my training was in theatrical combat, not in how to kill the enemy in a variety of messy ways. Chris and I had been at loggerheads over the fights ever since he joined Murder for Hire two months ago and I was beginning to suspect that we needed a drill sergeant, not a director, in order to get him to cooperate. Damn good thing he didn't have a problem taking orders from a woman or I'd have killed him by now.

"Okay! Let's try that part from 'Take him, Tiny,' okay?" I smiled encouragingly at Brad, who clutched his stomach protectively and nodded.

"Take him, Tiny!" Scarface shouted as the big gorilla lunged …

"Wait a moment!"

The three actors stopped in mid-action.

"We haven't even done anything yet," protested Shaun.

"That's my point. I've told you guys before that you have to be a lot quicker on that first punch!" I stood up and paced as I talked. "Shaun, you have to lunge the second Chris says 'Take him, Tiny!' "

"Okay." Shaun was not one for wasting words.

"Try it again."

They did so. This time Shaun lunged immediately, but Chris mixed up the order of his punches and blocks and clipped Brad sharply on the jaw.

"Shit!" Brad grabbed his chin and stumbled back a few paces.

"Oh, jeez, I'm sorry!"

"Chris," I said very carefully, "it's duck, block, *then* hit, not duck, hit, then block. We've been over this section before."

"I know, Connie! I'm sorry! But in the Marines they trained us to always be on the offensive so these moves just aren't natural!"

I took a deep breath, trying to ignore the voice in my head chanting that line from the song *Alice's Restaurant*, 'Why do you want to be a Marine, young man? Because I wanna *killllllll*.'

"It's not supposed to be natural," I finally said as patiently as was possible, given the circumstances and my temperament. "It's supposed to be stylized."

"Yeah, but *realistically* stylized," Chris said insistently. If his brow lowered any further, we'd be able to use it for shelf space. "It shouldn't be unnatural."

"Hey, that would make our fight an unnatural act," Shaun said helpfully. "Isn't that illegal in California?"

Brad rubbed his jaw. "It should be."

I massaged my temples, feeling the first stirrings of a headache. Great, and we'd only been rehearsing for a half hour.

"Guys, let's take a break, okay?"

No arm twisting was necessary to convince them. All three immediately headed for the kitchen, drawn, no doubt, by the wafting odor of brewing cocoa and recently baked chocolate chip cookies. I'd join them, but not quite yet.

Collapsing on an over-stuffed sofa next to JD (short for Jack Daniels), a large black, spherical feline of sanguine temperament, I enjoyed a few minutes of solitude. I shut my eyes, willing my headache to fade back into oblivion, and listened to the comforting sounds of the clink of crockery as Daphne filled mugs with her latest variety of hot cocoa. I idly wondered what she'd added this time. Grated orange peel? Mint? Perhaps cinnamon. Daphne's creativity knew no bounds when it came to two things: bad forties dialogue and cocoa.

Both talents are a definite asset to Murder For Hire, of which Daphne and I are the owners, producers, writers and directors. MFH is a theatrical group dedicated to parodying various genres in the mystery field. Our floating troupe of actors can and have done just about everything in the way of mystery-oriented entertainment. We've done full-out murder mystery weekends, staged kidnappings at parties, and pastiched, parodied and lampooned everything from gothics to Sherlock Holmes. No author, however revered, is safe from our heavy-handed pen and sometimes sledgehammer humor.

Our specialty is the classic 40's hard-boiled detective story, allowing Daphne to come up with such dialogue as:

> ... *the solution to this case was gnawing at me, hanging around my subconscious like a fart in a phone booth.*

I've been known to come up with a few gems myself, but Daphne is really the evil genius behind our '40s parodies.

We usually feature Carl Club, toughest P.I. this side of Frisco. Club is your basic lone-wolf gumshoe, a guy whose job is to nail crooks and send them to the slammer without getting his own belly ventilated by the various scum who inhabit the mean streets of Emerald Cove. Club, with the able assistance of his loyal secretary, Betty, has solved mysteries on trains, in hotels, at private parties, wherever MFH has been hired to perform.

We were currently rehearsing for our latest job, the Emerald Cove Shay Randell Festival designed to celebrate the opening of the new community library. The late Shay Randell was a famous author who'd lived and worked during the late fifties in our seaside community of Emerald Cove. As the creator of the now famous PI. Mick O'Mallet, Randell was a legend in our town and was thus being honored posthumously with a week-long festival that included lectures, film adaptations of his work and walking tours of local landmarks mentioned in his books. We were scheduled to perform scenes during the walking tours at various points, ending up at the Emerald Cove Hotel where, rumor has it, Randell used to drink himself into a stupor on a nightly basis.

The culmination of the Festival was going to be a Charity Ball held at the new library, featuring local—and a few national—celebrities, and a presentation of MFH's most popular original piece, *The Peruvian Pigeon*.

Of course, if I couldn't whip the fights into shape, this might be the last time we performed *Pigeon*, at least with Brad as Carl Club. And that would be a shame because Brad, with his craggy face and tall, barrel-chested build, was probably the best Carl Club we'd had. He also looked older than his twenty-eight years, which helped sustain the illusion of a down-and-out private dick.

I heaved a heavy sigh, causing JD to stretch out one black paw towards my chin and *mrrrp* inquiringly. "Sorry, baby." I scritched under JD's chin, prompting a buzz sawing purr that threatened to choke her with happiness. She rolled onto her back, exposing a fat stomach with a single white tuft of fur amidst the black. Giving into the impulse to rub my face against the softness of JD's fur and eliciting an indignant squeak when I flugaled her stomach, I decided to take advantage of Daphne's culinary talent and have a strong, fortifying cup of cocoa before the impending arrival of our other actors, including my current boyfriend, Grant Havers.

Just thinking of Grant turned the niggling headache from a hint to a serious threat. I hurried to the kitchen for a comforting cup of cocoa and a couple of Excedrin.

Daphne was in the midst of putting fresh baked cookies on a rack to cool and the guys were lounging around the kitchen table, partially filled mugs of cocoa in front of them. A plate that had undoubtedly once been full of chocolate chip cookies, but now held only the crumbs, sat in the middle of the table next to a bottle of Laphroig.

I stared at Brad and Daphne accusingly. I knew Brad's fondness for single malt scotches was rivaled only by my own, but only Daphne knew where I'd hidden my scotch. It wasn't so much that I minded sharing—although the cost of Laphroig was not often within my budget—but drinking during rehearsals, *especially* when we were running fights, was a no-no.

Daphne hastily handed me a steaming mug of cocoa, strong enough to put hair on my chest and said, "Drink this, Connie. You'll need it when I tell you who called. You might even want some of the scotch."

This didn't sound good. Didn't look good either because Daphne kept pushing her hair back. This was a sure sign of turbulence as Daphne normally loved to wear her dark, glossy mane over one eye, a la Veronica Lake (or Jessica Rabbit, take your pick). It usually ended up covering half her face.

"You mean it wasn't Guido begging for a minute of your time?" I asked, taking a careful sip of the cocoa. Mmmmmm … Cinnamon this time. "Daph-a-nee, I luv you, mia bella!"

Daphne scowled. "No. And for once it wasn't Grant telling us that he was going to be late because of a 'call from his agent'."

"She shoots, she scores." Brad hooted from the table.

I gave him a look and then glanced at the clock above the stove. Twenty after 5:00. "He's already late, along with Barry. And where the hell is Tasha, Brad?" Tasha, our costumer and part-time actress, was Brad's live-in girlfriend. I took an evil satisfaction in the fact that she was late, along with Grant.

Brad shrugged. "She's working late, remember? Off at 6:00, be here as soon as she can. Told you last week." He toasted me with a shot of my expensive scotch. I thought about telling Chris to do the fight choreography the way they did in the Marines. The thought made me smile at Brad, who eyed me warily. Wise man.

Daphne tapped me on the shoulder, distracting me from jolly visions of Carl Club lying in a pool of his own tomato sauce. "Connie, Barry isn't going to be here."

"What?!" My cocoa sloshed over the edge of the cup and Daphne stepped back a pace. I tried to moderate my tone. "He's not going to be here at all? We're not just talking late? What about tomorrow?"

"He got a part in some play at the Quarry Theater and rehearsals start tonight."

I sat down at the table, shut my eyes and took a deep breath. Then another. A friend of Brad's, Barry was fresh out of college, theater degree clutched in his fist and hot to make his splash in the local scene. He had just joined MFH, making it clear all the while that his interest lay in *real* theater, not in a 'performance troupe'. Only the fact that Barry was an excellent actor and that we were short a necessary male kept the rest of MFH from killing him. I did not, however, refrain from pointing out that MFH paid much better than most *real* theater in the area, including the prestigious and pretentious Quarry Theater. The Randell Festival would've been Barry's first actual performance with MFH.

Oh, but he would fit in well at The Quarry. Their plays tended to run for three hours, usually included a strong theme of misogyny—their version of *Taming of the Shrew* included black-eye make-up for the actress playing Kate, and *Hamlet* had a graphic rape scene that made even The Quarry's staunchest supporters wince—or were so experimental in theme as to be unintelligible. Imagine, if you have a strong stomach, a play consisting of five actors dressed in black sitting with their backs to the audience the entire time. For two and a half hours. The theme? Alienation.

When all was said and done, however, this left us short one actor three days before performance time. Goddamn actors ... Flaky, narcissistic, obsessed with the prevention of age and weight gain, actors were convinced that it was both their privilege and their nature to be temperamental.

I should know. For several years I'd done the routine myself as an actress and stuntwoman in Hollywood. I am proud to say that I resisted the temptation to get a boob job (maxing out my credit card for a couple of bags of saline just didn't seem worth it), but after too many rejections based on the wrong color hair (dark auburn) and breasts the wrong size (34B), I decided to put my energy into other areas. I had better luck getting stunt work, but a close call doing a fall while doubling a lousy actress (blonde, 38C) on a low-budget film gave my self-esteem a battering that required a strategic retreat and a long, hard look at my career goals. So at the age of 29, I'd gathered up my belongings, which included two cats, far too much clothing and an extensive music collection, and headed back to my hometown of Emerald Cove to reconsider my life.

But now was not the time or place for introspection. It wasn't doing a damned thing to solve the current crisis and it might lead to the question of why the hell I was currently dating an actor, given my knowledge and experience.

Opening my eyes, I accepted the shot of Laphroig that Shaun was silently holding out to me in hopes of averting an explosion.

I downed half the shot with one flick of my wrist. "Okay ... better now. So we need another actor. Someone who can pick up lines, blocking and fight choreography in three days. Any ideas?"

The silence was deafening. I slammed back the rest of the scotch. The boys, as Daphne and I refer to our male actors (out of their hearing, of course), sipped their respective beverages and looked thoughtful. Well, Chris looked pained, but I'd learned from experience that this was a sign that the thought process was indeed engaged. Daphne tried to fuel her brain by eating three cookies in quick succession, all calories and fat undoubtedly going straight to her already ample bosom.

Daphne, you see, is built like Monroe in her younger days, with more curves than Lombard Street. And no matter how assiduously she avoids exercise, she never seems to put on weight in areas that detract from her figure. I, on the other hand, out of necessity am a firm believer in exercise in order to eat those extra chocolate chip cookies without fear. I ate one, hoping it would give me inspiration not supplied by the Laphroig.

Letting the buttery, brown-sugary, chocolate-studded delight fill my taste buds, I waited for the proverbial creative light bulb. Sorry, my brain said snidely, your electric bill has *not* been paid this month.

Shaun, however, was evidently up to date on his internal utility bills. "I've got a friend whose brother's staying with him for a few weeks, taking a break from work." He paused and looked at all of us before finally adding, "He might work out." Shaun sometimes has a way of weighting his words, pausing so that the simplest sentence seems fraught with deep inner meaning. We've learned that it usually isn't.

"Is he an actor?" Daphne asked.

"Kind of. I mean, Chas said Alex—that's his brother's name—has done some acting, but I think he's mainly a stuntman."

I groaned. A stuntman? I now had proof that God *did* hate me. 75 percent (and I offer an apology in advance to that oh too small 25 percent that's left) of all stuntmen are nothing but chauvinistic egos with legs. Usually well-muscled legs, mind you, but that was not enough compensation for having to deal with their attitudes, their tantrums, and a boys club atmosphere so thick with testosterone that you can feel hair growing on your chest just by breathing in the same air as more than one of them. When I'd been working in stunts, the trend had been a deplorable tendency for the men to build up their bodies to the extent that their heads perched upon these massive shoulders with comic disproportion. 'Pinheaded' was a perfect description.

"What's wrong with stuntmen?" Shaun asked, offended that his suggestion had met with resistance.

"Nothing, if you like pinheaded, chauvinistic dickheads," I growled, eating another cookie.

"Like Marines," grunted Chris.

"Don't hold back, Connie, tell us how you *really* feel," Brad said under his breath.

I shot him a look, then turned back to Shaun. "*Reader's Digest* Version—"

"Thank God," muttered Daphne.

"—as a woman in the stunt business, I found most of them to be total jerks. The ratio of macho to intelligence is way too high in favor of macho, they're condescending towards women …"

"Kind of like Connie is towards men," Brad interjected, deftly ducking the piece of cookie I promptly threw at him even as I continued my tirade.

" … and they all have a much higher opinion of their fighting skill than reality warrants. Scratch a stuntman who says he knows how to swordfight and you'll find an extra who waved a sword around in the background of *Swashbuckler.*"

I paused, out of breath. Brad poured us both another shot of scotch while shaking with suppressed laughter. My tirades have that affect on him, just as his laughter clues me in on the fact that I'm overreacting to the situation at hand.

Daphne drank some cocoa and put in her sensible two cents. "Connie, they can't all be that bad. You've said yourself that you've worked with some nice ones. You can't just assume this guy is going to be a jerk."

"Yeah," said Brad. "Maybe he's of the non-pinheaded variety."

I laughed at that. Brad always did a good job of puncturing my bad moods, no pun intended.

"Okay, guys. We don't have much choice," I conceded. "Let's try giving this guy a call, Shaun. If he's interested, see if you can get him over here tonight."

Shaun made the call, but Alex wasn't in. "Chas said he'll have Alex call if he gets in tonight." Shaun looked apologetic.

"Good enough," I replied. "Let's get back to those fights for now. When Grant and Tasha get here, we can ask them if they know anyone else to call."

"Perhaps we might be lucky enough to get another out-of-work Soap star," Brad said to no one in particular.

"Brad, you are *such* a bitch," Chris commented in mincing tones. Being a Marine had done nothing for his sense of political correctness. He ambled back out into the living room, followed closely by Brad, Shaun and Daphne.

I shook my head as I reluctantly stood up, resigned to another session of frustration with the fight choreography no doubt enlivened by more snide comments about Grant, the soon-to-be out-of-work Soap star Brad was referencing. The worst part was that most of the comments were deserved, so there was nothing I could say in Grant's defense. I used to try to justify his behavior, but time and proximity had shown me the futility of my efforts.

Grant Havers, my current flame. My boyfriend. My significant other. My—dare I say it?—lover. We'd originally met on the set of a 'B' horror movie, Grant playing the charismatic head of a satanic cult, myself stunt doubling for his high priestess of evil. There was definitely an attraction between us, but immediately after the shoot ended, Grant got cast as a broodingly attractive doctor in *Tomorrow's Secret Search,* a daytime soap, I'd gotten involved in another low-budget film, and we'd gone our separate ways. And if I had known what I knew now, it might have stayed that way.

Not being particularly gifted with psychic ability, when I ran into Grant at a party thrown by some wealthy 'theatah' friends in Emerald Cove and discovered that the mutual attraction was still strong … Well, I'm not a saint. And neither is Grant.

So when I found out that Grant was staying with the same friends for an extended period of time as TSS was 'temporarily on hold', its fate being decided by the Network Scheduling Gods, it seemed like a natural thing to ask if Grant wanted to be part of MFH's troupe for the time being. He could still attend auditions, the time commitment was minimal and the pay, while nowhere near Union wages, was decent.

Grant was gorgeous, intelligent, talented, sophisticated, and—so I thought—had a sense of humor. I was in heaven. So when the other actors, including Daphne, starting complaining that Grant was condescending, didn't take them seriously, while taking himself *too* seriously, I defended him. It was his *art* he took seriously, not himself, I argued. And sure, he could be a little bit pompous on occasion and tended to dominate conversations at times, but he was so *interesting.* And no one could fault his acting. He was much better than Barry, who was *really* annoying.

"But, Connie," Daphne had said patiently after listening to my Ten Reasons Why Grant Is An Asset To MFH And To Connie Garrett, "he's treating you like a possession, not a person."

"Jeez, Daphne," I'd retorted impatiently, "I actually find a guy who likes to buy me clothes and you think he's *bad* for me?"

Ah, the blindness of love … I still cringe inwardly when I remember my justifications and rationalizations of Grant's subtly belittling behavior towards everyone in MFH, the definite attitude that he was the only *real* actor in the troupe. He and Barry had a lot in common.

Bottom line, Daphne was right. Grant was one of those men who feel obliged to try and change the very things that supposedly attracted them to a woman in the first place. My independence was a challenge, something to be broken down and controlled. My creativity? Something he encouraged and undermined at the same time, a subtle campaign to make me believe I couldn't do it without him. And yes, he did buy me clothes and jewelry, not to mention perfume. All high quality, very expensive. Every woman's dream, right? Wrong. It soon became apparent that Grant was on a campaign to dress me to his taste (conservatively tasteful, designer labels on everything), not mine (flamboyant and/or comfortable, label irrelevant).

As all this became slowly apparent even to my love-struck brain, my personality and common sense began to reassert themselves. This in turn led to an increase in friction between us and the deepening conviction on my part that Grant and I were nearing the end of our relationship. Sensing my growing distance, Grant was becoming more possessive in his affections, making me increasingly uncomfortable. My mind was made up. After the Randell Festival, I intended to break it off between us. As for his involvement in MFH, I hoped that Grant was correct in his belief that something *big* was going to happen in his career within the month.

In the meantime, I could hear Brad going over the dialogue leading up to the fight scene. I needed to go and make sure that our resident ex-Marine didn't do permanent damage to Brad, no matter how great the temptation to let Chris do his worst. Or his best. Be all that you can be … No, wait, that was the Army. Or was it the Navy?

I shook my head to clear it of irrelevant jingoistic jingles. No doubt about it—the combined strain of dealing with the Festival and Grant were causing me to lose it.

Chapter Two

Twenty minutes later, Grant and Tasha had still not arrived, but the fights were looking much better. Daphne and I sat on either end of our sofa and watched as Brad effortlessly disarmed Chris without taking a blow to the gut or to the jaw. He then started to work on Shaun, keeping up a steady flow of descriptive narrative as he went along.

> *The goon dropped his roscoe when I crunched my grinders into his mitt. I cold-cocked him with a right to his smeller. The other baboon lunged for me and my legs turned to limp pasta as he sank a fist in my belly. As I grabbed for the bozo's ...*

The phone rang mid-monologue. Happy with the way the fights were shaping up, I left Daphne to oversee the rest of the scene and went in the kitchen to answer it. Maybe it was Shaun's friend's brother, the stuntman. I could hardly wait to see if he could use words of more than two syllables.

I grabbed the receiver on the fourth ring, knocking over a stack of dirty plates that had been set on top of the cord. Tucking the receiver under my chin, I caught the dishes before they slid off the counter, giving a brusque 'hello' as I did so.

"Hello ... Daphne?"

"It's Connie. Hi, Andy." The second that I heard Andy Stewart's voice I knew that this conversation was going to bring trouble. Not because I had any sixth sense warning me of impending doom, mind you, but because every call we'd gotten from Andy since he'd hired us to perform at the Randell Festival had held some problem or another. Not that it was his fault. Head librarian at the new Emerald Cove Library, Andy was also the poor sucker who had to deal with all the various headaches that came with trying to organize something as complex as the Randell Festival. The whole shebang had been Andy's idea in the first place, but had he known what he was in for I bet he'd have kept his bright idea to himself.

Like so many other good ideas that should be relatively simple to plan and execute, the Randell Festival was plagued by bullshit and politics. Andy may have been head librarian and Chairman of the Festival Committee but he still had to pass everything through the rest of the Committee. This committee was composed of a dozen or so wealthy and influential Emerald Cove residents who also made up Friends of the Library, the organization responsible for funding the new library in the first place.

While many of the Friends were reasonable people who were content to put the running of the Festival and the library in Andy's capable hands, there were those who felt the need to stick their nose and fingers into every nook and cranny of both operations. And, like all organizations, there were the inevitable cliques and each one wanted things done *their* way, sometimes just to spite another faction. I was profoundly grateful we had Andy as a buffer between MFH and the Committee. If Andy was to believed, and I had no reason to doubt him, the War of the Roses had nothing on the Randell Festival Committee for political machinations and power plays.

Andy had hired MFH on the recommendation of our landlady, who was a volunteer at the library. Ever since our first meeting with Andy, during which he decided we were *simpatico*, Daphne and I averaged two calls a day from him; one to discuss the latest problem to be faced, the other to fill us in on the gossip and to allow Andy to blow off steam. This was not one of the latter.

"Connie, you're not going to believe this!" Andy's normally quiet tone was replaced by the voice of a man on the brink of a nervous breakdown. It seemed that each new stumbling block led Andy's nerves further down the path of slow deterioration.

"What's up, Andy?" I started stacking dishes in the sink. I might as well accomplish something during the call because I could tell this was going to be a long one.

His next words were unexpected, to say the least. "Damien Duran is dead. Drowned!"

This was a line worthy of a MFH production. All that alliteration was impossible to take seriously. So I laughed. "Boy, you must have spent all day thinking up that one, Andy. Seriously, what's up?"

"I *am* serious, Connie. Damien Duran is dead."

Andy's tone of voice left no room for doubt. Laughing had not been in good taste. Chastened, I said quickly, "I'm sorry, Andy. I didn't mean to be tacky. I thought you were joking."

"I wish I was." We were both silent for a moment, a respectful pause for Damien Duran, may he rest in peace. Whoever the hell he was.

"Do you know—" Andy said indignantly, breaking the silence, "—how much this throws my schedule off?"

"Your sched ..." I stopped. Obviously Andy and old Damien had not been close. So why was he telling me about this in the first place? Then suddenly my brain made the connection. Or, as Club would say, a clue crawled up my thigh and bit me on the ass. "Duran was a member of the Festival Committee, right?"

"That's right," Andy replied glumly.

Daphne and I had met most of the Committee members at one time or another. I remembered Duran as being an elderly man, very quiet and polite. Not an obvious player, if you'll pardon the Industry lingo, but I'd gotten the impression that his opinion carried weight. And he'd liked our writing, which automatically put him in my good graces.

"That's awful! Do they know how it happened?"

"They're not sure. His body washed up below the library by the caves."

"But what was he doing in the water in the first place? I mean, it's November."

"Damien liked his evening dip. And he was a good swimmer, by all accounts, but the currents must have been too strong for him last night."

"I'm sorry, Andy. You and he weren't good friends, were you?"

"Not really. I just let him use the library access to the beach. He is—or *was*, rather—a friend of Jason Downs."

"Ah." Jason Downs, a nationally syndicated newspaper columnist, was the main benefactor of the Randell Library. Downs was also a long-time Emerald Cove resident and took an active interest in any project that would benefit the community. He not only had a lot of clout, but was also supposed to be one hell of a nice guy. Daphne and I had as of yet to meet him.

"I know that Duran donated a great deal of money towards the building of the library, but I didn't really know him very well. He never seemed to have much to say, but whatever he did say usually carried the day. He seemed like a really nice guy." There was a brief pause before he added, "He was organizing the gala with Lucille. They didn't get along. Had a doozy of a fight at yesterday's board meeting."

Reason enough right there to be sorry the man was dead. More about Lucille later, but suffice it say that any enemy of hers was a friend of mine. Or would be if he were still alive.

"You know", Andy continued, "I feel like a real schmuck worrying about my schedule when the guy just bought the farm. But the show has to go on, and I'm the one who has to take up the slack."

Feeling that some comment was called for, I murmured something non-judgmental and encouraging, and waited for Andy to go on, which he did.

"Duran was supposed to pick up Jonathan Burke from the airport tonight and now I've got to cover for him."

"Who?" I had no idea what Andy was talking about.

"Jonathan Burke, the guy who's been commissioned to write the screenplay for Randell's last novel! *You* know, Connie, one of our guests of honor! Where have you *been* the last few weeks?"

"Sorry, Andy, I'm no good with names. But I'll take your word for it." I didn't have the heart to tell Andy that my interest in the Festival just didn't extend past the immediate job at hand for MFH. I love mysteries and I was overjoyed that Emerald Cove had a new library, but the life and times of Shay Randell left me cold. Daphne was the real forties aficionado of the group and probably knew all there was to know about Randell's last novel *and* Mr. Jonathan Burke.

Andy heaved a huge sigh. "Oh well, I guess I'd better get my butt in gear if I'm gonna get back in time for the program tonight. Are you and Daphne going?"

My mind went over the Festival agenda and drew a blank for tonight's scheduled entertainment.

"What's going on tonight?"

"They're showing *Down These Mean Streets* at the Museum. Starts at 8:00. The best adaptation of Randell's work ever brought to the silver screen. I'm sure Daphne's seen it."

"Oh, I'm sure we'll be there," I said without enthusiasm. The thought of going anywhere after rehearsal did not appeal to me, but Daphne would drag me there kicking and screaming if I put up a fuss. She'd already seen the film, and no doubt she'd be hot to see it again.

"Great! And there's a party in Jonathan Burke's honor being held at Jason Down's house afterwards. Naturally, you and your cast are invited."

"Are you sure that'll still be happening?" I asked dubiously. "I mean, on top of Damien Duran's death and all, will Mr. Downs still want to throw a party?" I knew I wouldn't if I were in his shoes.

"Oh, it'll still happen," Andy said firmly. "Emerald Cove society takes its social affairs very seriously. I'll see you tonight! Gotta run!"

"Bye, Andy."

I hung up the receiver and shook my head. What a soap opera this festival was becoming. Television and movies just didn't hold a candle to reality when it came to unbelievable events.

I looked in the cocoa pan. There was just enough left for half a mug, so I turned the burner on to re-heat it, skimming the skin off the top.

Waiting for the cocoa to warm, I took a moment to gaze contentedly around the roomy kitchen with its numerous oak cupboards, appreciating how lucky Daphne and I were to be able to live in such a nice house. The floors throughout the house were hardwood, comfortably scuffed with wear and covered in areas with throw rugs scavenged from second-hand stores or inexpensive antique markets. The ancient kitchen table and matching chairs were oak, sturdy and worn with age. Most of our furniture was old, actually, with the exception of the kitchen appliances and plumbing. The charm of an old house ends with decrepit stoves and corroded pipes.

When I'd first moved back to Emerald Cove, I'd stayed with Daphne in her one-bedroom apartment, putting my stuff in storage until I found my own place. A quick look at local rentals made it obvious that we'd be able to find a nicer place if we shared than either of us could afford on our own. And since we'd managed to come up with the idea for MFH without killing each other in such cramped quarters, the prospect of being roommates suited both of us quite well. Daphne's phlegmatic personality made a nice counterbalance to my undeniably volatile temperament.

It'd taken some time, but we'd finally lucked into a cozy two-bedroom, two-story Victorian within walking distance of Emerald Cove's central business district, as well as the beach. The place was owned by an eccentric woman by the name of DiSpachio. Mavis had a passion for theater and mysteries and was delighted to rent to the co-creators of a theatrical mystery organization. Credit check? Hah, not for us. Rent just a little more than we could afford? Not a problem, she'd lower the price. In short, Daphne and I got the bargain of a lifetime, although like most 'seems too good to be true' situations there were drawbacks. One was the presence of a guest cottage in back of the house, which rented out as a separate apartment, thankfully currently between tenants. The last renter had been an aspiring banjo player. Need I say more?

I poured the last of the cocoa into my mug and started for the living room just as Daphne stuck her head through the kitchen door and said, "Thought I'd warn you. Grant just pulled up outside."

I stopped mid-stride, sloshing cocoa over my baggy gray sweats. "Shit." Was there really a time where the mere sound of his name made my heart sing instead of my stomach hurt? I froze, total Bambi in the headlights time. The doorbell rang, blaring through the house in a horrendous homage to Big Ben. At least it didn't ring four times an hour like its namesake. I heard the front door open and Grant's deep, mellifluous voice greeting Brad, Chris and Shaun.

The phone rang. Daphne looked at me. "Shall I?"

"I'll be out in a sec," I replied, grabbing the receiver like a lifeline. Anything to avoid seeing Grant for a few more minutes.

"Pathetic," was Daphne's comment as she went back into the living room, selectively forgetting her own avoidance tactics when dealing with men who had worn out their welcome.

"Hello?"

"Uh … is Shaun there?" A deep, masculine voice, not as smooth as Grant's, but definitely appealing. It had to be the stuntman.

"Is this Alex?" I tried to put all prejudicial thoughts out of my mind.

"Uh, yeah."

Hmmm, two uh's in as many sentences. Not a good sign. Maybe he'd fallen on his head one too many times. I'd talk slowly.

"I'm Connie Garrett. Did your brother tell you why Shaun called?"

"Uh …" I winced. "Sort of. It was kind of garbled, though. Chas was into his second six-pack by the time I got back."

Oh, great. His brother was a party animal. Did it run in the family?

"Maybe I'd better explain," I said, not particularly hopeful that this was going to work out. "We have a theater group, Murder For Hire, and one of our actors bailed on us this evening, and …"

"Are you guys that hard to work with?" I recognized this as a joke, even if I didn't appreciate it.

"Depends on how much trouble our actors give us," I replied. "Which brings up my first question: Are you an actor or just a stuntman?" I did my best to avoid using any telltale inflection on my last four words.

I must have been unsuccessful, for there was a slight pause before Alex said, "I take it you don't like stuntmen much."

"They've got their uses," I said as noncommittally as possible. "But back to the question. Do you act?"

"What uses?" There was no hostility in his voice, just curiosity, so I tried to tone down my answer.

"If I had to pay someone to crash a car or set himself on fire, a stuntman would be my first choice. But we don't need anything that extreme in our show, just someone who can act a little, memorize lines, things like that." I couldn't stop myself from adding, "And no offense, but a lot of stuntmen I've met are lucky if they can memorize their own phone number."

There was silence from the other end of the line, so I continued, "Look, we really need to find an actor who can do some simple stage fighting as soon as possible, we have a show in three days and we're rehearsing tonight. It pays well, and the time commitment is minimal. Shaun seemed to think you might be interested. Are you?"

"Oh, I'm interested, all right. You've got my curiosity aroused."

Why did I get the feeling that he wasn't talking about the show? "Uh, can you come over and meet with us?"

"What time do you want me?"

He couldn't have meant it the way it came out, but I felt my face flush with color. There was something about his voice, an undercurrent of amusement mixed with a certain seductive quality that was making me flustered. "Uh …" Damn! " … as soon as possible." Oh, *that* sounded good, Connie. "I mean, could you be here in the next half hour?"

"Sure."

"Great!" I said far too heartily. "See you then." I hung up, wondering what the hell happened to my normal equilibrium. It'd been years since I'd gotten this flustered by a guy, let alone during a phone conversation.

The phone rang again. I picked it up. "Hello?"

"You want to give me your address or is mind reading a requirement as well as memorization?"

I shut my eyes, humiliated, and gave him our address. Served me right for being a bitch.

He repeated the address once, along with the directions I gave him.

"Do you have something to write with?" I had to ask.

"Nope. I'm working on my memorization. See you soon."

A reluctant grin curved my mouth as I hung up the receiver. If he had a sense of humor, this Alex guy couldn't be all bad. But then I'd thought Grant had a sense of humor at one time too.

"Hello, darling." I started at the sound of Grant's voice, stiffening involuntarily as he slid his arms around my waist from behind and planted a kiss on the side of my neck.

"Jesus, Grant, don't *do* that!"

"What? This?" He kissed the side of my neck again, his mouth warm and skillful as he moved it up towards my ear. A week ago, his touch would've been enough to melt any annoyance I felt at being taken by surprise. Even now it had an undeniable physical affect. But I wasn't in the mood for Grant or his kisses. I tugged at his arms, saying, "I've got to get back to rehearsal, Grant."

Grant ignored my resistance other than to tighten his grip ever so slightly as he turned me around to face him. Frustrated, I stared up into Grant's incredibly vivid blue eyes, part of his Black Irish inheritance. They were the kind of blue one normally only sees on cobalt glass, framed with thick black lashes that were the envy of all his female co-stars, as was his thick and carefully tousled mane of black hair. His features were chiseled with just enough ruggedness to save him from the pretty boy syndrome, and at six foot, four inches, his build was muscular without being grotesque. You know, the broad shoulders tapering into a slim waist, muscular thighs, blah blah blah. No doubt about it, Grant was certified hunk material.

Combine all the above with a large amount of facile charm and a voice that could melt butter without benefit of a burner, and it's easy to understand why it took me so long to see how much of Grant's charm was purely surface and how much of both his interest and his interesting conversation related to himself. It was almost flattering to watch his focus shift as he tried to figure out how to win me back when I started distancing myself. Flattering until one figured out that it had more to do with his ego than any real feelings for me.

"Grant, I have to …"

My words were stopped by a demanding kiss, the sort that you see on the steamier evening soaps. It was the kind of kiss that's hard to ignore if there's any physical attraction at all, especially if the blood's already been heated up by several shots of scotch. But then I thought of how many times Grant must have practiced this very kiss on his leading ladies and hardened my heart, not to mention my libido.

Placing my hands against his chest and shoving, I managed to gain about two inches of distance between our bodies as I said a trifle breathlessly, "Grant, I've to go watch rehearsal."

"Rehearsal will still be there in a few minutes," Grant responded in the faint British accent he'd cultivated after spending a year in England … when he was 10. He effortlessly closed the distance I'd gained, giving me the full benefit of that stormy blue gaze that had garnered him so many fan letters from Soap devotees. It was effective, I admit it, but I had to stifle the urge to jerk away from him.

"We're running the fights and they need work," I insisted, my hands still pushing against his chest.

"Darling, I'm sure that the boys can rehearse without a baby-sitter. For amateurs, they *are* quite competent." Grant smiled down at me, sure of his power to charm me.

I remained uncharmed, glad that the kitchen door and their noisy rehearsal had prevented 'the boys' (why did it sound so much worse when Grant said it?) from hearing Grant's condescending assessment of their skills. Turning my head to avoid another kiss, I snapped, "Grant, I'm the damned fight choreographer, as well as co-director. I've been stuck on the phone talking to Andy, not to mention trying to arrange for another actor to replace Barry—"

"Yes, Brad mentioned that." There was a great deal of contempt in the one syllable of Brad's name. Grant had not yet come to terms with the fact that Brad, not he, was playing the lead in *The Peruvian Pigeon*. The animosity between the two was barely veiled.

"Then you'll understand why I need to put as much time as possible into rehearsal right *now*." I gave an emphatic shove and managed to break away from Grant's tenacious embrace.

"You say something, Connie?" Brad's voice came from the living room. I guess my own voice had gotten rather loud.

"Not to you, Brad," I called. "Sorry!" I turned back to Grant, trying to contain my temper. After all, Grant didn't *mean* to annoy the hell out of me.

From his expression, I could tell Grant had decided Injured Lover was the required role of the moment. He was leaning against the counter wearing a distinctly sulky expression, arms folded across his chest as he stared accusingly at me. I prepared to be conciliatory. Call me a wimp, but there was too much work to be done to have Grant in a bad mood.

Laying a hand on his arm, I looked up at him with a remorse I didn't feel. "I'm sorry to snap at you, babe. I'm just so stressed out right now ..." I let my voice trail off as Grant decided if he wanted to stick with his current role or play the part of a sympathetic confidante.

Ever one for a challenge, Grant put an arm around my shoulders and drew me against him as he soothingly stroked my hair, pulling it out of the confines of the askew pony-tail I'd had it in for rehearsal. "It's all right, sweetheart," he murmured soothingly, kissing me gently on the forehead. "I understand. When this show is over, we'll go away for a week, maybe down to San Diego, stay at the Hotel Del ... Would you like that?"

I muttered something vague in reply, trying to just enjoy the sensation of his hand running through my hair while wishing that the reality of Grant matched the fantasy that he presented to the world. He was *so* damned attractive. And he did play his parts well, including that of a superlative lover. If only I could believe that he wasn't always subconsciously waiting for someone to yell 'CUT' when we'd finished making love ...

My response was enough to satisfy Grant for the moment. Depositing one last kiss on the top of my head, he put an arm around me and said, "Let's go get to work. We have a show to do."

We went back in the living room where the boys were taking a break from their physical workout. Brad was sprawled out comfortably on the couch, one hand draped protectively across his stomach. Shaun had somehow fit his entire length into a small ebony rocker, his long legs sticking up at an alarming angle, while Chris was sitting in the middle of a plush, hunter-green throw rug, methodically finishing off a plate of cookies. Daphne occupied one of the padded window seats in the front bay window, ignoring my other black cat, Renfield, who was perched on the windowsill above. From the intensity of his golden gaze, I guessed that Daphne had evicted Renfield from his favorite spot on the window seat.

Everyone looked up expectantly when Grant and I entered the room. I managed to snag one last cookie before Chris shoveled it into his mouth, and plopped down in my favorite overstuffed rocker, partly because it was so comfortable and also because it prevented Grant from sitting next to me. He contented himself with lounging at my feet. It was quite a picture, Grant gazing up at me with stormy adoration, wearing relaxed-fit jeans (CK) and crisp white cotton shirt (The Gap), his hand wrapped possessively around one of my legs. Just like an ad campaign for expensive champagne. Or would have been had I not spoiled the effect with my non-designer sweats topped by a black thermal shirt two sizes too big, exposing part of my red dance bra. As for make-up? What little lipstick I'd had on had been removed by Grant's kiss and my hair … well, I didn't want to know what my hair looked like, but I imagined it would make the Top 10 of bad hair days.

Lately I hadn't been making much effort towards my appearance when I knew I was going to see Grant. We'd gone out to dinner the other night and I'd worn leggings and an oversized men's workshirt rather than one of the outfits that Grant had purchased for me. It was a sign of his determination to keep me that he'd forbore commenting on my choice of wardrobe.

"That was Chad's brother," I said, trying to resist the impulse to pull my leg out of Grant's grasp.

"Is he interested?" Daphne leaned forward slightly, unknowingly barely avoiding a playful swipe from Renfield's paw.

"Interested enough to come over here to check things out."

"Was he a jerk?" This was from Brad, who continued, "Although I suppose you couldn't really tell the shape of his head from a phone conversation."

I ignored Brad's last comment and added, "Andy called as well, and I guess that one of the committee members drowned this morning, Damien Duran." This was greeted by a few 'Oh, that's too bad,' type comments, as well as some blank stares.

"Darling, that's terrible!" said Grant, in a decent facsimile of concern. "How did the poor man drown?"

"Probably inhalation of water," said Brad.

I bit my lip so I wouldn't laugh. "They think it was an accident."

Daphne, always pragmatic, asked, "Is this going to affect the show?"

"I don't think so. I just thought you all should know about it just in case it should come up, especially since there's a party at Jason Down's house tonight after the screening at the Museum, and we're all invited. You can even bring Guido, Daphne."

Daphne grimaced. "No thanks. He's starting to get on my nerves."

Not surprising. He got on my nerves the first time I met him.

Everyone look interested at the prospect of going to the party, even Grant. No doubt the thought of mingling with some of Emerald Cove's richest and most influential citizens—some who might even have connections in the Industry—appealed to him.

"That's right, they're showing *Down These Mean Streets* tonight!" Daphne's tone was rapturous. "It's my absolute favorite Mick O'Mallet film! 'Her legs were long, lean and went all the way to the floor, which was the best place for a woman's legs to go.' "

Brad took over. "Her breasts were firm and ripe and reminded me of twelve summer nights in a Moroccan bordello."

"How could anyone forget such deathless prose," I said with more than a touch of sarcasm. "Every now and then it really hits home just how chauvinistic this stuff really was."

"And now you write it." Brad grinned at me.

"No," I corrected, "I make fun of it."

"Well, we'd better get back to rehearsing if we're going to have time to clean up," Daphne said, motivated by the thought of seeing her favorite movie and a chance to wear one of her many black dresses. "I think I'll wear my new Ralph Lauren." Sure enough. "What are you going to wear, Connie?"

"Jeans and something on top." I felt Grant flinch. Good.

Daphne stared at me in disapproval. "No, you're not. All kinds of people are going to be there tonight who might hire us in the future, so we're both going to dress for the occasion."

I sighed. She was right and I knew it. "Okay," I said meekly. "I'll find something."

"I'll help you pick something appropriate," Grant whispered against my ear.

I leapt to my feet, moving away from Grant's possessive grip. "Well, let's get back to rehearsal, gang!" Any more forced pep in my voice and I could be a Mary Kay saleswoman.

"This won't run too late tonight, will it?" Grant stood up in one graceful move. "I have an audition tomorrow and should really put in some time on my craft." He looked condescendingly towards the other men. "You know how it is, I'm sure."

Chris and Shaun looked at him. Brad's grin became even wider. "Hey, did I read in Variety that *Tomorrow's Secret Search* has been canceled? You must have mentioned it earlier, Grant, but I guess I missed it."

Grant looked as though he'd bitten a lemon. "Well, there have been rumors, but ..."

Brad steamrollered right over him. "Jeez, was I surprised when I saw that it was last in the Soap ratings. You were up against *Judge Judy*, of course, and those *Charmed* reruns on FX really slaughtered you, but ..."

The doorbell saved Grant from any more humiliation, at least for the moment. I could tell by his expression that he was not going to forgive Brad in this lifetime, especially since all he'd said was true.

I sighed, knowing the price would be an uncomfortable rehearsal unless I sacrificed myself. Leaving Daphne to get the door, I slipped my arm through Grant's and smiled up at him. "You have to tell me about your audition. I don't think I've heard about this one. But then you get so many, it's hard to keep track." Shit, if I'd added a 'y'all' in there, I'd be eligible for the Scarlett O'Hara Saccharin award. Nothing like a little hypocrisy in the name of expediency to inspire self-loathing.

Oh well, it worked. Grant's ego visibly expanded, appeased by my attention and apparent admiration. Nothing was guaranteed to improve his mood faster than an opportunity to talk about himself. Giving me an affectionate squeeze, Grant said in tones that promised the thrill of a lifetime, "I'll tell you all about it after rehearsal, darling." Be still my beating heart.

I resigned myself to a detailed and boring monologue later in the evening. Oh well, I'd be sure to share it with Daphne. I'd be damned if I was going to take the bullet all by myself.

The new arrival was Tasha, short blonde hair curling out from under a black beret. She greeted us in a high, breathy voice that had irritated me until I'd gotten to know her and discovered that it wasn't an affectation. The voice matched her petite blonde, blue-eyed looks to perfection, but the stereotype stopped there. Tasha had a sharp intellect and made no effort to hide it. As a bartender, she was used to being hit on by men who assumed that she was your basic dumb blonde. Tasha quickly shattered their illusions by being able to intelligently discuss virtually any subject, albeit in a voice somewhere between Jayne Mansfield and Betty Boop. Tasha had confided that the contrast 'scared off a lot of jerks.'

Brad, on the other hand, adored both her intellect and her looks. Any resemblance to the macho Carl Club vanished when Brad and Tasha were together. The two were the most cloyingly cute couple I'd ever seen. If they ever procreated, the resulting offspring would be Care Bears.

Now they had their arms wrapped around each other and were exchanging endearments more suited to a reunion after six months apart. Luckily, most of it was unintelligible to the rest of us, but the words 'Boo Bear' and 'Cuddly Kitten' were clearly audible.

Daphne and I exchanged pained looks. Can you imagine a hard-boiled P.I. saying, "She had the kind of body that stopped traffic. Yeah, she was a real cuddly kitten, all right. My kind of boo bear."

The doorbell rang again, causing us all to wince.

"I'll get it," I volunteered. Anything to get away from Grant's intensity for a moment. "It must be Alex." This made Brad pause from his billing and cooing with Tasha to join Chris and Shaun, who were eyeing the front door with anticipation.

"Don't forget to check out his head for that special pin shape." Brad grinned at me. Making a face back, I opened the front door to greet the latest arrival.

I found myself staring up at six feet plus of well-built male clad in faded 501's and a hunter green-plaid flannel shirt. Wow.

I'm ashamed to say it, but it took me a few seconds to move my gaze up to his face, but at least I managed to say, "Uh … Hi. You must be Alex," without too much of a pause when I finally got there. Alex Barnett looked like Grant's tougher brother. Same basic coloring, except Alex's eyes were blue-green instead of stormy cobalt. His features weren't nearly as well-chiseled as Grant's, yet he was none the less attractive because of it. Alex wore his thick, dark hair a bit longer than Grant's and it showed no sign of being carefully groomed, a mark in his favor. I'm sure it looked neater than mine.

Talk about instant chemical reactions. When our eyes met, I felt as though someone had hit me over the head and my face flushed with heat. Meeting Grant for the first time had been similar, but if that had been getting hit by a rock, this was akin to being slammed by a boulder. My only consolation was that Alex looked equally thrown for a loop.

"Uh, yeah. You're Connie?"

I nodded. We stared at each other, having evidently exhausted our conversational ability for the time being. Who knows how long we would have stood there exchanging pheromones if Grant, obviously sensing a disturbance in the Force, hadn't stepped in.

Putting an arm around my shoulders a way that clearly marked me as his property, Grant held out his free hand in greeting. "I'm Grant Havers. You must be the stuntman."

Alex took the proffered hand and replied easily, "Part of the time, yeah. You look familiar."

At which point Brad stepped forward, saying, "Grant here's part of the late, lamented cast of *Tomorrow's Secret Search*. Maybe you've seen him there."

Alex laughed. "Nah, I hate soap operas. Must be something else."

I didn't look at Grant's face, but I felt his body tense up. Great, another alpha male for him to fight with.

"Brad Tandy." Brad and Alex exchanged handshakes, Brad continuing with, "Connie here's been on pins—" Emphasis on 'pins' "—and needles waiting to see if you were a stunt prick or not."

I gave Brad a look that should have incinerated him — and the dead horse he kept flogging—where he stood. He ignored it and cheerfully introduced Alex to Shaun and Chris, who had emerged in the front hall surreptitiously eyeing the shape of Alex's head. Alex gave me a quick sideways grin as he acknowledged the introductions. The brief eye contact was enough to set off butterflies in my stomach. This was ridiculous.

Daphne and Tasha joined us in the already crowded hall as Grant said speculatively, "Maybe we've worked on a film together … that is, if you're Union."

"Oh, I'm Union all right," Alex replied cheerfully. "Were you by any chance on *Time To Kill* that Johnny O'Brien directed for Corman?"

Grant nodded. "I was the lead."

"Then I was your stunt double."

"And you two didn't recognize each other?" I looked at them in disbelief.

Grant smiled down at me in a rather patronizing manner. "I don't normally pay much attention to the crew, sweetheart. I'm too busy immersing myself in my part. You were an exception."

I looked at Alex. He raised an eyebrow and said equably, "All those actors look alike to me."

I stifled a laugh, not wanting to make things any worse than they were already heading with Grant.

Daphne held out a hand expectantly. "And I'm Daphne Graves, Connie's business partner. This is Tasha, one of our actors."

Alex shook Daphne's hand and nodded politely to Tasha. "Do you share your partner's phobia against stuntmen?"

"Since she's the only one I've ever known, not really."

Alex looked at me in genuine surprise. "You're a stunt woman?"

"*Was* is the operative word," interjected Grant before I could answer. "We decided it was time for her to move on to better things."

I instantly seethed. How dare Grant try and mark his supposed territory by taking responsibility for my career decisions? Before I could give an outraged, 'What's with the 'we', white man?', Grant was once again saved by the bell.

The shrillness and volume of the doorbell was increased by our proximity and I was beginning to get claustrophobic as the seven of us stood packed in the hallway like Norwegian sardines.

Daphne managed to squeeze past Grant and reached for the doorknob. Before she had a chance to turn it, the door swung open and the perky voice of our landlady exclaimed, "Goodness, such a crowd! There you are, Daphne, Connie. May I?" Without waiting for an answer, Mavis inserted her tiny form into the front hall, followed by Sam Spayed, Daphne's extremely large tabby-striped cat. Mavis shut the door behind her and I groaned. Maximum load had been exceeded and I was suffocating.

Managing to insinuate herself between Daphne and me, Mavis seized us both by an arm. She fixed us each with a knowing look and said in conspiratorial tones, "So, girls! Who murdered Damien Duran?"

Chapter Three

I'd had it. Extricating myself from Mavis and Grant, I practically fell into the living room in my effort to get away from both of them and get some elbow room. I needed some breathing space if I was going to keep my temper and sense of humor at this point. The others trailed into the living room, Alex looking around with interest while Grant stayed as close to me as possible. Tasha headed off in the direction of the downstairs bathroom.

Mavis held onto Daphne's arm and repeated her question. "Well? Let's have it, girls! Who murdered Damien Duran?"

Remember those other drawbacks I mentioned to Daphne's and my near fairy-tale rental? Well, Mavis herself was Numero Uno.

Our landlady owned several houses on our block and lived in the one right next door. Warm-hearted, generous, kind to small children and animals, Mavis was also a relentless busybody and thought nothing of popping over to visit at all hours of the day and night. She usually knocked if she knew we were in, but both Daphne and I had caught her going out our kitchen door after we'd arrived home. She liked to keep an 'eye on things for us' and insisted on feeding our three cats special goodies, claiming the poor cats seemed so *hungry*. She ignored the fact that our three feline con artists ranged in shape from chubby to serious blimpage.

But the thing I hated most of all was Mavis's insistence that, because Daphne and I wrote and performed in the mystery genre, we were somehow more qualified to solve mysteries than any member of the FBI or Scotland Yard. Put together. Considering that Mavis thought Scully and Mulder from *X-Files* were real people, this was not too surprising. I could only be grateful that Mavis thought that any mystery with supernatural overtones should be left to those two experts.

The fact of the matter is that neither Daphne nor myself are any good at intricate plotting or figuring out solutions to the most simplistic Whodunits. Grafton or Christie we are not. I mean, let's face it. Whenever we're stymied as to explain how our detective came to his conclusions, all we have to do is have him toss off nonchalantly, 'I had a hunch.'

I listened as Daphne launched into our time-worn response of "We only write and *perform* mysteries, Mavis. We have no ability or interest in solving real ones." She stopped suddenly, doing a mental double take, and stared at Mavis. "Mavis, what on earth are you talking about? Damien Duran wasn't murdered. He drowned!"

"That's right, Mavis," I said reasonably. "Nobody killed him. It was a natural death. I mean, it was terrible, he drowned, but it was a *natural* drowning." That didn't sound right.

Mavis cocked her graying head of corkscrew curls to one side like a demented parakeet, sending a conspiratorial look around the room. "That's the story as *they* tell it. But you and I know differently, don't we? The man swam like a dolphin. It looked like he'd been koshed on the head."

I rolled my eyes. "Come on, Mavis, the guy was probably thrown up against the rocks after he died."

"And he had a *very* suspicious mark on the back of his neck."

"How can you possibly know that?"

"I have my sources," said Mavis smugly.

I was sorry I asked. The worst part was, Mavis really *did* seem to have sources in places and with people with whom she had no business having them, like police dispatchers, mortician's assistants and god knows who else.

"And my sources tell me that he had a U shaped mark on the back of his neck. I'm telling you, girls, if Duran drowned, my mother was a virgin." She finished this sentence with a hopeful glance in Daphne's direction, like a puppy seeking approval. It cut no ice with my partner, who had more than once regretted trying to teach Mavis forties slang.

"Jesus, Mavis, give it up!" Daphne exclaimed irately. "That's not even original."

Alex looked understandably confused. I was surprised he hadn't already run screaming out the door. He probably felt like a visitor to Bedlam at this point; all the loonies were in the asylum, with Mavis our very own Professor Tar and Professor Feather combined. All we needed for complete madness was Guido to arrive, proclaiming his love for Daphne in a fake Italian accent and crying copiously at the sight of the sunset. (Guido claims he feels things 'more deeply' than the rest of us on account he's an artist. Personally I think Prozac would work wonders.)

Brad noticed Alex's expression and explained, "One of the old guys on the committee for this Randell Fest thing drowned yesterday." He then turned to our landlady and added, "I guess you suspect foul play, huh, Mavis."

"You hit the nail right on the head, Brad." Mavis beamed at him. Brad had always rated high with Mavis and I've always suspected her of harboring a crush because he plays Club. It didn't seem to bother Brad, who was always willing to exchange hard-boiled wisecracks with her. But I could've killed him for egging her on tonight, especially when she went on to say, "And it's up to our girls—"

God, I hate when she calls us that.

"—to find out who killed him." Mavis finished up with a triumphant nod. Brad returned the nod solemnly, keeping an admirably straight face until he turned around to Chris and Shaun, who were both huddled in a corner trying desperately not to laugh. Grant's sense of humor did not extend to this sort of occasion.

Fortunately—or perhaps not—Alex's did. Turning the charm of his crooked smile on Mavis, he got into the game with, "So, these girls—"

I was going to kill him, too.

"—don't just run a theater company, but a detective agency?"

Mavis gave Alex an approving once over as she replied with reluctant honesty, "Well, no, just the theater company." She looked reproachfully at Daphne and me. "But I've often told them they should be private dicks as well. Think of the publicity that it would generate for their shows!"

"And vice versa," said the ever helpful Brad. "We could do commercials during the shows to advertise the private eye side of the business."

Oh, he was *so* dead …

Mavis beamed. "That's a wonderful idea! Don't you think so, girls?"

Daphne threw up her hands in exasperation. I covered my face with both hands and sat down on the window seat, grateful that there was no room for Grant to sit by me. Renfield immediately leaped onto my shoulder, digging his claws in for balance. I winced, but the pain was nothing in comparison to the humiliation of the moment. Part of me knew that the situation was funny, but that part was buried deep—like six feet underground in a coffin—at the moment. I was tired, wrung out by my problems with Grant, stressed over the upcoming shows, and thrown totally off-kilter by my unexpected reaction to Alex Barnett.

Daphne's sense of humor was obviously buried in the same graveyard as mind. Placing her hands on her hips, she glared at Mavis and said in uncompromising tones, "Mavis, we don't have time for this, we have got to rehearse!"

"That's right, Mavis." I stood up again, Renfield still balanced on my shoulder. I must have looked like a grouchy witch, complete with feline familiar. "We have a new actor to work in—" I glanced at Alex. "—that is, if we haven't scared him off already."

"No fear there." Alex settled down on the sofa with the air of one planning to stay for awhile.

"And we want to get finished in time to go to the screening tonight, so we'll have to talk about this later, okay?"

Mavis was nothing if not accommodating. Giving us all a beaming smile, she turned to leave with a cheery, "Well, I'll see you all tonight at the Museum! We can discuss the case more after the movie. Good luck with your sleuthing!" With that, she was out the door and temporarily out of our hair.

To give them credit, the boys waited a full beat after the door closed before bursting out into hysterical laughter.

"Graves and Garrett Agency, I love it!" Brad wiped tears from his eyes.

"Or they could shorten it to G&G," suggested Shaun in between snorts of laughter.

"Golly Gee P.I.'s," howled Chris. The three collapsed again.

Alex grinned, looking right at home.

Daphne and I maintained a dignified silence until Grant finally cast a damper on the group by saying, "If you three are finished, let's get on with rehearsal, shall we?"

Funny how one's sentiments can change when echoed by a pompous boyfriend. But he was right. We had too much work to do to waste time on juvenile jokes. Especially when Daphne and I were the butt of them. We knew our shortcomings and didn't need our cast to point them out.

I glanced at the clock. 6:15. Didn't leave us a lot of time if we were going to catch the screening. "Daphne, why don't you take the guys through the Von Krump stuff before Vilmer enters and I'll go over the script with Alex and show him what he'll be doing."

Grant didn't look particularly happy with this plan, but the professional within won over the jealous lover. He satisfied the latter by saying, "Don't be too long, Darling. We need to work the Von Krump/Vilmer scenes."

"I won't." I looked at Alex. "We'll go in the kitchen for this." He got to his feet with an alacrity that was flattering.

"Make some more cocoa, would you?" Daphne held out the empty cookie plate. "And maybe put some more of these on to bake."

Alex intercepted the plate before I could take it, examining the crumbs with an expert's eye. "Ah, chocolate chip!" he exclaimed. "Craft service couldn't be better if this is what you serve." I caught Daphne's eye as she beamed approvingly at our newest cast member. At least she had enough subtlety not to say, 'Go for it, girlfriend!' but her look spoke volumes.

I noticed Grant glowering at Alex and sighed inwardly. "Grant," I said solicitously, "can I get you something besides cocoa to drink? Some Espresso?" Grant did not care for our cocoa habit, yet another strike against him in Daphne's eyes.

The storm clouds in his gaze dissipated somewhat at my attention. And my question gave him another opportunity to show Alex just who belonged to who around this joint. "No, thank you, sweetheart. I stopped at Starbucks on the way over. You do what you need to do to integrate … Allan?" Grant gave a patently insincere shrug of apology at what was certainly a deliberate memory lapse.

"It's Alex," said the man in question. "But call me whatever you want, Greg."

Brad snorted.

Grant smiled with bared teeth. "That's *Grant*. But don't worry about it. We'll only be working one show together anyway."

Alex smiled back. "Yeah, I guess I could get lucky."

Who knows how long the two of them would've stood there flashing enough insincere tooth enamel to re-enact a scene from *Top Gun* if I hadn't lost patience. Snatching up my script, I pushed Alex towards the kitchen, nearly dislodging Renfield from his perch on my shoulder. "Let's get going, okay? You two can compare testosterone levels later."

I shut the kitchen door after us. I didn't want to have Grant eavesdropping in the dining room, trying to see if his territory was being encroached upon. And then I wondered if Alex would take it the wrong way and think I was just trying to be alone with him. My face flamed at the thought. I told myself to stop being an idiot and get to work. The flush subsided as common sense took over. We were here for one reason, I told myself firmly, and we both knew what that was: work.

During this internal dilemma, Alex set the cookie plate down on the counter and picked up the bottle of Laphroig. Turning towards me, he indicated the scotch and said, "Someone here's got good taste. This your boyfriend's?"

Instantly riled, I snapped back, "No, it's not!" Renfield jumped from my shoulder to the counter as I started grabbing ingredients for cocoa out of the fridge and cupboards. "Why does everyone assume that only a guy can appreciate single malt, huh?" I slammed the saucepan down on the counter. "And what makes you so sure he's my boyfriend, anyway?"

Alex raised an eyebrow and held his hands up as if to fend off a blow. "Calm down, would you? First of all, I apologize for the assumption, I just haven't known many woman who liked Laphroig. Consider my horizons broadened. And second—" He paused and gave me a rueful look. "—the master thespian did everything but lift a leg to mark his territory."

I concentrated on the cocoa for a moment, knowing full well that Alex was the one that deserved an apology and that I needed to summon up the humility to offer one. My temper had a habit of flaring up out of proportion to the offense and I'd been trying very hard to work on curbing it, and saying the words 'I'm sorry' when needed. The fact that his mere presence had me as skittish as a pre-teen with her first crush did nothing for my curbing ability or my diplomacy. I'd already been a total bitch to this man on the phone, based solely his profession, and he'd handled things with more good grace and humor than I deserved.

As I used a whisk on the cocoa with far more vigor than necessary, Alex scratched Renfield under the chin and changed the subject. "What's her name?" Renfield collapsed on his side in an ecstasy of purring, bones evidently melting within and unable to support his weight any longer.

"It's a 'he' and his name is Renfield." I hated the stiff sound of my own voice and tried to think of something conciliatory I could say. I pulled a bowl of cookie batter out of the fridge and turned the oven on. It was still warm from the previous batch.

"Renfield, huh?" I could hear the grin in his voice. "Why do you call him Renfield?"

I started to explain, then stopped as Renfield leapt to his feet, bones miraculously restored to normal as his attention was caught by movement in the kitchen window. "Watch." was all I said. Renfield ignored both Alex and me as he stalked an unsuspecting housefly buzzing around in the curtains above the sink. Alex started chuckling as he got the joke and watched in amusement as Renfield made a spectacular twisting leap in the air, landing on the counter amidst the dishes without upsetting any of them.

"Too bad, little fellah." Alex reached out to give Renfield another scritch on the head. "You lost your dinner."

Renfield backed away from Alex's outstretched hand and growled, a proprietary look on his face.

"He didn't miss," I said.

"Huh? You're kidding!" Alex looked around for the fly and then took a closer look at Renfield, who stared back at him calmly. A faint buzzing could be heard from within Renfield's closed mouth. He looked quite pleased with himself. The buzzing was cut off with a decisive crunch. Renfield gave a dainty little lick around his mouth to catch any stray pieces and jumped off the counter. I burst out laughing at the expression on Alex's face as disgust warred with amusement.

"Answer your question?"

"OH yeah. Does he eat spiders too?"

I smiled at him, the ice broken. I love a man who knows his Bram Stoker. Alex shook his head and laughed, watching Renfield saunter over to the back door and then suddenly bolt through the cat flap. "Quite a character." He gave me a sideways glance. "Like the rest of the household."

"Eccentric is a word that's been applied to most of the people currently in the house," I admitted. Pausing long enough to gather my courage, I took a deep breath and then plunged ahead. "Look, I'm sorry I snapped at you about the scotch and Grant. It's been a bitch of a day and as a result ... I've been a bitch."

"Apology unnecessary but accepted." He sat down at the kitchen table and looked at the Laphroig. "Of course, a wee drap o' this would go a long way towards soothin' me tattered feelings ..." Dropping the pseudo-Scottish accent, he continued, "Not that I don't love cocoa, mind you, but ..." He trailed off, giving me an ingenuous smile. My stomach did another flip-flop as I looked into those aqua eyes.

I turned to the cupboard and grabbed a shot glass, wondering if there was some imbalance going on with my hormones. I started to set it down in front of him, but he took it from my hand instead, our fingers brushing. The resulting charge of electricity, or whatever you want to call it, nearly caused us both to drop the glass before he had a secure hold on it. I jumped back abruptly, laughed nervously and gestured towards the Scotch. "Uh, knock yourself out. I'd better stir the cocoa."

"Thanks." Alex poured himself a shot and picked up the copy of *Peruvian Pigeon* that I'd set on the table. "What part should I look at?"

"Let's see," I mentally inventoried the characters that Barry had played, readying a sheet of cookies for the oven as I did so. "Jimmy the Weasel, The Frenchman ... I think that's it."

"Jimmy the Weasel. Very Mick O'Mallet."

"You're familiar with Randell?" I was surprised, pleasantly so. If he understood the genre, it would make integrating him this close to the wire much easier.

"Yup." Alex's eyes closed in a blissful expression as he took his first sip of Scotch. "Damn, that's good."

I looked wistfully at my shot glass sitting empty on the counter. A few drops of Laphroig still clung to the sides. No, I had to be strong. I slid the cookie sheet into the oven, shut the door, and set the timer. The cocoa was simmering, so I turned the burner down to 'warm'. I could have another cup of cocoa without feeling too unprofessional. But the thought of Scotch was so much more enticing, especially with Alex emitting little groans of pleasure every time he took a sip.

"Oh, hell!" Giving in, I grabbed my glass and sat down across from Alex. He had the bottle open before I'd even reached for it and poured me a healthy shot. "So you *are* a mind reader after all, hmmm?"

"Nah. I just saw the way you stared at my glass." Alex raised the object in question in a toast. "Here's to the hopes that someday you'll look at me with that much desire."

I choked on the sip I'd started to take. My face must have been as red as my dance bra. Somehow I managed to regain enough composure to say, "Get real. We're talking Laphroig here."

Alex laughed. "Point taken." He looked at me hopefully. "How about if it were Glenfiddich?"

I did not admit that I would toss out my entire bottle of Laphroig, let alone any Scotch beginning with 'Glen' for a date with this man. Instead I said sternly, "Let's get back to the show, shall we?"

I was almost disappointed when he took the hint and concentrated on the script. "How about finding me the pages where these characters come in?"

I did so, letting him read while I checked the cookies. The heavenly smell from the oven permeated the kitchen and I took a deep breath, sighing with contentment. A crisp autumn night, the scent of chocolate chip cookies, a shot of first-rate Scotch … and the most attractive man I'd ever met, stuntman or no. What else did a girl need? My more pragmatic inner-self answered that immediately: get rid of the boyfriend you've got before settling on a new one. Fine, I told myself, I was planning on it! But I can look, y'know! My inner self sniffed skeptically. I ignored her and took the cookies out of the oven, setting the sheet down on the cutting board.

Alex chuckled. I glanced over and saw with pleasure that he was reacting to our script.

"You like?" I couldn't resist the question.

"Very much." He turned the page, chuckling again. "You and your partner have a very male sense of humor, which is kind of required for this sort of stuff. No offense meant, mind you. It's just a very misogynistic genre."

"No offense taken." I looked over his shoulder to see what part he was reading. The Scotch had imparted its warm glow, leaving me relaxed enough to get within touching distance without worrying that I'd spontaneously combust or something equally embarrassing.

He was on the first Jimmy the Weasel scene in which the Weasel interrupts Club's questioning of Irene, the Weasel's moll. "There's a second Weasel appearance near the end." I reached forward and flipped the pages to the scene. The lovely smell of Laphroig wafted up from Alex and his glass, mixing nicely with the scent of the cookies. What a great aftershave … I inhaled deeply, causing Alex to swivel his head around towards me and inadvertently brush his lips against my cheek as I leaned over his shoulder.

The Scotch hadn't numbed me *that* much. I froze—a difficult thing to do with so much heat zinging through my body, starting at the point of contact and circulating through all erogenous zones—and stammered, "Ex ... excuse me ... I didn't mean ..."

"Neither did I ... but I wish I'd thought of it."

We stared into each other's eyes like the leads in a romance novel, the only place where things like this were supposed to happen. I knew if I didn't move away, something else would happen that couldn't happen until I resolved things with Grant.

I took a step backwards, stumbling into one of the chairs. I sat down with a thump, still holding my Scotch in a tight grip. "Umm ... we'd better talk about the walking tours and the pay and all that stuff." My voice sounded a little weak, but nothing compared to how I felt. I looked down at the table, too rattled to look at him as I spoke. "Aside from the Sunday evening performance of *The Peruvian Pigeon,* we're also doing three walk-ing tours on Saturday."

"And those involve ..."

"A guide will be leading groups of people around Emerald Cove, show-ing them the different places that Randell frequented, and MFH is going to be re-enacting scenes from one of his novels at various spots, like the Emerald Cove Hotel, along the cliffs, things like that."

I watched as Alex ran a finger along the edge of his glass. He had very strong looking hands ...

"Do you have the script for that?"

Distracted from my study of his digits, I replied with some disgust, "No, not yet. We're waiting for the Festival Board to finish selecting which scenes they want us to perform. I don't even know what parts we'll be playing. Are you any good at improv?"

"Considering that this whole evening was unplanned and unrehearsed, I'd say so."

I couldn't think of anything to say to that.

"Sorry." Alex sounded rueful. "I'm not usually like this."

"Neither am I." I did look up at that point. "I'm ... I mean, I don't know what to say."

"Makes two of us." We were both silent for a moment until Alex said, "So, *is* he your boyfriend?"

I hesitated, not wanting to go into that right now. But I really didn't want to blow it with this guy and he deserved some sort of answer. "We've been dating for a few months," I admitted, choosing my words carefully. "But there's been problems, at least from my point of view, and I'm not sure that it's going to last much longer than this Festival."

Alex studied his glass. "I take it he doesn't know how you feel."

I sighed, taking a healthy swig of my drink to bolster my nerves. "I've tried talking to him about things, but Grant's really good at ignoring what he doesn't want to notice. He's kind of possessive. Something you've already noticed."

"Sorry about that. Didn't realize how sore a spot it was."

"Yeah, well ..." I trailed off, not knowing what else, if anything, there was to say on the subject of Grant.

"So, we'll wait until after the show's over." Alex nodded with the air of a man who's made a firm decision.

"Wait for what?" I couldn't resist the question.

The look he gave me made my knees go weak even though I was sitting down. "For whatever we decide we both want."

Oh, my ...

I finished my Scotch in one gulp.

Chapter Four

The darkened auditorium of the Emerald Cove Museum of Contemporary Art was packed with people, many standing against the wall at the back. They were all intently watching Randell's *Down These Mean Streets,* which Daphne says is arguably the best film noir ever made and without a doubt the best screen adaptation of a Randell novel. She thinks it's due to the fact that it was the only screen adaptation scripted by the great Randell himself. Give me *The Maltese Falcon* any day.

Sitting in between Daphne and Grant in a surprisingly comfortable theater-style seat, I was probably the only one in the auditorium whose attention was not glued to the action on the screen. I was too busy pondering a number of things, such as my reaction to Alex Barnett, what I was going to do about my relationship with Grant and, of course, the show.

Alex had quickly proven that he was going to be an asset to MFH. His acting was at least as good as Barry's and his physical capabilities exceeded those of everyone else in the group. Considering my initial reaction to Shaun's suggestion, I was a bit embarrassed that Alex lived up to none of my expectations regarding stuntmen, even though I was thrilled with his talents.

I was also relieved that Grant would be hard put to complain about Alex's skills, because he was actively looking for something wrong the entire length of rehearsal. Grant's rivalry with Brad was purely professional. His reaction to Alex, however, was pure alpha-male 'stay away from mah woman', bristling hackles and all.

Ironically, after our little discussion in the kitchen, Alex had treated me with the same friendly charm he showed everyone else—— excepting Grant, of course—— and I somehow managed to get myself under control and not blush every time Alex came within touching distance.

I'd even kept my temper when Grant put an unnecessary kiss in a bit between our two characters, Von Krump and Lila Vilmer. Daphne was the one who pointed out that it changed the context of the scene. "Sorry," Grant had replied, "I just couldn't pass up the chance."

In one of his rare displays of deadpan humor, Chris had said, "Glad I don't have any more scenes with you." Even Grant had laughed, although I doubt he found Chris's remark particularly funny. I think he was just trying to prove that he was 'part of the gang'.

As if he knew I was thinking about him, Grant gave my arm a squeeze and brushed a kiss on the top of my head. I tried to enjoy it for what it was worth and focused on the screen once more.

We sat through O'Mallet's confrontation with Slash Mahoney in a darkened alley, along with his final shoot-out with Stinky Joe Maddon, the 'lowlife hophead who plugged O'Mallet's girl, Honey LaSalle, in the pan'. (Translation: drug-user who shot Honey in the face). Finally, the closing shot as the camera came in for a close-up of O'Mallet taking Honey in his arms for a passionate kiss as the two were reunited after Honey's long stay in the Emergency Ward. Miraculously, there were no visible scars so we were able to savor the picture of Honey's lovely, smooth-skinned face next to O'Mallet's strong-jawed profile as the story flickered to a close.

The lights came up and Daphne sighed with satisfaction. "That was great!" she enthused. "God, what a man! I hope Brad was paying attention to the way O'Mallet raised his fist to his mouth just before he punched someone, that is *so* right for the period! Where is Brad, anyway?" She twisted around in her seat, trying to decipher individual identities out of the huge mass of people in the auditorium.

"I think he's somewhere down in front," I replied. "I saw him and Tasha talking to Shaun as we came in. They got here much earlier than we did."

"Connie, *everyone* got here earlier than we did. We're lucky Andy saved us seats."

We'd nearly missed the opening of the movie because I'd misplaced my keys. I admit it, this is not a new phenomena. I'm always leaving my keys in restaurants, on counters, in locks, in my car, or just tossing them down in odd places around the house. It's the flakiest thing about me, I don't know why I have this problem. I'm sure a therapist could make big bucks figuring it out, something like 'Yes, vell, you haf a fear of unlocking ze secrets in your mind.' It's become such a joke that Daphne made a special hook in the entryway with a huge sign reading: CONNIE'S KEYS so that whoever retrieved the keys knew where to put them. This time it was Brad who found them on the couch, under J.D.'s tail.

I chose to ignore Daphne's aggrieved comment, however justified it might be, and discreetly scanned the audience for Alex, who had said he'd try to make the screening. He was definitely attending the party at Jason Down's, and had needed to go back to his brother's to change clothes. No sign of him yet.

I sighed with disappointment and leaned back in my chair, letting Grant rub my shoulders. I was tired. The stress of the evening combined with the Scotch had taken its toll.

"Oh, no ..."

I glanced over at Daphne. "What's wrong?"

"It's Franklin. He's heading for the podium. And I think he's going to give a speech. Ah, jeez ..."

I sympathized with Daphne's reaction. If Franklin Grace was going to give a speech, I didn't want to get stuck listening to it either. Franklin had just finished grad school and was a Randell scholar, if such a term could be used. He was teaming up with Andy to lead the Walking Tours on Saturday and probably knew more about the life and works of Shay Randell than anyone currently alive. His dissertation had been on Jungian Archetypes within Randell's writing and he was currently finishing a second draft on The Great Man's biography. How did I know all this? Franklin had imparted this information—and much more—within the first ten minutes when Andy introduced Daphne and me at one of the Committee meetings.

Now don't get me wrong, I like Franklin. Good-looking in a tall, gangly sort of way with mild brown eyes and messy blonde hair, Franklin was energetic, animated and very friendly. But like all obsessions, his discourses on the life and times of his hero could be pretty tedious.

I stood up and scanned the immediate vicinity for a discreet exit, spotting an easy out through a side door on my right. But before I could warn Grant and Daphne that I was heading for the hills, Franklin began speaking in his pleasant voice. The crowd grew silent and I reluctantly sat back down, unwilling to save myself from boredom by being blatantly rude.

Grant, on the other hand, had no such inhibitions. Pulling out his $600 Verizon cell phone, he leaned over and whispered, "Darling, I have to call my agent. I completely forgot about it and it *could* be important. I'll meet you in the lobby in a bit." Naturally, he whispered just loud enough to insure that the people sitting around us would hear and perhaps recognize him.

Grant would never be one of those actors who shunned the press. He craved publicity and recognition the way some people crave alcohol or chocolate. Sure enough, as he stood and made his way up the center aisle to the lobby, he created quite a stir among the female audience members, many of who probably subscribed to *Soap Opera Digest*.

Glad to have him gone, I settled back to listen to Franklin's speech, boring or no.

"As I'm sure you're all aware, this weekend will mark the two final

events that will close Emerald Cove's Shay Randell Festival." Franklin paused
as if to make sure that the crowd understood the enormity of his words.
"The last event will be the Gala dinner Sunday evening held at the newly
opened Emerald Cove Library. This will feature gourmet dining and dancing to the Billy 'dem Bones' Brewster Blues Band. There will also be entertainment provided by Murder For Hire, an original piece entitled *The Peruvian Pigeon*."

Daphne and I grinned smugly at each other.

"Of course," Franklin continued, "that sounds much closer to Dashiell
Hammett's work than anything Randell ever wrote. But this group has a
very good reputation and I'm sure whatever they present will do the memory
of Randell justice."

Daphne elbowed me in the ribs, turning my impending laugh attack
into a coughing fit.

"But it's the Walking Tours on Saturday that I'm chiefly interested in
telling you about." Franklin looked around the audience, his enthusiasm
on high wattage. "As you know, we will be conducting three two hour
tours—"

Under my breath, I started singing, "With passengers set sail that day,
for three two hour tours." Daphne elbowed me again, harder this time. I
subsided.

Franklin continued. "The times are posted out in the lobby and tickets
are still available. Now on these tours, we will be covering various locations
in Emerald Cove, locations which Randell—" It was fascinating how he
uttered Randell's name in the sort of reverent tones a man usually reserves
for God or Pamela Anderson. "—wrote about in his last novel, *Play To
Win*, such as the bar at the Emerald Cove Hotel. I believe he had a particular booth that they reserved for him at the Hotel."

An undercurrent of laughter greeted this last remark as Randell was
well known as an alcoholic. Franklin, however, wasn't being facetious. He
plowed ahead. "Again, the marvelous actors from Murder For Hire will be
performing for us, only this time their skills will be enhanced—" Oh, I
wish Grant had heard that one. "—by excerpts from *Play to Win* along the
way. Rumor has it that a murder or two just might occur!"

A ripple of interest ran over the auditorium. I smiled and silently
thanked Franklin for the publicity, even if he thought our skills could only
be enhanced by the words of Randell.

"And I myself," Franklin announced proudly, "will be reading passages
from the novel in their appropriate settings. This will indeed be an exciting
event, ladies and gentlemen, not just for Emerald Cove, but for any lover
of great literature!"

My, oh my, Franklin was really getting revved up here.

"Randell was one of America's greatest writers. He lifted the detective mystery up from the ranks of pulp fiction and placed it amongst the masterpieces of modern literature. For Shay Randell possessed a genius not unlike that of Poe, Hemingway or Dickens! Forget Hammet, he couldn't touch Randell's terse prose, a prose that was lyrical, yet grounded firmly in reality …"

My brain shut down at that point.

Like I said, Franklin is a nice enough guy, but when it comes to the subject of Randell, I think his little red choo choo has gone 'round the bend. To be fair, even Daphne will say that Randell had a hand in raising the image of detective fiction to a higher level, but she also admitted that his work rapidly deteriorated in proportion to the worsening of his drinking problem. And one thing that Randell could have never claimed to be was a writer rooted in reality.

Jeremy Kensington, the Museum's film curator, quickly ascended the stage as Franklin's talk began to take on the tone of a memorial sermon. Deftly commandeering the microphone, Jeremy thanked Franklin and reminded everyone that Jason Downs was hosting a party that evening, "in honor of Jonathan Burke, the writer chosen to adapt Randell's last book, *Blood Spurts High,* into a television pilot." Jeremy gestured to the back of the auditorium as the audience began applauding.

Daphne and I craned our heads around along with everyone else to see the great man. Burke wasn't hard to spot, bearded features set in a sullen scowl as he surveyed the delighted faces now turned towards him. He was standing next to Andy, whose craggy face was only slightly less glum. Burke gave a brief wave of one hand, more of a dismissal than an acknowledgment, and glowered at the crowd before him. I was not impressed.

Jeremy went on to say that the party was also to be a wake for Jason Down's "dear friend, Damien Duran who would have not wanted the festivities to stop just because he could not attend." He then thanked everyone for their attendance and stepped off the stage.

"Burke seems like a real creep," I whispered to Daphne. "And judging by the look on Andy's face, it must have been a total hell drive from the airport."

"Yeah, but I have to meet him!" Daphne hurriedly got to her feet, grabbing her purse from under her chair.

"Oh, c'mon, he looks like he doesn't give a shit about his fans. Why bother?"

"He can't be a total pig," Daphne replied. "His scripts for *American Mystery Theater* were the best in the series."

Talk about chop-logic. As it was, Daphne was heading up the aisle with the rest of the audience before I had a chance for a rejoinder. Me? I'd already had my fill of Hollywood egos, some quite talented and some whose only asset was a daddy who could buy them a part no matter how undeserved—provided it was on the right network.

Oh well. I decided I might as well make my way up to the lobby and see what there was in the way of refreshments. I also figured it was the easiest way to meet up with the rest of the cast as they would undoubtedly gravitate to the food and drink.

I leaned down to grab my bag, which I'd stored under my chair. My fingers brushed velvet, but before I could pick up the black drawstring pouch I was using as a purse, someone snatched it from my grasp.

"Hey!" I looked behind me, ready to lash out at whoever was trying to snag my bag. Before I could let loose with whatever string of invectives was waiting to escape, the bag was swung in front of me by its ribboned ties. "This yours, lady?" I looked up and found myself staring at a grinning Alex.

All thoughts of catching a purse-snatcher fled as my mouth curved in an answering smile. "Well, it does match my outfit better than yours."

"I don't know about that." Alex eyed me consideringly. "You'd better stand up so I can make sure you're not trying to pull a fast one."

I obliged, suddenly glad that I'd taken the time to do my hair and make-up. I no longer resented the fact that I'd had to forgo the comfort of jeans, conscious that the rich crimson of my low-necked, flowing rayon dress suited me perfectly. I didn't even regret the discomfort of my black suede Louis XIV-style heels.

Alex looked at me with frank appreciation. "You look fantastic." He dropped the bag in my outstretched hand, adding, "And this must be yours."

"It just doesn't go with your jeans," I smiled. He'd changed into a pair of new Levi's and a raw silk shirt the same aqua as his eyes. He looked great. It only rankled a *little* bit that he could get away with wearing jeans and still be considered dressed for the occasion.

There was a pause. "So … you made it." Oh, what this man did to my witty banter ability.

"Wouldn't have missed seeing you in a dress for a job on a Bond film."

"You really know how to turn a girl's head."

"I hope so." He reached out and brushed a stray lock of hair that had escaped from my chignon. "So where's Don José?"

I laughed at that. "Calling his agent. If he's Don José, I assume that makes me Carmen. Do you think he'll kill me in a jealous rage?"

"Depends on his character interpretation, I suppose."

I felt vaguely guilty even as I laughed and looked around to make sure no one from MFH overheard me making fun of Grant. Not that they'd object, mind you, but considering the fuss I'd made whenever anyone else did it, I felt like a first-class hypocrite.

Alex must have sensed my discomfort because he immediately changed the subject. "How about checking out some of that great fruit punch in the lobby?"

I grimaced. "You're joking, I hope."

"Okay, I lied. It's Ernest and Julio's finest boxed wine. Comes in two colors. White and blush." He took my arm as he talked, leading me up the aisle and deftly steering us in between the hoards of people crowding the upper part of the auditorium, presumably trying to meet the great Jonathan Burke. I hoped we'd have a few more minutes to ourselves before Grant found us.

I heard Lucille before I actually saw her. The jingle of her ever-present bangle bracelets and the clickety-clack of her stiletto heels were audible even over the noise of the crowd. "Oh, God, it's Lucille." I clutched Alex's arm.

He looked understandably confused. "Who's Lucille?"

"Lucille Monroe. Head of the Gala Dinner," I whispered. "And the biggest bitch I've ever met."

There she was, headed right for me, a royal pain in the ass disguised as a petite 50-something brunette. Daphne and I had met her briefly at one of the Committee meetings and the hostility between her and Andy had been palpable. It soon became clear that since MFH had not been her idea, and worse yet, had been *Andy's* idea, we were therefore a *bad* idea. Lucille had a very Hollywood notion about what actors and directors should look like and we were not it. She'd taken one look at my baggy khaki pants and oversized thermal top and had given an audible sniff. As for Daphne, her silk sweater and wool skirt made an even worse impression because she looked good. Lucille was obviously a woman with no close female friends.

She also had the worst fashion sense I'd ever encountered. You've heard of fashion victims? Lucille was a fashion terrorist. And tonight she was using all the weapons at her disposal.

Hair dyed jet black and lacquered into a helmet that would've looked at home on a Duracell battery commercial, Lucille was wearing a form-fitting lime-green suede jumpsuit that assaulted the eyes. Her huge designer earrings and multiple gold bracelets did their best to compete for attention. But her chest upstaged everything else. Encased in fluorescent green suede, her breasts jutted out like two silicon missiles poised for an impending launch. The crowd parted around her, probably afraid of being dented.

"I think I know her," Alex whispered back to me.

"God, I'm sorry. Maybe you were really bad in a past life or something."

"Maybe we were bad together," Alex retorted, "because she's definitely headed our way."

The bracelets fell silent as Lucille stopped before me. I felt my hackles rise before she even opened her mouth, mainly because she was doing her best to appear as if she'd only just noticed me and that I was barely worth her notice at that. "Oh," she said in a disdainful tone. "So you attended the showing, hmmm? How convenient. I wanted to speak with you."

Alex stood quietly slightly behind me, one hand resting lightly on my back. Normally I would have just waited for her to get to the point, but instead I said, "It's sad about Mr. Duran, isn't it?"

"Hmm?" she paused as if searching her memory banks for the proper response. "Oh. That. Yes, very sad." With a reading like that, it was good thing Lucille wasn't trying to make it as an actress because she obviously didn't give a shit. She continued. "Did Andy tell you that I wish to attend one of your rehearsals at the library?"

My hackles rose even further. "No, he didn't."

Lucille smiled, the cold soulless smile of a shark. It was even scarier considering that her facial muscles barely moved. The woman was a monument to the perils of plastic surgery. "I suspected as much. Never trust an *underling* to deliver a proper message."

I lifted an eyebrow by way of response. It was either that or punch the bitch.

"Now, Daphne—"

"*Connie,*" I corrected.

"What was that?"

"I'm Connie. My partner's name is Daphne."

"Oh. Yes. Well, whatever." Lucille seemed vaguely astounded that I would bother making such a trivial correction. "At *any* rate, as I mentioned, I will be attending one of your little rehearsals."

I decided to be blunt. "Why?"

Again, Lucille looked amazed that I would dare to question her. "I think I need to *impress* upon you how important it is that I actually *see* what your little show has to offer in order for me to seat people so that they can get the full benefits of the evening. You *do* know that there are people paying five thousand dollars a *plate*, don't you?"

"I believe Andy mentioned it." I kept my voice neutral.

"Well, we want to make sure they can see everything. The little people can just make do." She laughed at her own words, but I knew she wasn't joking. This woman was a consummate snob.

"And of course I want to see full dress, with all props. Since Andy hired you *without* consulting me, I just want to make sure we're not getting a pig in a poke, so to speak. You *do* understand, of course, Connie." She smiled again. If you could call the slight lifting of the bottom corners of her lower lip a smile.

"Oh, I certainly do." I smiled back, the sort of tight little smile that usually comes before I lose my temper.

"Good. Then I'll—"

"You can certainly come for part of a rehearsal," I cut in, "but you won't be able to see a full dress because we won't be doing one."

"*No* full dress?" Lucille would've sneered had her facial muscles allowed. "Isn't that ... *unprofessional?*"

"Considering how many times we've performed this piece, a full dress is hardly necessary. Our rehearsal tomorrow night at the library is primarily for blocking purposes so we know how to best utilize the space."

"I see." It was obvious that she didn't, but before she could pursue the matter, Alex threw himself in front of the bullet.

"Mrs. Fife?"

Lucille's head snapped around and her Arctic gaze settled on Alex for the first time. When she saw that he was an attractive male, the chill thawed a bit. "I haven't gone by *that* last name for a year. It's Lucille Monroe now."

I wondered briefly what had happened to Husband #1. Of course, it sounded as though she'd had multiple last names, so Mr. Fife might not have been the first. Images of black widow spiders and their mating habits flashed through my mind.

"You look familiar, though," Lucille continued, giving Alex the once-over and obviously liking what she saw. She placed a red-taloned hand on his arm. "Didn't you work on one of my late husband's films?"

Alex nodded. "I was the stunt coordinator for two of Mr. Fife's films."

Lucille thawed further. "I've always *adored* stuntmen. They're so ... *virile*. I'm surprised I didn't get to know you better." She squeezed his arm suggestively, her tone implying that she'd be more than willing to make up for lost time.

I watched with interest to see how Alex would extricate himself without causing offense. I could tell that Lucille was the sort of woman who didn't take an easy 'no' for an answer. But as luck would have it, fate intervened in the form of one of the Committee members demanding Lucille's immediate attention. And since this particular member was Barbara Dubray, wife of one of Emerald Cove's elite, Lucille had no option but to respond graciously. Well, as graciously as the framework of her personality allowed.

Giving Alex's arm a final squeeze, Lucille reluctantly relinquished her prey with a quick, "We'll talk later," before turning her attention to Mrs. Dubray.

Alex and I made a quick escape across a row of seats to a side aisle that wasn't as congested as the one leading to Jonathan Burke. I was giggling uncontrollably by the time we reached the lobby door whereas Alex looked like a man who'd just escaped from being eaten alive.

"I'm glad *you* can laugh," he said with a shudder as we went through the door and into the crowd of people milling about the lobby. "That is one scary woman."

"I don't know *how* you missed getting to know her," I choked out between giggles. "You're so ... so ... *virile!*"

Alex contented himself with a quiet, "Just remember I know where you live. And where you keep your scotch."

I gave a toss of my head, turned and immediately collided with Chris, completely ruining the moment. Giving Alex a look that just dared him to say anything, I apologized to Chris.

"No problem," Chris replied. He had dressed for the occasion in ragged jeans, weathered army boots, a black T-shirt with the arms and neck cut off and a leather jacket with the Grim Reaper painted on the back, a bloody scythe reaching around over his front right shoulder. "You gonna meet Burke?"

"I'm not in any real hurry." I looked over Chris's shoulder, spotting Grant on the other side of the lobby talking to several women who obviously recognized him from TSS. He was looking in our direction with a scowl. I gave him a vague smile and turned back to Chris. "Daphne's the fan so she can represent MFH and schmooze with the guy."

Chris raised an eyebrow. "He's a real asshole, if you ask me. Called me a militaristic skinhead."

I couldn't believe my ears. "But ... you have hair, Chris."

Chris nodded calmly.

Alex gave a bark of laughter as I went on, "I can't believe he said that! Did you hit him?"

"No. I just told him he was a dried up little prick who fulfilled his frustrated fantasies by writing about and identifying with a sado-masochistic macho PI who overcompensates for his lack of self-esteem by crushing the nuts and skulls of moronic bad guys. It didn't go over too well. I need some wine. See you guys later." With that, Chris turned and walked off.

I stood still in amazement. That had been the longest and most eloquent speech I'd ever heard from Chris. I only wish I'd been there to see Burke's reaction.

"Connie, you made it!"

I turned to find Andy towering above me, light blue eyes partially hidden behind black wire-framed glasses. Andy resembles nothing more than a depressed St. Bernard, his face all crags and droopy jowls. I've never seen him in anything other than khaki pants and shirts with some sort of cat theme. Tonight was no exception, a bevy of tubby kittens chasing string all over his short-sleeved cotton shirt. His face was drooping more than usual and I suspected that close proximity to Jonathan Burke had something to do with it.

I introduced Andy to Alex, briefly explaining the reasons for our change in cast. Andy rolled his eyes when I told him of Barry's last minute defection, saying, "I swear, these people with their goddamn artistic temperament. You'd think that someone issued them a license giving them permission to be an asshole." He looked towards the center of the lobby. I followed the direction of his gaze and saw that Burke was now holding court, Daphne at the front of the eager throng waiting to introduce themselves to one of Hollywood's elite.

"Fun ride from the airport, huh?" I made an educated guess.

Andy shook his head in disgust. "Don't get me started!"

"Is Burke really that bad?"

Andy looked around quickly to make sure no one would overhear him, then said, "He's an arrogant, inconsiderate jerk. And I figure that one out *before* I met him. Do you know what he did?" I knew this was a purely rhetorical question and waited for Andy to continue, which he did almost immediately. "I got to the airport early, waited at the security checkpoint so I'd be sure not to miss him. Even had one of those stupid signs with his name written on it. Made me feel like a goddamn chauffeur or something."

I made appropriate sympathetic noises.

"The flight arrives, I stand there for 45 minutes, no sign of him. So finally when it's obvious there's no way he could still be on the plane, I go to the ticketing counter and check the passenger manifest. Turns out he wasn't on this plane because he came in on the same flight last night!"

"So he changed his flight plans and didn't bother to tell anyone?"

Andy nodded again.

"What an asshole!" Several people turned and looked at me. Lowering my volume, I said, "How did you find him?"

"I called the Hotel Emerald and found out that he'd checked in a day early."

"Unbelievable."

"Oh, it gets better."

"Evidently he didn't like the room we'd booked for him and demanded a suite instead. Do you know how much that'll add to the budget?"

"Um … whatever happened to just say no?" I asked.

"Well, I would have if it'd been up to me. But it seems that he ran into Lucille at the hotel bar, and she just said yes."

And probably to more than the hotel suite, I thought. Aloud, I said, "I think I'll definitely skip an introduction to Burke."

"Oh, don't waste your time," Andy assured me. "The man is a walking ego! He's the kind of person who uses his intellect as a bludgeon. He's pompous, arrogant and seems to think that the rest of us poor mortals should be thrilled to do nothing but listen to him spout off about himself."

Andy paused for breath and I took the opportunity to say, "It'll be over Sunday, Andy." I patted him on the arm comfortingly. "And then you won't have to see Burke or talk to Lucille again. Talk about a pair made in hell."

Andy sighed. "Isn't that a thought straight from heaven. I'd pay a lot of money if both Burke and Lucille would just vanish off the face of the planet, you know?"

"I know. Oh. That reminds me. Lucille informed me that she will be attending our rehearsal tomorrow evening."

Andy smacked his forehead with an open palm. "God, I forgot all about that!" He looked at me apologetically. "Sorry I didn't warn you, Connie."

"You've had plenty of other things to think about, my friend. Besides—" I imitated Lucille's affected diction, "One should *never* trust an *underling* to do a job."

Andy grimaced. "Don't ever do that again, Connie. I'd hate to confuse the two of you in the dark and kill *you* by mistake." He wandered off in the direction of the refreshments table, no doubt planning on easing his pain with a glass of cheap wine.

Alex tapped me on the shoulder. "Don José's headed this way, slowly but surely. Do you want me to do a discreet fade away?"

"Hell, no!" I glared at him indignantly. "I'll be damned if I'll let anyone dictate who I can socialize with. Besides," I added, my attention caught by the sight of Jonathan Burke's arm around Daphne's shoulder, his hand slowly wandering south, "we have to go rescue Daphne."

Alex looked in that direction and nodded. "Let's go."

We managed to wade through the crowd and got several feet away from Jonathan Burke, who was no more prepossessing at close range than he'd been from a distance. Burke's skin was tanned and leathery, his heavy, sullen features partially obscured by a beard and mustache several shades darker than the salon-sun-streaked brown hair that surrounded his heavy features like a lion's mane. He was a big man, at least six feet and built like an ox, but the indulgences of food and drink gave him one of those stomachs that bulged out like a woman in her third trimester. It showed clearly beneath his multi-colored Hawaiian shirt and white sports coat. I suppose that he might have been attractive to certain women but I was not one of them. Jonathan Burke reminded me of nothing so much as an overcooked honey-glazed ham.

I pushed my way right next to Burke in time to hear him say, "It's always a pleasure to meet a fellow writer, Miss Graves." His hand had by this time made its way to Daphne's black-velvet clad rear and on 'pleasure', he gave it an overly-familiar squeeze. Daphne's eyes widened with surprise as Burke continued, "We'll have to have a drink together later. We can exchange ..." He paused, savoring the last word, " ... techniques."

"What a charmer," Alex whispered in my ear.

I just shook my head and stepped forward to rescue my partner, who'd never been good at confrontations of any sort. Despite her ability to spout tough-guy slang at the drop of a hat, Daphne is a wimp.

Daphne saw me and immediately said with unmistakable relief, "Connie!" She gave a nervous little laugh and continued overly brightly, "I'd like you to meet Connie Garrett, Mr. Burke. Connie's my partner, the other half of Murder for Hire!"

A brief flash of annoyance at being interrupted crossed Burke's face, but he had enough social grace beneath the arrogance to acknowledge Daphne's introduction. The annoyance vanished as he looked me up and down, his gaze lingering on my chest in a way that made me sorry I'd worn a Wonderbra. "So, Ms. Garrett," he said in tones oily enough to make drilling seem profitable, "I see that the other half is as attractive as the first."

"Pleased to meet you, Mr. Burke," I said without enthusiasm.

The hand that wasn't massaging Daphne's backside reached out. I shook it once and would've let go had Burke not wrapped his fingers around mine in a death grip. I tugged ever so slightly. His fingers tightened even more.

Considering my tolerance for sexual harassment—zip, zilch, zero—things would've gotten ugly very quickly had Alex not stepped in, shoving his hand forward and saying, " I'm Alex Barnett, one of your many fans. An honor to meet you, Mr. Burke."

Burke had no choice but to release my hand in order to shake Alex's. I took advantage of the moment to say, "Daphne, turn around. I think you've got something on the back of your dress."

Daphne twisted around, effectively ridding herself of Burke's unwanted massage. "Where? What? Is it a stain? God, I hate trying to get velvet cleaned, it's such a pain."

"It's okay, Daphne." I took her by an arm and pulled her out of Burke's reach. I looked squarely at him as I added, "It's gone now. A pleasure meeting you, Mr. Burke."

Burke's eyes narrowed as he acknowledged my hit with a little nod, his mouth twisting in a smile of grudging admiration. "Likewise, Ms. Garrett. And Ms. Graves." He leered at Daphne. "I hope to see more of you."

Daphne gave another little nervous laugh and quickly stepped behind Alex and me. At that point Burke was accosted by none other than Mavis, resplendent in innumerable layers of purple chiffon. She gave us a cheery wave, said, "I'll talk to you girls later!" and then turned her full attentions back to the unsuspecting Burke—no pun intended. I would've felt sorry for him if he wasn't such an asshole.

"God, I need some wine!" Daphne exclaimed as soon as we were out of Burke's hearing. She headed straight for the refreshment table, Alex and I close behind.

"That makes three," Alex commented.

"Burke does seem to have that affect on people," I agreed. Sure enough, Chris and Andy were both at the table, wine in hand.

"So," Andy said when we reached the table, "how did you like the famous author?" There was no doubt as to the sarcasm underlying his last two words.

"He's awful!" Daphne sounded truly disillusioned, like a kid who's been told there's no Santa. She grabbed a plastic cup of White Zinfandel, downing half of the wine in one gulp.

"Teach you to judge a writer's personality by his work," I admonished.

"Yeah, well." Daphne sipped her remaining wine disconsolately.

Alex reached out and got two cups of the same, handing one of them to me. I started to take a sip when Grant materialized beside me and grabbed my wrist, causing wine to slosh out onto the floor.

"Darling, you don't want to drink this." He took the cup from my hand and nodded to Alex, combining greeting and dismissal in the one gesture. Alex raised an eyebrow and stayed where he was.

I stared at Grant in disbelief. "Grant," I said with unnatural calm, all things considered. "Please give me my wine back."

"But sweetheart, you know that cheap wine always gives you a headache. I'm sure there'll be plenty of quality wines at the party."

"But we're not there yet and I'm thirsty *now*."

"Then let's go to the party now." He set my cup of wine on the table.

This was becoming slightly surreal. Grant had always been somewhat controlling, but his current behavior was bordering on the ridiculous. He must've been watching when Alex and I were joking around and felt the need to assert himself. Whatever the reason, he was really starting to piss me off.

Who knows what would've happened next if we hadn't been interrupted by an unfamiliar voice hailing Daphne and me from across the lobby.

"Miss Graves! Miss Garrett!"

Everyone at the table turned and watched as a short, sandy-haired man with a cherubic face and bright blue eyes approached us eagerly. He had a camera clutched in one hand, a notebook and pen in the other. Every instinct I possessed cried out 'trouble' and it didn't take long for my sixth sense to be validated.

Stopping before us, the man looked at me and said, "Miss Graves?"

"I'm Connie Garrett," I corrected him. "This is Daphne Graves."

"I'm Arthur Sloan, from *The Emerald Post*. I'm doing the features on the Randell Festival and I was wondering if I could have a moment of your time for an interview."

Daphne and I exchanged glances. We'd actually read some of Mr. Sloan's articles in the *Post*, often sharing the opinion that his writing style was more suited to *The National Enquirer* than a respectable community newspaper. But surely a simple interview about MFH couldn't give him much grist for his mill and the publicity could get us more work.

Daphne evidently felt the same way. "We have a few minutes, don't we, Connie?"

I nodded. "Why don't we go outside where it's a bit less crowded?"

Sloan nodded eagerly.

"We'll be back in a few minutes, guys." I said, not addressing anyone in particular. I just hoped that Grant wouldn't get in Alex's face during our absence. The look on his face didn't bode well for the rest of the evening, unless …

A stroke of genius hit me. "Mr. Sloan, when you're done interviewing Daphne and me, you might want to talk to Grant Havers here." I indicated Grant, who immediately turned on his patented photo-op smile. "He's a Los Angeles actor with some major credits. It might be an interesting angle for you to get his perspective on the Festival." I didn't add that it would also get Grant out of my hair for at least half an hour.

Sloan took the bait. "That'd be great! Would you mind, Mr. Havers?"

"Not at all." Grant was all charm, his scowl eradicated by the thought of talking about himself to a member of the media. "I'll be here when you're done talking to the girls."

I gritted my teeth and worked my way through the crowd to the front doors, shoving them open with more force than was necessary. Daphne and Sloan were right behind me so I let the chill autumn air cool my temper.

"This is great, girls!" Sloan enthused.

I wondered briefly why everyone called us 'girls' when we were both nearly thirty.

Sloan continued, talking at the pace of a machine gun. "I'm a big fan of you two—even though I've haven't seen a show yet—but I know all about your work in the community. I'm a big fan of mysteries, especially all those forties films, so I'm sure I'll love your show on Sunday night! Do you want to tell me about your group? How you got started? How many members you have? Of course, I already know a lot about it, but it would be great to hear it from the horse's mouth, so to speak."

Both Daphne and I opened our mouths to answer, but before either of us could get a word out, Sloan kept going. "Let me ask you this: the two of you are pretty much in the thick of things, right?"

"Uh, well—" I looked at Daphne for help. She shrugged helplessly.

Sloan didn't seem to need an answer. Dropping his voice to a conspiratorial whisper, he leaned in close and said, "I got a hot tip that there was some major league dirt going down at the Randell Fest, so I got on the speedtrack and stretched strides over here to get the scoop from you two!"

"What?" I was totally lost. Daphne, while equally confused, looked somewhat impressed by Sloan's use of '40s vernacular. It *did* sound frighteningly normal coming out of his mouth, especially with the reporter's rapid fire, slightly nasal delivery.

Sloan looked at us with disappointment. "I thought that you two, of all people, would understand the lingo."

"Oh, we understand the lingo—" Daphne assured him.

"—we just don't know what the hell you're talking about!" I finished. "I mean, what major league dirt?"

Sloan leaned in even closer. The smell of Old Spice permeated my nostrils and I stifled a sneeze. "Well, confidentially, there's been some talk that Damien Duran's drowning *wasn't* an accident."

All became clear. "You've being talking to Mavis DiSpachio, haven't you?"

"I tried to reach the two of you earlier this evening," Sloan continued quickly, "but you weren't home. Mrs. DiSpachio kindly clued me in on your investigations into the matter so far."

"Investigations!" Daphne squawked.

"Sssshh!" he hissed, looking from side to side in the manner of a stoolie in an old gangster film. "Anyone could be listening!" This was getting totally ludicrous. But Sloan wasn't finished yet. "The mark on the neck, have you got any leads on that so yet?"

"Look, the first we heard about the mark was from Mavis, so that doesn't really—"

Sloan barreled right over me. "Right, the mark shaped like a 'U.' Any ideas?"

"Of course not!" I didn't add that even if I *did* have any ideas, he'd be the last person I'd share them with.

Sloan looked at the two of us with admiration. "You're just as modest as Ms. DiSpachio said you'd be." Before either of us could respond to that remark with the contempt it deserved, Sloan continued. "What about the bruises on his back? There were bruises on his back, you know!"

"No, we *didn't* know," I said. "But there are a lot of rocks on that part of the beach, so it wouldn't really surprise me if the poor guy was bruised from head to toe."

Sloan ignored my logic. "It may also interest you to know that Lucille Monroe has reportedly received several threatening phone calls over the last two days and—" He looked at me. "Did you say something?"

I had, in fact, laughed. "Threatening phone calls? What sort of threats?"

"She wouldn't get specific, just said that the threats concerned her involvement with the Festival. From my vantage, it looks like trouble. Maybe even a connection with Duran's death."

From the way he was speaking, it was obvious that Sloan relished the thought that there might be trouble. The only trouble I saw from *my* vantage was the thought of what Sloan might write. The man was a throwback to the days of muckraking. I wondered how he'd take it if I suggested he submit a resume to *The Weekly Globe*.

Daphne, in the meantime, had no hesitation in giving Sloan her opinion. "Well, this is the first we've heard of any threats to Lucille, Mr. Sloan, although it wouldn't surprise me considering what a bi ..." Daphne caught herself as Sloan began scribbling down every word. " ... what a difficult person she can be. Have you considered the possibility that it might be a publicity device on her part?"

"Now *that's* an interesting thought." Sloan scribbled furiously. "This throws a whole new slant on the story."

Great, I thought. Just what we needed, more bad blood with Lucille. I figured I'd better step in. "As for Damien Duran, we don't know anything more about that than you do."

Sloan looked at me in sympathy. "Investigation not going so well?"

"There *isn't* any investigation, Mr. Sloan!" I was beginning to get angry. "The man drowned! The police say it was an accident, so let's ..."

"You've been in contact with the police, then!" Sloan's pen flew across the paper.

"No! I didn't say that!"

"Oh, *I* see." Sloan nodded wisely. "You can't divulge your contacts, I understand." He looked at us conspiratorially and added, "You know what I mean?" He went back to his writing. I was speechless.

"The birds fly south for the winter," Daphne murmured.

"What was that?" Sloan looked up from his notebook, startled.

"Nothing," Daphne replied sweetly. "Just babbling."

"Hmmm." Sloan scribbled a few more words and then shut his notebook with a decisive 'snap'.

I finally recovered my voice. "If that's all, Mr. Sloan, we need to get back inside. And you have another interview waiting for you."

"That's right!" Sloan looked eager at the thought of a fresh victim. I didn't know who to feel sorry for, Sloan or Grant, so I decided not to waste my pity on either of them. "This was just great, girls! I'll be in touch." He headed back into the museum. "Keep me posted on any pertinent evidence that might come your way!" With that, he vanished back inside.

Daphne and I looked at each other. "What did we just do?" she asked me.

"I'm not sure," I replied. "But I have a really bad feeling that it's gonna be in the newspaper."

"Yeah, straight from the horse's mouth," she said glumly.

"And written up by a horse's ass," I finished.

Chapter Five

Alex and I stood by a bay window in the living room of Jason Down's opulent Emerald Cove residence. The house was set back from the cliffs overlooking the ocean, providing a magnificent view. And even though it was eleven o'clock, we could still see the pounding surf foaming up on the rocks, courtesy of Mr. Downs' backyard lights. These weren't ordinary lights, mind you, but high-powered spotlights set in a rim along the back wall, illuminating the seascape below. A set of French doors led to an outdoor courtyard set at the top of a terraced garden, which descended in well-tended steps to the beach.

The house itself was comfortably opulent, done up like a hunting lodge with dark wood paneling and thick hunter-green carpeting. The furnishings were all leather and more dark wood, old-fashioned lanterns casting a soft illumination on oil paintings depicting English hunting scenes. If there were a Mrs. Downs, either she didn't exert much influence in the decorating, or she liked living in a house that was reminiscent of an exclusive Men's Club. I found it soothing, a different world from the boisterous crowd that we'd left only a half hour ago back at the Museum.

A glass of expensive champagne had gone a long way towards improving my mood, that and the fact that Grant had still not arrived. If I hadn't already decided to break up with him after the Festival, the fact that I felt trapped when he was in the same room would've told me it was time.

Daphne and I had gone back in the lobby after our disastrous interview with Arthur Sloan, and Grant had once again been surrounded by adoring fans and was more than ready to give an interview. When I'd told him that Daphne and I were going to go ahead to the party, he'd kissed me absently on the head, saying he'd join me later. Between Sloan trying to dig out all the dirt on the Festival and Grant promoting himself, I was sure he'd be at least an hour. So Daphne and I had driven over and met Alex there. The three of us were practically the first ones at the party.

"Quite a view, isn't it?"

I smiled up at Alex. "Yeah. I could get used to this sort of lifestyle. Now if I could only figure out how to obtain it."

"Here's to obtaining our dreams." He paused, giving me a meaningful look over the rim of his glass. "Whatever they might be."

We clinked expensive crystal champagne flutes. I lowered my eyes as I sipped, wondering if there was such a thing as love at first sight. I had no doubts about the reality of lust at first sight.

"Hey, Connie, have you tried these stuffed mushrooms?" Daphne's voice broke the mood. "And the baked cheese puffs are delicious!" She held out her plate, which was piled high with hors d'oeuvres of all types, a stuffed mushroom threatening to tumble off the side.

"Thanks, Daphne." I rescued the mushroom, only to send it to its doom between my teeth. "God, that's good!" I took a cheese puff. "Have you met Jason Downs yet?"

Daphne shook her head. "Nope. I haven't even seen him. Not that I'd know what he looks like if I did. Have you?"

"No. I wonder if he's even here yet."

"You know," Daphne said thoughtfully in between bites of stuffed mushrooms, "it's kind of weird that we've been working on the Festival for three weeks and still haven't met this guy."

"That elusive Scarlet Pimpernel," I replied absently, more interested in the contents of her plate than the elusive Jason Downs. "Are there any crab cakes left?"

"Are you kidding? Tons!" Daphne gestured around the sparsely populated room, sending a bit of cheese puff flying. "There's enough food for an army over there and hardly anyone's arrived yet."

Scarcely had the words left her mouth when the doorbell rang, signaling a slew of new guests and the end of our peaceful little interlude. Flamenco guitar started up, replacing the innocuous New Age music that had been playing since we'd arrived.

Burke, Mavis and Lucille were among the latest guests, with Andy trailing in a safe distance behind them. Mavis still had Burke in her purple-chiffon draped clutches, oblivious to his bored mien. Lucille cast a predatory gaze around her, but luckily her view of Alex was blocked by the growing crowd of people. I decided I needed food and a lot more champagne if I was going to deal with any of the new arrivals.

"Time to refuel," I said to Daphne, grabbing Alex by the hand and pulling him over to the food-laden buffet tables at the other end of the living room. I started piling hors d'oeuvres on a plate.

"I'll get more champagne." Alex snagged my glass and intercepted one of two tastefully clad waiters circulating with buckets of cold Perrier-Jouet champagne and crystal flutes.

More people poured into Jason Down's house as I loaded my plate with food enough for two. Among the stuffed mushrooms and cheese puffs there were also luscious crab cakes, finger sandwiches, smoked salmon, fresh brie, all kinds of crackers and spreads including caviar and sour cream, and an entire table devoted to nothing but desserts. I'd raid that one later.

Alex reappeared carrying flutes brimming with champagne. He looked at my ladened plate. "I could go kill a deer if you're that hungry."

"Hey," I protested, "I hunted for two."

"Better than eating for two."

"Let's find a place to sit down, shall we?"

The house was filling up rapidly, but we found a place on one of the leather and plaid couches in the living room. Daphne had already settled herself in one corner, happily occupied with her food. The three of us sat and ate in companionable silence for a few minutes, watching the stream of guests as they came in through the front entranceway.

Brad and Tasha came in, saw us, waved, and headed straight for the champagne. Tasha looked quite elegant in a navy blue silk dress and heels, while Brad held true to the male creed of 'jeans and nice shirt a dressy outfit make'. Shaun, on the other hand, arriving minutes later, was actually wearing dress pants and a black rayon shirt. He was in between girlfriends and was dressed to impress. If he was lucky, Lucille wouldn't notice him.

Many of Emerald Cove's elite walked through Jason Down's front door in the space of fifteen minutes. Sandwiched in between the elite was Chris with his tattoos and leather jacket, looking at ease enough to have been born to the crowd with which he was mingling. I recognized some of the Festival Board members, all dressed to the nines in designer labels and sparkling jewelry, and wondered how many of them, if any, mourned for Damien Duran. Not many, unless this was the Emerald Cove high society version of a wake.

"Why so thoughtful?" Alex looked at me quizzically.

"She's trying to figure out if she can eat another crab cake without exploding," said Daphne.

I ignored that. "I was just thinking about Damien Duran … wondering if anyone here actually gives a rat's ass that he's dead."

Daphne shrugged. "Hard to tell."

"And more to the point, I wonder if anyone here is actually happy about it." My gaze flickered over to Lucille, currently monopolizing Jonathan Burke's attention, all of which was focused on her chest.

"Like, 'happy he's dead' or 'happy they killed him' happy?"

"Considering that he had a huge fight with Lucille, I guess that anything's possible," I said flippantly.

Alex raised an eyebrow. "Do I detect a bit of previously denied interest in, well, detecting?"

Daphne and I looked at each other and laughed. I shook my head and said, "That'd be like someone with ADD deciding they wanted to be an air traffic controller."

Daphne nodded. "Not our forte."

"Forte, huh? Pretty fancy word from a tough talkin' dame like yourself." Brad, a plate full of food that made my previous pillage of the hors d'oeuvres table spread seem stingy, sat down on the arm of the sofa. Tasha was right behind him, with two flutes of champagne. We scooted over to make room for her on the couch.

We were soon joined by Chris and Shaun and another ten minutes passed by, during which the MFH crowd congregated on and around our sofa, drinking an abundance of champagne and eating food that Jenny Craig and the late Dr. Atkins would have run from, screaming in terror. It was refreshing to hang out with our cast without the stress of rehearsal and I was thankful Grant hadn't arrived yet, as he would've been hot to mingle with the crowd.

I was actually starting to wonder if Grant had decided to blow the party off when he hadn't shown by the time I was ready to hit the dessert table. Come to think of it, Sloan hadn't made his appearance yet either, although maybe Lady Luck and Jason Downs had decreed that he wasn't invited. Whatever the reason, who was I to question the will of the Gods?

"Time for dessert?" Alex looked pointedly at our empty plate.

"You read my mind," I said as we both stood up.

"Yeah, and it's just this repeated cry for chocolate."

"Jeez, Connie, he *can* read your mind." Daphne grinned up at me. "How about getting me some, too?"

"We won't be able to carry enough for both of you," Alex said, pulling Daphne up by one hand and giving her a gentle push towards the buffet tables. "Besides—" Alex reached out and caught my arm as I headed after Daphne, "—I think we'd better dance off some of the crab cakes before we go for the big guns."

He pulled me back into a passable spin, putting his hands on my hips as he proceeded to follow the rhythm of the music. The sound system was now giving us Gypsy Kings and I'd had just enough champagne to throw caution to the wind and go with it, my hands resting on his shoulders and back as we moved in time to the music. Alex moved his hand over the curve of my hip as we danced, a subtle, erotic gesture that could have been deliberate or accidental. It didn't matter. By the time the song ended, we were staring into each other's eyes, out of breath from more than the exertion of dancing.

"So," Alex said softly, hands still resting lightly on my hips, "If I feed you chocolate, will you tell me what you have against stuntmen?"

I burst into laughter, his words effectively quelling the sexual tension. "Feed me chocolate and you might even change my mind."

"Promises, promises."

Hand in hand, we threaded our way through the now-large crowd to the dessert table. Daphne was still selecting from the wide assortment of goodies spread out before her, completely oblivious to the admiring gazes of several men trying their best to get a better glimpse of her cleavage as she leaned over the table to study the desserts.

"Tell you what." Alex handed me a clean plate. "Why don't you be in charge of the desserts while I get us some more champagne?"

I felt for any sign of an impending hangover. Not even a twinge, so I said, "Sounds good. I'll meet you back at the couch, okay?"

"Best offer I've had all year." With that, Alex vanished into the crowd.

I turned back to Daphne with what must have been a really dippy smile. She took one look at my expression and shook her head. "Disgusting."

"You're just jealous," I teased as I reached for a mini-éclair coated in dark chocolate, oozing cream from all sides.

"Damned right I am," she shot back, stealing the éclair from under my outstretched fingers. "I bet *he* doesn't cry every time the friggin' sun sets!"

I took another equally tempting éclair. "I thought you thought that was romantic." Oh my, three-layered chocolate mousse …

"It is. Once." There was a definite note of finality here.

"Does this mean that the sun is setting on Guido?"

Daphne nodded. "Tomorrow first thing. After we get back from blocking out the Walking Tour, that is."

I toasted her with a petit four, popping it into my mouth. "I heartily endorse the move," I said in between bites.

She looked at me slyly. "And does this mean that we're going to see the end of …" Daphne stopped short as a hand clamped around my wrist, turning me around with a hard tug. Luckily I'd set my plate down on the table or my pastries would have gone flying. And that would've meant war.

Grant stood glowering down at me, his cobalt eyes flashing a storm warning. "I'd like a word with you, Connie." He bit each word off with a decisive snap.

I did not like the sound of this, especially as I had no idea what I'd done or *not* done to bring this on. I was completely taken aback, and just a little embarrassed. People were staring. "I'm getting dessert, Grant, can't it wait a bit?"

"I don't think so."

"Um, okay. Daphne, can you take my plate till I get back?"

Daphne did so, giving Grant a look of pure dislike as she said, "God, Grant, you are *such* a control freak!" There was no love lost between those two.

Grant ignored her. Still holding me by the wrist, he wrapped his other arm around my shoulders and said, "Let's go outside, shall we?" Not waiting for a reply, Grant practically pulled me towards the French doors. I went without argument because I had the feeling he would have dragged me out anyway and the last thing MFH needed was a public scene between two of its members.

Once outside in the courtyard, Grant steered me to a bench and sat me down with enough force to make Alex's reference to Don José seem less laughable. Angry words at Grant's arrogant behavior formed on my lips, but he beat me to the punch.

He leaned over me and said, "What the hell did you think you were doing?"

I stared up at him, completely taken aback by the intense anger in his voice. "I was about to have some dessert before you interrupted."

"That's not what I'm talking about and you know it."

Good God, dialogue straight from a Soap. Well, I wasn't in the mood. I started to stand, saying, "You know, Grant, if you're going to be obscure I'm going back inside."

Grant grabbed my shoulders and pushed me back down. "You're not going back in there without me, and we're not going back in until we get a few things straight."

"Well, get *this* straight," I shot back, furious at his high-handed treatment, "I don't appreciate being manhandled!"

"Oh? I can remember several occasions where you seemed to enjoy it quite a bit."

I blushed, knowing full well that he was referring to certain past sessions of rambunctious love-making that had left both of us enjoyably exhausted. "That was different, Grant, it's called role-playing. It's not the same thing as being bullied!"

"You certainly seemed to enjoy it when Alex manhandled you. Or was that role-playing?"

"Do you mean … are you talking about the fact that we *danced*?" Grant was silent. This was going from the ridiculous to the ludicrous and I'd had just about enough. "Because if that's what all this fuss is about, you'd better …"

He cut me off. "I don't like walking in finding you in the arms of another man."

I couldn't believe this. "Jesus Christ, it was just one dance, Grant, it …"

"I'm not blind and I'm not stupid, Connie." Grant sat down beside me, hands biting into my shoulders as he continued, "There was more than dancing going on between the two of you."

I was silent for a moment, partly due to the fact that he was right and partly because I'd never seen Grant quite so … *realistically* angry before. I decided that offense was the best defense in this case and went straight for the jugular. "You know, Grant, I never say a word when you're surrounded by adoring fans and that happens a hell of a lot!"

It worked. Taken by surprise, Grant's fingers loosened slightly. He recovered quickly and came back with, "That's not the same thing, Connie, and—"

"The hell it isn't! You flirt with dozens of strange women every day because it's part of your job and don't tell me you don't enjoy it, because it's obvious that you do!"

Grant started to interject something but I was on a pleasantly self-righteous, if slightly hypocritical roll and had no intention of stopping. "So why are you giving me grief because I flirted with Alex? He's a nice guy, I enjoy his company!" I stood up, pulling away when Grant tried to catch hold of me again. "More importantly, he's new to the group, and I want him to feel comfortable! So sue me!"

I fully intended to go back inside, but my grand exit was ruined when one of my heels caught in a cobblestone, twisting my ankle slightly. I might have fallen had Grant—in true romance hero style—not leapt to his feet and caught me in his arms. Oh hell, I thought, seeing the gleam in his eyes.

"I didn't realize you were jealous," he said softly, still holding me. We looked like we were posing for the cover of a trashy romance. I briefly wondered if any of those heroines ever discovered the joys of chiropractors because they'd sure as hell need them. There was nothing comfortable about my current position.

"Grant, this is killing my back." I pushed against him. He straightened up slightly. "And I'm not jealous. I just hate double standards."

"If you say so." He sounded so smug, I just wanted to slap him. But better to let him believe what he wanted and get this whole unpleasant little scene over with.

I knew a kiss was inevitable so rather than fight it, I accepted it passively. The lack of enthusiasm on my part didn't seem to bother Grant, who wore a satisfied smile when he finally let me go.

"Now let's get you that dessert you wanted," he said magnanimously, one hand resting on my lower back as we walked back inside.

Gee, thanks, I thought. But I kept it to myself. Grant was history after Sunday night's performance and that was all there was to it.

Back inside, we were immediately approached by Irene Matthias, one of the mutual theater friends with whom Grant was staying. Irene's a theater junkie, the sort of person who (and I quote) 'just adores the creative stimulation circulating within the environs of a theater.' An attractive brunette in her mid- thirties, Irene had just enough talent to get small parts in local productions, which kept her stimulation circulating. She's nice enough, once you get past the pretentious outer layer.

Irene had several society matron types with her, all eyeing Grant the way I had eyed the dessert table. Introductions were made all around, myself included, although it was obvious that the interest was in Grant, not me. To give Grant credit, he went out of his way to let the women know that he was with me, even as he proceeded to charm them with his easy and superficial chatter.

I took the opportunity to surreptitiously scan the room for Alex. He was not on the couch nor could I see him anywhere in the crowd. I saw Chris, who looked to be in deep discussion with a young woman wearing a very conservative and very expensive satin dress. They both wore expressions of intense concentration and seemed fascinated with each other. Oh, to be a fly on the wall for *that* conversation.

Daphne was also on the missing in action list, along with my dessert plate. I wondered if she'd told Alex that I'd been shanghaied at the buffet. I hoped so, I didn't want him to think I'd stood him up.

I saw Brad and Tasha float by, both carrying flutes of champagne. They stopped briefly when I waved. "How's it going?" Tasha inquired, brushing back a curl of pale blonde hair that had escaped from her French braid. Her wide blue eyes were somewhat unfocused, as were Brad's. I suspected that they'd downed a lot of champagne since last I'd seen them.

"Fine," I replied, maneuvering out of the small circle of women surrounding Grant. He kept an eye on me even as he continued regaling his admirers with an anecdote about his days in drama school. "Have you spoken to our host yet?"

"Sure," said Brad. "He was in the library showing off his collection of antique toy soldiers." He waved one arm towards a door at the other end of the living room, nearly knocking a glass out of the hand of another guest.

"Did you by any chance see Daphne?"

Tasha took a sip of her champagne. "We were telling her about the soldiers and I think she and Alex went in to see if they could find Mr. Downs."

I tried to act nonchalant at that bit of information, conscious that Grant's attention had shifted towards us with the mention of Alex's name.

Brad tugged at Tasha's arm. "C'mon, schnooks, let's get some more food."

"See you later, Connie!" They both waved and floated back towards the buffet.

I slipped an arm through Grant's and pretended an interest in his anecdote that I'd heard several times before.

" … and when we'd finished the scene, the director stood there for a moment and said, 'I have to apologize, folks. I was so fascinated watching Grant clean his nails that I didn't pay attention to the rest of the scene.' Then he turned to me and told me that it was the best bit of improv stage business he'd ever seen, but I'd have to cut it or all the focus would be on me instead of the action."

I waited until Grant uttered the deep, falsely self-deprecating laugh that always followed this story, and let his audience's high, shrieking giggles of appreciation die down to manageable decibels before saying softly, "Grant, I'm going to go hunt down Daphne. She has my dessert plate and there's such a crowd around the table now."

He glanced over to verify my story before saying, "You don't mind if I stay here for a minute, do you, darling? Irene has some other people she really thinks I ought to meet."

I shook my head. "Not at all. Business first."

Grant smiled approvingly down at me, giving a little shake of his head as if to say, 'that's my brave girl.'

I smiled back through gritted teeth. Fine, let Grant think I was putting on a brave front to hide my jealousy if it made him more reasonable. No skin off my nose. But ye gods, his patronizing manner was infuriating!

Irene touched my arm before I could leave. "Connie, is it true that you and Daphne are actually investigating poor Mr. Duran's death?"

I started to ask Irene where she got such a ludicrous idea, but before the words left my mouth, I saw the obvious answer waft by, swathed, mummy-like, in layers of purple fabric. *Never mind.* I thought of Eddie Murphy's old SNL comedy routine, the one where he's a convict, reciting his poem "Kill My Landlord." I glared at Mavis as I tried to come up with a reply that didn't include the words 'kill my landlady.'

The problem was taken out of my hands — or mouth, rather — by Grant. "Now there's a ridiculous notion if ever I've heard one." He put an arm around my shoulders and gave a squeeze. "It takes a complex mind to solve a murder." Grant gave another little laugh, on doubt intended to take the sting out of his words. It didn't work. "The only way Connie and Daphne would be able to solve a mystery is if they had a script to refer to. Isn't that right, sweetheart?" His admiring audience tittered. Grant smiled down at me, inviting me to share the joke.

Daphne says that having something like that said to you is the verbal equivalent of being slapped in the face out of nowhere with a wet haddock. It takes you totally by surprise and you can't believe it actually happened until you have some time to process the event. An apt comparison, because I could not bring myself to accept that Grant had just insulted me so completely in front of a crowd.

I looked at Grant and gave a laugh that had nothing to do with levity. "Well, there's your answer, Irene." I shrugged out from under Grant's arm. "Excuse me."

As soon as I left Grant's side, the women all moved in closer, cutting him off from my view and vice-versa. Fine. At that moment, if I never saw or heard Grant Havers again, I'd die a happy woman. And, if the next time I *did* see him, he was on the receiving end of a baseball bat, I'd die an even happier woman. I headed off towards the library in search of my friend, my dessert, and Alex.

When Tasha and Brad had talked about a library, it had conjured visions of a cozy little room lined with books, a single leather arm-chair and a table with a reading lamp. Well, it was a room lined with books and there was indeed a leather armchair. However the room was the size of Daphne's old apartment, and the bookshelves were alternated with glass walled curio cabinets, inside of which were the fabled antique soldier collection. The leather armchair was one of four, each with its own reading lamp. There was also a couch strewn with plaid cushions.

While not as crowded as the front room, the library was still pretty packed with people, but I managed to spot Daphne curled up on one end of the couch. She was deep in conversation with Franklin, of all people. He was holding a bottle of Perrier and gesticulating broadly as he spoke. I walked up to them, catching bits and pieces of their discussion. Every sentence I heard included the words 'Randell' and 'genius'.

"Hi, guys," I interrupted.

Franklin looked up, his face as open and eager as a puppy's. "Connie! What a pleasure it is to see you! Daphne and I were just talking about the Festival! Isn't this great?" A lock of shaggy blonde hair fell forward at the same time as his wire-rimmed glasses. He shoved the hair back out of his face and the glasses back onto the bridge of his nose in a mechanical gesture.

Franklin reminds me of a poor man's Clark Kent, one who'd never emerge from a phone booth as Superman. "I can't wait until the Walking Tours, they're going to be just fantastic! Are you girls—" That word again.

"—ready for them? Of course you are, I'm sure you're just as excited as I am!" He beamed at both of us.

No reply seemed necessary, so I smiled at him and then turned to Daphne. "Please say you still have my plate. Because I really, really need it right now." She pointed to a small side table next to the couch. There it was, my plate still piled high in all of its caloric, fat-filled glory. "You are a true friend," I told Daphne. "Did you tell Alex that I was ... er ... detained?"

"No." Daphne took a sip of champagne. "I told him you were dragged outside by a creep with a control complex."

"Oh, you have *no* idea ..." I gave her a succinct and admittedly vituperative account of what happened with Grant, including his disparaging comments about our deductive skills. Which, true to the delayed reaction of the wet haddock effect, made me angrier each passing minute.

"That son of a bitch!" said Daphne. "He actually said that in *front* of people?"

I nodded grimly.

"And you didn't kill him?"

"Wet haddock."

"Ah." Daphne nodded in complete understanding.

Franklin listened to all of this with great interest, if little comprehension.

"But I swear," I said, "if I thought if Damien Duran was really murdered, I would be SO tempted to try and figure out who did it, just to make Grant eat his words!" I shoved a mini-éclair in my mouth for emphasis.

"Asshole," muttered Daphne. "Even if he *is* right."

"How do we know he's right? We've never tried to solve a murder before! So how do we know we couldn't do it?" I was righteously indignant, not to mention high on sugar. Sensibly, Daphne had no answer for this, and my newfound faith in our non-existent deductive capabilities subsided as fast as it had risen. I looked around the room. "So where'd Alex go, anyway?

"We came in here to find Mr. Downs, missed him by a minute according to Franklin here—"

"That's right," Franklin interjected. "He's a great guy, too. Has a very comprehensive Randell collection. You'll have to meet him."

I nodded absently as Daphne continued, "At any rate, Alex decided to see if he could find him so he went that a way." She pointed towards a door at the other end of the library that led to yet another room jammed with people.

"I'm going to see if I can find him. Just let me know when you want to leave, okay?" Daphne nodded and went back to her conversation with Franklin. I picked up my plate full of its precious cargo and wandered into the next room, which appeared to be an entertainment center dominated by a huge plasma screen television currently showing *The Maltese Falcon*. Hmmm, Jason Downs *did* have good taste.

Success! I saw Alex across the room in animated discussion with Shaun, who looked pleasantly tipsy. Alex still had two glasses of champagne and I hoped one of them was for me.

Alex looked up and glanced in my direction. His face lit up when he saw me. He said something to Shaun and started towards me.

Before he was even halfway across the room, however, he was stopped in his tracks by Lucille. I could feel my hands curve into claws as she slipped an arm through his, smiling intimately all the while. Alex looked decidedly uncomfortable as Lucille leaned up and whispered something in his ear.

The question here was, did I want to act like a lady and let Alex extricate himself or did I want to go over there and punch Lucille's lights out? The matter was settled when Lucille plucked one of the glasses of champagne from his hand and ran one red-lacquered nail up his thigh. I saw red and took a step forward.

"Connie!"

My bloodlust was thwarted when Andy unwittingly stepped in front of me, his mood much improved. Like everyone else at the party, he carried a champagne flute. If the rosy glow suffusing his jowly face was anything to go by, I suspected the glass had been refilled many times that evening.

"Are you having fun? I know this is the most relaxed *I've* been in weeks! I'm going to enjoy it while it lasts, because tomorrow is going to bring nothing but grief, let me tell you!"

"This is great, Andy. I'm just trying to find a friend ..." I tried to peer over Andy's shoulder, but his tall, heavy-set form blocked my view. Even standing on tip-toe didn't help.

"Just watch out," he said with quick look around. "Lucille and Burke are both around here somewhere. And there isn't enough champagne in the world to make their company bearable!" With those sage words of wisdom, Andy wove his way into the library, leaving my field of vision wide open.

Alex had somehow managed to extricate himself from Lucille's red-taloned clutches and was edging away from her as quickly as politeness allowed. She had my champagne glass. Bitch.

Just as Alex ended the conversation with Lucille, a hand caressed my rear with a familiarity that caused me to jump. I whirled around and saw

Jonathan Burke holding forth to a group of guests. He was smirking in such a way that made me sure that he was the culprit and the satisfied glance he gave me out of the corner of his eye confirmed my suspicion. He was paying me back for interfering with his pursuit of Daphne, and he knew that I knew it. I silently vowed vengeance.

And then Alex was at my side, casting a quick look back to make sure that Lucille was not in pursuit. "Quick," he said under his breath, "Let's get out of here."

"Good idea. Cruella De Ville is still looking your way." And I didn't want to remain in the same room with Burke a second longer.

We went back through the library where Daphne and Franklin had been joined by Andy.

"Do you want to stay in here?" Alex asked as I hesitated before going back into the front room.

I peeked out the door to see where Grant was. He was still carrying on a conversation with Irene and her friends, periodically scanning the room with a slight frown. I ducked back inside the library before he saw me. "It would probably be a good idea." I gave him a slightly edited version of what had happened with Grant.

Alex frowned. "I'm liking that man less and less."

"Well, the feeling's mutual on his part." I leaned against the wall, setting my plate down on a nearby table. "I swear, he's never been so irrational or possessive before."

"Maybe he senses that he's losing you."

"The operative word here is 'lost'." I took an éclair off the plate and nibbled on it. "Tonight was the last straw. Now I just have to tell him. But not until after Sunday night. The rest of the cast has a hard enough time working with him without adding that kind of tension to the pot." I sighed. "Right now I could really use that glass of champagne that Lucille stole."

Alex grinned. "Sorry about that. But I'm not going to steal it back, if that's what you're angling for."

I grimaced. "Please. I'd rather have a fresh one. Who knows where that woman's been? Never mind, don't answer that."

"Wasn't even going to try. I'll be right back." Alex vanished into the front room, reappearing moments later with my champagne and a tense expression.

"Yours truly is headed this way," he warned me dramatically. "I think he suspects."

"Oh, hell! Let's go hang out by Daphne. It won't look so …"

"So sordid?"

I elbowed him in the ribs. "Call it what you will, but I'm *not* up to another fight tonight, so just cooperate! Besides," I added with a certain touch of malice, "Lucille just made an appearance and there's safety in numbers."

In one of those rare moments of perfect timing, we managed to position ourselves on opposite ends of the couch with Daphne, Franklin and Andy just as Grant entered the room. And even better, the crowd cleared out just enough for Lucille to have a clear view of him as he came through the door. Her eyes narrowed, her hunting instincts—among other things—clearly aroused.

Lucille intercepted Grant before he'd taken more than two steps into the library. I tried not to be too obvious as I watched Lucille imposing her dubious charms on Grant. I noted the set look on Grant's face as Lucille murmured something in his ear. She then ran one finger up the side of his champagne flute in a blatantly suggestive manner, her gaze boring into Grant's. He looked pretty tense, struggling manfully not to let his disgust show. He managed a somewhat forced smile as she said something else in his ear.

Grant stood it for about five minutes, no doubt not wanting to offend anyone who might possibly be able to help his career, even when that anyone was as repugnant as Lucille. Only the appearance of Jonathan Burke distracted Lucille's attention long enough for Grant to excuse himself.

He joined me at the couch, his mouth a grim line. I knew better than to ask what they'd been talking about. Grant looked ready to explode again. Instead, I smiled as though I was happy to see him and said, "I'm thinking about heading home. It must be getting close to 1:00 and I'm wiped."

I was afraid that Grant would want to go home with me and was already prepared with the litany of reasons why I needed to go straight to sleep. To my relief and surprise, he didn't suggest that he join me. Still looking annoyed, he replied in a distracted manner, "I'm going to do the same. I may have an audition tomorrow and I need to get some sleep. I'll walk you to your car."

Daphne looked up. "Are we leaving, Connie?"

"Do you mind?"

"Nah." Daphne stood up and stretched, an action that immediately garnered the attention of most males in the room. "We've got a lot of work to do tomorrow. See you at the library in the morning, right, Andy?"

Andy nodded cheerfully. "Sounds good. I'll have the stuff for the Walking Tours ready for you by 9:00. Just come around the side to my office because the library won't be open yet. I'll make sure to unlock the side-gate."

I looked at Alex. "We'll see you tomorrow at rehearsal?" I hoped my voice didn't sound too eager.

"Wild horses and all that." He nodded briefly to Grant, who barely acknowledged the gesture.

Daphne and I retrieved our purses from the front room, pausing only to say good-bye to Brad, Tasha and Shaun. Chris had vanished, along with the girl he'd been talking to. Maybe he'd gotten lucky.

Grant walked us to my car, promising to contact me in the morning and let me know about his audition. He then gave me a perfunctory kiss on the lips and vanished. Strange behavior from someone who'd been in a jealous rage only a short time ago. I didn't know whether to be insulted or relieved.

It wasn't until we were nearly home that Daphne said, "You know, we never did meet Jason Downs."

I shrugged. "Another time."

"No, but don't you think it's kind of weird? I mean, how come we seem to be the only ones who haven't met him? Maybe he doesn't exist."

I yawned widely. "You've been reading too many mysteries."

"Yeah," said Daphne. "Too bad we're not better at solving them."

Chapter Six

It was a chilly, gray Friday morning as Daphne and I sat at one of the small white tables dotting the outside patio of the Ginger Cottage Bakery. One of our favorite breakfast hangouts, Ginger Cottage was located on Cove Street, right across the street from the ocean. Along with the view, they also served the best cinnamon rolls this side of heaven, along with a wide selection of coffee and espresso beverages.

Having already ordered, we were leaning back in our chairs watching the early morning traffic go by, trying to wake up. Neither Daphne nor I are known for greeting each new day with enthusiasm. At eight in the morning, I desperately needed the sugar and caffeine jolt that only a cinnamon roll and a Blanco Espresso (white chocolate mocha by any other name) could bring.

Both of us were in unusually foul moods this particular morning, partially brought on by an over-indulgence in too much rich food and alcohol consumed way too late the night before. Being waylaid by a disgustingly chipper Mavis on our way out the door hadn't helped to improve our dispositions, especially considering that her first words had been, "Any new leads, girls?"

With a quick, "We're late, Mavis, we'll see you later!" Daphne had grabbed my arm and pulled me down the front walk before I could deliver the scathing response her question deserved.

I was also still seething over Grant's behavior and his disparaging comments, as well as indulging in a session of circular thinking concerning Alex and my unaccountable reaction to him. Was he *really* as attractive as I remembered? Did he *really* find me as attractive as I found him? Did I behave like an idiot teenager with her first crush last night? Did I want the answers to these questions? And back to the beginning again.

But the bulk of our bad temper had to do with this morning's edition of *The Emerald Post*. As we had speculated, we were indeed news this morning. The paper was currently spread out before us on the table as we read the article in disbelief.

Under the heading 'Death Takes A Bow', Arthur Sloan, budding crime reporter, had compiled an article on the Festival and the death of Damien Duran containing speculations that seemed more suited to a tabloid than a small local newspaper. Sloan made a fleeting reference to the findings of the coroner's verdict of accidental drowning, but then went on to fling vague innuendoes with abandon. He skirted, if not crossed, the line between justifiable speculation and grounds for lawsuits.

Sloan also cited the mysterious 'U' shaped mark on the back of Duran's neck as proof that foul play had occurred. Although no names were mentioned in direct conjunction with Duran's death, the impression I received from the article was that anyone who'd ever met Damien Duran was a possible suspect. Lucille's threatening phone calls were gleefully reported as well.

But the capper was in the final smarmy paragraph, where it stated:

> *Daphne Graves and Connie Garrett, the two lovely and talented heads of Emerald Cove's own "Murder for Hire," are said to be investigating the matter. Although the girls coyly deny this, one source informs us that they are working night and day on inside information pertaining to the case.*

"*Coyly*. He used the word *coyly?* I can't believe this. How did this idiot get a job writing for the *Post?*" I shook my head in disbelief. "He's got to be related to someone 'cause I can't imagine anyone wanting to sleep with him."

"And he called us 'girls'," Daphne reminded me glumly. "I really hate that."

I spotted something else. "Oh, and look at this," I said, stabbing a finger at Grant's picture, a scaled down version of his headshot, in the lower right-hand corner of the page. "Grant's interview got its own section."

Daphne looked. "I can't believe that!" she exclaimed irately. "Not one word about our organization other than to make us sound like a couple of idiot Nancy Drew wannabees, but Mr. Soapdish gets his picture in! And how did he get Sloan a picture on such short notice?"

"He carries extras in his car, of course. No actor in L.A. travels without them." I read the section on Grant aloud.

> *Well-known star of* Tomorrow's Secret Search, *Grant Havers, graces Emerald Cove with a special guest appearance in Murder For Hire's shows for Saturday's Walking Tours and Sunday night's Gala Dinner. Mr. Havers is taking a break from the rigors of Hollywood and enjoying the quieter pace of Emerald Cove's theatrical world with his fiancé, Connie Garrett ...*

I looked up at Daphne. "I'm going to kill him."

"Which one? Grant or Sloan?"

"Both." I read on.

> When asked what he thought of his fiancé's sleuthing activities,
> Mr. Havers refused to comment, cleverly steering the conversation
> back to his own career. I guess discretion is necessary when you're
> involved with an amateur detective.

I don't know which pissed me off more, being called an amateur or a detective.

"Discretion?" Daphne snorted inelegantly. "Try 'narcissism'. Is there anything else?"

I scanned the rest of the article. "Just a bunch of stuff about Grant's career. Nothing we haven't heard before so I'll spare you the repetition."

A gust of cool air blew in off the ocean and I shivered inside of my bulky forest-green sweater and jeans, wishing I'd worn my leather flight jacket as well. Daphne seemed comfortable in her jeans and short sleeved pink t-shirt, but then she's one of those people who seems to be able to adjust to any weather condition without discomfort. A good thing, because Daphne is a definite believer in vanity before comfort.

The arrival of our breakfast—warm cinnamon rolls dripping with frosting, accompanied by large cups of steaming mochas—went a long way in reviving our flagging spirits. One sip of my Blanco Espresso brought a contented smile as the caffeine and sugar hit the system and almost instantly drove away the lingering effects of last night's gastronomical indiscretions. Maybe life wasn't so bad after all. Although I still wanted Sloan's head on a platter. And I wanted Grant in a different country. Like Tierra del Fuego.

Daphne and I concentrated on our food for a few minutes until the initial feeding frenzy subsided. Then we went over the Walking Tours, discussing the various places where we might be performing, and whether or not our actors would have time to get from point A to point B. But as Daphne sensibly pointed out, we wouldn't really know until we'd gotten the information from Andy and walked the route ourselves. This is the sort of show I refer to as 'Kamikaze', having virtually no rehearsal time, no run-throughs. Our cast would be flying by the seat of their pants, so to speak, and hopefully we wouldn't crash and burn in the attempt.

"So …" Daphne paused, taking a sip of her mocha. "What do you think about Alex? I mean, aside from the fact that Disneyland could power up their Electrical Parade with all the sparks between you two."

"I'd say that answers your question." The thought of Alex brought a smile to my face and a pleasant warmth elsewhere.

Daphne looked pleased. "He's a step far above and beyond Grant, that's for damned sure. About time you get yourself a decent man."

"Now let's not get too optimistic," I cautioned. "I mean, I just met him, and technically I'm still dating Grant."

Daphne dismissed this with a wave of her hand.

"Besides," I continued. "He's bound to have some neurosis hidden somewhere. They all do."

Daphne shrugged. "At least the rest of us won't have to be bored to tears by stories of his career. Speaking of boring, when are you going to tell Grant it's over?"

"After the Festival."

"How do you think he'll take it?"

"After the way he's been acting? Let's just say that while I'm not looking forward to it, I really don't give a shit."

I finished up the last of my cinnamon roll, that lovely gooey part in the center that soaks up all the frosting and spices. Daphne, in the meantime, was using her finger to scoop up any vestiges of cinnamon goop left. Her hair hung down over one eye as she single-mindedly cleaned her plate, the ends falling dangerously close to her mocha cup. If vanity came before comfort in Daphne's philosophy, the needs of her stomach overrode both.

"Well, we'd better get going if we're going to finish the walk by noon." Daphne groaned as she stood up. She always groans when faced with the prospect of movement after a hearty carbohydrotic meal.

"And we still have to stop and see Andy," I reminded her, ripping out the articles from the Post and tucking them in my bag. "He promised to have the passages they want performed highlighted, along with a map showing the entire route."

We settled up on our bill and went down the wooden stairs to Cove Street. No sooner had we touched the sidewalk than my mood, vastly improved by caffeine and sugar, was once again shattered by the appearance of none other than Grant. He looked incredibly handsome in an Armani suit, attracting looks from all directions. A month ago my heart would've skipped a beat at the sight of his face. Now it just pounded from anger.

"Good morning, love." Grant enveloped me in a warm embrace and kissed my unresponsive lips. "Good morning, Daphne."

"Hi, Grant." Daphne stepped back a pace, no doubt leaving me room to swing.

Before I even had a chance to bring up the subject of the article, Grant started off on an enthusiastic roll that held no pauses for interruption. "I'm so glad I caught you here, darling! I tried calling you at home but you'd already left. I'm going to L.A. for an audition this afternoon, as well as a meeting with the casting director and producers of a CBS Movie of the Week, in which I'm up for the lead role. Sal thinks it has tremendous scope to it. Which reminds me, the Scope Mouthwash commercial I did back in June will start airing next week, so be sure to watch for it. At any rate, the part I'm up for is an environmentally concerned plastic surgeon who gets involved in a plot to ..."

I caught the glazed look on Daphne's face as she became stupefied by one of Grant's endless monologues on his career plans and strategies. I knew how she felt. He could be more effective than a sleeping pill. If only we could harness his powers for good instead of evil, Grant could be the patron saint for insomniacs worldwide.

I pulled my attention back to what he was saying, uttering 'uh huhs' at appropriate intervals. " ... and I don't want you worrying that I'll be caught in traffic and miss rehearsal, so I've arranged to take the train there and back. I might be a bit travel fatigued, but I'm nothing if not professional, so you know I'll give my all at rehearsal. All right, darling?"

I nodded, not that he would've noticed if I'd dropped to my knees, raised both fists to the sky and cried, "NO-O-O-O-O!" at the top of my lungs. Like the Energizer Bunny, Grant was still going.

"But I saved the most exciting news for last: I'm up for the lead in the Randell Pilot, *Blood Spurts High.*"

"What?" Daphne's focus was brought sharply back to reality with this piece of news. "*You're* up for Mick O'Mallet?"

"Grant, you're kidding!" I couldn't believe it.

He smiled smugly. "I knew you'd be thrilled. Sal submitted my headshot to the director, who'd seen my work before. I'm supposed to meet with him sometime next week. There's even an off-chance that he'll be attending the Gala. My only regret is that I won't be playing the detective. But having me play O'Mallet for one of the scenes in the Walking Tours could work out nicely. After all, Jonathan Burke will be attending those and I'm sure he'll put in a good word for me."

It was hard for me to imagine Burke putting in a good word for anyone but himself but I kept my opinion to myself. I also forbore to mention the old chestnut about the dumb blonde actress who slept with the screenwriter. Hey, if Grant wanted to sleep with Jonathan Burke, who was I to stop him?

Euwwww. I was immediately sorry the thought had crossed my mind.

"At any rate," Grant finished up, "I have to run if I'm going to catch my train. Wish me luck!" A quick kiss and Grant was gone.

Daphne and I looked at each other.

"Well," Daphne said after a moment, "I have to go on record of saying that if they cast Grant as O'Mallet, I'm not going to be able to watch it. It's like blasphemy."

"I wouldn't go quite that far, but I don't think he's right for the part."

"Grant's just too good-looking," was Daphne's final judgment. "I mean, *Nip/Tuck,* yeah, but O'Mallet? I don't *think* so!"

We started the four blocks to the library. "And I never even got a chance to call him on the article," I reflected as we strolled along.

"I noticed," said Daphne. "I'm actually kind of proud of you. There was a time when you would've thrown the newspaper at him before he'd even opened his mouth."

"I guess I am getting better at controlling my temper," I said thoughtfully.

"It's a sign of maturity."

"Yeah," I sighed, "but we'll always be 'the girls' to everyone else."

We reached Emerald Cove Library, which was also the beginning of the route for the Walking Tour. The library was Spanish-style architecture, with a red-tiled roof, white stucco walls and a verandah running in a 'L' along the front and one side of the building. A wide staircase led up to the front doors from the sidewalk. The far end of the large parking lot, following the same 'L' shape as the verandah, ended up against a brick wall twenty feet above the beach. There was a side courtyard on the opposite side of the library, which had a stairway leading down to the beach itself. This was guarded by a metal gate, which was usually kept locked at night. The same gate that Damien Duran had used when he took his final swim.

Daphne and I went up the side entrance. Andy had indeed remembered to unlock the gate. His office was right next to the courtyard. I could see him through the glass of the sliding door, sitting in a cracked leather chair with his back to us as he carried on an animated phone conversation. Large bookcases flanked either side of his desk like sentries.

I tapped on the door. Andy turned and gestured for us to come in. As soon as we did, it was apparent that the conversation he was embroiled in was an argument.

"I heard you the first time," he said in clipped tones. "Look, I already told you … Yes, I've read the letters …" His voice rose. "No, I don't *know* what I'm going to do with them, but I'll tell you what *you* can do with …"

"Lucille," Daphne whispered.

I nodded. Who else could bring Andy to the point of apoplexy?

We tried not to eavesdrop *too* obviously as he continued his battle. Daphne nudged me and pointed to the answering machine. The light was on, which meant this entire conversation was being recorded. As with me and my keys, Andy had his own particular foible. His was answering machines. He consistently picked up his calls after the machine had already answered and he never remembered to shut the thing off. As a result, he was always taping his conversation so I tried to be circumspect while on the phone with Andy.

"Look, Lucille—"

Daphne and I smiled.

"—I'll talk to you this afternoon at the meeting, but I just don't have time for this right now, okay?" From the indignant squawking clearly audible on the other end, it didn't sound like it was okay. Andy solved the problem by hanging up while his caller was in mid-squawk.

Taking a deep breath, he sank back in his chair and mopped his forehead with one hand. A couple of sips from a can of Tab further restored his composure. Andy looked at us solemnly and said, "If that woman was hanging off a cliff and needed a rope, I'd toss her one with an anchor attached to the bottom. And not a jury in the world would convict me."

"What's the Silicon Madame's problem now?" I asked.

"Well, let's see. There's the phone calls she's been allegedly receiving—"

"Oh yes, we've heard about those."

"Everyone in Emerald Cove has heard about those phone calls," said Andy. "Did you see the article in the *Post* this morning?"

"We saw it," Daphne replied glumly.

"It was something, wasn't it?" Andy shook his head, his jowls a quiver. "Sloan's just begging for a lawsuit."

"Among other things," I muttered darkly.

"Anyway, Lucille is now claiming Duran was murdered and that she's next on the list. Can you believe it?" Andy took another restorative sip of Tab.

"We should be so lucky," said Daphne.

I shook my head. "So she's trying to cash in on Duran's death and get publicity. God, that woman is disgusting. The poor guy drowned. Leave it alone and let him rest in peace."

"Well, it seems that his death might not have been as simple as the police first suspected."

"You mean there really was a 'U' shaped mark on his neck?"

Andy looked at me in surprise. "How did you know about that?"

I shrugged. "Something to do with a little bird named Mavis DiSpachio."

Any shook his head in admiration. "It's just amazing how Mavis finds out these things before the police ever release the information."

"I'd call it frightening," said Daphne.

"What does this mysterious mark have to do with his death?" I asked, not wanting to dwell on our landlady's possibly illegal connections with Emerald Cove's shadier populace.

"I guess that the coroner is now saying it's possible that someone pinned his head to the sand and held him underwater by the back of his neck."

I shivered. "That's grim. Do they have any idea what made the mark?"

Andy shook his head. "Nope. And he also had bruising on his back and shoulders that could have been made by a blunt object."

So Sloan *wasn't* just talking out of his ass last night. At least not about everything.

Daphne looked ill. "But why would anyone want to kill someone like Mr. Duran?"

Andy shook his head. "Your guess is as good as mine."

"Maybe he had some hidden secrets," I said. "Like an illegitimate kid or drugs."

"Or a bad gambling debt." Daphne jumped on the speculative bandwagon.

Andy looked doubtful. "I guess anything's possible, but I'd be willing to bet that Damien Duran had about as clean a slate as anyone would want. Like I told you, he and Lucille butted heads over the gala dinner, but other than that I hardly ever heard him talk, let alone raise his voice."

"I guess Lucille just brings out the worst in people," I said.

Andy rolled his eyes. "Can't argue with that. My blood pressure's gone through the roof since I met her."

"Too bad she's not really on the endangered list," Daphne muttered.

"Do you know what she and Duran were arguing about?" I asked, expecting the answer to be something like the color of the tablecloths.

"OH, yeah." Andy took another swig of Tab. "I can't believe I haven't told you guys about this already. It seems that Lucille had a fling with Randell in the '50s and ..."

"No!" Daphne exclaimed with real anguish.

Andy looked at her with sympathy. "Sorry, Daphne. But it's true."

"But Randell would've gone for dames with style, dames with class! Not dames that dress like an MTV bimbo when they're pushing fifty!"

I did some quick arithmetic. "That would mean that Lucille had to be very young at the time. And that now she's pushing sixty, not fifty."

"Right on both counts," Andy said. "They had a short but evidently passionate affair when Lucille was in her late teens, just past jailbait. Randell wrote her letters, which I've seen."

"Letters?" Daphne sounded ill.

"Yup. Love letters." Andy grinned wickedly. "You've got to see them. They're actually pretty funny." Daphne made a gagging noise. "But the thing is, Lucille wants them to be part of the Randell display in the library to show the softer side of Shay Randell, and I'm not sure that it's really relevant to the Festival."

"I shouldn't think so!" Daphne said with great finality.

"So what does that have to do with her argument with Damien Duran?" I asked, feeling that the subject had gotten off track.

"Well, not only does Lucille want them on display, but she wanted to put one in the program for the Gala dinner, preferably on the first page. I can't believe I didn't tell you about this." Andy shook his head again. "I mean, you should see these things! If I were Lucille, I'd just be embarrassed, but that woman will do anything for attention. Although the letters really do have a certain entertainment factor ..."

"Andy, you can't do it!"

I looked at Daphne with mild disbelief. She was taking this thing awfully seriously. I asked curiously, "Do you have the letters here, Andy? I'd love to see them."

"They're around here somewhere." Andy gestured to the jumble of papers on his desk. His entire office was probably a fire hazard. "I'll dig 'em up later so you can take a look. Don't worry, Daphne. I seriously doubt that I'll display them, and Damien Duran took the matter of the program straight to Jason Downs, who vetoed it."

"Good!"

Andy shook his head in amusement. "You sound just like Franklin. I read him one of the letters the other night, thinking he'd get a kick out of it. Not only did he not see the humor, but when I mentioned I was thinking of putting them in the display, I swear, I thought the man was going to kill me!" Andy chuckled. "Franklin is just too easy to con."

"But you won't really do it, right?"

"No, Daphne, I won't. Although I might wait a day before I tell Franklin. It's way too fun getting a rise out of him." Andy laughed again. "You Randell fanatics are something else. But you really do have to read the letters one of these days." He pulled a sheaf of papers off of his desk, handing them to me. "Take a seat, you two, and we'll go over the map and stuff."

Andy had given us photocopies from the book, highlighting the scenes that had been selected. He'd also circled points on the map that he felt would be appropriate for the different scenes, making our job a lot easier. "Of course, you can play with the scenes a bit, and if the areas I've chosen don't work out, I trust your judgment."

For the next twenty minutes, the three of us conferred on the passages that the Committee had approved for the Tour, deciding which of our actors were going to play what parts, along with the logistics involved. It seemed feasible on paper, but we really needed to walk the route to get a realistic picture.

Daphne had the same thought, saying, "I think we'd better walk this through now, Connie."

We stood up, gathering the make-shift scripts and maps as we did so.

Andy reached into a desk drawer, pulling out a brass key. "I also wanted to give you a key to the library because it closes at 6:00 tonight and I may not be able to get back by 7:00 to let you in." He handed me the key.

I took it, saying doubtfully, "Is this legal? I mean, we're not city employees or anything."

Andy gave a dismissive shrug. "Who's gonna know?"

I had another thought. "Is there an alarm system"

"Not yet. It's supposed to be installed tomorrow. I'm not too worried about it — I mean, this is Emerald Cove, not L.A—but it'll be nice to have before we get the Randell exhibit installed. Some of that memorabilia is worth a lot of money."

I slid the key onto my key ring, touched by Andy's trust.

"Thanks a lot," I said.

"Yeah, Andy, that's really sweet of you." Daphne poked me in the arm, adding, "I'll make sure Connie doesn't lose her keys again."

"Okay. See you tonight." Andy stood up to see us to the door. He stopped mid-way, smacking himself in the middle of the forehead and exclaimed, "I almost forgot! I've got some of your publicity pictures back, the ones you loaned us, plus the negatives. I also made a few copies of some articles that featured MFH and I wasn't sure if you'd seen them or not." He went to his desk, grabbing a folder with our names written on it. "Here you go."

"We can look at this all later," I said firmly, intercepting the folder as Daphne eagerly reached for it. I stuffed it into my bag. "We've got work to do."

Chapter Seven

It was 9:45 when Daphne and I hit the street and began the walk. We first headed towards the staircase marked with a sign reading "Scenic Walk" further down on Cove Street. It led down to a seacoast path on the cliffs overlooking the ocean.

Once down the stairs we paused for a minute to take in the scenery and listen to the sound of waves crashing onto the rocks below. The beaches below had a wild, rocky look more common to the coasts of Northern California, especially this time of year when the weather was gearing up for the rainy season.

"God, I'm glad tourist season is over!" exclaimed Daphne, "The beaches are practically deserted!"

'Practically deserted' was a relative term for Emerald Cove, even in off-season. There were always tourists, especially on the weekends, and today was no exception. There were also assorted joggers and other locals, in-cluding a woman walking her dog in defiance of Emerald Cove's strict 'no dogs on beach' laws.

"It's actually kind of weird," I said as we started along the steep, un-even path.

"What's weird?"

"The beaches in Emerald Cove are never empty during the day or early evening, for that matter. If Damien Duran *was* murdered, you'd think someone would have seen something."

"You know what's even weirder?" Daphne picked her way carefully through a patch of rocky dirt.

"What?"

"The way no one, including you, ever refers to the guy by just one name. It's always first and last, the way people refer to a movie star. Tom Cruise. It's never just 'Tom' or 'Cruise.'"

"I'm not sure how that relates to Damien Duran's death."

Daphne grinned at me. "See?"

Damn. She was right.

"Okay," I conceded. "You have a point. But if Damien Du ... er, if

Duran went into the water at sunset, don't you think someone would have noticed, well, foul play?" I felt like an idiot actually using those words outside of one of our shows.

Luckily Daphne didn't notice.

"But the beach he used was private, right? I mean, you can only get there if you have access through the library or one of the houses on the street."

"So what about the people that live in those houses?"

Daphne shrugged. "No guarantee anyone was admiring the view when he died, even if they *could* see anything after the sun went down. And I'm sure that the cops'll be interviewing anyone who lives there."

"I guess you're right," I said doubtfully.

Daphne rolled her eyes. "Jeez, Connie, you're kind of worrying me with this born again detective thing you've got going. I mean, I know that Grant's an asshole and I don't blame you for wanting to prove him wrong, but can you stop fixating until we're done working?"

"Fine," I said. "No more Nancy Drew action until we're done, I promise."

The participants of the tour had been advised to wear comfortable walking shoes and I felt a pang of pity for Tasha, the only actress who would actually be performing on the cliffs. She was going to have a great time navigating her way down the path in high-heels. I mentioned as much to Daphne, who said sensibly, "She's going to have to wear flats and bring her heels with her."

"Okay, here's where Tasha and Brad will be." I pointed to a rocky plateau directly overhanging the cliffs. It was about twelve feet to the right of the path, set about a foot lower than the actual walkway. Andy had chosen well, the audience would have a clear view of the scene. I just hoped neither Brad nor Tasha were afraid of heights. "Now we've got them doing which scene?"

Daphne consulted her notes. "This is the scene where the mysterious young heiress tries to convince O'Mallet to help her dispose of a dead body left on the balcony of her hotel room. But Mick isn't buying 'cause he knows this dame's as crooked as the seams on her stockings. But his supply of J.D. is getting low and his bank account is flatter than his ex-girlfriend, so he figures he might as well listen to her proposal."

I shook my head, amazed as always at how easily my elegant partner dropped into hard-boiled slang. No wonder she attracted such strange boyfriends.

"You know, we *could* have Grant play O'Mallet here," I said thoughtfully.

Daphne shook her head. "I don't think there's enough time for him to get from this point to the Cave. Besides, we promised Tasha and Brad a chance to play a scene together."

"Yeah, you're right. It just seems kind of odd having three different actors playing O'Mallet."

"You're the one who pointed out the logistic impossibility of doing it any other way."

We went further down the path, admiring the view and the houses that flanked the seacoast walk. "Look, Connie, there it is. Jason Down's house." Daphne pointed reverently to the beautiful dark wood house directly above us. It was even more magnificent in the daylight, looking like something straight out of *The Ghost and Mrs. Muir.* It even had a widow's walk running along the top story, winding upwards to a look-out tower. I wish I'd known about that last night. The view from the tower had to be incredible.

We kept walking. "I still wish they'd let us use gun shots," Daphne bemoaned as we navigated a particularly rocky bit of path. "It would add so much more authenticity to everything. I mean, why do we always have to resort to poisonings and stabbings for our murders?"

A lone jogger passing by at that moment swiveled his head and stared back at us, no doubt unsure if he'd heard Daphne correctly or not.

Daphne continued, "It just sounds like one of those effete limey mysteries. People are *always* getting shot in American pulp novels, either that or they get slapped around until they rupture something! Connie, can't you think of some way we can—"

"It's no use, Daph." I cut her off, having heard this particular complaint before. "You can't fight Emerald Cove on this one. We can't have simulated gunfire of any sort. No caps, no blanks, not in any public place. It could start a panic. The only place we can use blanks this time is in the library for the Gala."

We approached an isolated little walled plateau directly above a mass of rocks currently occupied by a bevy of seals lolling about in contentment. Some of the young and friskier pups were frolicking in the water, occasionally sliding up onto the rocks in what seemed to be futile attempts to get the lazier seals to play. Pelicans and seagulls soared above, diving into the water for their breakfast.

"This is the spot where Franklin is going to read Randell's description of Emerald Cove," said Daphne, checking the notes from Andy.

We looked out over the rocks at the slate-gray sea. "Andy couldn't have picked a better spot, don't you think?"

"I still wish we could fire blanks," Daphne said grouchily.

"Give it up."

We made our way down the path to the Children's Cove. This was a shallow, walled-off area of beach, specifically for kids to go wading in safety from rip-tides and rocks. It was another favorite hang-out of the seals and was also the site of a fight in which O'Mallet gets clubbed by a .38, the closest we could come to an actual gunfight on the Tour. Grant would play O'Mallet in this scene and Chris would do the clubbing. I imagined Chris would enjoy the assignment.

"HI, YOU GUYS!" Zooming down the sidewalk lining the Children's Cove were two identically-sized blonde girls. They wore matching rollerblades and expressions of unholy glee.

"Oh, shit." Daphne and I both uttered the profanity under our breath as we watched prepubescent trouble zip towards us. It was Morag McGregor and Rosanne "Banana" Jones, two girls who lived in our neighborhood. They were eleven year-old bosom pals and had been thorns in the side of MFH ever since we'd staged our gothic spoof, *The Wet Lake* for a local mystery club. We'd needed a small girl for the part of the obligatory troubled child (every Gothic has one) and the two girls had alternated in the role. Whoever had given the advice never to share a stage with animals or children must have worked with kids like Morag and Banana.

It wasn't they did a bad job on stage. It was the time off-stage that proved the problem. The two of them didn't mean to cause trouble—does a hurricane *mean* to rip your roof off?—but they could wreak as much havoc as any natural disaster ever concocted by Mother Nature. They'd accidentally pulled down the curtain and knocked the backdrop over during one show trying to keep an eye on stage because they'd both developed crushes on Shaun. They followed him around with round-eyed, unwavering stares of devotion that had given him the creeps.

Now they stood before us, smiles beaming from deceptively angelic faces. Banana's golden curls framed large hazel eyes while Morag's straight pale blond hair fell over a guileless sky-blue gaze. But they couldn't fool me. I knew what they wanted.

"You guys, when are you doing your show?" Morag hopped from one skate to the other in an amazing feat of balance. "It's this weekend, right? Can we help?"

"Yeah," chimed in Banana. "We really want to be in your thing. We'd be really good. We could kill someone, or scream, or die, or pretend to be really scared when something scary happens."

You had to hand to 'em, at least they came right to the point.

"How did you two monkeys find out about the show?" asked Daphne.

"Oh, we go visit Mavis 'cause she gives us cookies," said Banana cheerily. "She told us you were going to kill people on a walk!"

Trust Mavis to spill the beans. Why didn't she just sell nuclear weapons to third-world countries while she was at it? It would do less damage.

Oh well, the damage was done. "We're sorry, girls," I said with considerable patience, "but we don't have any parts for kids this show. So maybe during your Christmas break we could work you both in on something, but not this time."

"Very diplomatic," Daphne murmured.

"Well, at least we'll go to it," said Morag, her enthusiasm unfortunately undiminished. "Kids are allowed on the walk, right?"

Both girls looked inquiringly at us.

Daphne and I looked at each other in a mild panic. We hadn't foreseen this.

"There is no age limit," I began carefully, "but I think you might find this kind of thing boring."

"That's okay, we won't be bored." Banana skated around us in circles, like a shark. "We might be able to help you guys, you know. Like if something really scary or mysterious happens, we'll scream really loud. So people will know that it's supposed to be really mysterious."

"Oh, jeez …" Daphne turned away with closed eyes.

"Yeah," Morag took up the torch enthusiastically, "We can be your helpers like Bess Marvin and George in Nancy Drew!"

That was enough of that. "No way," I stated firmly. Giving them what I hoped was quelling glare, I continued, "Listen, rug rats, we really don't need your help on this one. No screams, no nothing! If you go, you behave. If you don't screw this thing up, we'll include you in a show at Christmas. If you *do* screw it up, you're history."

"Washed up," said Daphne.

"Finished in this town," I concluded.

They giggled, unquelled, and started to skate off. At the top of the incline Banana called out, "Good luck on your show! We won't screw it up, we promise! We'll just watch!"

"Yeah," added Morag. "We won't say anything. We'll just clap really hard for you guys whenever you do something really good!" The two waved cheerfully and skated away.

"I won't be able to take it," Daphne exploded. "I can take Lucille, I can even take Grant's posturing, but I will *not* be able to live through those two hellions screaming and clapping after everything we say!"

"Don't think about it," I said.

Nancy Drew indeed, I thought as we continued up the sidewalk. I hated Nancy Drew, stupid teenage wonder girl. How was anyone supposed to live up to that kind of perfection? And didn't the editors ever notice that her hair changed color in each book? In one book she was an expert water-skier with blonde hair. In the next, an accomplished equestrian with red-dish titian-haired locks. Entire generations of adolescent girls grew up feel-ing inadequate and spending far too much money at salons because of Nancy Drew. Oh well, there had to be something to keep us insecurely in place before anorexic super models, boob jobs and *Baywatch*.

We stopped in front of The Gnome's Den, a little gift store that cor-nered the market on quaint. Most of its traffic came from the fact that Gnome's Den housed the entrance to Davy Jone's Cave, an Emerald Cove landmark. Although Randell had used the Cave in *Play To Win*, he hadn't used it for the nefarious purposes we had planned: the discovery of the Body and the climactic scene of the Walking Tours. This was the only part of the tour that we had planned well in advance, with Andy's blessing. Grant was again playing O'Mallet and Chris was going to hide behind a rock and pull a body out of the surf for O'Mallet to discover. The 'body' was a CPR dummy, although Daphne had spoken wistfully of trying to get a cadaver from a medical school. Sometimes Daphne worries me.

"So," said Daphne as we stood outside the shop looking at the mixture of fantasy-based and nautical knickknacks in the display windows, "Do you want to go in?"

"We might as well double-check the lo—"

"—the logistics, yes I know. You sound like a broken record, do you know that?"

"Can't we use *real* bullets?" I shot back immediately.

Tossing her head, Daphne pushed open the door and went into the shop. I followed with a smirk.

We smiled at Betty, owner of The Gnomes Den, who was busy ringing up a customer. A pleasant woman in her thirties, Betty wore her red hair in crimped waves and favored layers of gauzy, multi-colored fabrics, ballet flats and ethnic jewelry, along with the occasional crystal pendant. She seemed like the sort of person who'd vacation in Sedona.

Betty was currently standing behind a counter festooned with netting, shells, miniature buoys, you name it. Trolls, elves and (of course) gnomes were nestled amongst brass sea animals, key rings in the shape of ship's wheels and t-shirts proclaiming "I (Heart) Gnomes!"

Wading through the relentless sea of cute, we made our way to the dank staircase at the back of the shop. A heavy wooden door was held open by a large keg and you could feel a gust of ocean breeze coming from the doorway. The whole effect was very Pirates of the Caribbean. All that was needed was an animatronic buccaneer seated on the keg swilling grog and menacing tourists with a flintlock.

The pungent smell of brine, kelp and decaying sea critters grew palpably stronger as we descended the narrow, slippery wooden steps curving down towards the ocean. The walls were carved out of rock and the air was noticeably chillier the further down one went. We passed a middle-aged couple on their way up. They were puffing and panting, but smiled broadly at us, saying, "It's much longer going up, girls!" as they toiled back up the stairs. I knew from experience that they were right.

We reached the bottom. "Oh, this is going to be great!" Daphne cried exultantly. "It's creepy down here!"

It was pretty dramatic. Dim electric lights caused shadows to bounce off the cave walls as the surf pounded and crashed against the rocks. We were sprayed by an incoming wave as we emerged onto the huge flat rock that formed a platform above sand and rocks. The platform had been rendered child and tourist-proof by wooden guardrails set into cement pilings. A person could climb over or under the rails if they were really determined, but most people didn't want to get wet. Daphne and I had no such compunction, however, and carefully clambered down onto the ground.

I could see out to the ocean as the cave opened up about ten feet away from the platform. To the left lay cliffs, with an isolated beach beyond. During high tide, water covered most of the sand and rocks below us, occasionally washing over the rock ledge itself. Unless we had a storm, however, I didn't foresee any real problem for our actors aside from wet feet.

To the right was a natural archway which led to the beach. Behind that archway was the rock where we wanted Chris to hide. It would require some wading, even during low tide, but I doubted he'd mind.

"Okay," I said. "Chris will hide over behind that rock, holding one end of the rope. The body'll be hidden around the edge of the archway, well out of sight. If he pulls on the rope, the body should follow the wash of the waves until it lands about here." I indicated a spot about five feet out from the platform where the waves were already washing in. "Grant will be at the edge of the platform giving his speech—we need to pick out the cue sentence for Chris—so he'll be able to react immediately when the body floats up."

"Grant's going to have to try and block the audience's view when he rolls the body over. He should stand in front of it while he's talking."

"What? And ruin his shoes?" I laughed at the idea. "He'll never go for it."

"He has to," Daphne insisted. "I've seen the dummy and no matter how much we dress it up, it's still going to look like the Pillsbury Doughboy!"

"All things considered with Duran's death, that's probably just as well," I said. "I'm a little concerned that people are going to think it's in bad taste."

Daphne snorted. "Oh, please. Most of the people going on the tour wouldn't blink an eye if a real body washed up. They're mystery fans."

She had a point.

"Grant'll still kick up a fuss," I warned.

Daphne dismissed my words with a wave of one hand. "Oh, just appeal to his professionalism and the 'truth' of his craft and I'm sure he'll do it."

I couldn't argue with that.

We were both standing below the platform. Daphne jumped back as a large wave rolled in, drenching us both to our thighs. She quickly retreated to dry safety up on the platform while I waded up to my knees over to the archway and the rock beyond, making sure the rock would conceal Chris's frame.

"Connie, you'd better hurry up." Daphne was trying to squeeze water from her leggings as she spoke. "We still have one more stop to make at the Hotel. God, I hate the thought of going in looking like this, I mean, they are such snobs in there!"

I rolled my eyes impatiently. As if I cared what the employees of the Emerald Hotel thought of our clothes. I had more important things to think about, like whether or not the body would really float the way we hoped it would.

"Why, hi there, Daphne!"

We both looked up in time to see Franklin descending the stairs at a gallop. He jumped the last six and landed on the slick rock platform without even stumbling. He bounded over to where Daphne was wringing out her leggings. A lock of hair fell over his forehead. He and Daphne could've been the Veronica Lake brigade.

"Scouting out the terrain, I see," he went on, grinning broadly as he looked around. "This is going to be so much fun! I can't wait to start the first tour. Is this where the body will be coming from?"

"Over there, behind the archway where Connie's standing." Daphne pointed. Franklin spotted me and waved. I waved back as he waxed enthusiastic. "Oh, great! Hi, Connie! Didn't see you at first! Isn't this *great*?"

I swear, the man made everything sound like an ad for Sugar Frosted Flakes.

"Just great," I replied in deadpan tones as another wave splashed over my hips.

"You know how much I love Randell and it's just so wonderful to be conducting tours on the very sites that Randell wrote about in his books." Franklin was speaking so rapidly I began to wonder if he had, indeed, consumed too many bowls of sugar saturated cereals. "The actual *ground* that Randell himself walked on—"

"What about the water he walked on?" I murmured.

Not hearing me, Franklin rambled on, "—and the thrill of seeing passages enacted from his great work, *Play To Win* … This is just great!"

I refrained from voicing my opinion that *Play To Win* was far from a 'great work'. It would be like kicking a puppy. A crippled, orphaned puppy.

"Well, we're both certainly looking forward to it," Daphne said diplomatically as I clambered back up onto the platform. "You're setting the scene down here with a reading, aren't you?"

"Yes, that's right." Franklin paced up and down the giant slab of rock. "I'm visiting all the sites where I'm giving readings tomorrow. That's why I'm here. To soak up atmosphere. To—" His voice deepened dramatically. "—to go down these mean streets. That's right, doll face. Because a man's gotta do what a man's gotta do. It's a cruel world, baby. It's a world where every corner hides a two-bit stoolie and every manhole shields a hopped up lowlife who'd snuff his own mother for two bits. Yeah, that's why I'm here, sister …"

I'd had enough. I went to the stairs, motioning for Daphne to follow me. She did so reluctantly, apparently enjoying Franklin's impromptu recitation more than I was.

Waving a cheery good-bye, Franklin continued to soaking up atmosphere. He was still pacing back and forth, Randellisms spewing forth a mile a minute as we left.

"Whoa, I think we've found our next Carl Club," I joked as we ascended the stairs.

"He's good, isn't he?" said Daphne quite seriously. "His readings are going to be fantastic, if that was any indication."

"You'd never know it by the speech he gave at the Museum."

We paused for a minute outside The Gnomes Den, taking gulps of fresh air and catching our breath after the climb. The hotel was several blocks away and Daphne was in no hurry to get there in her wet leggings. "We should've done this part in order," she griped. "The hotel first, *then* the cave. That's how it's gonna be in the show."

"But stopping here first we don't have to double back," I said reasonably. "And we have a lot of stuff to do. We're just going to check out the performance space and leave, okay?"

"I still wish we looked better," she said unhappily, pulling the damp fabric away from her legs. "My legs are soaked."

"It could be worse," I said, my own wet 501's making me callous. Nothing beats damp, briny denim for discomfort, unless it was wet socks in soggy Converse high-tops. "At least your T-shirt isn't wet and we won't be brought up on public display of obscenity charges."

"Are you saying my breasts are obscene?" Daphne asked indignantly.

"No, but since you aren't wearing a bra, you'd look like a contestant in a wet t-shirt contest."

"You should talk, Miss G-String."

"Well, you can't see my g-string through my jeans, can you?"

"You can't see those things *without* clothes. How the heck can you stand having a string going up your ..."

We bickered over the virtues of g-strings versus bikini underwear, an ongoing debate since high-school, all the way down Prospero Street until we reached the hotel.

Walking in through the pink tiled arches of the Emerald Hotel's entrance-way, we passed through the lovely rose-strewn patio courtyard and into the understated elegance of the foyer. Nattily attired guests strolled through the lobby. Daphne and I definitely stuck out like hookers at a debutante ball.

An elderly desk clerk standing behind the baroque reception desk was eyeing us askance, his thin lips pressed together in obvious disapproval. He looked us up and down, finally asking with frosty politeness, "May I help you two?"

Well, you could start by taking that stick out of your ass, I thought as Daphne faded into the background behind me. But I behaved myself. Squelching up to the desk, I said, "You might be able to. We're doing the entertainment for the Randell Walking Tours tomorrow. I assume you know about them?"

The clerk's expression thawed marginally. "Yes."

"We'd like to look at the space in which we'll be performing."

He looked at my wet jeans, trying to decide whether or not he should let us further into the hotel.

"It's just water," I said impatiently. "We aren't planning on sitting on the furniture, just looking at the space."

"Go up the main stairs and go right," the clerk said reluctantly. "It's the Oak Room, directly at the end of the hall."

"Thank you," I said. I squelched a childish urge to sit on one of the velvet-upholstered chairs in the lobby as we walked upstairs.

We took a quick look at the Oak Room, a huge, wood-paneled space with lots of leather chairs and glass-enclosed bookcases scattered about the room. The floors were hardwood with large oriental rugs scattered about at random. There was a wood-lined bar in the far back of the room set against a picture window with a panoramic view of the ocean. Plenty of room for audience and actors.

Daphne looked around. "I don't see any problem with the space. Do you?"

"Nope. Let's get out of here." We were both eager to go home and relax before the rigors of tonight's blocking rehearsal for the gala performance of *Peruvian Pigeon*. We'd think twice before agreeing to do two different shows for the same event again. It was way too exhausting.

At the bottom of the main stairway, Daphne nudged me and pointed over to the lobby entrance. "Talk about a match made in hell," she whispered. I looked and saw that Jonathan Burke had just come in, accompanied by none other than Lucille. The two were close together, walking arm in arm and looked as though they might be heading towards Burke's hotel room. My mind didn't want to go beyond that point.

Should we wait until they went on about their business or go ahead and brazen it out? I had no desire to encounter either Burke or Lucille separately, let alone in tandem.

The matter was taken out of our hands when Burke glanced up and saw us. A smile of recognition spread over his face. A smarmy, insidious leer of a smile that did nothing for his looks. Lucille saw us as well and she was not smiling.

"Ladies," said Burke as they approached us, "So nice to see you again."

"I wasn't aware that it was raining," said Lucille, her icy gaze dropping to our wet clothing. Her four inch turquoise heels dug into the carpet, leaving crescent shaped scars in the thick pile.

"We were checking out various locations on the Walking Tour," I answered coolly. "And as most of them are on the seacoast path, we got a little wet." I gave her tight sequined sweater-dress and four-inch heels a once-over of my own. I swear, when Lucille lay down her breasts would still be standing at attention.

"Well, I must say, the effect is quite charming." Burke leered at Daphne.

Lucille was pissed, her eyes narrowing under their heavy coat of iridescent green eyeshadow. "We'd better be going," she said to Burke in tones that brooked no contradiction. "Remember—" Her eyes flicked to us and away with the rapidity of a switchblade. "—I'll be at your little rehearsal this evening."

"Thanks for the warning," I said sweetly as they walked up the stairs.

"Hopefully you won't get a threatening phone call and miss it." Lucille did not deign to respond, but her shoulders stiffened slightly so I knew I'd gotten to her.

I waited till we were safely outside the hotel before exclaiming, "God, that woman is a bitch!"

Daphne nodded her agreement. "She and Burke make quite a pair, don't they? Connie, do you think the two of them are ..." She paused delicately.

"Daphne," I replied firmly, "We don't want to go there."

Upon arriving home, I immediately collapsed on the couch and covered myself with a plaid throw, intent on indulging in a long nap to make up for last night's decadence and sleep deprivation. My brain, however, not only refused to turn off, but whether I wanted to go there or not, was stuck on the Burke and Lucille channel.

As distasteful as I found the idea of the two of them in any kind of intimate relationship, I had to wonder what was going on there. It was possible that they already knew each other through film industry connections. Was it just a coincidence that they'd met in the Emerald Hotel bar when Burke showed up a day early? And why *had* Burke flown in ahead of schedule without telling anyone about his change in plans? Did he have something to hide? Or was he just an inconsiderate asshole?

While there was no doubt that the answer to my last question was a definite 'yes,' there could still be more to Burke's actions than having apparently been raised in a barn. It seemed suspicious that he arrived unexpectedly and unannounced on the same night Damien Duran was allegedly murdered. Of course, just because the man was an asshole also didn't mean he was necessarily capable of murder, but if called upon to make a snap judgment, I'd have said that Jonathan Burke was capable of almost anything. That being said, why would Burke want to murder a harmless old man?

Ugh. My attempts at deductive thinking were making my head ache. How did detectives — or mystery writers, for that matter — do it? Luckily my brain finally decided to take a time out and I drifted off to sleep before I could do myself any more damage.

Chapter Eight

When I woke up a few hours later, my incipient headache was gone. I was, however, immobilized by the weight of three cats and had a cramp in both legs. Ever notice how felines manage to shove your body into whatever position they find comfortable regardless of what it does to you?

Shedding the cats, I tottered around until my circulation returned to normal and then joined Daphne for a late lunch of homemade clam chowder and sourdough bread. The chowder had little pats of butter melting in it, large succulent clams vying for room with chunks of potato. The bread was fresh from a local bakery, fragrant and warm.

Daphne had been a busy little bee during my nap. Along with the cooking and shopping she'd also broken up with Guido over cappuccino at Espresso House. "He used up an entire dispenser's worth of napkins," said Daphne with callous indifference as she buttered a piece of bread. "He says the sunsets will always remind him of me so he'll never watch one again. That ought to make life difficult. Mmmm, I love fresh sourdough!" How was it Daphne was incapable of defending herself from the Jonathan Burkes of the world, yet she could break up with a guy without thinking twice? I wished I could dispense with Grant so easily.

Fortified by both nap and food, I was in a much better frame of mind and tackled the job of gathering up props for rehearsal without complaint. Daphne had already set out our costumes and props for the next day's Walking Tours, as well as organized the scripts for distribution to our actors. For the first time since we'd begun rehearsals for the Festival, I felt like we had things under control. Hah. Famous last thoughts.

Daphne and I arrived at the library at a quarter till seven, pulling in to the empty lot at the side of the building.

"Looks like we're the first ones here." I scanned the street for familiar vehicles.

"Big surprise." Daphne ran a brush through her hair. "When was the last time any of our actors arrived on time? It'll be a cold day in Sinnerland before any of 'em get here early."

"Sinnerland?" I looked at my partner with raised eyebrow. "Where'd you pick up that little gem?"

"Randell's third novel, *Saint in Sinnerland*. You know, the one where he introduces Chuck T-Bone."

"Chuck *T-Bone?*"

Daphne gave me an incredulous look. "Haven't you been reading your Randell? T-Bone is his other series detective. It wasn't as popular as O'Mallet, but Randell wrote at least five T-Bone mysteries!"

"And this affects me how?" I got out of the car as I spoke, slamming the door shut before Daphne could frame a withering reply about my lack of higher education.

Daphne joined me as I opened the trunk, saying, "I'll grab the shoe-shine kit and the trench coats if you can get the rest of the stuff."

"Sounds good." I gathered up several bags holding the rest of our props and followed Daphne around to the front of the library. Setting every thing down on one of the wrought-iron benches that lined the verandah, I searched for the library key on my key chain. "God, it's cold," I said with a shiver as a gust of icy wind blew down the street, cutting right through my jeans, sweater and leather flight jacket. "I could sure use some coffee."

"Me too." Daphne was actually wearing a man's tweed jacket over her jeans and T-shirt, a mute testimony to the drop in temperature that had occurred this evening. Although summer weather had hung on tenaciously throughout October, autumn had definitely arrived, bringing with it the cold, damp nights typical of Emerald Cove in November. There'd been forecasts of possible showers and you can bet that this was yet another of Andy's worries. Rain would cast a damper over the Walking Tours, reducing attendance or possibly canceling the tours altogether.

Finally locating the right key, I unlocked the large double doors, holding them open while Daphne carried our gear into the dimly lit lobby. When she was done, I shut the doors behind us, hitting the switches that illuminated the library.

The lobby was a large airy space with empty glass display cases, destined to hold Randell related items. To the left were the bathrooms, to the right the children's reading room. Directly in front of us, two wrought iron gates were propped open leading to the library proper. All of the floors were done in a dark brown tile that always made me think of slabs of chocolate.

I helped Daphne move everything into the main library, setting it all down on the registration desk. We spread all the props out and checked them off against a list to insure that nothing had been left behind.

"You got the roscoes?"

I rummaged through one of the bags and pulled out three Smith and Wesson Victory model .38's, along with several less impressive cap guns. "They're all here." I set the box of blanks for the .38's down alongside the guns. "And here's the scripts for the walking tours."

"Good." Daphne looked satisfied as we finished checking items against the list. "Now if everyone pays attention, maybe we'll have one smooth run-through and get out of here early."

The chorus to a certain song from *South Pacific* ran through my brain, the words 'cockeyed optimist' at the forefront.

A quick glance at my watch showed that it was 6:45. The sound of the front doors being opened caught my attention and I looked up to see Andy. He was wearing a windbreaker along with the long-suffering look that bespoke of time spent with Lucille. As Daphne would say, Andy's face looked like five miles of bad road and it was a safe bet that Lucille was personally responsible for 90 percent of the furrows running across his forehead.

"Hey, Andy!" Daphne greeted him cheerfully. "We didn't expect you here so early."

"Yeah," I said. "You beat all of our actors."

Andy sighed heavily. "The meeting was pointless. We spent forty-five minutes listening to Lucille bitch about all the extra work that Duran's death has caused her, as if she's not thrilled to be in control of it all." He threw himself into a chair, running a hand through his hair. His face drooped with exhaustion, reminding me more than ever of a St. Bernard down on its luck. "Ah, but you girls don't want to hear any of this."

"Sure we do," I hastened to assure him. "Especially if it's dirt about Lucille."

Daphne nodded, slamming a bedraggled mink piece, little paws still intact, down on the counter. It was old and mangy, straight from a Salvation Army somewhere, but we'd never consider buying a new one, even if we *could* afford it. I could just see us getting doused with red paint at one of our shows, headlines reading, 'Outraged animal lovers attack local theater group!'

Andy didn't need any more prompting. "Lucille just didn't understand how Damien could've been so careless and irresponsible to go swimming at his age when he had civic responsibilities to attend to."

"I don't know how Lucille can be so irresponsible as to *dress* the way she does at her age," Daphne muttered. "What a cow."

"Well, 'bovine' is one of the milder terms that come to mind when I think of Lucille." Andy picked up the mink and absent-mindedly fiddled with the paws as he spoke. "She was absolutely livid. Totally off the deep-end. From the way she was going off, you'd have thought the rest of the Committee had drowned the guy just for the sole purpose of inconveniencing her." The mink's paws wiggled faster as he concluded, "That woman is a menace to society, this festival and my blood pressure!"

"Why was she so bent out of shape over Duran's death?" I gently removed the mink from Andy's hands before he pulled the paws off in his agitation. He didn't even notice.

"Hell if I know. When they were working on the gala, they didn't see eye to eye on anything. And it pissed Lucille off no end 'cause like I told you, Duran's opinions carried a lot of weight."

"So you'd think she'd be happy with him out of the way, wouldn't you?" I said.

"Hell yeah," said Andy. "Like I said, I'd have thought she'd be dancing on his grave. Near as I can figure, Duran's death left some loose ends that Lucille has to wrap up, unless she can con some other poor sap into taking on the responsibility. Whatever, she's making enough of a stink to raise the dead."

"Methinks the lady doth protest too much," I murmured.

"If you mean Lucille," said Andy, "she's no lady."

"True. But I wouldn't be surprised if she was kicking up all this fuss to hide something."

"Like what?"

"Well—" I paused, picking my words carefully. I didn't want to come off sounding like Sloan. "Maybe she's actually glad Duran's dead and doesn't want anyone to know."

Andy considered this, then shook his head 'no.' "If it were anyone but Lucille, I might agree with you. Problem is, I've never seen her hide her feelings about anything. Why would she start now?"

Daphne nodded. "He's got a point. She's definitely lacking in the basic social skills department."

"Yeah, but even Lucille would hide it if she had something to do with his death." There. I'd said it.

Both Andy and Daphne looked at me.

"You mean, you think Lucille killed him?" Andy's expression was almost hopeful.

"Why not?" I said recklessly. "We don't have any other suspects. Except for possibly Jonathan Burke."

"Burke?" Daphne raised an eyebrow. "I mean, the guy's a jerk, but he's also a respected writer."

"I don't respect him," muttered Andy. "In fact, I think he'd make a great villain."

Daphne looked doubtful. "I don't know …"

"Neither do we," I said, "But he did come into town the night Duran was killed, without telling anyone his plans had changed."

"True," said Daphne. "But what's his motive?"

I'd asked myself the same questions before my nap and I still didn't have any answers. Defeated for the moment, I heaved a sigh. "I really have no idea. I guess it's just that Burke and Lucille are the closest thing to villains that we've got."

"It'd sure be nice if Lucille was guilty," Andy said wistfully. "I am counting the days, let me tell you. If I couldn't let off steam, I'd probably blow that bitch away."

"Why don't you just hide in your office when she shows up to watch rehearsal tonight?" I suggested.

Andy groaned. "Shit, that's right. I'd forgotten about that. I think I might do just that if you two don't mind. I've got to bone up on my Randell trivia if I'm gonna lead the third tour tomorrow and this may be my only chance."

He stood up, the chair creaking from the release of Andy's bulk. "In the meantime, I need a jolt of java. Anyone else for coffee?"

Both Daphne and I nodded emphatically. It was time to work and we both needed the caffeine.

Andy headed off towards the staff office, saying, "I'll give a holler when the coffee's done. Yell if you need me."

Brad and Tasha arrived. Brad was already wearing his fedora and trench coat over jeans and a sweater. He had an unlit cigarette dangling from his mouth. I raised an eyebrow at Tasha who shrugged and said, "He's been in character since dinner." She dumped an armload of '40s costumes on the counter and added, "I've finished with all of the repairs on these. We should be in good shape for tomorrow and Sunday."

I lifted up a vintage black satin evening dress cut on the bias. I'd found it at a thrift store in L.A., a jagged tear running up one side. Being at odds with a needle and thread, I'd had it in my 'to mend' pile for a year, along with various other flea-market goodies. Tasha had commandeered the pile and used such tiny stitches that the repairs were only visible if you knew where to look.

"Tasha, you are a genius." I held up another dress, this one a sleeveless silk-velvet cocktail dress in a rich hunter green. The material had all but disintegrated in places so Tasha had cleverly pieced new velvet over those spots, working in jet beads to hide the basted edges. The pattern of the beadwork was random, yet somehow looked like it was supposed to be exactly where it was.

"She's something, isn't she?" Brad uttered the words in his best Carl Club persona, grabbing Tasha around the waist as he did so. "And the doll's all mine."

Tasha gave Brad a quick kiss on the cheek and pulled away to help me sort out the costumes. Brad swatted her on the butt and strode off into the stacks to run his lines, taking an imaginary inhalation of smoke as he did so.

"Okay," I said briskly as Tasha and I placed dresses, men's coats, baggy zoot suit pants, fedoras and other assorted costume pieces in piles according to character. "Who are we waiting on?"

Daphne did a quick mental check. "Chris, Grant, Shaun, Alex ... oh, and Mart is supposed to show up between 7 and 7:30 to run music cues."

Martha Jacowski, better known as Mart, was our saxophone player, an invaluable addition to our shows. She'd done *Peruvian Pigeon* before, so Daphne and I felt secure about having her only attend the one rehearsal. There was something about a wailing sax that made the forties atmosphere complete. You know what they say, a show without sax ... Never mind.

"Coffee's on!" Andy stood at the staff office door, a steaming mug in one hand. "Cups, cream and sugar are all in the office. There's a fridge with milk as well. Help yourself. It's Peet's Viennese dark roast." He went into his own office, shutting the door partially behind him.

Neither Brad nor Tasha were interested, but Daphne and I followed the scent of fresh coffee into the staff office where Andy had brewed a 12 cup pot, borrowed two mugs off of a wall rack and helped ourselves. I added liberal amounts of Splenda and milk to mine, Daphne watching the process with the disdain of one who only drank her coffee black. I stirred in an extra spoonful of Splenda just to watch her grimace and provoke the inevitable, "I don't know how you can ruin good coffee that way. At least use real sugar!"

I headed back towards the lobby, saying, "I'm not asking you to drink it." I took a big swig of my coffee, hiding a grimace of my own as I found that I'd gone overboard on the sweetener, even for my taste.

The library door opened. My heart skipped a beat and then sped up as Alex walked in, dressed in jeans and a flannel shirt. I tried to act casual as I set my mug down and greeted him, a hard thing to do when your heart is drumming a mile a minute. What if he'd been lying? What if last night had been a dream? What if I just said hello and stopped acting like an idiot? I opted for Number Three.

"Hey there." I felt ridiculously shy, considering our easy interaction at the party. Oh, for a magnum of champagne ...

Alex's answering smile dispelled all doubt. "Hey there, yourself. Am I late?"

"Right on time," I replied, wondering if he knew how the muted greens of his shirt brought out the color of his eyes. I doubted it. Alex didn't seem the type to worry about it, unlike Grant who was aware of every nuance of his wardrobe. "Speaking of which," I said, my thoughts segueing into the matter at hand, "why don't you try these on and see if they fit." I handed him some baggy pants and a couple of jackets for the two characters he'd be playing.

"Sure." He slipped one of the jackets on over his shirt and hefted his arms to test the fit across the shoulders. "No problem. Is this other one the same size?"

"I think so. The pants are gonna be a little big in the waist because they fit Barry, the actor you're replacing, and he was a bit thicker through the middle."

"He had a beer gut," said Daphne.

"Ah."

Further conversation was forestalled by the arrival of Chris and Shaun, closely followed by Mart and her saxophone. Mart was short and skinny, her face capped off by a mop of short-cropped black curls and dominated by a huge smile. Mart is the only person I've run across who smiles all the time who's neither a beauty contestant nor a serial killer. At least not as far as I know. I introduced her to Alex and she smiled in greeting, treating each cast member to an excellent view of her teeth.

I looked at Daphne. "So now we're just missing Grant, right?"

"Well, he's not here, if that's what you mean," said Daphne with a smirk.

"His absence makes my heart grow fonder," said Brad, emerging from the stacks to join the rest of us.

"Not me," said Chris. "I still can't stand him."

I rolled my eyes. "Well, he doesn't come in for the first half of Act One, so let's get going. We have a ton of blocking to go over and I only want to have to do this once."

"Aye, aye, Cap'n Connie." Brad threw me a mock salute. He raised his voice. "Everyone! Line up for inspection!"

"It's okay, Connie," Alex interjected before I could respond to Brad's not-so-subtle allusion to my somewhat authoritative manner. "Some of us prefer strong women."

"Well," I tossed back, "you know what they say about working with animals, kids and actors, you gotta let 'em know who's boss."

"What works with stuntmen?" This was Brad again, watching the interaction between Alex and me with interest.

"A six pack of Coors and a whip." I smiled sweetly at both Brad and

Alex. "Shall we move on?" I turned back to the registration desk and retrieved my notes and blocking diagram.

"She's lying," I heard Alex telling Brad as I fished for a pen in the
depths of my bag. "Coors would never work with me. Have to at *least* be
Sierra Nevada."

"I'll remember that," I murmured just loudly enough to for the sound
to carry. "Daphne, do you want to start this or shall I?"

Daphne snorted derisively. "Like they'll listen to me? You're the one
with the whip. So to speak."

She had a point. Our actors tend to expect Daphne to be in charge of
public relations, schedules and munchies for rehearsals, a sort of glamor-
ous Betty Crocker. I'm expected to direct, which is fine except when they
treat me like a combination of Ridley Scott and Attila the Hun. I'm not
that bad. Really.

I took a deep breath. "Okay, everyone!" That got their attention. "What
we're going to do first is go through the script, skipping the dialogue except
for entrance and exit cues. We're doing it in chronological order to avoid
confusion. After that, we'll work out specific blocking and run whatever
scenes need rehearsing, probably any of the fight stuff and anything with
Alex so he has a chance to catch up with the rest of us. Also, make sure you
know exactly what costumes you'll be wearing so you know how long you'll
need to change." I paused briefly. "Any questions?"

"Hello, everyone, I'm here! Sorry I'm late." Grant's well-trained voice
rang throughout the library as he entered through the double doors with a
purposeful stride. His entire attitude reeked of 'here I am, never fear, the
show is saved!'

"Oh good, we can all stop worrying." Brad voiced my thoughts in an
uncanny imitation of Grant's theatrical tones.

Grant did not look amused.

As Grant made a beeline for me, I conjured up the closest to an enthusiastic smile that I could muster and said, "No problem, we were just getting started." Grant leaned down to kiss me on the mouth but I turned my
head just enough so that his lips connected with my cheek instead. Ignoring the slight frown that creased his forehead, I quickly asked, "How did
your audition go?"

The frown disappeared magically as I turned Grant's attention to the
one thing guaranteed to distract him from any minor peeve: himself. "I
expect a call from my agent within the next day." He gave me a smile that
excluded the rest of the cast and said softly in a voice fraught with innuendo, "I'll tell you all about it later tonight."

As I tried to frame a non-committal response, I noticed Alex turn away, a frown of his own clouding his face. I didn't know whether to be glad that he cared or worried that he'd think I was enthusiastic about the idea of a private tLte á tLte with Grant.

Daphne saved me by cutting in with, "We really need to get going here, guys. So if everyone could get their scripts and follow along so we don't waste time …"

I shot her a grateful look as Grant, ever the professional, pulled out his script and stood poised for action. Everyone else took their places as well.

"Okay." I looked at my notes. "Brad, you're going to start from this desk." I pointed. "We're going to move it slightly to the left so none of the action will be blocked by this pillar. Now—"

"Doesn't that keep most of my action limited to the outer perimeter of the space?" Brad leapt behind the desk. "See what I mean?"

"It'll only be for the first monologue," I explained. "When Daphne makes her first entrance as Megan you can take it out in front of the desk."

"But couldn't I start in the audience with the lights down and then move it to the desk as the lights go up?" Brad jumped back out from behind the desk and moved to a spot amidst an imaginary audience. "Like this:

> *It was a cold night, and the fog was rolling in off of the Thames, which was kind of scary since I was in San Diego.*

He moved towards the desk, continuing his monologue.

> *I was waiting for a new case to keep me in Jack Daniels. My bottle was getting low and so was my morale …*

I interrupted, "Yes that's fine. Now go to the desk and skip to Megan's cue line. Daphne, we have you entering from behind those stacks."

Brad did as directed and Daphne made her entrance without a hitch. Skipping to the end of the scene, she asked, "Do I exit the same way?"

I consulted the diagram Daphne and I had spent a good deal of time preparing. Each character was carefully marked in place with a neat little arrow pointing the way on and off the stage area. "No. You'll go off to the right of the check-out desk and back to the staff office." I pointed. "Just so everyone knows, most of the entrances and exits will be on either side of this main desk because the staff office is where we're changing and staging our props."

We continued. We got through my entrance as Betty, Girl Friday, and Chris and Shaun's entrance as the thugs, with no problems, which finished up Act I.

Act II, however, was hell from the start. Nobody was happy with their positions as set and Brad and Grant vied with each other to see who could come up with more creative ideas to make their entrances and exits more 'dramatically effective.' Our diagram was soon an illegible mess covered with hatch marks crossing out initials, arrows pointing this way and that to indicate new positions. Alex was the only cast member who refrained from adding his opinions, probably because he saw my temper fraying with each new hatch mark. Daphne did her best to help control the confusion, all the while casting apprehensive looks in my direction as she waited for the inevitable explosion.

It was Grant who finally set off my internal TNT. First he actually grabbed the diagram and pen from my hands while I was trying to decipher Von Krump's first entrance amidst the mess. He marked all over the paper while telling me why he wanted to exit out the front doors, stating that it would be "an infinitely more appropriate choice for Von Krump's character." All this in a tone so condescending it made me want to rip his eyes out.

"Grant," I said, holding desperately to the last shreds of patience, "All that you've said taken into consideration, you're going to have to exit towards the office."

Grant took me by the shoulders and stared into my eyes with great sincerity. "Connie, I recognize your need for final decision—" A nice way of calling me a control freak! "—but that doesn't fit into Von Krump's motivation."

I stared at him. "Motivation?"

"Yes, darling," he replied in the tones of an adult speaking to a very slow child. "I know you're familiar with the term, the times you've spent doing stunt work not withstanding. An actor should do nothing without discovering the truth of his character's inner motivation."

Daphne shut her eyes and turned away with a brief "Oh, God."

All of my good intentions of staying on an even keel with Grant till after the last performance went out the window. My temper, already simmering gently, hit full boil in a matter of seconds. I jerked away from his hands. "You want motivation? Fine! You are motivated to exit that way because this is a *satire* and Von Krump *has* no inner motivation!" My volume increased with each word. "And more importantly, you're motivated to exit towards the office because you have to be back on stage in five minutes in a different costume! So unless you intend on stripping down out front and giving the Emerald Cove locals a *really* cheap thrill, you'll need to exit towards the dressing room! I trust that's sufficient motivation!!"

If anyone felt the urge to laugh, they had the good sense to stifle it. There was dead silence as Grant and I glared at each other. I'd never seen Grant so furious, especially not with me. If I hadn't been angry and frustrated myself, the expression in his eyes would've actually intimidated me. The words 'you wouldn't dare strike a woman' flashed into my mind, but I stifled the urge to say it. Grant wouldn't have gotten the humor and at that moment I thought he might just dare.

I don't know what would've happened if the sound of a car pulling into the parking lot hadn't distracted both of us. Daphne went over to a side window and peeked out. She groaned out loud and said, "Connie, Lucille's here."

"Shit." The news was more effective than a bucket of cold water dashed in my face. I looked at everyone. "I forgot to warn you all ... she wants to see a rehearsal in progress."

A metallic slam followed my words as Lucille shut her car door. The jingle of bracelets and the staccato of heels on pavement were audible, growing louder when she reached the tiled floor.

Grant and I looked at each other and in a rare moment of mutual telepathy, agreed to table this particular argument until later. He raised an eyebrow. "Shall we continue with rehearsal?" His voice was calm, his manner purely professional.

I nodded and matched his demeanor. "Let's take it from your exit."

"That would be towards the office." Grant's smile did not reach his eyes but I gave him credit for trying.

I nodded again. "Yes, please." The hatchet was buried momentarily but I knew it'd be dug back out later that night.

As Grant did his lines and made his exit, I felt a brief, reassuring hand on my shoulder. I didn't have to look to know that it was Alex, but I smiled up at him anyway. At that moment, Grant turned around and saw us. His lips thinned and a look of pure hatred flashed across his face, but it was gone so quickly that I must have imagined it. Time for me to do an ego check if I thought Grant would waste that much real emotion over something so trivial.

The front doors were flung open and all worries about Grant were driven out of my mind as Lucille made her grand entrance. She was dressed in a too tight, too short red sweater dress designed to offend anyone with an iota of fashion sense. I was impressed that she could actually balance on the red four-inch heels that matched the dress. I briefly wondered why someone with as much money as Lucille would choose to shop at what appeared to be mail-order from Sluts 'R Us.

She stood in the doorway for a moment as if waiting for the butler to announce her presence. We smiled at each other in mutual dislike.

"Good evening, Lucille," I said coolly. "Make yourself comfortable. There's coffee in the staff room if you want some."

"Don't let me interrupt you," replied Lucille. "I'm anxious to see how your little show is progressing. Although some coffee would be lovely." The last sentence was directed in equal parts to Alex and Grant, her manner switching from condescending to coy in seconds.

Enough of *that* shit. "Help yourself," I said before either man could react. "I'm sure Andy won't mind. We're going to continue with our blocking, we have a lot to get through tonight. Grant, if you and Alex could take your places for the next scene switch?" I picked up the blocking diagram, effectively dismissing her.

Lucille's nostrils flared briefly as she realized she'd been outmaneuvered. "I believe I will have some coffee," she said coldly. "Hopefully you'll have something underway that I can watch."

"Big Brother is alive and well," muttered Chris to no one in particular.

Grant stepped forward. "Connie, I'll just take a moment and help Mrs. Monroe find the coffee. There's one scene before my next entrance." Grant held out his arm. Lucille shot me a triumphant glance as she took it.

As they vanished into the staff office, I looked at Daphne. "Was that supposed to teach me a lesson?"

Daphne shrugged. "Trust Grant to schmooze the money."

Alex shook his head. "Personally I'd rather hand feed a barracuda."

"How could you tell the difference?" Daphne asked him.

"That's easy," I said. "The barracuda would be more tastefully dressed."

Chapter Nine

For the next hour and a half, Lucille sat in a corner where her precious five thousand dollars a plate guests would be placed so she could no doubt judge every movement and angle from their perspective. She radiated scorn throughout the entire rehearsal. Everyone was on their best behavior, conscious that we had an unsympathetic audience of one.

Despite Lucille's oppressive presence, we managed to establish basic blocking, props placement and music cues for all three acts. All the actors knew where they were going, with or without motivation. It was time for a break.

"Okay," I said after Mart finished her last sax cue. "Let's take fifteen minutes before we run the fights."

Normally this announcement would have been greeted with huge sighs of relief and an immediate dispersal of whatever tensions rehearsal had caused. Tonight, however, everyone looked uneasily towards the corner where Lucille sat, a chilly, contemptuous smile on her face.

"We're just going to be doing fight rehearsals after this," I said with a brief glance in her direction. "You're welcome to stay if you'd like, but there's really nothing for you to see."

"I'd already come to that conclusion." Lucille stood up, balancing precariously on the tiled floor.

I didn't bother to play stupid. "I seem to remember telling you that this was only a blocking rehearsal, Mrs. Monroe. If you were expecting more, you were warned."

"Oh, I was warned all right." She strode towards me, her weight—all of it in her chest—dipping forward on her toes. Her astounding cleavage quivered with righteous indignation beneath red acrylic. I had an absurd urge to tell her not to point those things at me but I stifled it. The situation looked bad enough as it was. "I should have known better than to trust Andy to pick a *real* theater company instead of amateurs."

I felt a wave of shock and anger ripple through the cast. Daphne's eyes were wide and I saw her hands bunch into fists. I was still calm, the kind of calm usually seen in the eye of a storm.

Lucille continued, fingering the green silk velvet dress as she spoke. "Where did he find you two? The local high school?"

I gently but firmly removed the dress a safe distance from her nails. "Please don't touch these. They're vintage."

"Are they?" Lucille sniffed contemptuously. "Then they're the only thing about your company that warrants attention."

I was saved the immediate necessity of replying by the appearance of Andy, who must have been listening from his office.

"Is there a problem?" His voice was mild but there was an unmistakably warlike glint in his eye.

Lucille rounded on him. "I'll tell you what the problem is! I've had no cooperation from you since I was hired to run the gala. It was bad enough with Damien Duran sabotaging me, but being forced to endure your constant usurping of my position is just too much!"

"Lucille …" Andy got no further.

Lucille steamrolled over him. "And as for these amateurs that you hired … hired *without* consulting me, I might add, it's obvious that you have no idea what constitutes real theater!

I looked at our cast. Tasha, Mart, Daphne and Shaun looked stricken, while Chris and Alex appeared to be ready to toss for the honor of punching Lucille. Grant looked downright murderous, although I was sure it had more to do with the impugning of his talent rather than the insult to Murder For Hire. Brad just burst into loud laughter and walked away, shaking his head. It was his way of restraining himself from doing or saying something he'd regret later. I, on the other hand, felt no such constraint.

I felt my mouth drawing up into a tight little smile I only get when my temper's one notch below seeing red. Andy started to say something, but I held up one hand and said, "Please, Andy. Allow me." All of the members of MFH immediately drew back several paces and waited.

I faced Lucille, who looked triumphant, sure that she'd put us in our place. I stared at her for a few seconds, taking my time as a state of deadly calm enveloped me. She stared back, hostile and just slightly uneasy, like a gunslinger afraid that he'd finally met his (or her) match. All that was needed to complete the standoff was a tumbleweed blowing across the room.

When I finally spoke, my voice was smooth and dripping with contempt. "Mrs. Monroe, I have met a great many people during my time in Hollywood. What amazes me is that out of all the Industry sharks and sleazes that I've run across, I have never met such an ignorant, *rude* person before."

Lucille's face went red. "Why, you …"

I overrode her. "Excuse me, you've had your say and I intend to have mine. First of all, this is a *blocking* rehearsal. If you really knew anything about theater, you'd know you wouldn't be able to ascertain a thing about the final performance from watching it. If you need to look up 'ascertain', I'm sure Andy will loan you a dictionary."

"I don't have to listen to this, you bitch!" Lucille's face was now purple, an interesting contrast with her blue-black hair and red dress.

I stepped forward, my smile broadening. Lucille actually stumbled backwards a step. She probably expected me to hit her. I hit her, all right, with a verbal blow that was unquestionably below the belt. "Second, Mrs. Monroe, I suspect that your knowledge of real theater is about as genuine as your chest. Which means you don't know what the hell you're talking about."

Lucille was now white with fury. Amazing the range of colors the woman went through in a matter of minutes. "You *will* be hearing from the committee," she hissed with pure venom. "This is *my* gala. Now that that idiot Duran is gone, my contract gives me final say and I will personally see that you are not only out of the program but that you *never* work in this town again!" Lucille stormed past Andy and out the front doors. The squeal of tires on pavement was audible as she burnt rubber pulling out of the parking lot.

There was a moment of stunned silence. I stood with my fists clenched, the adrenaline of battle coursing through my body as I tried to assimilate the fact that yes, someone actually told me I'd never work in this town again.

"Gee," Brad finally commented. "All that and you didn't even refuse to sleep with her."

The tension broke as everyone but Grant burst into laughter. Mine was only slightly tinged with hysteria. Grant looked appalled, although whether at me or Lucille or both I wasn't sure.

I sat down as the adrenaline vanished as quickly as it had come, leaving me drained and queasy. Alex knelt by my side and asked, "Are you okay?"

"I think I'm gonna throw up."

"I'll get you some water." Alex started to stand, but Grant gave him a resentful glare and snapped, "I'll get it." Alex shrugged and stayed where he was, putting a comforting hand on my shoulder. I shut my eyes and took a few deep breaths to steady myself until the nausea passed.

"Oh my God ..." I opened my eyes and looked at Daphne and Andy, stricken with the knowledge that I might have just killed our show and ruined Andy's reputation along with that of MFH. "I am so sorry, Andy, I—"

"Don't you dare apologize!" Andy broke in vehemently. He clumsily patted my other shoulder. "If anyone ever deserved to be told off, it's that bitch."

"She wasn't exactly polite herself," pointed out Daphne matter-of-factly.

"No," said Grant, returning with a glass of water which he handed to me. Alex reluctantly stood up as Grant maneuvered himself between us. "But it was hardly politic to call attention to the fact that she'd had breast augmentation as a way of making your point."

I was taking a swallow of water and Grant's words made me spill some down my front. The criticism hurt because I knew he was right and tears stung my eyes.

"Oh, I don't know," said Andy with a surprising edge of anger to his voice. "I thought as comparisons went, it was a damned good one."

"Worked for me," said Chris in one of his rare conversational contributions.

Brad came up and took my free hand. "Connie," he said solemnly, "I'm sure I speak for all of us when I tell you that it was a privilege to witness you rip that bitch to shreds with as much class and restraint as you used." There were nods of agreement from everyone but Grant. Brad continued. "If I had some of your Scotch, I'd toast you with it."

I laughed. "Thanks, Brad." It made me feel better knowing that I had the support of everyone with the probable exception of Grant. I turned to Andy. "Can she really get us fired from the Gala?"

"Not to worry." Andy's eyes took on a determined gleam. "She'll try and get you out, but I'll make a few phone calls and see that the people who matter know what *really* happened."

"What about her contract?" The contract I'd love to shove down her throat.

A shadow of doubt passed over Andy's face. "Let me put it this way ..." He paused, and Daphne and I exchanged worried looks. "That contract does give Lucille a certain amount of say. But the bottom line is that if Jason Downs wants you, there's not a hell of a lot she can do about it." The determined air was back. "So I'd better get on the phone and circumnavigate Lucille before she can do any real damage."

Andy gave me one last reassuring pat and went off to his office. He paused at the door and turned back. "Are you going to do any more rehearsing?"

I looked at Daphne, and then we both looked at our cast. "As soon as we hand out the scripts for the Walking Tours, I think we're about ready to call it a night," I said. Daphne nodded in agreement. The general relief was palpable; we'd all had enough for one evening.

"Then I'll say goodnight. I'll call you as soon as I know anything." Andy waved and vanished into his office.

It took about ten minutes to deal with handing out the scripts and making sure everyone knew what they were wearing tomorrow, and the locations and times of their scenes. We'd planned on going over the scenes more extensively but that would have to wait until the morning. None of us had the energy left.

I stood up and looked at my watch. Was it really only 9:30? It seemed like midnight. "Let's gather up the props and get out of here."

Grant took me by one arm and pulled me into the stacks where we had relative privacy. "I'm going to talk to Mrs. Monroe and see if I can undo any of the damage already done."

"Thanks for the support, Grant."

"Don't be childish, Connie." Grant looked at me coldly. "She seems to have influence with Jonathan Burke and it would be foolish to alienate either of them at this juncture in our careers."

"You mean *your* career." I shook my head, too tired to care. "You do what you want, Grant. I'm packing up and going home. We have three walking tours tomorrow and I'm exhausted."

"I'll be over to see you when I'm finished."

I shook my head. "Not tonight, Grant, I'm …"

Grant cut off my words with a single hard kiss, one that held little affection. "Don't argue with me. I'll see you later." With that, Grant strode out of the stacks and left the library, leaving everyone else to pick up props and me staring after him open-mouthed. I stood there for a moment, shaking with anger. Did he really think that I'd respond to that caveman routine?

Daphne poked her head around the corner. "If you don't mind my asking, what was that all about?" I told her and she shook her head in disbelief. "You've got to get rid of that jerk."

I didn't argue. We went back out to find all of the props gathered neatly together and everyone gone except Brad, Tasha and Alex. Alex looked at me inquiringly and I gave him a weary smile in return. "I'll be back in a minute."

"Meet us outside," said Brad. "We'll take everything out to the car." I nodded gratefully, grabbed my bag and headed off to the ladies room.

My reflection in the bathroom mirror was less than flattering, even taking the fluorescent lighting into consideration. The makeup that hadn't faded had migrated to all the wrong places. I looked like a forlorn raccoon. One with pale lips.

A little bit of lipstick took care of part of the problem, but even after wiping away the errant mascara with some tissue and water, I still had dark circles under my eyes. The stress of maintaining the balance between my desire to tell Grant to go to hell, and knowing that MFH would be screwed if he left on this short notice, had me in a permanent crisis mode. I was barely holding onto my sanity. The confrontation with Lucille threatened to send me over the edge.

I took several deep breaths. If I were lucky, I'd get a decent night's sleep and maybe that would help me regain my equilibrium.

When I got outside, there was no sign of Alex. He hadn't even waited to say good-bye. A wave of sudden sharp depression swept over me. I got out my keys and turned to say goodnight to Brad and Tasha, so tired I could barely see straight.

Daphne held out her hand and said, "Give me the keys, Brad's gonna drive me home and Tash'll meet us there. I'm going make us all some co-coa."

I stared at her blankly. "That's nice. What about me?"

She nodded to a dark green Mustang convertible parked in the corner. Alex stuck his head out of the driver's side window and called, "Can I give you a lift?"

The depression lifted as rapidly as it had descended. I hesitated. "Our first show's at eleven tomorrow …"

Daphne gave me a little push towards Alex's car. "It's early. We've already got almost everything together for tomorrow anyway. You don't want to be home when Grant shows up, do you?"

The decision was easy. I turned to Brad and Tasha. "I'll see you guys tomorrow. Thanks for all your help." Then I walked over to Alex's car where he waited, leaned down on the driver's side window and said, "So show me how you stunt boys drive."

He grinned. "I intend to."

Chapter Ten

Alex actually drove very well, taking the streets of Emerald Cove at a leisurely pace and with none of the aggressive automotive maneuvering I'd come to expect from stuntmen. I told him so and he looked at me in amusement. "What did you think I was going to do, try and jump the car onto a train?"

"Heck if I knew what to expect," I admitted. "Most of the guys I worked with always drove like they were filming a car chase. You know, something to prove."

Alex shook his head. "No thanks. My testosterone levels are normal unless I'm being paid big bucks to do something stupid."

I laughed. "Well, it's a nice change."

"Glad to hear it."

We reached Prospero Street and Emerald Cove's business district. Alex threaded his way through the usual Friday night traffic of tourists, trendy college kids and well-dressed yuppies out for the evening.

"Where are we going?" I asked as he narrowly missed being side-swiped by a BMW pulling out of an underground parking garage.

Alex looked at me ruefully. "I had ideas about stopping for a relaxing drink, but everything looks packed. Hardly my idea of relaxing."

I eyed the hordes of people. "Mine either."

"Any ideas?"

I thought about it for a moment. "I like the beach … unless it's too cold for you."

Alex smiled. "Sounds perfect."

How about that, I thought. Getting Grant to walk on the beach with me had been a major achievement, always spoiled by the fact that he acted like royalty bestowing largess on the poor peasant wench (me) the entire time we were there.

"You up for breaking a minor law?" We pulled to a stop at a red light.

"How minor?" I asked warily. Last thing MFH needed at this juncture was for one of its founders to be arrested. I thought of what Arthur Sloan would do with such a scoop and inwardly shuddered.

"We could buy a bottle of wine at the grocery store, find a quiet spot on the beach …" Alex trailed off and looked at me as he waited for the light to change.

"There's a Jonathan's Grocery up a couple of blocks on Jewel," I said instantly, the idea no doubt appealing to the juvenile delinquent in me. "Take a right up here. You'll see the store on your left. I think it's open until ten."

Alex looked at his watch. "Ten till ten."

"We should just make it."

We managed to make it to the store and buy a respectable bottle of red zinfandel before the store closed. In the parking lot on the way to the car, I stopped short and said, "We forgot to get cups. And what about a cork-screw?"

Alex shook his head, cradling the wine, which was wrapped in a brown paper bag. "Swiss army knife in the car. And who the hell needs cups?"

"We're gonna look like a couple of winos," I said, getting into the car.

"I don't mind if you don't mind." Alex handed me the wine as he started the engine. "Where to?"

We ended up parking down on Cove Street where the scenic walk began, the only place in Emerald Cove not crawling with activity. Most people were sensible enough to try negotiating the rocky path only during daylight hours. I pointed to the same staircase that Daphne and I had descended earlier today. "This walk's a little tricky at night."

"Hey," said Alex. "I'm a stuntman."

"You're gonna trip," I predicted as we started carefully down the stairs. "You know that, don't you? The gods *will* punish you."

"As long as the wine doesn't break." Alex tucked it safely beneath his left arm, holding onto the bottom of the bottle with one hand.

We passed a bench overlooking the ocean. Alex turned to me. "Not what you're looking for?"

"I want to be closer to the water." I loved feeling the salty spray of the crashing waves on my face and it'd been a few days since I'd been afforded the time to enjoy that particular pleasure. Getting soaked up to my waist at Davy Jones Cave didn't count.

We walked in companionable silence along the edge of the cliffs, our eyes growing slowly accustomed to the dark. The houses above afforded a little bit of light, especially Jason Down's home, but the footing was still treacherous. Alex, somewhat to my disgust, was as sure footed as a mountain goat while I slipped on loose rocks every now and again. On the other hand, the wine was safe.

"Here." I turned off the path and went down a gradual slope that became a narrow track of sand and rock. It led to a little patch of beach in between cliffs and jagged rocks. It was too small to warrant a stairway so we had to step carefully on rock and sand that became increasingly damp the further we descended. This was my favorite private spot in Emerald Cove, usually deserted by tourists and locals alike in favor of more readily accessible locales.

The track ended abruptly in a four-foot drop off to the sand, which was slowly being covered by the encroaching tide. The beach itself was about twenty feet long and only a few yards wide during low tide. It was tucked between two cliff faces jutting out into the water and had several smooth shelves of rock running its length.

Alex whistled in appreciation as he watched the waves crashing over the rocks in front of us, curling back out to sea with a gentle hissing sound. "This is nice," he said simply. He handed me the wine and leapt down to the sand, landing lightly on his feet. I started to hand back the wine in preparation for my own jump, but Alex forestalled me by catching me around the waist and lifting me down to the beach instead.

I stumbled against him, slightly off-balance and breathless as I said, "Thanks."

He steadied me, hands still about my waist. "I didn't think you'd feel up to stunt work after this evening."

It was funny. If Grant had done and said the same thing I would've been pissed off at his condescension. I didn't get any sense of that from Alex, but maybe I was just enjoying having his hands on me too much to notice.

We climbed up on a small rock shelf down the beach, just big enough for the two of us and our wine. I leaned back against the cliff face and watched Alex pull out his handy-dandy Swiss Army knife, one of those with eight million attachments.

"How did you know which one was the corkscrew?" I asked as he flipped the little bugger right up on the first try.

"Practice makes perfect."

"Oh? Do this sort of thing a lot, do you?" I tried to keep my tone light, part of me seeing green as I thought of Alex opening bottles of wine to share with countless other women.

"I traveled through Europe with a buddy and this——" he waggled the knife at me. "——and being fresh out of college, you bet the corkscrew got a lot of use." He pulled out the cork with an easy twist of one hand. "Shall we let it breathe?"

"Hell, no!" I held out my hand imperiously.

"How about a toast?"

"Kind of hard to do without glasses."

"Au contraire." Alex rested the bottle in my hand, keeping his own hand right above mine. His face was dim in the shadowed rocks but I heard the smile in his voice. "To the show."

"To the show," I echoed. We lifted the bottle to the sky and then took turns drinking. He kept his hand on the bottle as I took a swallow. I was conscious of his proximity the entire time.

I started to let go when it was Alex's turn, but he put his hand over mine and said, "Not till we finish the toast." He drank and then set the bottle down in a niche in the rock. My skin still tingled from his touch. Or maybe it was the wine. I hadn't eaten anything since the clam chowder and bread that afternoon.

We sat in comfortable silence for a few minutes and watched the waves froth over the sand and rocks in front of us, hissing gently as they retreated out to sea. This was exactly what I needed after the stress of the day. Listening to the sounds of the ocean I could feel the tension brought on by rehearsal, Lucille and Grant slipping away with each receding wave.

I took another sip of wine, enjoying the mellow, slightly spicy flavor. Grant would've called it fruit-forward, along with a number of other textbook descriptions in an effort to 'improve my educational palate.'

I gave my head a shake, willing all thoughts of Grant back in my mental file marked 'Tomorrow is another day.' Or was it 'Frankly my dear, I don't give a damn?'

"You cold?"

I looked up at Alex, startled by the question. "No. Why, are you?"

"No. But you shivered, so ..."

I laughed. "Sorry about that. I was just putting unwanted thoughts in their proper place."

"Don Jose, perhaps?" Alex took his turn with the wine, downing a hefty swig after he asked the question.

I shrugged, not wanting to go there. Alex, however, was persistent. "Is he going to give you hell for tonight?"

"Only if he finds out about it." And even if he didn't, I thought. Grant would certainly think the worst when he arrived at the house and I wasn't home. The thought made my stomach hurt. "Hand that over." I grabbed the wine and brought the level down by a good two inches.

"Do the two of you come down here often?" Alex's tone was carefully neutral.

I snorted inelegantly. "Are you kidding? Too much sand."

"What exactly do the two of you have in common?" Alex sounded genuinely curious. "Besides acting, that is."

I shrugged. "If you'd asked me that a month ago, I'm sure I could've written you a list. Now? Beats the hell out of me."

Alex shook his head. "You really need to tell him it's over. Even if I didn't have my own agenda, I'd give you the same advice."

"As soon as the show's over." My voice was much sharper than I meant it to be, but I didn't want to talk about Grant any more.

There was a brief pause before Alex said, "Sorry. You have your reasons."

"Yeah, I do," I shot back, still on the defensive. "I can't think about anything but the shows right now. I'm sorry if it seems cowardly, but—"

"Hey, it's okay." Alex reached out and touched my hand. "You don't have to say another word," he added as I started to reply. "You're thinking about the show and you're right. And I'm a jerk for stressing you out even more."

I drank some more wine and handed him the bottle. There was another brief pause as I stared at the waves, my mood suddenly bleak. "I seem to make a habit of snapping your head off."

"Two times does not a habit make. I'll start to worry after the third."

"Maybe I should just get it over with," I sighed. "I don't seem to be dealing with anything very well these days."

"You've got a lot to deal with. Lucille is enough to make anyone ..." He paused, searching for the right word.

"Bitchy?" I said helpfully.

"I didn't say that. I was thinking more along the lines of homicidal?" I gave him a look and he hastily handed me the wine. "Just kidding."

"Mm hmm." I took a sip. "Although it's too bad that Damien Duran died and not Lucille."

"Yeah, that woman's a real piece of work."

"Do you think she's capable of murder?"

Alex chuckled. "Sure, if looks could kill."

"Are you talking about her evil stare or her wardrobe choices?"

"Both."

We both laughed this time. "Seriously, though. I mean, I'm asking you to make a snap judgment here, but do you think that Lucille could have killed Damien Duran?"

To his credit, Alex gave my question serious consideration before replying. "I'd have to give you a two-part answer. First, I have no idea if Lucille could have killed the guy. I don't have enough background on either of them. But I personally think anyone is capable of murder, given the right set of circumstances."

"I'm not sure I buy that," I said, trying to picture, say, Mavis as a cold-blooded killer. Sure, Mavis could *irritate* someone to death, but murder? Nah. I said as much.

Alex shook his head. "No, I'm not just talking about something that's been premeditated. What about self-defense? Or killing to protect someone that you love?"

"I don't define killing someone in those types of circumstances as murder."

"Fair enough," said Alex. "But the point I'm trying to make remains the same. Anyone, given the right provocation, is capable of taking the life of another human being—" he paused to take a sip of wine. "—with the possible exceptions of Gandhi and Mother Teresa."

I still wasn't sure I agreed with him entirely, but it added another possible dimension to Duran's death. Although I doubted an elderly man taking a swim could pose a threat to anyone, let alone how deliberately pinning someone under water could be construed as self-defense.

My head started to ache again. Obviously too much deductive reasoning was bad for me. I could feel the muscles in my neck and back coiled up in knots. I rolled my head from side to side in an effort to loosen things up.

Alex noticed and looked at me with concern. "You okay?"

"Just a little tense after the day."

Alex put a hand on my shoulder and squeezed, giving a low whistle as he did so.

"What?"

"Good lord, woman, you've got more knots in your back than a pine tree."

I laughed. "How many knots does a pine tree … ohhh … never mind …" Alex had set the wine bottle down and began to rub my shoulders, easing my flight jacket down so that I could get the full effect of his strong fingers as they worked their magic on my tense muscles.

"Here, move this way a little." He shifted us both slightly so that I was sitting between his legs as he massaged my back.

"Works for me." I closed my eyes and let myself relax, the combination of wine and backrub doing their job. It seemed the most natural thing in the world to be here with Alex, so unlike the theatrical quality that spending time with Grant had to it. Had I ever felt this easy intimacy with Grant? I honestly didn't think so.

Conversation was sporadic as Alex worked on my back, many of my utterances being little sounds of contentment as yet another knot dissolved under his skill. We talked a little bit about stunt work. I told him why I'd finally quit and tried to explain my prejudice against the breed as a whole. Alex summed it up with "stunt work attracts a certain type of guy. Let's face it, the majority of people who want to throw themselves off buildings, crash cars and set themselves on fire for a living have to have either more than the normal dose of machismo or less than your average IQ."

"Testosterone junkies," I retorted. "What's your excuse?"

"Got dropped on my head too many times as a baby."

I laughed but it turned into a purr as he threaded his hands through my hair and kneaded my scalp.

At least twenty-five minutes passed, by which time the consistency of my muscles had gone from ropes of steel to limp Fettuccini a la Connie. When he finally stopped the massage, Alex wrapped his arms around me, hands clasped at my waist and pulled me against him. Oh well, I thought to myself as I leaned my head back on his chest, no harm, no foul. It wasn't as though we were actually *doing* anything.

"Do you want some more wine?" Alex's breath was warm in my ear as he spoke. It sent a pleasurable shiver up my spine. I nodded 'yes', wondering if he knew what he was doing. I decided I didn't care.

He handed me the bottle. I drank, holding it up inquiringly after I'd had my fill. Alex wrapped one hand around mine on the bottle. "How about another toast?"

"What are we drinking to?" I inquired lazily.

His hand tightened on mine. "To getting rid of excess baggage."

Startled out of my mellow mood by the vehemence of Alex's tone, I turned my head sharply to look up at him. In doing so, my lips inadvertently brushed against his. The contact sent a jolt of electricity straight down through to my toes.

Alex drew in his breath sharply, drawing back as if he'd been burned. Misreading the action, I felt my face flush with mortification. "I ... I'm sorry," I began to stammer, "I didn't mean ..."

"Connie, don't be an idiot." With that, Alex turned me around so that I was half lying across his legs and kissed me.

His kisses were warm and expert, flavored with wine. His fingers knew the exact places on my neck and face to make my knees go weak even though I was reclining. If I'd felt a little frisson of electricity before, this was a complete meltdown.

I don't know how long we kissed or how long we would've continued if nature hadn't put a stop to it by sending a particularly large wave crashing against the rocks below. Frigid salt water sprayed over both of us, effectively dampening our passion. Talk about cheap symbolism.

We broke apart, water dripping down our hair. I looked down at the beach, now covered by the encroaching tide. "Oh my God," I said breathlessly, "Have we been here that long? We're gonna have to wade out of here."

"That's what we get for not paying attention." Alex reached out and pushed a strand of wet hair out of my face. "Not that I mind."

"Me either." We smiled at each other, that silly irrepressible kind of smile only seen on people suffering from extreme infatuation or a good dose of laughing gas.

Another large wave rolled in, sending spumes of water into the air. We huddled back against the rocks, managing to avoid the worst of it this time, but it was definitely time to go.

Alex grabbed the wine bottle and took a long swig. "Not too much salt water," he grinned. "Here, finish it up."

I did so and handed it hastily back to him as water slopped up onto the ledge, soaking our feet. "Let's get out of here."

There was no way up off the beach other than the way we'd come down. This meant jumping down off the ledge into the water and wading as waves rolled in around us, the tide tugging at our legs. By the time Alex boosted me back up to the path and easily pulled himself up after me, we were both soaked to the waist. I was spending a lot of time in wet denim today.

We made our way back up to the car, Alex putting an arm firmly around my shoulders as we walked. I slid one arm around his waist, grateful for the support. The wine and the day had finally taken their toll in sheer exhaustion, and I could barely put one foot in front of the other by the time we reached the top of the stairs.

We were quiet on the drive home, neither of us feeling the need to make conversation. Every now and again Alex would brush my face lightly with one finger and I'd smile drowsily, my eyelids at half-mast. For the first time in weeks, I felt totally content with the world, confident about the shows and positive about the future.

This state lasted approximately ten minutes at which point Alex pulled up to my house and I saw Grant's black Lexus parked in the driveway. My eyes snapped open.

"Oh, shit."

"What?" Alex followed my gaze. "Is that Don Jose's?"

I nodded grimly and glanced at the car clock, which read 11:30. "I can't believe he's still here. Daphne must be pissed as hell." I retrieved my purse from the floor and started to open the door. Alex put a hand on my arm.

"Do you want me to come in?"

I shook my head. "That would add enough fuel to the fire to burn down Emerald Cove." I turned around and looked at him. "Will you take a rain check?"

Alex smiled. "You bet." He paused before adding, "You sure you'll be okay?"

"Don't worry about me," I said with confidence. "Grant is annoying but I don't think he even knows how to throw a punch. He always uses a stunt double." I reached out and touched his shoulder. "Alex, I had a great evening. Thanks."

"Me too. I'll see you in the morning, okay?"

"Okay." Getting out of the car, I slammed the door shut and waved as he pulled away from the curb and drove off into the darkness. I squared my shoulders, took a deep breath and went into the house.

Daphne was curled up on the couch, a book in one hand, a cup of what was no doubt hot chocolate in the other. As soon as she saw me, she put the book down and stood up, hissing, "Grant's in your room."

"What?!" I took off my damp bomber jacket and hung it up in the front entryway, noting that my keys were hanging on their designated hook. I'd actually know where they'd be in the morning.

"Shh!" Daphne glanced upstairs to make sure the coast was clear. "He got here at 10:30, demanded to know where you were and then refused to leave until you got home. He said he'd wait upstairs."

"Shit." I felt every knot Alex had dissolved coil right back up in my muscles. "Did you tell him where I was?"

"I didn't know, so I couldn't tell him."

"Does he know that I went out with Alex?"

Daphne nodded miserably. "He asked me straight out who you were with and caught me off guard. I'm really sorry, Connie, I ..." She paused as she finally took a good look at my soaked clothing. "Jeez, what happened to you?"

"We went for a walk on the beach, got caught by the tide." I took another deep breath, my heart racing a mile a minute. "I'd better get this over with."

"Connie, he's really angry. And I think he's been drinking." Daphne actually looked worried.

My apprehension increased. Grant rarely drank to excess. And more significantly, I'd never seen Daphne take any of Grant's emotions seriously.

I tried to ignore the butterflies putting on an aerial show in my stomach and said lightly, "What's he gonna do, hit me?"

"If he does, I'll kill him." Daphne wasn't joking. "I'll wait up, okay?"

"Thanks."

The door to my room was closed, which made me even angrier than I already was. How dare he appropriate my room without my permission? The anger dispelled a few of the butterflies and I opened my door with more force than necessary, figuring that the best defense was a good offense.

Evidently Grant had figured the same thing because the second I walked in the door he grabbed me by the shoulders and flung me unceremoniously onto my bed. I barely had time to catch my breath and struggle to a sitting position before Grant had shut and locked the bedroom door. It was looking as though my best defense might be karate.

Grant looked very much like the villain in a soap opera. I would've laughed except for the fact that Daphne was right; Grant was royally pissed off and there was nothing remotely theatrical about his rage. It made our argument at Jason Down's party seem laughable by comparison. I thought of the final act in *Carmen* and half wondered if I should look for a knife.

"Where the hell have you been?" The fact that water from my sodden clothes was now soaking into my goose-down comforter made the answer to his question seem rather obvious. It also made me angrier than ever. Now the damned thing would have to be dry-cleaned.

I shook my head in disgust and swung my legs over the edge of the bed, fully intending to get to my feet and oust Grant from my room for the night and my life after Sunday.

Grant, unfortunately, had other ideas. In an almost repeat performance of the other evening he shoved me back down before I could stand. To-night, however, instead of leaving it at that, he actually pressed me down to the bed before I knew what he intended. Holding me down with the weight of his body, he clamped my wrists with both hands and pinned them to the mattress. What really worried me, however, was the fact that he didn't seem to care that his expensive trousers were going to be ruined by salt water. This was definitely *not* normal behavior.

I made one brief attempt to throw him off but I might as well have been trying to budge a concrete statue as Grant countered easily by in-creasing the pressure on my wrists. I stared at him in disbelief. "Grant, damn it, you're hurting me!"

"Answer my question." He continued to hold me with painful strength, his face inches from mine. Yup, he'd been drinking. I could smell tequila— the only hard liquor he favored—on his breath.

This was ludicrous. "Grant," I said between gritted teeth, "My jeans are soaking wet—which should give you a clue as to where I've been, by the way—and the water's ruining my comforter."

He ignored my words. "What were you doing at the beach this time of night? You knew I was coming over."

I glared at him. "I told you I didn't want to talk tonight, damn it! And if I want to go to the beach to unwind, that's my business!"

Grant's mouth twisted to one side. "With another man? Coming back looking like you've just re-enacted a scene out of *From Here to Eternity?*"

This only served to remind me of my ruined comforter. "God damn it, you let me up right now!" I thrashed beneath him and nearly succeeded in getting one wrist free. Grant merely shifted his hands momentarily, lifted my arms and upper torso off the mattress and slammed me back down. I pulled my wrists impotently against his grip, furious at both him and my own helplessness. I'd been in this position with Grant before, albeit under much more pleasurable circumstances, and if he chose not to let me up there was exactly nothing that I could do about it. And we both knew it.

The absurd thing was that I was also feeling increasingly guilty. Even though I firmly believed part of his fury was caused by damaged ego, I was forced to consider the possibility that maybe he really cared about me. Warped thinking, I know, considering the circumstances, but I'd never seen Grant this upset about anything, even a bad audition. Technically we hadn't broken up and if I hadn't exactly been rolling around in the surf with Alex, the evening hadn't been entirely innocent.

But I was not about to admit any of this to Grant, who had no business being in my room without my permission, much less touching me without same. A semi-guilty conscience was not enough to make me stupid.

I willed myself to calm down and took a few deep breaths to clear the red from my vision. I heard the phone ring downstairs and waited until it had stopped before finally looking up at Grant. I noticed with a new detachment how dark his eyes became when he was angry. Anger did nothing to detract from his looks, but his remarkable handsomeness no longer had the power to affect me. "Grant," I finally said as calmly as I could, "Alex and I went for a walk on the beach. We had some wine and talked. We got caught by the tide and a few big waves. That's it." And except for the last two words, strictly the truth.

I looked for some softening in his expression, but he was still seething. "What were you doing going out with him in the first place?"

"Jesus, Grant, I needed to unwind, he offered to take me out for a quick drink. We went to the beach because Emerald Cove was crawling with night life and there wasn't a restaurant or bar that didn't have a line two miles long." I hoped this would satisfy him because my wrists were going numb.

He stared down at me as if trying to discern the truth behind my words. Evidently none of my periphery guilt showed because his face finally began to lose some of its white-lipped fury. There was, however, still a load of resentment in his tone as he said, "You knew I wanted to see you tonight."

I sighed. "I tried telling you at the library that I didn't want to have any serious discussions tonight, Grant. The whole scene with Lucille was more than enough for one evening." I tried to sound conciliatory as I added, "Look, I'm sorry I pulled a no-show on you, I just wasn't thinking about it, okay?"

Grant nodded slowly and loosened his grip, although he still didn't let me up. "Don't do it again, Connie."

"I'm not planning on it." That's right, I thought, because after the show you are *history*, you bastard. Right now I just wanted him off of my bed, not to mention my body. There was just a *little* bit of an edge to my voice as I said, "Can I please get up now?"

He didn't answer but I saw the shift in his mood as a small, sensuous smile played about his lips. Oh no, I thought. We are *not* going there. I tried again, turning my head slightly as he closed the gap between us so that his lips landed on my cheek instead of my mouth. "Grant, there is nothing more uncomfortable than denim that's been soaked in sea water. I'm cold, wet and exhausted."

He ignored me, abandoning his grip on one wrist to twine his fingers through my damp hair in what could have been meant as a lover-like gesture. But it seemed more like he was trying to hold my head still so he could kiss me, which he did, roughly and possessively. I endured the kiss but when his hands moved down to my jeans and started fumbling with the zipper, I made a sound of protest.

"You said you wanted to get these off." The innuendo in his tone made me want to smack him.

I might have actually done so if we hadn't been interrupted by a knock on the door. A frown of annoyance crossed Grant's brow. I tried to hide my own smile of relief.

"Connie?" Daphne sounded concerned.

"Don't answer," whispered Grant.

"What's up, Daphne?" I said loudly, not bothering to dignify Grant's suggestion with a response.

"That was Andy on the phone with the scoop on the show. Want the update now?"

"Yeah. I'll be right down. Give me a few minutes to change my clothes." I looked up at Grant and said quietly, "This is important, Grant. And then I need to get some sleep. We've got shows to do tomorrow."

Grant finally let me up, his professionalism winning out over his need to prove his desirability. He rolled off of me and got to his feet. Not taking any chances, I immediately scrambled off the bed, forcing back words of anger as I saw just how much water my comforter had absorbed. I pulled it off and threw it in a corner for the time being. I then grabbed my warmest flannel robe, unlocked the bedroom door and said, "I'll see you in the morning, Grant." Not waiting for a response, I stalked down the hall to the bathroom, shutting and locking the door firmly behind me in case he had any ideas about a romantic shower for two.

I turned the water on full blast and hurriedly stripped off my wet clothing. I was starting to shiver, either in reaction to my anger or the chill from being forced to stay in my soggy garments far too long. Probably both. I stepped under the cascade of hot water, anxious to forestall a cold. I swear, if I had so much as a scratchy throat in the morning, I was going to murder Grant. I hoped he'd taken my none-too-subtle hint and left. Maybe by tomorrow I'd be able to treat him with civility, but tonight was open season on pompous actors/jealous boyfriends as far as I was concerned.

The quick shower helped take the chill away and restore my nerves. By the time I'd rubbed lotion into my skin and wrapped myself in cozy black and red flannel, I was nearly calm.

Renfield greeted me as I descended the stairs, twining about my ankles with a rumbling purr. I managed to avoid either tripping or stepping on the cat by scooping him up. I draped him over one shoulder and took a cautious look around. Grant was nowhere in sight.

Daphne was in the kitchen seated at the table, two fresh mugs of cocoa set in the middle. Melting marshmallows bobbed gently on top of the frothy chocolate and the fragrance of the combination wafted gently through the air straight to my nose. Sitting down, I took my mug and cradled it in both hands, holding it away from Renfield as he leaned over and sniffed.

Daphne looked at me. "You wanna tell me what happened up there?"

I sighed. "Is he gone?"

She nodded. "Didn't look too happy about it, but he left."

"Did he say anything?"

"Nope." Daphne took a sip of cocoa, gaining a mustache of marshmallow as she did so. "He and I don't talk much."

"Lucky you." I drank some cocoa and gave her a brief rundown of the evening, starting with Alex and ending with Grant's little 'me Tarzan' routine in my room.

Daphne raised an eyebrow. "Weren't you scared?"

I shook my head, disturbing Renfield, who promptly jumped off of my shoulder and onto the table where he sauntered across its surface before leaping to the floor. He vanished out into the dining room with a flick of long, black tail. "Grant would never hurt me. He may have been angry, but I still think a lot of it was acting. Besides, I was too furious to be scared."

"What an asshole."

"I'm not gonna argue." I took a sip of cocoa. "It just really pisses me off that I've let myself get into the position of having to cater to him, or risk screwing up our shows. I should have dumped him ages ago."

"I'm not gonna argue." Daphne grinned at me. "Alex, on the other hand ..."

I smiled. "I'm *definitely* not gonna argue." I let my mind wander back to the beach for a moment, then gave myself a little mental shake and said, "What did Andy say? Are we still in?"

"Unofficially, yes."

"Unofficially?"

"Andy managed to get a hold of Jason Downs before Lucille did. Downs really likes our script, plus he checked our references before we were actually hired."

"So what's the problem?" I drank some cocoa, trying to catch a marshmallow oodging over the rim of the mug before I lost it. I caught the marshmallow but spilled cocoa on the table.

"Well," replied Daphne as she tossed me a napkin, "as I said, unofficial status is that we're in. Downs and the Festival Board have dealt with Lucille enough to know what she's like and they're inclined to take Andy's word for what really happened."

"And the official status?"

"Officially the Board members have to listen to Lucille's side of the story before making a final decision since she's in charge of the Gala. And since we don't have Damien Duran on our side any more, there's a small chance we could get kicked off the job."

"Great," I groaned. "I'm gonna come off worse than Osama bin Laden by the time she's finished."

"She's going to do her best to make us all sound like a bunch of no-talent amateurs," said Daphne. "But yeah, you'll probably get the worst of it."

I shrugged fatalistically. "Oh well, there's nothing I can do now. We'll know tomorrow?"

"Yeah. Most of the committee members will be attending the Walking Tour, so unless we really screw up I think we'll be okay." She paused before adding, "I'd really like to kill that woman."

"Get in line," I muttered darkly.

Chapter Eleven

"Salaciously smooth … salac … salacious … salaciously smooth oil on your … salaciously smooth oil on your sun-kissed skin …"

I took a deep breath and counted to ten, adding another five to my mental tally as Shaun continued to dissect one of his lines as gumshoe Mick O'Mallet, pacing the entire length of the Oak Room as he did so. White jacketed waiters ignored him as they arranged the buffet and set glasses out on the bar in preparation for the tour.

Shaun was an excellent actor and a perfectionist. Unfortunately he was also prone to extreme cases of stage fright if not given adequate rehearsal time. Considering that we'd just gotten the Walking Tour pages from Andy yesterday and only had this morning to rehearse the scenes from *Play to Win*, Shaun was a mental wreck. Reassurances that there was plenty of room for improvisation were not helping. I wondered if our other O'Mallets were having this much trouble.

The entire line as written was:

> *What happened to the Riviera, doll-face? You know, that expen-*
> *sive hotel where we were going to stay and soak up the sun, where*
> *I'd salaciously smooth oil on your sun-kissed skin and we'd stare*
> *up at the stars and sip sangria.*

Shaun could not get it right to save his life. And with each repetition, the expectancy of said life was decreasing because my nerves couldn't take much more.

"C'mon, Shaun, let's try it from the top." I smiled encouragingly. Shaun responded with a glower. His irregular features and dark eyes set under heavy brows gave him a face well-suited to glowering.

Daphne, Alex and I each had a scene with Shaun as O'Mallet. Daphne's was brief and uncomplicated. She was playing Ginger, the sassy secretary to Mr. Big (Brad, who would theoretically come flying in from his own turn as O'Mallet on the cliffs in time to make his cue). The scene consisted of one-liners, Daphne and Shaun breezed through a quick rehearsal with no problems. The same was true with Alex's scene as a suave Englishman mysteriously involved in the case. Shaun had flung snappy repartee back at Alex with nary a stammer or hesitation. Nope, it was just my scene that was being turned into a bigger trauma than a blind date.

Admittedly, my mood wasn't helping matters. I was still more or less emotionally hung over from my encounter with Grant, whom I'd seen for a mercifully brief time this morning when the cast met at our house. He'd behaved as though the previous evening had never happened. He'd dropped a casual kiss on my cheek when he'd come in and had even been polite to Alex. All in all, Grant had the air of a man who'd reached a decision that made him very happy. I only hoped he wasn't planning our wedding.

There wasn't much I could do besides match Grant's demeanor, although I hadn't come close to forgiving him and didn't think I would. I just kept telling myself, 'two more days …'

Once again Shaun and I took up our beginning positions as Daphne and Alex sat on the side-lines and tried not to laugh.

"What are you doing here?" I turned on O'Mallet furiously.

"You're my client," retorted O'Mallet. "You're payin' me to protect you, in case you've forgotten."

"The only thing I'd like to forget is *you!*" I turned on my heel, O'Mallet's hand on my arm forcing me back to face him. "Let go of me!"

"Not so fast, doll." O'Mallet grabbed my other arm. "What happened to the Riviera, Angel? You know, that expensive hotel where we were going to stay and soak up the sun, where I'd salaciously smooth your skin and … shit!" Shaun stalked over to the bay window and began muttering, "Smooth oil … smooth oil on your sun-drenched … sun-*kissed!* …" and on and on.

I turned in frustration to Daphne, who was laughing silently as Alex sang "Moses supposes his toeses are roses" under his breath. I glared at them both, exerting considerable effort over my rising tension. I reminded myself that I did indeed possess a sense of humor. I glanced at the clock. Ten till eleven. Ten minutes until hordes of Randell fans descended on us. Ten more minutes to fight our way through the Line From Hell.

I heaved a huge sigh and nearly popped a button off my dress, the pride and joy of my costume collection. It was black chiffon, with an intricate design of gold, bronze and dull green bugle beads spiraling out on each of the padded shoulders. The dress ended in a full, flowing skirt that conformed gracefully to the legs with each step. The fact that I'd found it at a thrift store in Los Angeles for only three bucks was frosting on the cake and annoyed Daphne no end. Sheer black nylons and black ankle-strap heels completed the outfit, my hair carefully styled by Tasha in a forties chignon. Not my usual look, but catching a glimpse of myself in one of the Oak Room's decorative mirrors, I didn't think I looked half bad.

Evidently Alex didn't think so either as I looked down to see him eyeing me with a distinctly appreciative gaze.

"You like?" I asked, spinning around to make my skirt swirl around my legs.

"Not bad for a moll, let alone a stunt babe." He grinned at me and adjusted his white Panama hat to a rakish angle over one eye.

"And you're looking kind of *clean* for a stuntman," I retorted in reference to his white summer suit. He could've played the debonair villain in an Indiana Jones movie in that outfit.

"Let's try it again, Connie." Shaun left the window and joined the group, a determined look on his face.

"Before we start," I said, choosing my words carefully, "I think we ought to agree that we continue through to the end of the scene even if one of us drops a cue, okay?"

"You mean when I slaughter that stupid line again?" Shaun smiled ruefully. "I appreciate your tact, but let's call a spade a spade here."

I looked at him. "Okay. Then you're taking this way too seriously and I don't care if you say 'smoothing salacious saliva on my sun-soaked sarong,' let's just run this thing through!"

Shaun laughed. "Okay, Connie, point taken. I'll lighten up."

It worked. We barreled through past the trouble zone to the part where O'Mallet kisses Claire passionately—after she tries to slap him, of course. In Randell novels, dames are always slapping and O'Mallet is always smooching them.

We reached the end of the scene where I do, in fact, slap him and make my exit, leaving O'Mallet to his famous quote, "Dames … they're like boomerangs. You throw 'em away but they keep comin' back, twice as fast."

Daphne and Alex applauded.

I glanced at the clock. Four minutes before detonation.

Alex tossed me my purse. "Here, you hussy. Fix your lipstick."

After fixing my makeup, I looked around to make sure everything was in place for the final show. One of the Oriental rugs in the middle of our stage area was bunched up on one end. That was an accident waiting to happen so I got up to straighten it. My gaze was caught by little umbrella shaped dents in the floor next to the carpet, no doubt caused by customers in heels, the female cast of Murder For Hire among them. Yet another reason *not* to wear the damn things unless absolutely necessary.

Picking up the end of the rug, I gave it a brisk shake and it settled back to lie flat on the floor. The heel marks once again caught my eye, this time flipped upside down so they looked like little U's with lids on. Something about them niggled at the back of my brain, but before the niggle could turn into a nag (a naggle?), the door burst open to admit Tasha and Brad, hustling their chops to beat the tour. Both looked hot and tired and Tasha's hair was wind-blown, her white trumpet-skirt dress decidedly disheveled.

Brad had to change for his brief appearance in this scene as 'Mr. Big.' "Quick!" said Tasha as she helped him out of his trench coat and tossed it in the linen closet we'd appropriated to store props and personal belongings. "They're about three minutes behind!" She grabbed Mr. Big's jacket.

"You guys cut it a little short," Daphne commented. "You should have at least 20 minutes while Grant and Chris do their scene at the Cove."

Brad looked sheepish. "We stopped for coffee and then got caught in the crowd on the way over. There's a lot of people on the tour."

"How many of them?" I hastily tucked my lipstick into a small black velvet handbag.

"About forty." Brad mopped at his perspiring face with the sleeve of his jacket. "We're lucky Franklin talks so much, otherwise they would've beaten us here."

I threw my purse in the closet, almost nailing Tasha on the head as she reached to shut the door.

We all hurried out of the Oak Room and down the back staircase, barely avoiding the tour. Franklin was at the forefront, gesturing expansively as he talked. I just caught the words ' … his favorite spot to reflect on the many facets of life that are woven throughout his novels' before Franklin vanished into the Oak Room and his voice mercifully faded from auditory range.

"How long should we wait?" Daphne whispered as we watched what seemed like an endless stream of people go into the Oak Room.

"At least five minutes or so for them to settle and get a drink."

"I wish *I* had a drink," muttered Shaun, his normally ruddy complexion a rather interesting shade of green. It reminded me of those old Italian Renaissance portraits where everyone has that unhealthy greenish white skin tone.

"You'll be fine," Brad said encouragingly. "I'd bet my buttocks on it."

"Oh shit!"

Everyone turned and looked at me as I stared in horror at the backs of two small blond girls as they followed the rest of the tour into the room.

Daphne followed my gaze and groaned. "Oh hell!"

"What? What?!" Shaun demanded.

Daphne and I looked at each other. Should we tell him or leave him mercifully ignorant until they made their presence known, as they undoubtedly would. Daphne gave an imperceptible shake of her head and I agreed.

"Uh, nothing. I just snagged my stocking."

In this case, ignorance was bliss.

Five minutes passed, Shaun pacing up and down the stairs the entire time. His nervous energy was catching, and I finally couldn't take it any more. "Let's go for it."

Daphne nodded, relieved. "Ready, Shaun?"

Shaun straightened his shoulders and gave a terse "Yes," in reply. He marched up the stairs with the air of a man going to meet the guillotine.

Daphne entered the Oak Room first and Shaun followed shortly after her. He left the door slightly ajar so the rest of us could hear our cues. Brad had the next entrance, so he took up the position directly by the door, his ear pressed up against the crack.

We all listened closely; they'd started the scene.

"I wanna see your boss, babe," growled O'Mallet.

"I'm not your babe, buster," sassed the secretary.

"Tell it to the Marines, sister. I hear you're anyone's babe that can spring for the cost of a cup of java."

"Why, you no-good ..."

"Can the repartee, cupcake. I ain't got the time. I'm working an a case and ..."

They continued. So far so good. Good audience response, no sign of life from Banana or Morag ... Oops, spoke too soon. A high-pitched hyena-esque giggle announced the presence of Morag, who had the most lunatic laugh I've ever heard, let alone from a ten-year old. Oh well, at least the rest of the audience was laughing, too.

"After I'm finished talking to your boss, maybe we can talk about us," said O'Mallet, propositioning Ginger. No surprise there. If there was a female in an O'Mallet novel that didn't get propositioned, she was either under 16, over 60 or butt-ugly.

"You're a no-good, two-timing, low-life bum," smirked Ginger in response. "My favorite qualities in a man."

"Yeah, toots? well, you're not exactly sugar and spice yourself. But I'll tell ya, Ginger, I like a little bit of snap to my women."

"Kiss me, ya louse."

This was Brad's cue to burst into the room and burst in he did. Throwing the doors open with a crash that made even the other actors jump, Mr. Big strode into the room, unlit cigar in one hand.

Alex, Tasha and I flattened ourselves against the wall as all eyes turned towards the open doors. There were piercing shrieks from the Terrible Two, making sure that everyone else was sufficiently aware that this was a startling event. I groaned silently.

"You messin' wit' my secretary, O'Mallet?"

O'Mallet started to answer, but Mr. Big bulldozed right over his lines, moving to the center of the room as he continued his rant. "No one touches this doll but me, O'Mallet, especially not some low-life, nickel-and-dime-store detective who's on my payroll! You got that, O'Mallet? Huh? Huh?"

O'Mallet finally got a word in edge-wise with "I'm not on your payroll yet, pal, and I ain't likely to take the case if you don't shut your yap ..."

I moved back so I wouldn't get slammed in the face by Brad's upcoming exit. Alex's scene was next and he looked about as nervous as a cat stretched out in the sun as he leaned against the wall on one side of the doors. He caught me looking at him and gave me a slow smile that made me catch my breath. Damn those pheromones.

The doors exploded from within as Brad stomped out, followed by Daphne and a vigorous round of applause.

"That's my cue," said Alex, having narrowly avoided getting slammed against the wall by one of the doors. With more adjustment of his Panama hat, Alex (a.k.a John St. Romney) strolled into the room. Daphne shut the door this time, turning to me with a slightly harassed expression.

"Watch out for Jones and McGregor," she warned. "They're sitting dead front and center of our performance area."

"Are they behaving?"

"As well as can be expected. I mean, I suppose some people might find it flattering to have someone hanging on your every word, going 'oooh, shafted,' after each zinger."

"Oh, God."

Daphne patted my shoulder. "We can kill 'em later."

Alex re-emerged shortly, shaking his head. "Watch it, Connie, there are these two little girls in there that you would not believe."

"Oh, yes I would," I assured him. It was time for my entrance. I went in, taking my time as I picked my way through the crowd towards the bar. The audience gazed at me expectantly. I heard Morag hiss, "It's Connie! Look, it's Connie!"

If they shrieked or applauded now, I *would* kill them.

O'Mallet was across the room watching me intently. I glanced in his direction, did a double take and turned back to the bar, visibly upset.

"Water, please," I said haughtily to the young blond waiter manning the bar. He looked startled but poured me a glass of water and put it in front of me.

The crowd watched.

I took the glass and turned, finding O'Mallet at my side. I glared at him and walked away quickly. He followed at a leisurely pace.

Reaching the designated 'stage' and steadfastly ignoring the ear-to-ear grins of the two blonde demons sitting right in front of me, I set my glass down and turned angrily towards O'Mallet.

"What are you doing here? I thought I told you to stop following me!" Morag gasped.

"You're my client. You're payin' me to protect you, in case you've forgotten."

"The only thing I'd like to forget is you!"

Sure enough …"Oooh, shafted!"

I glared straight at the girls with a look that said 'one more sound and you're history.' Morag grinned and waved. Banana gave me a thumbs up.

"Not so fast, doll." O'Mallet grabbed my arm and turned me around in time to prevent a possible double infanticide. "What happened to the Riviera, dollface? You know, that expensive hotel where we were going to stay and soak up the sun …" He continued, spitting out each word with evident relish, ending with 'sipping sangria.'

I nearly applauded, catching myself just in time. "I don't—"

"C'mon, sister," he interrupted. "Don't play innocent with me. Or do things just look different in broad daylight out of bed?"

I raised my hand to hit him, he grabbed it and pulled me into his arms for a he-man style kiss. As was standard procedure for a Randell dame, I resisted for approximately five seconds before succumbing to the virile masculinity that was O'Mallet.

Morag and Banana giggled. We ignored them, pausing for air and our next lines.

"You're a dirty, low-down gumshoe …"

"And you love it."

Kiss. The entire audience laughed at that, Morag's hyena giggle rising above the rest.

We broke the kiss, my hands on his shoulders, his arms still around me. "What changed your mind this time," O'Mallet said softly and cynically. "Find another corpse you need to hide?"

"Why you no-good louse!" I shoved him away and slapped him across the face, the sound ringing out like a pistol shot. It elicited gasps from everyone except the girls, whose simultaneous 'ooh, burned him!' made me wince.

I stormed out to the welcome sound of applause, leaving O'Mallet to get a huge laugh with the boomerang line.

As I exited, Brad entered, a theatrical changing of the guard as Mr. Big went in for his death scene. The rest of us gathered around the door again. We had to go in and help drag out his corpse.

I could hear Brad harassing the audience as well as O'Mallet, saying things like, "What are you all doin', sittin' around on your cans and eating? You work for *me*, remember, so get off your duffs and work" And "What the hell are these two brats doin' here? Jeez, I hate kids!" Morag's giggle rang out loud and clear.

"Die, already, would you," Daphne muttered. Time was growing short and Brad showed no signs of stopping. He enjoyed improvisation far too much for our own good.

I was about to suggest that Alex go and strangle him when Brad finally upped and died. Or *started* dying, rather, after taking a bite of chip and guacamole. "Aaaaugh!" he gurgled amidst other fascinating noises.

I couldn't stand it. I had to see. We all peeked in and watched as Mr. Big lurched all over the room, clutching people by shoulders and shirtfronts as he gasped, "Poison … It was … poison!" He staggered toward Franklin who backed away with a bemused expression.

Finally, Brad sensibly picked a sturdily built woman and expired slowly and dramatically by sliding down her tweed-trouser clad legs. One hand was outstretched as he uttered his mercifully final words "It was … the dip!" followed by a convincing death rattle.

O'Mallet stood over Mr. Big's thankfully silent corpse, shaking his head. This was our cue to clear the body so Shaun could give his closing speech and lay out the plot for the final scene in the Cave. Before we could move, however, Banana and Morag began shrieking "He's dead! He's dead!" in decibels guaranteed to wake even the unfortunate corpse.

Brad opened up one eye, grabbed each girl by an ankle and snarled, "Yeah, I'm dead and if you don't shut up, I'm takin' you with me!" Having effectively shut the hellions up for the moment, he died again.

"Quick!" Daphne hissed. We moved in to snag the corpse and high-tail it out of there before anything else could happen. As each of us started to take a limb, Morag and Banana said eagerly, "We'll help you!" They both grabbed the leg that Alex was about to pick up and stared at him with worshipful gazes.

"No, really." Alex kept his British accent and composure while trying to regain the leg. "I appreciate it but it's quite all right." Determined to be of assistance the girls hung on grimly and tried to haul Brad's prone body out of the room by themselves.

Morag gave an especially enthusiastic tug and succeeded in removing Brad's shoe as well as propelling herself backwards into Alex, knocking *him* off balance and sending him into the refreshment table. He managed to steady himself with one hand, unfortunately in a dip bowl.

Alex pulled his hand out of the bowl. Chunks of guacamole dripped onto the table. Banana immediately dropped Brad's leg and rushed over to Alex, shrieking, "Don't lick it off, it's poison!"

This brought down the house with the exception of Franklin. Wearing a distinctly 'we are not amused' expression, he glared at Daphne and me as if we'd planned this.

Abandoning Brad's shoe, Morag grabbed a handful of napkins, knocking a bowl of tortilla chips onto the floor in the process. She ignored the litter of chips as she and Banana began wiping frantically at Alex's hand. Mr. Big's corpse was now shaking with barely suppressed mirth.

"They're dead," Daphne whispered fiercely.

I nodded and grabbed Brad's abandoned limb, leaving Alex to his fate. Daphne grabbed the other leg while Tasha hastily took an arm and the three of us began valiantly trying to haul Brad out of the room. Brad being solidly built, it was hard work for those of us in high heels. A heavy-set man in his mid-forties finally took pity on us and nudged Tasha out of the way, lifting Brad under both arms.

Our rescuer had tears of laughter running down his face by the time we got Brad out of the Oak Room and the doors safely shut behind us. He wasn't the only one. Brad had nearly choked trying to keep quiet and the second the doors had closed, he burst into unrestrained hysterics. Brad has a laugh like Mr. McGoo and the sight of him lying on the ground braying with laughter was enough to set Tasha off.

Daphne and I stared at the trio, too annoyed to be amused. I was consumed with a deep inner need to slaughter Morag and Banana before they could grow up and reproduce.

"That was great," chuckled our helper, wiping his eyes. "You oughta make those kids part of your act." He shook his head and re-entered the Oak Room, saying in parting, "I gotta see what they'll do next."

"Oh, that's just great!" Daphne exploded quietly yet vehemently. "We do all the work, those monsters come in and screw up the show and *that's* what people are gonna remember!"

"There ain't no justice," I agreed, while a smile tugged at my mouth at the memory of Alex trying to hold the girls at bay while his hand dripped mashed avocado. "Let's wait in the lobby, shall we?"

"Get up, Brad." Tasha nudged her still prone and giggling boyfriend with her toe. "You're going to be trampled if you don't move."

As Brad complied, Alex came out and slammed the doors behind him. "They're right behind me. Let's move!"

None of us needed to ask who 'they' were. Leaving Shaun to follow when he could, the rest of us dashed downstairs to the lobby to wait in relative comfort until the first Tour vacated the hotel.

Chapter Twelve

Standing inside the chocolate laden interior of the unimaginatively but accurately named 'Chocolate Shoppe,' Daphne and I stared at the mouth-watering selections while waiting for our turn to order. Along with a variety of gourmet truffles and other less pretentious chocolates, were holiday displays running the gamut from a dark chocolate haunted house with orange jack-o-lanterns, white chocolate ghosts and licorice cats to a snow-covered village, constructed entirely out of white, milk and bittersweet chocolate confections. Normally my attention would be entirely on my surroundings, but at the moment my mind was busy dissecting the second show.

We had all dispersed for a well deserved break between the second and third tours, so Daphne and I had made a beeline for the nearest chocolate supplier, happily less than a block from the Emerald Hotel. Alex and Shaun had gone over to the Cave to watch the last scene with plans to hunt for coffee afterwards. We were all under orders to bring back enough for everyone, including Chris and Grant, neither of whom had made it to the hotel before we'd left.

All in all, things were going well. The second show had gone relatively smoothly compared to the first, no doubt due to the absence of Morag and Banana. What it had lacked in demonic children, however, was made up for by the presence of Burke and Lucille. The pair had stood smack in the center of the crowd, Burke grinning malevolently like Satan at a church picnic. I'd made the mistake of inadvertently locking gazes with him and his lips had moved in what had no doubt been an uncomplimentary and/or obscene remark.

As for Lucille, her expression had been one of contemptuous amusement as she added her own derogatory comments to Burke's throughout the show. She'd been dressed as tackily as usual in a tight fuchsia dress with matching four-inch heels. Did the woman own any shoes that didn't look like Barbie's rejects? I hoped her feet hurt. Franklin had actually had the temerity to shush them at one point, drawing poisonous glares from both. He returned the favor with a look of venom that seemed totally incongruous on Franklin's normally friendly face..

Thanks to the rest of the crowd, Burke and Lucille failed to ruin our performance. The applause and laughter from the enthusiastically rowdy audience drowned out most of their biting remarks. And Brad proved his true worth as an improviser by directing most of Mr. Big's theatrical venom towards the pair. Like a guided missile, he only needed a target to be deadly.

Both Andy and Mavis had been there as well, Mavis being surprisingly unobtrusive as she watched every scene with avid concentration. She was almost certainly memorizing the dialogue for later use. Andy had a tiny notepad and was scribbling in it whenever Franklin talked, no doubt planning on borrowing from Franklin's immense storehouse of Randell trivia when he led the third tour.

"Did you notice Lucille's outfit?" Daphne's question ended my mental recap.

"It was hard to miss, especially in the middle of all the jogging suits, jeans and tennis shoes."

"Speaking of shoes, those stilettos of hers! Who the hell would wear high heels on a walking tour, for chrissake? Especially fuchsia ones?"

I looked at Daphne and raised an eyebrow. "This from the girl who once wore ankle strap sandals with three inch heels to Disneyland?"

"You wore a cinch belt."

"Yeah, but at least I had on flat shoes."

"Fine," snapped Daphne, "but we were both 18 and stupid. What's Lucille's excuse? Besides bad taste, that is."

"Well, she sure as hell isn't 18 and ..."

I stopped as that little niggle that had been picking at the back of my brain suddenly smacked me upside my head. Heels. Crescent shaped heel marks ... the U shaped mark on Damien Duran's neck and Lucille, queen of the 'fuck me but don't ask me to walk' shoes ...

"Daphne, I think—"

"Next!"

Daphne and I had reached the front of the line and it was our turn to order. All other considerations were momentarily shunted aside to make room for the weighty decision of What To Buy. Call me shallow, but my blood sugar was digging the proverbial hole to China.

Five minutes later and several dollars poorer, Daphne and I headed back to the Emerald Hotel with our purchases; a pound of assorted chocolates to share, a quarter pound of butterscotch squares for Daphne and a small box of bittersweet chocolate truffles enrobed in creamy ivory-white chocolate for me.

"So what were you going to tell me?" asked Daphne, happily munching on a free sample.

I told her my theory about the heel marks as we walked back to the hotel. Daphne stared at me with new respect and said, "Connie, do you realize you've made a real honest to goodness logical deduction?"

I nodded. "Mavis must never find out."

We reached the Emerald's entrance and saw Franklin approaching us from the opposite direction. "I'll tell you later."

Franklin's shaggy hair was windblown and the cuffs of his khaki trousers were noticeably wet. His topsiders left damp prints on the sidewalk. He smiled and waved when he saw us, meeting us at the doors. "Girls!"

"Hey, Franklin." I tried to project some enthusiasm in my voice, but my immediate goal was to settle down and relax with a hot cup of coffee and a truffle. At this moment, Franklin was nothing but an impediment to my desires. And a soggy one at that. "You decide to go wading or something?"

He glanced down at his wet pants with a rueful expression. "I stood too close to the edge of the platform during the last stop at the Cave. A bunch of us got soaked. You should see your actors."

Oh great. Just what we all needed, Grant on a rampage because his Gucci loafers got wet.

Franklin continued, "I just wanted to let you both know that the tours are going well and that the audiences really seem to appreciate my lectures and your acting. The feedback has been quite positive."

"That's nice." Enthusiasm was conspicuously lacking in my response.

Daphne took up the social slack and said brightly, "That's great, Franklin! How are your readings from the book going over?"

Franklin beamed at her and replied, "Better than I'd hoped! Other than Burke and Lucille—" His tone was downright venomous when he uttered the names. "—the crowd seems to love everything!"

"Just one more show to get through," I said, practically tapping my feet in my impatience to get back to the Oak Room and dive into my chocolates.

Franklin's enthusiasm was undimmed. "I especially enjoyed the scene on the cliffs that your two actors did. It was great! They really captured the essence of Randell without deviating from the book at all."

Daphne and I exchanged looks. We both caught the implied reproach, conscious or not.

"There were some nice bits done here as well—" now Franklin's tone definitely held a hint of condescension "—although I noticed a bit of straying from the original text." From the reverence with which Franklin uttered those last two words, one would think he was talking about the Guttenberg bible. He continued. "Didn't Mr. Big actually die when he was pushed out of his office window?"

"Well, yes," Daphne replied with a sideways glance at me, "but ..."

"But we thought that'd be taking realism a bit far," I broke in with a laugh. "Kind of difficult to do more than once, not to mention hard on the actor."

Franklin considered this seriously. "I suppose you're right. Although I did feel that the death was a bit over-done with the dip and all ..."

"The crowd enjoyed it," I said, a slight edge creeping into my voice.

"Oh, them." Franklin dismissed the paying audience with a flick of one large hand. "Those two ... girls won't be part of the act again, will they?" He looked as though he'd bitten the mother of all lemons.

"NO!"

Coming from Daphne and me in unison, our emphatic response caused Franklin to take a step back. "They never *were* part of our act," said Daphne firmly, insulted that he'd even consider the possibility.

"Nope, just an act of God," I added.

"Well! That's a relief." Franklin took yet another step away from us and glanced at his watch. "I'd better get everyone moving. You'll have an hour before the next tour starts. Andy will be leading that one." Franklin's tone left no doubt that he considered Andy a pinch-hitter at best. I wondered if he remembered whose idea this whole shebang had been in the first place.

Whatever, I wanted my coffee. "Well, I need to, uh ... fix my make-up. I'll meet you upstairs, okay, Daphne?"

"Oh, I'll come with you," she said quickly. "We'll see you later, Franklin. Thanks for the input."

Franklin smiled at her, an instant transformation to the eager puppy person, which was a welcome improvement over his former smug superi-ority. "Are you going to Burke's lecture this evening?"

"No" and "Yes" were uttered simultaneously and respectively by my-self and Daphne. She gave me a look that brooked no argument, saying, "We'll definitely be there."

I kept my mouth shut and tried not to wince when Franklin exclaimed "Great! I'll see you there then!"

We both waved as he walked off, presumably towards the library to join the last tour. I wondered if he'd be able to keep quiet on the sidelines as Andy played tour guide. Probably not.

As soon as he was safely out of earshot, I turned to Daphne and said, "I guess all things considered we're lucky that Franklin didn't yell 'heretics!' during the show."

Daphne laughed. "C'mon, he's not that bad."

"Oh yeah? Hey, if we'd told him that the rugrats were actually our idea, he'd be stacking the wood around our ankles and tossing a lit match."

"I don't know … he's kind of cute." Daphne's comment had a speculative tone that worried me. She *was* in between boyfriends, after all, now that she'd given Guido the boot.

We turned to go inside but stopped when Shaun hailed us from across Prospero, a cardboard carrier filled with cups bearing the Starbucks logo held in both hands. We waited as he crossed the street with his precious cargo, steam curling up from the small openings in the safety lids.

"You are a god," I said with feeling as the smell of fresh java wafted towards me.

"I wish all women were so easy to please," Shaun said with a grin, a great deal more relaxed now that we'd gotten two shows out of the way. The three of us went inside.

I tried to sound casual as I asked, "So where's Alex?"

Shaun nodded towards his feet. Daphne and I looked and saw that his shoes and cuffs had suffered the same fate as Franklin's. "Alex got soaked so he buzzed back to his place to change pants. He should be back any time. I think Grant had the same idea; he got pretty wet examining the body."

"What about Chris?" I asked, holding the door to the Oak Room for Shaun and the coffee.

"What about me?"

Chris was already seated in one of the leather armchairs, seemingly oblivious to the fact that his pants were soaking wet up to crotch level. Well, obviously not *totally* oblivious as he'd thoughtfully put a towel down on the chair before sitting on it. I looked around warily for Grant, but he was nowhere in sight.

"Chris, don't you want to change your pants?" Daphne stared at him dubiously.

"Nah. The surf's pretty high. I'll just get wet again next show. Thought I'd rough it until then." His attention focused on the trays of coffee and he leapt to his feet with alacrity, soggy trousers and all. "One of those mine?"

Shaun set the carriers down on one of the side-tables and pulled out a cup marked with a big 'C.' "Lemme check … I think this one's yours … black, right?"

"Yup."

"And here's two mochas … Daphne and Connie, these must be yours." Shaun handed each of us a large cup. "Non-fat for you, Connie, regular for Daphne."

Brad and Tasha came in as Shaun sorted out the who-got-what of the coffee. Daphne and I pulled out our bounty of riches from the Chocolate Shoppe to round out the nutritional value of the moment. Enough caffeine and sugar to get us all through the last show and then dump us down into a hypoglycemic pit shortly thereafter. Oh well, I'd had some carrot sticks earlier.

Mocha in one hand, several truffles in the other, I curled up on one end of a large settee and relaxed for the first time that day. Daphne settled herself comfortably on the other end and we toasted each other silently with our cardboard cups before tucking into our refreshments.

I was happily sipping my mocha a few minutes later when Daphne said in an undertone, "So? Is Lucille still your number one suspect?"

I looked around to make sure no one else was paying attention. I didn't want anyone reporting this conversation to Mavis, even as a joke. They didn't understand the forces of evil that would be unleashed—namely my temper—if they gave Mavis any more ammo. Satisfied that none of the other cast members were listening, I leaned across the couch and hissed, "Absolutely. She's the only one with any kind of motive that we know about and she's definitely got the heels."

Daphne nodded, unsurprised. "I suppose it makes the most sense," she said. "Unless Burke cross-dresses in his spare time."

Now there was a mental picture I could have done without.

Just then Alex walked in. "We'll talk more later," I told Daphne as my fickle brain gratefully jumped from an unwelcome image of Burke wearing lingerie and heels, to matters of a more hormonal nature.

Alex's pants were now a slightly different shade of white than his suit jacket. He caught me looking at them and shook his head ruefully. "I guess Shaun told you what happened, eh?"

"You play with fire, you get burned. You play with water, you get wet."

"You play with Connie, you get killed," said Chris, giving me a dead-pan expression as I glared at him.

Alex laughed. "I'll take my chances, thanks."

I gestured towards the unclaimed coffee. "One of those is yours."

"Thanks." He smiled at me, holding eye contact for an instant longer than necessary before turning his attention to his cup of coffee. I smiled after him until I realized that Chris, Brad and Shaun were watching the proceedings with interest and more than a little approval. I suspected they'd be delighted to see the last of Grant.

I briefly contemplated a career in demon conjuring when Grant, his pants dry and perfectly creased, strode into the room barely a second later. He looked pleased with himself. I guess his shoes hadn't been ruined after all. Nodding briefly to the other actors, Grant came over to my side and placed a proprietary hand on my shoulder, saying, "I'm sorry I took so long. I had a message to contact my agent and spent quite a long time on the phone with him."

Not wanting him to sit down by me, I smiled and said, "That's okay. There's a Cappuccino on the table for you."

"Thank you, darling." Grant bestowed a lingering kiss on the top of my head before joining Alex at the table. Alex's expression was carefully neutral.

I made the mistake of asking Grant how his portion of the shows had gone, thus condemning all of us present to a detailed description of same. To hear Grant talk about it, he'd done the entire scene by himself. Chris's participation seemed negligible, if not non-existent. I wondered that Chris hadn't given into his marine training—not to mention the understandable temptation—and turned the staged fight moves into real ones. Grant was lucky that he didn't have a pistol grip shaped indentation in his skull. From the expression on Chris's face as he drank his coffee, I suspected he was entertaining the same line of thought.

Grant's self-aggrandizing monologue was interrupted by Brad clearing his throat and saying, "Tasha and I are going to go to our spot now. It's about that time."

I glanced at the clock. "You still have at least twenty minutes, though."

"Yeah, but we could use the fresh air. It's kind of thick in here." His glance flickered briefly to Grant, who was thankfully oblivious to the insult.

It turned out to be a good thing that Grant's pomposity had caused Brad and Tasha to go to their places early. It seemed they'd barely left when the door burst open and Brad ran in, a flustered Tasha following close on his heels.

"Sorry we're late ... the streets are jammed ... there are millions of people in the tour and they really slowed us down ... gotta hurry ... they were heading down the street as we ran in the front door ..." Brad hurriedly doffed his trench coat and put on Mr. Big's plaid jacket.

Daphne and I stared at him in bewilderment. "Late? But the tour's only just now supposed to have started."

"Yeah," said Daphne indignantly. "We're supposed to have at least another fifteen minutes before they get here."

"Andy started it early because there were so many people, he was afraid it would take twice as long to get them from place to place," Tasha explained.

"Why didn't he call on his cell?" I asked indignantly, ignoring my own tendency to leave my cell phone turned off ... and at home.

"The battery wasn't charged."

"Oh God ..." Daphne moaned.

That was the signal for all of us to rush around wildly, grabbing personal belongings and shoving them in the closet, disposing of coffee cups, adjusting costumes and make-up. Daphne checked in her mirrored compact to make sure her hair was falling over one eye in correct film noir manner while I re-did my lipstick. She and I then dashed to the door to join the rest of the actors as they left the room. Talk about your unwelcome adrenaline rush.

We'd only made it a few feet from the Oak Room when we found ourselves face to face with the final tour group. It was a bizarre parody of a standoff in a spaghetti western, only instead of gunslingers versus bandits we had eight actors against hundreds of townspeople.

Brad wasn't kidding about the size of the group. Okay, maybe there weren't exactly hundreds but there were at least eighty people standing in front of us, the tour snaking down the hall and onto the front staircase.

Directly in front of us was a group of elderly women, all wearing knee-length khaki shorts, Shetland sweaters and sturdy walking shoes. One of them had a walking stick as well and she used it to potentially dangerous effect, waving it in the air as she boomed in a voice that could be heard for miles, "Here they are!"

Acknowledging the crowd with a few half-hearted waves and a collective glare at Andy, who smiled cheerfully from his position as group leader, we dove en masse towards the back staircase in the opposite direction, tearing down it in about four seconds flat.

Grant made a sound that sounded suspiciously like a whimper. He was probably thinking about how he had to wade through that mass of humanity to the Cave. Chris grinned.

I thought quickly. "Let's give them ten minutes to settle in and get drinks." I turned to Shaun. You'd better just follow Daphne in or you'll spend an hour looking for her in that sea of people."

"No problem." Shaun shook his head. "Did you see some of those women? They looked like they were ready for a week-long trek through the country."

"I've worked with audiences like this before," Grant said with a shudder. "Back in my days of summer stock. They're full of bright asides to each other, booming encouragement to the actors at regular intervals ... they utterly destroy any subtleties of emotional depth present in the work!"

"Bummer," said Chris.

Lack of emotional depth aside, the show was an unqualified success. Maybe it was just that after the horrors of Morag and Banana in the first show followed by Burke and Lucille in the second, the cheerful audience participation offered by the last crowd was easy to deal with. Even the sight of Arthur Sloan busily snapping pictures and taking notes failed to disturb me. Maybe for once his purple prose would be used for good, not evil, and we'd get some decent press out of this.

As the last of the crowd trickled down the stairs, the actors gathered up all props and belongings, which Alex offered to take to his car so the rest of us could go down to the Cave and watch the final scene where Grant discovers the body and gets coshed on the head by Chris. I really wanted to see that second part.

Daphne, Brad, Tasha and I made our way down Prospero towards the seawall, several blocks away. Shaun had passed, having already seen the scene, so to speak. The sunshine was hazy, fog already starting to roll in off of the ocean. It made for great atmosphere, but no doubt Grant would have something to say about the damp air affecting his health.

I shook my head. I had to stop thinking about what Grant would or would not say. I listened with half an ear as Brad indulged in one of his favorite after-show activities: discussing the pros and cons of every minute stage business in the show, comparing it to the previous performances and suggesting new, improved ways to do it in the future. Daphne and I were used to this après-show analysis and had learned to just let Brad ramble without our feedback. Sooner or later he'd run out of steam, whereas if we participated he'd never stop. He was still going strong halfway to our destination, so Daphne and I tuned him out and continued our interrupted discussion under the protective white noise of Brad's babbling.

"Why do you think she would have done it?"

"Other than the fact that they argued over the Gala, I can't come up with a good reason," I admitted reluctantly. "I mean, aside from the fact that she looks and acts like a Disney villainess and really just *should* be guilty."

"If that's all there was to it, they'd have found Andy's body with a fuchsia stiletto buried in his head."

"Maybe she just hasn't had the chance yet."

Further speculation would have to wait, however. We'd reached the section of seawall directly overlooking the cove. "They've got the audience on the beach instead of on the platform," said Daphne in surprised tones. "I guess they couldn't fit everyone down there."

"I hope the placement of the body still works," I said worriedly, looking over the edge of wall to see the beach covered with our audience, Grant standing directly beneath the natural archway that led to the Cave.

"We'd be better off going down and watching from the platform," said Daphne. "It's just too crowded down there."

Considering that audience members were still making their way down the access staircase leading onto the beach, I had to agree with Daphne. Some of the people were even venturing into the water to get a better view of the action.

The four of us dashed into the Gnome's Den and negotiated the treacherous stairs as quickly as was safely possible. When we reached the bottom and edged out onto the platform, Grant was just beginning the scene. He was explaining about the dropper who had fogged him the night before and how he'd been tipped off that it was the same Hard Harry who'd be showing up on the beach any moment now to pick up Mr. Big's blackmail money. And how he, O'Mallet, would be there for the kill.

The audience was eating it up, even if some of the vintage Randell vernacular was going over their heads. They waited expectantly for the confrontation between O'Mallet and the dropper. The dropper, alias Louie the Sap (aka Chris), was currently waiting, unseen by the audience, behind the rock formation I'd picked out yesterday. I peered out from the far edge of the platform and caught a glimpse of Chris slumped against a rock holding on to the rope that was attached to the 'corpse' out from under the rock ledge. Chris's character didn't actually appear until after the discovery of the body.

As Grant hit the cue line " … and this town won't be safe until Simon's pushing up daisies," Chris tugged on the rope with both hands. Daphne and I watched with satisfaction as the 'corpse' emerged from its hiding place, rounded the corner of Chris's rock and floated into audience view amidst gasps and a smattering of applause. I sighed with relief. It had worked as well as I'd envisioned.

Then Daphne gasped sharply. "Connie, that's not the same dummy that we borrowed!"

"What?" I took a close look as the dummy floated gently in the surf, limbs moving with each rise and fall of the water. Daphne was right, it wasn't the same dummy. It was the wrong gender for one thing. We'd dressed ours in '40s era masculine attire. This one was wearing a jarringly contemporary dress. Soggy fuchsia fabric clung to a pencil thin frame that boasted a surprisingly large pair of breasts. Jet black hair fanned out in the water, making a grotesque curtain for the mottled face, oddly blackened in places. The rest of the skin was deathly white and a tongue protruded darkly from the lips. My attention was drawn to a length of seaweed that was pulled tightly about the neck.

I heard several sharp intakes of breath, mine included, and a flashbulb went off as Arthur Sloan began taking pictures. Several screams came from the audience as the realization hit.

It was a genuine corpse and it was Lucille.

So much for my theory.

Chapter Thirteen

"All right, people! Listen up! Listen up, people!"

Those of us still gathered in the library to give information to the police duly listened up as Detective Ron Honey prepared to let loose with another self-important speech. Honey, along with his partner and superior (in every sense of the word) officer, Detective Sergeant O'Donohue, had arrived on the scene shortly after two uniformed policemen responded to the phone call placed by a shaken Andy.

I had a strong suspicion that this was Detective Honey's first really big case. There is a particular physical type of male cop marked by a pallid complexion, dull brown hair and a receding hairline matched by an equally receding chin. This description usually goes hand in hand with an officious attitude that makes getting a speeding ticket from one of these guys feel like you're being charged with a felony.

Honey fit the stereotype to a T, intent on making up for his unfortunate surname and lack of chin by being as pompous and authoritarian as possible. He was watching everyone and everything suspiciously, writing down copious notes in a little notebook. He'd stare at something, snap the book open with a flick of his wrist—a move you just *knew* he'd practiced at home—and scribble on the pages, no doubt proof of guilt. He did this after glaring intently at a full book cart and I wondered which unlucky library book was the culprit.

Detective Sergeant O'Donohue, on the other hand, was quite a hunk. He may have been Irish on his father's side, but a certain cast to his eyes and darkly handsome features made me think his mother's family must be Asian, maybe Korean or Vietnamese. Whichever, he was a cutie and a hell of lot more charming than his partner. Maybe they took turns playing Good Cop/Bad Cop, although it was hard to imagine Honey pulling off charm under any circumstances.

O'Donohue had instructed all of the audience members, along with the actors and tour guides, to assemble at the library while the police went over the crime scene with their team of experts and did whatever it was they did when a murder occurred. My knowledge of police procedure was the same as Daphne's: non-existent. Carl Club never needed it, why should we?

Most of the audience members had given their names and relevant information to the detectives and been released. A few still lingered, no doubt hoping to be on the scene when the murderer was apprehended. Mystery lovers are a ghoulish bunch of people, that's for damned sure.

Sloan was also there, even though he'd been one of the very first people to give a statement. I could tell he was torn between feeling disappointed that he wasn't still at the crime scene with the rest of the media, and satisfaction that he was an eyewitness. When the police had shown up he'd still been taking pictures of Lucille's waterlogged corpse, muttering under his breath about the "scoop of the century." I was surprised that he hadn't thought to try and interview anyone while waiting in the library. I thought it was against police procedure, but Sloan had shown a remarkable lack of regard for reality up to this point and I wouldn't have put it past him. He'd actually glanced hopefully in our direction a few times, but I refused to let him catch my eye.

All of our actors were still in the library, congregating quietly in the Children's Corner. I sat at a table with Daphne, Alex, Shaun and Chris while Brad and Tasha took up one of the small couches. Grant, whom I was avoiding as much as possible, sat in a window seat, alternating between gazing moodily out onto the courtyard and staring broodingly at me. The overall effect was diminished by the huge stuffed animal rug that shared the window seat with him. He didn't seem particularly shaken by the appearance of Lucille's body. Maybe he felt she had ruined his performance.

At another table sat Andy, Franklin and Betty from the Gnome's Den. Betty was almost certainly going to be grilled about anyone and everyone who'd paid the fee to risk their necks on the stairs leading to the cave, as well as any of the performers during the tours. She looked nervous, fingering a necklace of heavy blue glass beads, a Celtic cross dangling from the center. Poor Betty. Someone who surrounded herself in 21st Century Cute seemed singularly unequipped to deal with something as gruesome as a murder on her back porch, so to speak.

I'd already done an internal search to figure out honestly how I felt about Lucille's gruesome death. Going past the sheer horror of it, I found that beyond a certain amount of pity, I didn't feel much of anything. That was a relief; I don't think I'd have liked myself very much if any part of me had been happy that she was dead even if I had suspected her of murder.

I also wondered how Andy was dealing with it. As much as he'd professed to loath her, I couldn't imagine him getting any actual satisfaction from Lucille's demise.

I suspected that those of us from MFH were going to be asked more than our names and phone numbers, given the fact that Lucille's body had appeared in lieu of our dummy. I just hoped they'd get around to it soon. The shock of Lucille's death was wearing off and I was now aware that my feet were demanding to be let out of my three inch heels.

Heels. Thoughtfully I took off one of my shoes and stared at it, flipping it over this way and that. I picked up a paperback from the shelf, one of the *Goosebumps* series. Apologizing to the Library Gods (but not to R.L. Stine), I surreptitiously pressed the heel of my shoe into the cover, careful to put the pressure on the curve at the back. It left a perfect little U shape. Dammit, I knew I was on to something! Except now my number one suspect was out of the running. Permanently.

Jeez, I was beginning to think in Carl Club monologues. This was not good.

Honey started up again. "We want every one of you who worked on this Randell Walking Tour to remain where you are. The rest of you lookeeloos can vamoose on home."

Lookeeloos? Vamoose? I looked at Daphne and Alex, who wore identical expressions of disbelief. Was this guy for real? Maybe he and Arthur Sloan shared the same caricatured gene pool. Daphne shook her head and picked up a book from the stack on the table.

"We're going to question each of you, one at a time," Honey continued. "So make sure you keep your stories straight. We just want the truth from you," he finished with a fierce sweep of his pale blue gaze over the assembled group. "Just the truth."

Detective O'Donohue stared at his underling with all the enthusiasm Chuck T-Bone would show for a glass of cherry Kool-aid. When Honey opened his mouth again and started to let out yet another "All right, people!" O'Donohue cut him off with a terse "That's enough, Honey" and gestured emphatically towards our group. "Why don't you get names and addresses while I start taking statements." He turned to Andy, having already established his identity as Head Librarian. "Is there an office we can use?"

Andy nodded, eager to be helpful. "Mine's right behind the front desk. I'll show you."

"We'd appreciate it. Why don't I take your statement first?"

As Andy led the detective towards his office, I could hear him add, "I can make some coffee when you're finished with me," and O'Donohue's grateful response, "I could sure use it." They disappeared into Andy's office and the door shut behind them.

The rest of us were left to the tender mercies of Det. Honey, who glared at each and every person in the room before finally snapping open out his notebook to take our names. He headed straight for Daphne, no doubt irritated by the fact that she was deeply engrossed in *Samantha Jenkins, Girl Detective*.

"Name!" he snapped.

Jolted back into reality, Daphne looked up at him, tossing her hair out of one eye. "Excuse me?"

"Your name, young lady!"

Daphne stared at him coldly and supplied the requested information, followed by our address and phone number. I was next in line and gave him my name when asked.

"Address and phone number?"

"You already have it."

Honey eyed me suspiciously. "Are you trying to get smart with me, young woman?"

I took a deep breath, willing my temper to stay calm. Not wanting to dignify him with his title, I began, "Look, Honey—" only to be cut off by a red-faced Honey proclaiming in a loud voice, "And flirting won't get you anywhere either!"

I flinched as everyone in the library turned and looked in my direction. I'd had about enough. "Not in your wildest dreams, pal!"

"Are you going to give me your address and phone number or ..." he paused and leaned forward to emphasize his next words, " ... would you rather go down to the station?"

Daphne intervened at that point, saying, "Connie and I have the same address and phone number, Detective. We're roommates."

Honey looked at me accusingly. "Why didn't you tell me that in the first place?"

"I was waiting for the truncheon action," I snapped.

Chris turned the beginning of a laugh into an unconvincing cough, drawing Honey's fire on himself.

"Do you find murder *funny*, young man?"

Chris gave the question a moment of serious consideration before replying, "Might be if the dead person was a clown."

I shut my eyes as Honey exploded.

"You're the kind of punk kid that gives Emerald Cove a bad name!" he yelled, his face turning an unbecoming shade of red. At this rate, the man was going to have a heart attack before he hit forty.

Chris stared unblinkingly back at him. "Aren't you going to call me a Commie bastard?"

Honey was too flustered to go for the notebook. "Watch it, buddy boy," he began. "I ..." But his words were cut short by the welcome appearance of O'Donohue, who had finished with Andy and no doubt come to see what the commotion was about. He took his subordinate by one arm and led him to the foyer, speaking in a low voice the whole way. I caught something about "checking with the forensics people," I had a suspicion, however, that O'Donohue was just getting rid of Honey before he could totally annihilate public relations between the law and the citizenry of Emerald Cove.

Chris was giggling helplessly over being referred to as 'buddy boy' and I was still fuming when O'Donohue returned and politely requested that I accompany him to Andy's office. As I stood up, Alex gave my hand a quick reassuring squeeze under the table, safely out of Grant's line of vision.

I followed O'Donohue back to Andy's office. It felt weird to be sitting in there with someone else in his place behind the desk. Of course, the fact that I could be considered a possible suspect in a murder investigation didn't help the weirdness factor one bit.

"Would you like some coffee?" O'Donohue smiled at me from Andy's leather chair.

I shook my head. "No thanks. I'd like to get some sleep tonight."

"Do you normally have trouble sleeping?"

An innocuous enough question, but I didn't think it was paranoia that made me think he was trying to find out if I had a guilty conscience.

"Only when I have too much coffee."

He looked at his notebook. "Connie Garrett, correct?"

I nodded.

"And you and Daphne Graves are the producers of …" He checked his notes again. " … Murder For Hire?"

"That's correct. Although all things considered, I'm wishing we'd named it something else." Now why did I say that? Maybe I should've taken him up on the cup of coffee and cleared the fuzz out of my brain.

"Can you tell me a little about what happened? Or rather, what was supposed to happen in your show at the point that Ms. Monroe was found?"

This, at least, was comfortable ground. I launched into a detailed description of the scene in the Cave, including the CPR dummy and its intended participation. O'Donohue listened intently, writing in his notebook all the while.

"So Chris Giametti was the person who set the dummy under the ledge after the first two shows?"

"That's how we had it set up," I replied. I tried to keep my voice neutral as I added, "The only other actor on the scene would've been Grant. Grant Havers. And I can pretty safely say that he wouldn't have volunteered for the job."

"Why not?"

How could I explain to an outsider what was self-evident to anyone who'd worked on a show or film with Grant that he was too selfish to do anything that might be construed as manual labor? I settled for "he wouldn't like getting his shoes wet unless he had to" and left it at that.

O'Donohue just nodded and made another notation in his book before asking, "When was the last time you saw Ms. Monroe alive?"

That was easy. "She and Jonathan Burke attended the second tour. I suggest you speak to Mr. Burke. The two of them seemed to be on fairly intimate terms." I honestly didn't mean to sound like I was accusing Burke, but I knew my distaste for him was evident in my voice.

"I plan to do just that." O'Donohue spoke amiably enough but I felt rebuked, as though he thought I was trying to tell him his job. "Would you tell me where you were between 2:30 and 4:00pm?"

I thought for a moment. "I was in the Oak Room for most of that time."

"Were the other actors there as well?"

"All of them were there at some point or another. I don't remember the exact times, though. Is it important?"

"Very." O'Donohue's voice was uncompromising. "We need to establish the whereabouts of all parties involved. Once the autopsy is done and we get a time of death, I'm hoping we can eliminate most of you from the list of possible suspects."

I gulped. The members of MFH really *were* being considered as suspects.

He continued, "So I need to know if and when you left the Oak Room, and whether or not anyone was with you. I need to know as exactly as you can recall who showed up at the Oak Room and when. The smallest bit of information, which may seem trivial to you, could be important to this case."

I hate being lectured. He wanted detail? I'd give him detail. "Fine. Immediately following the second tour, Daphne and I went to Le Chocolate Shoppe, stood in line for ten minutes, selected and purchased a large quantity of chocolates. I believe they were Bordeaux's, bittersweet truffles and a pound of mixed. You can check with the proprietor. She can verify our purchases. We then went back to the Emerald Hotel, where we ran into Franklin Grace outside the front entrance. We talked to him for five *very* long minutes and he left. Shaun arrived with coffee right before we went inside and the three of us went upstairs together. Chris was already in the Oak Room when we got there." I paused for air and then continued. "Tasha and Brad showed up about ten minutes later, followed shortly by

Alex, who had gone home to change pants. Both he and Shaun had gotten wet while watching the last scene in the second show. Grant and Chris had *also* gotten wet during the show, so Grant also went to his current residence to change and schmooze with his agent. Chris didn't bother."

"Anything else?" O'Donohue didn't bother looking up from his notebook.

"Nope. That's my story and I'm sticking to it."

O'Donohue did look up, staring at me steadily. "You're not taking this seriously, are you, Ms. Garrett?"

"I take Lucille's death very seriously, Detective. But the thought of one of our actors being involved? No, I can't take that seriously." He didn't say anything. I sighed, ashamed of myself. "Look, I'm sorry. I know this is necessary. It's just … this has been a really long day and I'm about done in." Oh, bad choice of words, Connie …

"You and Ms. Monroe weren't close then." This was a statement, not a question.

I was too tired to be anything but direct. "Lucille Monroe was a rude, pushy, abrasive woman. She alienated just about everyone she came into contact with, including me. I could give you a list longer than the Begets in the Book of Genesis of people who don't like Lucille, but I can't think of anyone who would actually kill her."

"Fair enough." O'Donohue scanned his notes. "I think that's all I need from you for the moment, Ms. Garrett. If you'd ask your partner Ms. Graves to come in next, I'd appreciate it. You'll be at home this evening in case we have any further questions?"

"Damned straight," I said with feeling. I started to stand, then hesitated. O'Donohue looked at me inquiringly. "This may seem silly, but I think I know what made that mark on Damien Duran's neck."

O'Donohue looked at me sharply. "Where did you hear about the mark? We haven't released that information to anyone."

Not wanting to incriminate my landlady, I said, "Don't you read Arthur Sloan's column in the *Post*?"

He groaned. "I must have missed this one."

I took off my shoe again and showed him the heel. "I was looking at the marks that these left on the floor of the hotel. If someone just pressed down with their weight towards the back …" I demonstrated on Andy's wooden desk.

O'Donohue was silent, staring at me with an intensity that made me very nervous. He finally spoke. "That's a remarkably perceptive observation, Ms. Garrett."

"Uh, thanks."

"And one that hasn't been presented yet."

Uh oh, I thought. Was I about to be arrested? "Um, can I put my shoe back on?"

He nodded, still staring at me thoughtfully. "Have you told anyone else about this?"

"Just Daphne. But the weird thing is, the only person I can think of who wore these kind of heels on a regular basis and had any animosity towards Damien Duran is … *was* Lucille. And she's out of the picture."

"We'll look into it. In the meantime, get some rest, Ms. Garrett."

I got to my feet. "You read my mind, Detective O'Donohue."

He raised an eyebrow. "I wish it were that easy. This case would already be closed."

Chapter Fourteen

"Connie, why aren't you dressed?"

I looked up at the sound of Daphne's voice. "What are you talking about," I said innocently. "I'm wearing sweats."

"You're not wearing those to the lecture!" She stood in front of me as I sat curled up in the over-stuffed rocking chair in the living room listening to the Gypsy Kings and reading *Where The Chill Waits*, a horror novel by T. Chris Martindale. Renfield sprawled contentedly across my lap.

I stared at her resentfully. I couldn't believe that Daphne wanted us to attend Burke's lecture, especially after the events of the day. Okay, to be fair, she didn't exactly *want* to attend, but she insisted it was important for us to both make an appearance. "If we don't go out," she'd said in the library parking lot when I'd made my protests loudly known, "people might think we've got something to hide. After all, Lucille died during our show."

I'd started to retort that the thought was ridiculous but had stopped myself when I'd realized that she might have a valid point. While O'Donohue hadn't exactly told us not to leave town, I had the feeling that none of us were off the hook at this point.

I'd tried another tack on the drive home. "Don't you think that it's disrespectful to Lucille to go out when she's only been dead a few hours?"

"Well, if I thought that either one of us felt that Lucille deserved re-spect, dead *or* alive, I might agree with you. But we both know it's bullshit."

She'd had me there. By the time we'd pulled up to the house, I'd reluc-tantly agreed to go to the damn lecture.

Now, however, as Daphne stood there in yet another of her elegant black dresses, I was furiously regretting my earlier lack of backbone. The thought of changing out my comfy sweats just to go listen to that pomp-ous, self-serving asshole was intolerable.

Daphne was implacable. "It's 7:00. The lecture starts at 8:00. I want to get there in time to get a seat."

Renfield made a small mrrping noise and burrowed his head under one paw. "How can you possibly expect me to disturb my little boy?" I asked, running a hand down Renfield's plush black fur.

"I'll do it for you." Daphne unceremoniously scooped the cat out of my lap and dumped him on the couch.

"Hey!" I protested.

Renfield stared around sleepily for a moment and then promptly curled up into a tight little ball with his nose hidden in his tail. He fell back asleep almost immediately.

Having lost my excuse, I got grudgingly to my feet. "I'm *not* putting on stockings," I said firmly.

"No one said you had to." Daphne spoke the way she would to a three-year-old.

"I'm wearing jeans," I added for good measure.

Daphne rolled her eyes. The doorbell cut off any further comment on her part.

"God," I groaned, "It's probably Mavis wanting to find out if we've solved the case yet …"

"I'll get it," said Daphne in a rare instance of philanthropy. Or so I thought until she added, "You get changed."

Grumbling, I headed up the stairs while Daphne went to the front door. I was at the top of the staircase when I heard Daphne say with surprise, "Alex! What are you doing here?"

I halted in my tracks and listened as Alex replied, "I heard you two talking about the lecture and thought you might like some moral support." He paused briefly. "Connie *is* going, isn't she?"

"She's getting ready," said Daphne. "You want something to drink?"

I bolted into my bedroom, not waiting to hear any more. I sure as hell didn't want to be caught listening through the banisters like a child banished upstairs while the adults partied. Besides, I had to change into something nice now that I had worthwhile incentive.

A quick once-over through my closet produced a black rayon dress with black crocheted lace and taffeta ribbon trim. The style was vaguely Regency; sort of Jane Austin goes Goth. I added black stockings, a pair of vintage black satin shoes, and topped it off with a delicate silver and onyx necklace. Somehow the choice of black seemed appropriate if vaguely hypocritical.

As I got ready, I thought about my interview with O'Donohue. I still wasn't sure whether I'd done more harm than good by sharing my heel theory with him. So far I'd kept my word and not told anyone else about it.

I did a quick make-up job, just enough to cover the ravages of the day, scrunched my hair with some mousse to give it curl and grabbed my velvet bag.

When I came downstairs fifteen minutes later, Alex and Daphne were talking about film noir, Daphne's favorite topic. I was glad they weren't discussing Lucille. We'd no doubt get an earful after the lecture.

Alex was seated in my rocking chair with a glass of red wine and a lapful of felines. Both J.D. and Sam had decided he was acceptable bedding and were yin-yanged across Alex's black pants. Daphne was sitting next to the still snoozing Renfield on the couch, also drinking wine.

Alex looked up as I reached the bottom of the stairs, an appreciative look in his eyes as he saw me. I was glad I'd made the effort. "I'd stand up and say hello properly, but ..." He scritched J.D. under her chin. She reached up and placed a trusting paw on his chest, her purr audible from across the room.

"You're going to need a lint brush," I commented as I sat down on the couch in between Daphne and Renfield.

Daphne handed me a glass of wine. "We should leave in ten minutes. Do you have your keys?"

"They're on the hook," I said smugly, having actually remembered to hang them up after we'd returned home.

"Connie always loses her keys," Daphne added for Alex's benefit.

"It's chronic," I admitted.

"Why don't you make an extra set so you'll always have one on hand?" Alex suggested quite reasonably.

"She did ..." Daphne looked at me. I shrugged, so she finished, " ... but she lost them."

"Drives Grant crazy," I added with a small smile.

"Silver lining to every cloud," said Alex, raising his glass in a small toast.

There was a moment of companionable silence as the three of us drank our wine.

Daphne glanced at the wall clock. "We should get going if we're going to get seats."

"You think it's going to be that crowded?" Alex started dislodging the cats as gently as possible.

Daphne nodded. "Everyone's going to know about Lucille by now. And you know how morbid people can be."

"Lookeeloos." Alex did a credible Detective Honey imitation.

"This whole thing is so weird," I said. "I was sure that Lucille had killed Duran."

"Yeah," said Daphne, "but it does seem more likely that the same person murdered both of them. Do you think there's any chance that Andy ..."

"No." I shook my head vehemently. "Although I wouldn't blame him if he did kill Lucille. That woman was enough to drive anyone to murder."

"True," said Daphne solemnly. "But who?"

The three of us stared at each other for a beat, a tableau straight out of a cliché-ridden drawing room mystery … and then burst into laughter.

"And on that note …" Alex unhooked Sam's claws from his shirt and got to his feet.

Daphne and I stood as well. I finished my wine in one last gulp and handed the glass to Daphne, who took it along with the other two and headed towards the kitchen, saying, "I'll grab your keys." She disappeared through the kitchen door.

"Do you want to take one car?" I asked Alex, not looking at him directly. This was the first time we'd been alone since last night's trip to the beach and I felt suddenly shy.

"Only if you think Daphne would object to riding by herself." Alex moved in front me as he answered, reaching out to pull me into his arms for a kiss that made shyness seem a little hypocritical. "I'd have done that sooner, but didn't want to get you in more trouble with Don José." Alex gave me another kiss. I tried to feel guilty about it and failed miserably. "He won't be there tonight, will he?"

I shook my head. "Nope. He was going out with the people he's staying with, some dinner party. He was pissed that I wouldn't go with him. Told him I was too tired."

I hadn't told Alex any details about Grant's behavior of the previous evening, only that he'd been upset that I'd been gone. Why borrow trouble when it seemed to gravitate towards me of its own accord?

Daphne came back into the living room with my keys and we left for the museum, leaving all three cats napping contentedly on the couch. I would've envied them more if Alex weren't walking out the door with me.

When we reached the museum, the parking lot was filled to capacity and the streets were lined with cars in a mute testimony to parallel parking skills. More autos inched their way along Prospero, their occupants searching optimistically for an empty space. Almost everyone on foot seemed to be heading towards the museum.

"I didn't know there were this many Randell fans in Emerald Cove," I mused aloud.

"Or lookeeloos," Alex muttered.

"They've heard about the murder," said Daphne in disgust. "I bet they stare at traffic accidents too."

My watch said quarter till eight and it took us at least ten minutes to find a parking place on a tiny side street several blocks away from our destination. It would have ultimately been quicker to walk from the house. I was glad we hadn't risked it, though, because the slightly overcast day was now fulfilling its promise with heavily clouded skies.

A light mist of rain began to fall as we walked to the museum. Daphne glared at the heavens. "This is gonna kill my wave."

Sure enough, by the time we got through the throng at the front doors and picked up our complimentary tickets from the box office, Daphne's hair fell straight and damp and she looked resentfully at Alex's natural curl. Everyone's clothing was slightly soggy. I hoped my mascara hadn't run.

Once inside, I almost longed for the chill night air. The museum's auditorium was packed and the heat from so many bodies was stifling. I swear I saw steam rising from damp clothing. It was like being in an indoor swamp.

It was 8:00 on the dot and people were settling into their seats. Words like 'murdered,' 'strangled,' 'Lucille' and 'that bitch' were clearly audible in the constant hum of conversations going on throughout the room.

"Where do we sit?" I wondered out loud, scanning the auditorium in the vain hope of glimpsing three empty chairs.

Daphne shook her heard wordlessly. This was more than even she had bargained for.

"Looks like standing room only, ladies," said Alex.

"I think you're right," I agreed reluctantly. The prospect of standing at the back of the auditorium with the rest of the latecomers did not thrill me. I was already uncomfortably hot and sticky.

"Look, there's Andy!" Daphne pointed over the crowd down near the podium where Andy was deep in conversation with Franklin. "Maybe he can snag a couple of chairs for us." She set off determinedly down the crowded center aisle.

Alex and I followed in Daphne's wake, the three of us dodging elbows, purses and other assorted obstacles. I stumbled on a leg that was carelessly stuck out in the aisle and would have tripped headlong if Alex hadn't steadied me with a strong hand on one arm. The leg's owner—a hennaed matron with enough make-up to give Tammy Faye a run for her money—glared at me. "Watch where you're going," she said stridently. "You almost snagged my nylons!"

The apology I'd planned to make shriveled and died. Someday I'd learn to control both my tongue and my temper, but this wasn't the day. "You might try putting your leg where it's supposed to be," I snapped back. "Haven't you ever heard that a lady keeps her legs closed in public?" I moved on before the outraged woman could respond.

I felt Alex's hand tighten on my arm and immediately regretted the outburst. I risked a quick glance at him, expecting condemnation or at least the mortified anger Grant always had in these situations. To my surprise, Alex was laughing silently.

"Are you laughing at me or near me?" I asked.

Alex shook his head. "Lady, you're what my dad would call a pistol."

"Is that good or bad?"

Alex put an arm around my shoulders and squeezed. "What do you think?"

I smiled and leaned against him for a minute before continuing our slow progress to the front of the room. What a difference a sense of humor made in a man!

When we finally reached Andy, it was easy to tell that something was wrong because his brow was furrowed like a Sharpei pup. Franklin also seemed unusually tense, although considering that both of them were technically suspects in a murder case, they had a pretty damned good reason to be upset.

Andy saw us as we approached and broke away from his conversation with Franklin. "Girls, girls! You would not *believe* this mess! Burke hasn't shown up yet and here we have a crowd larger than *anyone* had anticipated!" He rubbed his forehead in what could've been a vain attempt to smooth out the lines.

"Burke isn't here?" Daphne sounded devastated. I kept forgetting that she actually admired the jerk. On an artistic level, that is.

"You've got to be kidding," I added. "I can't believe the guy'd pass up an opportunity to be publicly worshipped."

"No. And he was supposed to be here at seven." Andy paced back and forth as much as the crowded space would allow. "We had several of our committee members here to meet him for cocktails and he just didn't show up!"

Burke pass up free drinks? Curiouser and curiouser. It certainly didn't jibe with his reputation. Supposedly, he drank almost as much as the man whose work he was adapting to the Silver Screen.

"Did you call the hotel?" asked Alex.

"I've left so many messages that the gal at the front desk recognizes my voice. There's no answer in his room."

"When was the last time anyone saw him?"

Franklin answered me this time. "I spoke with him briefly after I left the library. You see, we've been corresponding since he was chosen to adapt *Blood Spurts High*. At one point he was actually quite open to discussing the work with me."

Big surprise, I thought, since Franklin was probably more qualified to adapt Randell's work than Jonathan Burke.

Franklin continued. "I wasn't happy with some of his latest ideas, though. I wasn't sure if he was really staying true to the Randell ideal and I wanted to discuss it with him."

I was amazed. Franklin either had a great deal of courage or a total lack of tact. Possibly both.

"Where did you see him?" asked Daphne.

"I met him in the lobby of the hotel."

"What did he say?" I asked in fascination.

"Well, he wasn't exactly courteous," Franklin admitted. "In fact, I'd have to say that he was rather hostile. I'll spare you two ladies the details—"

Damn.

"—but suffice it to say he wasn't amenable to suggestions."

No shit, Sherlock.

"He did mention that he intended on going back to the Cave to soak up some atmosphere for the screenplay. He seemed to think that today's ... murder—" Franklin looked rather queasy as he spoke. "—would give him inspiration."

"That's really sick," I said in disgust. Talk about warped. It's one thing to soak up atmosphere, oh, say in Whitechapel where the victims were long-dead. But Lucille hadn't even been *embalmed* yet, let alone buried, not to mention the fact that she and Burke had been lovers. The man was grotesque.

Franklin nodded. "And then I believe he was planning on returning to the hotel until it was time for to him to come here. I can't imagine where he could be."

"Probably in a bar getting smashed like Shay Randell," Andy muttered darkly.

"So what now?" asked Daphne.

Andy shrugged. "Yours truly here, and Franklin are going to speak instead. Franklin did a lot of research on Burke and his work and he knows more about Randell than anyone I know."

Or would ever want to know, I added silently.

"We'd better get going." Andy wiped sweat off his forehead. "God, what a mess!"

I had a feeling he was referring to more than just Burke's no-show.

"Where are you three sitting?"

Daphne, Alex and I shrugged in unison.

"Well, you can sit at the side here if you don't mind looking at our profiles." Andy gestured to three chairs on the stage sidelines, two with suit jackets draped over the backs. "Franklin and I won't need ours and if Burke shows up he can stand."

We gratefully accepted his offer and settled into the chairs while Andy approached the microphone. The view wasn't bad at all and the smells of wet clothing and too many people were less overwhelming up on the stage.

Andy tapped the microphone and the buzz of conversation in the auditorium immediately faded. There was an expectant silence as the crowd focused its attention towards the podium.

After the inevitable whine of feedback followed by minor adjustments that occur at any public function involving a sound system, Andy cleared his throat and began. "Good evening, ladies and gentlemen. My name is Andy Stewart and I'd like to welcome you to the second-to-last evening of Emerald Cove's first annual Shay Randell Festival."

And possibly the last, I thought.

"It's gratifying to see so many people in attendance this evening, so many more than we'd actually anticipated. Or have room for …"

There was some laughter at this, mostly from those people comfortably seated. Andy continued. "We at the Library appreciate your support. For those of you that don't already know it, all proceeds from the Festival are going to the continued upkeep of the Emerald Cove Library. It's especially gratifying that you would all come this evening given that it follows in the wake of a tragedy: the unfortunate death of our Charity Ball coordinator, Lucille Monroe."

Everyone leaned forward in his or her seats in anticipation. If they were expecting anything juicy, they were sadly disappointed by Andy's next words; a brief statement to the effect that the death was under investigation by the local police, followed by the summation, "Lucille's death was a sad and unfortunate tragedy, especially after the unequivocal success of the Walking Tours." Here he firmly turned the subject away from the murder. "Thanks again to Franklin Grace, our informative guide—" Franklin smiled shyly at the light smattering of applause that followed Andy's words. "—and Murder for Hire."

Andy turned and smiled in our direction. There was more applause and an almost palpable air of speculation. Could we possibly have staged Lucille's murder to gain publicity? Or were we indeed the Nancy Drew-esque heroines as portrayed by the likes of Mavis and Arthur Sloan?

"And now I have an announcement that may come as a disappointment to some of you. Jonathan Burke, noted author and our scheduled speaker for this evening, has been unavoidably detained."

A collective groan of disappointment swelled through the auditorium, and several people actually stood up to leave. Andy forged on. "We apologize for this unexpected turn of events but we hope you'll decide to stay for the program. Mr. Burke will be replaced by Franklin, a noted Randell expert in his own right."

I glanced at Franklin. He seemed unperturbed by the disgruntled mutters that were clearly audible.

"Franklin can probably tell you more about Randell than Mr. Burke could have, including anything you'd ever want to know about the film adaptations."

Franklin positively beamed.

"Now I'm not sure why anyone would *want* to know as much about Randell as Franklin does ..." A ripple of laughter ran over the room. " ... since by all accounts, Shay Randell was a rather unpleasant person, especially when he was drunk. Which was apparently ninety-five percent of the time."

I turned to Daphne and whispered, "He's good. Look, most of the jerks that got up to leave have sat back down."

"Yeah," Daphne whispered back. "But I don't think Franklin appreciates the stuff about Randell being a drunk. Check him out."

I looked. Franklin's beam of satisfaction had been replaced by a look of self-righteous indignation. If he'd been a teakettle, he'd be steaming.

Andy went on, oblivious to the reaction his words were getting from his back-up speaker.

"I've read most of Shay Randell's work and it never ceases to amaze me that a man with his capacity for drink could write the books he did, brilliantly turning out characters and plots that are now world-famous. I guess it just goes to prove that it's always possible for a man's art to transcend his personality."

More laughter. I didn't dare look at Franklin.

"And I'd say that's enough from me. Again, we're sorry for the change in program, but we hope you'll welcome Mr. Franklin Grace.."

This time the applause was much warmer. I stole a glance at Franklin as he approached the podium. He appeared calm when he accepted the microphone, nodding coolly at Andy, who stepped away from the podium and joined us at the sidelines.

"Thank you." Franklin smiled as the last of the applause died down. "I realize that it must be a disappointment to those of you here to listen to Mr. Burke, but I hope you'll bear with me and perhaps even find my words of interest. I've spoken to and corresponded with Mr. Burke and we've discussed many of his ideas for the adaptation of *Blood Spurts High* ..."

I tuned Franklin out when he started blathering on about Randell's 'gut wrenching prose.' I mean, he was nice enough and not even bad looking but it was no small wonder that he didn't appear to have a girlfriend. What woman could hope to compete with gut-wrenching prose? Franklin's obsession with Randell left little time or room for anything else.

My mind turned to the missing Burke—an appropriate turn of phrase,

I thought. I bet he was off in some bar, picking up on some stupid bimbo who hadn't the taste or the brains to say 'no.' Burke wouldn't want them with brains anyway …

But even as these rather rude thoughts ran through my head, common sense told me that anyone as vain as Jonathan Burke would not have passed up a public appearance, especially one guaranteed to add to his notoriety since it followed so closely on the heels of a murder.

Daphne nudged me. "Are you listening to this?"

"Huh? What did I miss?"

"Just listen."

" … sure that the reports of Randell's drinking have been greatly exaggerated. A man as sodden with alcohol as the Shay Randell so many people seem to delight in portraying, could never have written the works of genius that Randell has given the world. It's a sad but true fact that those who have failed to reach the heights of a creative genius such as Randell feel it necessary to belittle the man himself, as his art is so blatantly beyond the reach of their criticism."

Whoa. Talk about turning a podium into a soapbox.

Luckily, Franklin seemed to have expended his burst of self-righteous anger on that last sentence. He went on in milder tones; giving interesting details of Randell's life and works before finally opening up the floor for questions. He received quite a few and answered all of them competently. In fact, the only thing missing from his skills as a lecturer was a sense of humor.

Franklin got a solid round of applause as he left the podium and turned the microphone back over to Andy.

"Thank you, Franklin, for an interesting and informative lecture." Here Andy led another round of applause, remarkably generous in my mind as Franklin had all but called him a failure in public.

An additional 'thank you' to the audience and a quick reminder that there were free refreshments in the lobby ended Andy's speech. He got a large round of applause himself before stepping down from the podium.

As the audience began trickling out of the auditorium, presumably to take advantage of the free grub, Alex, Daphne and I stood up. Alex gestured towards the crowd. "How about I do that he-man thing and fight my way to the food before it's all gone? You two can follow when it's thinned out."

As Alex dove in with the other salmon swimming upstream, Andy joined us with a sardonic smile. "How'd you like the lecture?"

I looked over towards Franklin, who was happily talking to a crowd of admirers. "Let's just say I don't have much to say to Franklin right now. At least nothing that would be polite."

Daphne was a little kinder. "Well, he certainly knows his stuff. But don't you think he's a bit … delusional?"

"Totally whacked is more like it," I muttered.

Andy laughed. "He doesn't bother me. Franklin's basically a nice guy with one major blind spot. I've learned that he doesn't pull any punches if you push the wrong Randell button. We've had some wrangles over it in the past, no big deal."

You're a bigger man than me, Gunga Din, I thought. Noticing the way his buttoned suit jacket strained at the waist, I was glad I hadn't said that out loud.

Andy was then accosted by several people who proceeded to grill him about Lucille's death with a lack of tact that would've made Jonathan Burke feel right at home. Daphne and I looked at each other and heartlessly abandoned our benefactor to the wolves before they started grilling us as well.

The crowd had thinned out enough to make negotiating the aisles a little less comparable to salmon trying to reach their spawning grounds. The lobby, on the other hand, was packed, people squashed together like canned anchovies. I hoped Alex had managed to snag some food. All of these aquatic similes were making me hungry.

I spotted Mavis across the lobby waving madly in our direction. I waved back with an insincere smile pasted on my face and muttered, "Any way we can avoid her?"

Looking up to see which 'her' I was referring to, Daphne shook her head. "I think," she said reluctantly, "that the only way we could do that is to move to another state. Besides," she added, "we have worse problems than Mavis. Emerald Cove's answer to Jimmy Olsen is looking our way."

She was right. Arthur Sloan was perched inappropriately on the edge of one of the refreshment tables, notebook in hand. He was staring at us with definite intent. I knew if he cornered us it would be like an encounter with a Moray eel; he wouldn't let go unless we chopped off his head.

Damn. More seafood imagery. My stomach growled resentfully as we moved away from the refreshments, telling me in no uncertain terms that I was going the wrong way. Seeing how Mavis was zeroing in on us like a heat-seeking missile from that direction, my stomach might be right. I glanced back towards the table. Sloan was standing up, eagerly heading our way. I swear, he and Mavis were like a pair of velociraptors, attacking from either side.

Suddenly my view of Sloan was blocked by a much more welcome sight; Alex bearing plates of food, plastic cups teetering precariously on the edge of the plates. He balanced his load as skillfully as any waiter, deftly avoiding the constantly shifting crowd as he made his way to my side. Plucking two cups off the plates before his luck ran out, I said, "Quick, let's take this outside."

Daphne grabbed the third glass and the three of us beat a hasty but tactically sound retreat out the front doors and around the side of the building. We settled on a ledge sheltered from the rain by the overhanging lip of the roof.

The food was an uninspired assortment of chips, cookies, raw veggies, cheese squares and crackers, but at the moment it looked as appetizing as the gourmet spread presented at Jason Downs' house. We each raised our cup of cheap wine as Daphne said, "Here's to avoiding unwanted company."

We drank, all three of us grimacing at the astringent taste of a supposed Burgundy that had never seen France. It wasn't the taste that made me choke, however.

"I thought you were too tired to go out, Connie."

Grant stood framed beneath the concrete archway, the light from the front porch catching the carefully placed —- and expensive—highlights in his hair. He looked very photogenic. And *very* pissed off.

Guess Daphne made that toast too soon.

Chapter Fifteen

It was 10:30 by the time I walked in my front door. My head was throbbing from hunger; the only things I'd eaten in the last couple of hours were my pride and words bitten back before they could escape.

I'd just spent an acrimonious hour in Grant's car hashing out the end of our relationship after being hauled to my feet, spilling my wine down the front of his expensive shirt and slacks. That hadn't helped matters.

Daphne had tried to take the blame when Grant showed up at the Museum like an avenging cross-gender Fury. She'd said—truthfully, mind you—that she'd insisted I go to the lecture even though I'd wanted to stay home. But Grant wouldn't buy it, not with Alex sitting so close to me on the ledge. No one cares about truth when circumstantial evidence is so clearly damning.

When Grant had grabbed my arm, out of the corner of my eye I could see Alex tense for action. That's when I'd lost my grip on my wine glass and Grant had immediately released me in order to inspect the damage to his clothes. I'd found something reassuring in this sign that his vanity was stronger than his anger. His out of character behavior the night before had disconcerted me. "Connie," he'd said as he wiped distastefully at the stain of cheap Burgundy, "We need to talk. Now."

Normally these words from Grant would've sent me heading for the hills. However, the pause had given me enough time to give Alex a warning 'I'll handle this' shake of the head as I'd resolved at that moment to stop being such a wimp and get the inevitable confrontation and conversation over with. Tossing my keys to Daphne, I said, "I'll meet you at home, okay?" Daphne looked dubious, but nodded anyway.

"Connie, are you sure?" Alex had still remained unconvinced. Grant, of course, bristled angrily. The two might have exchanged words or even blows if Daphne hadn't taken Alex by an arm and said, "We know who to blame if she doesn't come home," followed by an evil look at Grant.

Grant ignored her and stalked off towards his car, which was illegally parked in front of the museum. I'd followed slowly, wondering if it was humanly possible to find and train a replacement for Grant for tomorrow night's Gala performance.

It was this thought that had not only kept me from being brutally frank with Grant as to why I wanted to break it off, but also from punching him when he didn't use the same restraint when telling me what an 'idiotic little tramp' I was for preferring Alex to him. There was a lot more along those lines, including a few choice tidbits about how I was throwing away my opportunity to better my situation and learn how to appreciate the finer things in life.

Maybe it was because he was wording things like a character in a Regency Romance, but I managed to keep my temper and even apologize for not being totally up front when I became interested in Alex. I did tell him that I didn't want to play Eliza Doolittle to his Professor Higgins. I used that comparison instead of Galatea to his Pygmalion because I figured he was more likely to get a stage play reference than a classical one. I was not quite the uneducated peasant he seemed to think I was. At any rate, the upshot was that he was still going to do the Gala tomorrow night, but after that he thought it best if he left MFH even though he realized that his absence would 'sadly affect the overall quality of the troupe's performance.'

Ladies and gentlemen, I held my tongue. The words 'one more night' played in an endless loop through my brain as I waited for the red mist to clear from my vision. Then I calmly and deliberately said, "Well, that's it then. I'll see you tomorrow night" and got out of the car, much to his surprise.

"Don't you want a ride home?"

"No, I don't think so. I'll walk, it's not far." I gently shut the door before he could say another word. Possibly the word that would tip me over the edge into homicide. Or at least car abuse.

By the time I walked the five blocks home, Alex's car was gone. Part of me was disappointed, but it was just as well. I was cold, damp, pissed off and hungry. Not my most attractive state.

I shut the door behind me and dumped my purse on the couch, narrowly missing the cats, who were all still curled up in an Escher-esque jumble of heads and tails with no discernible starting point. They all went into auto-purr the moment I touched them. It was nice to be home.

The scent of simmering cocoa was in the air, so I followed my nose and joined Daphne in the kitchen. She looked up from her cooking. "Is he dead?"

I shook my head. "Unfortunately we need him for tomorrow night. But it's definitely over." I looked around. "You've been busy." A plate stacked high with Russian tea cookies sat in the middle of the table and a pot of leftover clam chowder bubbled on the stove. My stomach growled menacingly as the various smells reached me. I patted my middle gently and said, "Soon, my pretty. Soon."

Daphne handed me two mugs brimming with cocoa. "None of us actually ate any of the food at the museum, and I figured you'd be starving after dealing with Grant. So? Tell me about it."

I gave Daphne an edited accounting of the last hour as she ladled out two bowlfuls of hot chowder, butter already melting into the cream. Comfort food. I only gave her the highlights, so to speak, but those were enough.

"Man, I would've kicked him right in the balls!" said my ladylike friend.

"Kinda hard to do when you're sitting in a car." I sat down at the table and took a sip of cocoa. My grateful stomach gurgled in contentment.

"Clawed his face, then!" Daphne looked disappointed that I didn't have Grant's blood on my nails, but she gave me a bowl of clam chowder anyway and sat down across from me.

I laughed. "That would've done it. He'd never forgive me if I marred his classic good looks." I shook my head. "Y'know, part of me really hates the fact that I didn't tell him off, but I'd never be able to forgive myself if I let my personal life screw up the show. And it's my own fault for waiting so long to deal with it."

Daphne looked at me for a moment. "I think they call that maturity."

"Yeah ..."

"On one hand, it's a good thing. On the other ..." She shook her head regretfully. "It's a lot less entertaining."

As we ate our late night supper, we went over a quick check list of all the things to remember for the Gala. Had all the actors been informed of the call time? They had. Were all props and costumes accounted for and ready to be taken to the library first thing in the morning? They were. And so on.

"I'm so glad today's over." I reached for a cookie and scattered powdered sugar all over the table. "I swear, if I had to deal with one more problem, one more bit of drama ..."

"All we have to do for the rest of the night is relax. And get some sleep."

"Here's to that." We raised our mugs in a toast and the doorbell rang. The gods have a cruel sense of humor.

We groaned in unison.

"That's got to be Mavis."

"We'll tell her we don't have time to talk."

"Right."

Neither of us made a move to stand. Daphne looked at me. I looked back. Somewhere the theme to *The Good, the Bad, and the Ugly* played in the background. It was a stand-off.

The doorbell rang again. Big Ben's theme blared throughout the house, grating on my already shredded nerves. I cracked first, as Daphne knew I would.

"Oh, shit, I'll get it," I growled, slamming down my mug with enough force to slosh liquid over the sides.

"I'll clean up the dishes," Daphne said generously. She could afford to be generous. After all, I'd be the one dealing with our crackpot landlady determined to turn us into dime novel detectives.

The doorbell sounded once more as I reached the front hall, the piercing tones making me wince. My headache, which had been fading away quietly, suddenly made its reappearance. "All right!" I yelled through the closed door. "I'm coming! Don't ring the damn bell again!"

Unlocking the deadbolt I flung the door open, fully expecting an excited and inquisitive Mavis. Instead I found a somber-faced Detective-Sergeant O'Donohue and his supercilious side-kick, Detective Honey.

My surprise must have been obvious, and I could tell that Honey took it as immediate proof of a guilty conscience. He gave a small, self-satisfied nod, flipped open his ever-presented notebook and scribbled in it.

Recovering the use of my voice, I said, "Can I help you?"

"I hope so." O'Donohue's somber expression was replaced by a smile as he continued, "May we come in, Ms. Garrett? I apologize for the late hour, but we need to speak with both you and Ms. Graves."

"I suppose so." I stood back and let the two police officers in. Closing the door, I ushered them through the living room, saying, "We're working in the kitchen, so why don't we just go in there?" I sorely needed my cocoa for this encounter. And I was going to add a shot of Irish Cream even though Honey would no doubt take another note, something along the lines of 'suspect consuming alcohol to steady guilty nerves.'

As I led them through the dining room, Daphne yelled, "Did you get rid of her?" just as we reached the kitchen door.

"Not exactly."

Daphne looked past me to our visitors and put her mug down.

"Oh." She raised an eyebrow. "Isn't it a little late for a visit? I thought we'd covered everything we needed to this afternoon."

"It's never too late for a visit from the Law," replied Honey. The capital 'L' was obvious.

O'Donohue shot him a look and continued, "This isn't in regards to Lucille Monroe's death, although it may well be connected. Uh … may we sit down?"

"Sure." Daphne waved them into the empty chairs. Honey sat down after giving his chair a suspicious once-over. Did he think it was booby-trapped? Evidently not. It didn't warrant a flip of the notebook.

Oh well, it wouldn't hurt to be polite. "Would you like something to drink? Tea or coffee? We're having cocoa if you'd like some."

"Coffee'd be great," replied O'Donohue. Honey declined.

O'Donohue eyed the cookies. "May I?"

"Go ahead." I pulled out our French press and put some water on to boil. I then nabbed the bottle of Irish Cream from the liquor cabinet and poured a shot into my mug, giving Honey a defiant stare as I sat back down. Daphne and O'Donohue both reached for cookies. Daphne managed to spray powdered sugar all over the table as she bit into it. O'Donohue was more fastidious, although he still got sugar on his face.

I felt more at ease. If they were going to arrest us, they would've already done so and certainly wouldn't be having coffee and cookies at our kitchen table. Besides, it's hard to feel intimidated by a man with powdered sugar coating his five-o'clock shadow like a light snowfall. And he was so good looking, with such a nice, warm smile. I wondered about the possibilities of setting him up with Daphne. A nice detective would be so much better than another tortured artist like Guido …

O'Donohue reached for another cookie, saying, "These are great! You'll have to give me the recipe for my wife. Sonia'd love 'em. Although I hate to think of the mess the kids would make with the sugar."

Married? With children? Oh well, to be honest Daphne didn't seem that interested. She never was interested in the nice, normal guys. Oh, no, she always had to go for the ones who cried at sunsets or showed up in the middle of the night to read a poem dedicated to her beauty, one that just couldn't wait until morning when the rest of us had had our coffee. I should be grateful she'd never taken up with a banjo player.

Daphne downed the last of her cocoa as if it were a shot of bourbon, wiped her mouth with the back of one hand and said, "So! What's the word on the street, Detective?"

Great. She'd slipped into film noir mode. O'Donohue looked fascinated if somewhat taken aback.

Honey picked up a cookie, sniffed it and put it back on the plate.

"You touch it, you eat it," Daphne snapped.

To my amazement, he reluctantly retrieved the cookie and gingerly took a bite. A look of almost comic surprise appeared as he said in unflattering wonder, "It's good!" He promptly took another.

This was getting way off the track. "Why don't you tell us the reason for your visit? We've got work to finish before our show tomorrow." Like going to bed.

O'Donohue nodded. "An hour ago Jonathan Burke's body was found in the same location and condition as Lucille Monroe's.

Daphne's and my shocked gasps mingled with the shriek of the tea kettle as the water came to boil.

I got to my feet and turned the burner off. My hands didn't shake too much as I poured hot water into the press and made the coffee, but the news of Burke's death had blown away what little was left of my equilibrium. I got out a mug for O'Donohue as Daphne said, "Burke was strangled?"

Honey pounced on this. "How did you know that? We didn't mention that!"

"Oh, please," I said in disgust, setting down the mug of coffee in front of O'Donohue. "Sergeant O'Donohue just said that Burke's body was found in an identical condition as Lucille's, and we already knew she'd been strangled. We were there, remember?"

Hmmm, maybe not the best thing to say to couple of homicide detectives.

I grabbed the cocoa pan and portioned out the remainder between Daphne's and my mugs, adding a very liberal portion of Irish Cream to mine. It might be time for the Laphroig to make an appearance if they didn't leave soon.

"Burke was strangled," confirmed O'Donohue, "but he'd also sustained trauma to the back of his head. I suspect that the head injury was done first in order to make it easier for the murderer to finish the job."

"When was he ... the body ... found?" I asked. There was something particularly gruesome about the thought of all those people gathered to hear Burke speak while his body floated in the tide at that damned cave.

"He was found approximately a half hour ago."

"And you're sure he was knocked off?" Daphne wasn't being flippant at this point; her tone was subdued. Slang is just second nature to her.

O'Donohue didn't seem put off. "We don't have the full Coroner's report yet, but I think it's safe to say that Mr. Burke was murdered. Unless he was in the habit of wearing seaweed knotted around his neck."

"Sea of death ..."

We all looked at Daphne in puzzlement.

"*Sea of Death!*" she repeated, then went on to clarify. "It's a Randell novel. The victims were found in a secluded cave, strangled with seaweed! Randell even based the location in Emerald Cove, so it can't just be a coincidence!"

Honey's notebook was open, his pen flying furiously across the pages.

I nodded slowly. I'd read the book too at Daphne's insistence. "She's right. And I don't think it's a coincidence either." I was impressed. Daphne and I were two for two with logical deductions.

"What makes you say that?" Honey kept up a steady flow of scribbling as he asked the question.

I stifled the urge to say 'elementary, my dear Honey,' and settled instead for, "We're in the middle of the Shay Randell Festival, Detective Honey. The people murdered were both closely involved with it and the style of murder for at least two of them is lifted directly out of one of Randell's books. And not one of his better known or better written ones, either. The killer would seem to know his Randell quite well." I had, in fact, only read it because Daphne had insisted. She set a much better example to our actors than I did; to prepare for the Festival, the majority of them had read more Randell novels than I did.

"Why do you say 'knows *his* Randell', Ms. Garrett?" The pen paused as Honey popped a cookie in his mouth.

"A nasty habit I picked up from society." I grabbed the last cookie before he could. "You know, assuming that if you're referring to anyone of importance, it must be a male. I really hate it when I do that too ..."

This shut him up for a moment, so O'Donohue took over the questioning.

"Could you please both tell me when you last saw Jonathan Burke?"

I answered first. "At the second walking tour this afternoon."

Daphne nodded.

"Did either of you speak with him?"

"Nope. In fact, I'd say we both avoided him. Burke was not a pleasant person to talk to."

"Can you be more specific?"

"The few conversations we had with Burke consisted of sexual innuendoes on his part."

"He was a sleaze," said Daphne with great finality.

"I see." O'Donohue took a few notes of his own. "I don't suppose you heard him mention where he planned to spend the afternoon?"

I did remember. "He told Franklin Grace that he was going to go down to the beach by the cave to soak up some atmosphere for his writing." My tone was neutral, my feelings were not. If anyone deserved to be bashed on the head and strangled with seaweed, it was Burke.

"Franklin is the young Randell enthusiast, correct?"

Daphne nodded.

"Where did you go after you left the library?" O'Donohue addressed both of us.

"Right here."

"The kitchen?" Honey looked skeptical.

"At home, in general." You twit.

"Both of you?"

Daphne answered this time. "Yup."

"Anywhere else?"

"To the Museum of Contemporary Art to hear Burke speak … well, of course, he wasn't there. And then back here." She stopped and looked at me. "Well …"

I stepped in. "I was talking to Grant Havers in front of the Museum for an hour. I got back home at 10:30."

"Can anyone verify this?"

Coming from O'Donohue, the question didn't set me on the defensive. I got the impression it was merely routine whereas with Honey, I felt like he'd be first in line to pull the lever on the hot seat for both of us without a second thought. Or without any real evidence against us, for that matter.

"Mavis DiSpachio, our landlady," I replied with some certainty. "She lives next door."

"She knows what time you arrive home?"

Daphne and I exchanged martyred looks. "Oh, yes," I said grimly. "Mavis doesn't miss much of anything. In fact, if you want to question her, just stick around for a few more minutes."

"That's for sure. Your car will attract her like a hooker to a sailor on shore leave." Daphne looked pleased with herself.

O'Donohue grinned. Daphne caught his expression and I could tell she didn't like the fact that he didn't take her seriously.

The phone rang and I settled back in my chair, waving a hand in Daphne's direction. "Your turn."

She glowered at me and grabbed the receiver.

"Hello … this is she. Who's this? … Ah. Mr. Sloan."

Oh, no.

"Yes, we've been informed of Burke's death."

"Why is he calling?" O'Donohue's undertone carried a wealth of accusation as Daphne continued to chat with the intrepid boy reporter. I gathered O'Donohue had dealt with Arthur Sloan in the past.

"How should I know?" I snapped. "I didn't ask him to call."

"It's good publicity for your little group, though, isn't it?" Honey's voice dripped with unflattering insinuations.

"Oh, right, like we arranged this whole mess just to get some publicity!" Me and my big mouth.

"Murder has been perpetrated for less."

"Now look here, Honey—" I stopped as I realized how ridiculous both the argument and my words were.

O'Donohue stepped in before Honey could say anything else. "Drop it, Honey."

Honey subsided.

"Uh huh, that's right. *Very* similar to the method used in *Sea of Death*. But don't quote me on that." Ooh, O'Donohue was not happy. You've heard of the expression 'a cloud passed over his brow?' Well, O'Donohue's face took on a veritable thunderstorm when Daphne continued with, "Yes, we've spoken to Detective-Sergeant O'Donohue. As a matter of fact—"

O'Donohue gestured emphatically, slashing one hand horizontally through the air as he mouthed, "No!"

But it was too late. "—he's right here." She smiled at O'Donohue and handed him the receiver. The look he gave her did not bode well for future goodwill from the local police department. Daphne just smiled, her look clearly stating 'Take *that*, copper!' She sat down, exuding self-satisfaction and listened to O'Donohue's end of the conversation with unabashed curiosity.

"Mr. Sloan, I really don't have time for ... What? Yes, Ms. Graves told me her theory, but ... What?! ... I haven't read the book, Mr. Sloan, so I can't really comment on that with any ... WHAT?!! Consulting? No, we are certainly *not* consulting with ... No, they are *not* officially working on the case with ... Mr. Sloan, I think we're capable of solving this case without the help of two amateur detectives!" Daphne gave an outraged squeak as O'Donohue took a deep breath and continued, "Look, Mr. Sloan. I don't have time for this. The press will be informed of any new developments on the case when it's appropriate for the knowledge to be made public. Yes, you can quote me on that!" O'Donohue hung up. He turned around and glared. "You two are dangerous."

I thought that was more than a little unfair, but didn't think it would be a good time to argue the point.

Daphne, on the other hand, was more than ready to wade into battle. "I just answered his questions," she said with a glare of her own. "No one said we couldn't talk to the press and it's not my fault if he makes assumptions."

"You didn't exactly discourage the assumptions," O'Donohue shot back.

"Yeah? Well, referring to us as 'amateur detectives' won't help matters either."

"That's true," I agreed. "Have you ever been taken out of context?"

O'Donohue groaned as the implications of my words sunk in. Daphne caught my meaning as well and smiled. "Thanks for the press, Detective. I'm sure Sloan will make the most of the quote."

What O'Donohue might have said or done at that point was to remain a mystery. There was a quick obligatory knock at the back door and, true to our predictions, Mavis burst into the room. She'd obviously dressed for our visitors seeing as she was wearing her favorite red velour housecoat. She labors under the misconception that it makes her look like a femme-fatale. The desired image was completely shot by her Nike high tops sticking out from beneath the hem line.

"Hello, girls, I hope I'm not bothering you, but—" She stopped, pretending that she'd just now noticed our guests. Mavis is a very bad actor. Putting a hand up to her mouth in a gesture as broad as a mime, she continued, "Oh! Dear me, I didn't realize you had visitors!"

I was resigned to our fate. "Hi, Mavis. This is Detective-Sergeant O'Donohue and Detective Honey. They'd like to ask you a few questions."

Mavis fluttered her lashes coyly. "Of course, officers. Anything I can do to help." She fluffed her hair up with one hand and hitched the hem of her housecoat up with the other, affording us all a glimpse of her bird-like calves and dirty white high-tops. I wanted to smack her.

"Would you please tell us if you happened to notice Ms. Graves and Ms. Garrett arrive home this afternoon?" O'Donohue smiled encouragingly. Mavis was entranced.

"Oh, yes," she simpered. "I always keep an eye out for my girls."

That was certainly true.

"And what time did you see them?"

"Oh, I'd say it was about fivish. In fact, I remember quite clearly because I was waiting for *Predator* to start on USA and it was scheduled for 5:10. I heard Connie's car pull into the driveway right as Arnold flashed on the screen." Mavis giggled. "Of course, I didn't mean that literally. He would never do anything like that in a movie. He IS our Governor, after all. And such a hunk!"

O'Donohue and Honey looked confused, a natural state for anyone trying to follow Mavis's train of thought for the first time. I guess O'Donohue managed to sift through the dross and extract the pertinent facts because he went on to a new question. "What about later this evening?"

Mavis considered this. "Well, I saw the girls at the Museum around ten till eight, at least twenty minutes after I got there, although they were at home when I left, so don't get any naughty ideas about their whereabouts—"

Thanks a lot, Mavis.

"—and then I got home at, oh, I'd say 9:30, and naturally I noticed Connie's car in the driveway."

"Did you know Jonathan Burke?"

Mavis dropped her hemline, looking genuinely shocked. "You don't mean to tell me he's been murdered!"

"Why would you assume he's been murdered?" came the inevitable question from Honey.

Mavis turned an innocent brown gaze on him. She must have been some coquette in her youth. "Well, Detective O'Donohue asked if I *did* know Mr. Burke, not if I *do* know him. So it's really very obvious. And Lucille was knocked off so it stands to reason that Burke was kacked as well."

Honey had nothing to say in the face of Mavis's reasoning. O'Donohue winced at the bad slang. "Do all of you talk this way naturally?"

"Oh, Daphne's taught me all sorts of lovely expressions."

O'Donohue shot Daphne a look. "I see."

I doubted it.

"As it stands, Ms.—" He paused, at a loss for her name.

"Mrs. DiSpachio." She paused. "Widowed." Up went the hemline. "But you can call me Mavis."

"Well, Mavis. Mr. Burke was murdered sometime this evening."

Mavis looked less shocked than gratified that her logic had proven correct. "That poor man."

"How well did you know him?"

"Oh, not well at all. I only met him twice. Once at the Museum two nights ago and once during the second Walking Tour."

"Did you notice anyone acting in a suspicious manner?"

Mavis thought about this carefully. It was with some regret that she finally replied, "No, not really. Except that Mr. Burke was rude to everyone. He even corrected our tour guide, Franklin Grace. And Franklin does know his Randell!"

"I see." Again, I doubted it. O'Donohue took one of Mavis's hands and smiled again. "Thank you for your help, Mavis."

"Any time, Detective!" Mavis's lashes fluttered again. So did my stomach. "If you need any more help, please feel free to contact me! Although with my girls on the case, I'm sure you'll have the perp in the slammer in no time! Bye, now!"

Mavis exited, her last words leaving O'Donohue looking as though he'd bitten a particularly sour lemon.

"Do you have any other questions?" I asked, hoping to hurry them on their way. At this point, I just wanted to crawl into bed before things got any worse. My headache was back with a vengeance, the specter of a migraine lurking behind one eye.

"Is tomorrow the last day of the festival?"

I nodded, wincing as the movement sent a knife-like pain running down the left side of my head.

"And your group is performing at the Gala Charity Ball thing?" This was from Honey.

"Yes."

"I see …"

I had no idea what special significance Detective Honey placed in this innocuous piece of information and at this point, I didn't care. I stood up and began clearing dishes from the table. O'Donohue took the hint and got to his feet as well, Honey following suit. Daphne, on the other hand, leaned back in her chair and gave a little wave. "Let us know if you need any help cracking the case."

O'Donohue handled the provocation admirably. "You'll be the first to know, Ms. Graves."

I could only hope he was joking. With Burke's death, Daphne and I had run out of suspects.

Chapter Sixteen

"Oh, shit …" These were the words with which I greeted the next morning. Rain was spattering down on the roof and a sharp blade of pain knifed through one eye down the back of my neck when I tried to sit up. A migraine. A goddamn migraine. Of all the headaches on all the days, this one had to walk into my head today …

Silently apologizing to the Epstein brothers, I oh so slowly and carefully crawled out of bed and into the bathroom where I splashed cool water on my face in futile hopes of alleviating the pain. Only then did I risk a glance in the mirror, the reflection confirming my fears. Bloodshot eyes glared at me from behind a tangled mass of hair, my face strained and pale even in the rose-colored lighting insisted on by Daphne. Luckily the nausea hadn't set in yet and I had some prescription medication that would make life bearable in short order.

I got the pill bottle out of the medicine cabinet and then slowly negotiated the stairs down to the living room where Daphne was curled up under a plaid throw rug in front of the fireplace. She'd lit a small firelog and was gazing moodily into the flames, an Edward Gorey mug clutched to her chest. "It's too cold," she muttered to no one in particular. "Too cold and too wet to go out. I wanna go back to bed."

"Don't even think about it," I snapped.

My tone made her look up. One glance at my face told the story. "Migraine?"

I nodded, wincing at the additional bolt of pain that accompanied the movement.

Clutching her throw around her shoulders, Daphne followed me into the kitchen and poured me a mug of cocoa, refilling her own as well. I accepted the offering gratefully and washed my pill down with a gulp of the rich liquid. I wanted to add a shot of espresso, but there's no way my head could take the sound of the coffee grinder. Maybe later.

I looked at the clock. 9:30. Had I really slept that long? The cast was due to arrive in fifteen minutes for a final line read-thru and I was still in my bright red thermal pajamas. I wasn't quite ready for Alex to see me in anything quite so goofy, so I headed upstairs and took a quick shower.

As I threw on jeans and a heather green fisherman's sweater, I reflected that had I still been with Grant, I would've no doubt left the thermals on just to irritate him. This was a definite sign that breaking up, while hard to do, was the right thing. Why didn't anyone ever write songs about the upside of these situations?

A little bit of lipstick brought some color back into my face and the headache started to recede; I was ready to face the day, possibly even the coffee grinder. Nothing short of Valium could make me look forward to facing Grant, of course, but I counted on his professionalism—and mine— to get us both through the day. Then we could go our separate ways, he to a no-doubt successful career and an appropriately fashionable trophy wife, and me … well, I'd worry about that after the show.

I went back downstairs with a little more spring to my stride to find that Brad and Tasha had arrived. They were sitting in the living room discussing both the murders and tonight's performance.

"Do you really think that any of us are serious suspects?" This was Daphne in a disbelieving tone.

"Sure!" Brad sounded positively cheerful as he continued, "I mean, c'mon, we're all directly involved because Lucille died during our performance. If the cops had seen Connie tell her off the other night at rehearsal, they'd have booked her by now."

"Oh, thanks," I growled.

"Just kiddin', Con." Brad grinned at me. "Seriously, I doubt anyone is seriously considering any one of us as the murderer. None of us knew Jonathan Burke, why would we kill him?"

Why wouldn't we? I thought. But I kept it to myself.

"To be honest," Brad went on, "Andy appears to be odds on favorite if you take a good look at things, but that's almost as ridiculous as it being one of us." We all nodded in agreement as he continued. "It'll just be kind of weird performing in front of a bunch of people who're wondering whether we're actors or murderers."

"Jeez, Brad," I said, "Please don't bring that up in front of Shaun. He gets nervous enough as it is."

"Sorry, Connie."

"It's okay. But we have to remember that even though there's going to be a lot of conjecture and a lot of press coverage tonight, it won't center on us beyond our performance. We just do our job and leave."

"Lookeeloos," Daphne muttered.

"Yeah, well, they won't be looking very much in our direction. I hope."

My headache was definitely on the way out, and I was nearly convinced that we'd be in and out of the evening relatively painlessly.

The front door opened without warning. "Hey, guys." Shaun, looking dashing in a black leather jacket and olive khaki pants, stood in the hall brandishing a newspaper in one hand and a moist paper bag in the other. "Did you see the paper this morning?" He tossed the bag in Daphne's direction.

Daphne looked inside. "Blueberry muffins!" I was beside her in a flash and we took our pick before generously handing over the remainder to Brad and Tasha.

"Thanks, Shaun," everyone chorused, mouths full.

Shaun, meanwhile, already had the Emerald Post unfolded and was pointing to a front page photo of Jonathan Burke under a headline reading 'Cove Killer Strikes Again!' There was a smaller picture of Lucille in one corner. The unkind thought crossed my mind at how pissed Lucille would've been that Burke got more coverage than she. I didn't have to ask if the article was under Arthur Sloan's byline. As soon as Shaun read the opening sentence, it was painfully apparent that Sloan's puerile pen was responsible.

"It seems," Shaun read, "that Emerald Cove has its own Jack the Ripper. The modus operandi may be different, but the body count is rapidly rising to match that of Springheel Jack—"

"Jack the Ripper only killed prostitutes," Daphne commented to the room at large.

"Well, Lucille did dress like a hooker," I said.

"But Jack the Ripper killed five of them."

I shrugged. "I guess that two victims constitutes rapid rising in Sloan's book. What an ass!"

"It gets much worse," Shaun assured us.

> The body of renowned mystery writer, Jonathan Burke, was found at the base of Davy Jones Cave. He had been dead for several hours before the discovery of his body and police reports confirm that foul play was involved. Murder is also suspected in the death of Ms. Lucille Monroe, the coordinator of the Randell Festival's Gala dinner. Ms. Monroe was found earlier the same day in the same location at the climax of Murder For Hire's Walking Tour, also part of the Randell Festival. Both of these deaths follow closely on the heels of the supposed accidental drowning of Damien Duran, also involved with the Festival.

Shaun paused for breath and Daphne said somewhat doubtfully, "That's not so bad."

Shaun looked at her and continued.

*The murders of Lucille Monroe and Jonathan Burke were both
made to resemble murders in Randell's famous novel 'Sea of Death',
right down to the killer's gruesome calling card, a length of slimly
seaweed draped like a noose around the victims' necks. Police are
releasing very little information at this time, but Detective Sergeant Bernard O'Donohue of Emerald Cove's P.D. has made it
clear that he expects to make an arrest shortly. With his partner
Detective Honey as a loyal Watson—*

"Watson? Lestrade, maybe, but Watson? I don't *think* so," said Daphne.

*—our fine boys in blue should apprehend this criminal soon and
once again make the shores of Emerald Cove safe for its citizens. It
is also rumored that working closely with the police are those two
cuties in crime—*

Daphne and I both choked on our muffins as Shaun enunciated the
last three words with great precision.

*—Connie Garrett and Daphne Graves, of Murder for Hire. With
these two amateur sleuths on the scene, the killer better resign
himself to Justice!*

"Cuties in crime?" I said slowly, still unable to believe what I'd just
heard. "Is Sloan totally insane?"

"Boys in blue?" Daphne had the same stunned look I did, slowly replaced by rising anger. "Sloan writes like something out of an old *Police
Gazette!*"

"You gotta wonder why he hasn't been canned by now," said Brad.
"Who the hell is he sleeping with?"

"I don't know," I said grimly. "But I think that after that article, the
guests will be looking for a lot more than a performance out of us. This
isn't the kind of publicity that I had in mind." I turned on Daphne. "Did
you really have to talk to that idiot last night?"

She shrugged, embarrassed. "It seemed like a good idea at the time."

"Why?" I shot back in irritation. "Just so you could piss off
O'Donohue?"

"He was being condescending!" Daphne said defensively.

"Well, what do you expect when you start talking like Carl Club, for
crissake?"

Daphne countered with an attack of her own. "Well *you're* the one
who's been trying to solve Duran's murder!"

"Yeah, but you don't see me shooting my mouth off about it to a reporter with a bad case of National Enquirer-itis, who then refers to us as 'cuties in crime!'"

Daphne and I glared at each other.

"Golly Gee P.I.'s," murmured Brad. Daphne and I turned our glares in his direction. He looked back at us innocently. My irritation deflated immediately as I realized how silly we were being. "Sorry, Daphne," I muttered. "It's not your fault that Sloan is an idiot."

"No, you're right," Daphne sighed. "I shouldn't have talked to him. Sorry, Connie. I'll go make some more cocoa."

Knowing that it was her way of making amends, I let Daphne go off to the kitchen to work her culinary magic without another word.

I turned to find Brad looking at me with what I can only call an unholy gleam of mischief in his eyes. "I thought you swore off crime fighting in favor of show business."

Oh, crap, I thought.

I looked pleadingly at Shaun and Tasha. "You guys, promise me, you won't tell Mavis that I'm even *thinking* about the murders. She'll never let up!"

"Not a word," said Shaun. Tasha made the Girl Scout's promise with one hand and nodded solemnly.

Brad just grinned at me.

"Looks like Mavis was right about you after all."

"I swear, one word to Mavis about any of this and you're a dead man," I told him between clenched teeth.

Brad held up his hands in a 'who, me?' gesture. I looked at him suspiciously. "I'll keep my mouth shut ... but you gotta tell us what prompted this new *Murder She Wrote* mentality."

I heaved a huge sigh. "Grant," I said simply. "He said I couldn't do it."

"Ah," said Brad. "Your secret identity is safe with me, Batgirl."

I heard a car drive up and peered out the window, hoping to see Alex's green Mustang. Instead, Grant's black Lexus was backing into a spot in front of the house. Turning to Brad, I said, "I'm gonna help Daphne with the cocoa. Can you get the door?"

"Anything for our resident Miss Marple," said Brad.

I resisted the urge to kick him. All teasing aside, I knew that Brad would keep my secret, especially if there was a possibility it would eventually piss off Grant.

Daphne was adding freshly grated orange rind to a fresh pan of cocoa. "Grant's here," I said. "I'd better make some espresso."

"Let him drink cocoa," said Daphne.

"He doesn't deserve your cocoa," I replied. "Besides, I really need the caffeine myself."

Getting the canister of coffee beans out of the fridge, I ground enough beans for several shots of espresso, more than ready for my first java jolt of the day now that the migraine had faded to a memory.

I was adding water to the espresso machine when the kitchen door flew open and Mavis rushed in, soaking wet and dripping water all over the floor. Mascara was running down her cheeks to match the rain drops running off her wet mackintosh. She looked like an emaciated panda.

She looked from Daphne to me and back again in expectation. "So? Who did it"

I rolled my eyes and turned back to the espresso machine. Let Daphne handle this one. She did, managing to keep all but the faintest hint of exasperation from her voice. "Mavis, why on earth would you think we know anything about the murders?"

"I read this morning's *Post*, of course!"

That did it. My patience was shot. "Mavis, you're the one who told that idiot, Sloan, that we were 'hot on the trail' in the first place." Never mind that I thought we *were* hot on the trail until Lucille and Burke turned up dead.

"Right!" she answered brightly.

Daphne stepped into the breach. "So clearly, you of all people should realize that neither Connie nor I have any idea who the murderer could be." This much, at least, was true. And we weren't about to let her know that we were even speculating as to who it *might* be either.

"But you must have *some* idea by this time," Mavis insisted. "This is your business! All those books you read, it must give you some idea, some insight into the twisted minds of demented criminals!"

It was on the tip of my tongue to say that I didn't even understand the twisted workings of Mavis's demented mind, but once again, what would be the point? I suspected that the migraine drug was having a mellowing affect on me because I was starting to see some humor in the situation. Not a lot, but enough to be able to pat her on the shoulder and say lightly, "If we figure anything out, you'll be the first to know, we promise. But now we have to get ready for the Gala, so we'd better get back to it, okay?"

Mavis sighed in disappointment, but headed back out the door, having been around us enough to know not to push her luck when we were prepping for a show.

"Let's see," I said as I helped Daphne fill mugs with cocoa and put them on a tray. "I woke up with a migraine, the local police force probably wishes they had a legitimate excuse to lock us up, there's a killer on the loose … and we're now known as 'cuties in crime.' Does it get any worse?"

Grant walked into the kitchen. "Connie," he said coldly. "May I have a word with you?"

I had to ask.

Chapter Seventeen

The staff room of the library had probably seen more activity in the past few hours than it had in the combined six months of its existence. Cast members of *The Peruvian Pigeon* were spread out from one end of the cubicle-filled office to the other, setting props, changing costumes and running lines for the next act, all while trying to scarf down our dinners (filet mignon and fresh steamed vegetables). Big band and jazz music filtered in from the band through the closed door.

We'd completed the first act during the latter half of a very lavish cocktail hour, the applause and laughter increasing with every drink served. Act Two was scheduled to start immediately after dinner was finished and, as usual, all the preparation beforehand didn't prevent props from being misplaced and actors' nerves from acting up. Shaun was huddled in one corner, eyes glued to his script as he muttered his lines under his breath. He took his role as Thug #2 very seriously.

I'd managed to put all thoughts of Lucille, Burke and Duran out of my mind for the moment as I had a more immediate problem. I rummaged through the fedoras and slouches piled on one of the tables Andy had cleared for our costumes and props, looking for my Smith & Wesson '38. "Has anyone seen my gun?" I said to the room in general. "I thought I'd put it down by the hats, but it's gone." I flipped over a fedora and peered underneath. Nothing.

"I've got mine," said Brad.

"Check the miscellaneous props table. I loaded all three as soon as the first act was over." Alex spoke up from a corner where he was adjusting the lapels of his Jimmy the Weasel suit, a red, white and blue checked monstrosity that'd come out of someone's father's closet. I'd lost track of who'd donated it; no one wanted to admit to being related to anyone with such horrible taste. It suited the character of the Weasel to a 'T,' though, and if anyone could wear it and still manage to look appealing, it was Alex. I doubted that Grant could've carried it off; he took himself far too seriously.

This morning's talk hadn't been too bad, although definitely irritating. Grant had just wanted to assure me that he fully intended to behave in a professional manner and would do his best to make sure that the show was as good as possible. The implication, of course, was that without his cooperation the rest of us would suck, but I wasn't about to pick another fight.

Alex had arrived shortly thereafter and we'd managed a quick moment alone in the kitchen, during which he'd practically done a body check on me for bruises. I assured him I was fine and that I'd fill him on the details after the show. For the rest of the morning and afternoon, he and Grant managed to treat each other with glacial civility. I tried to help matters by being as professional as possible to both of them.

Still no gun. This was ridiculous. All of the blanks were in their boxes but there was no sign of two of the three working guns. By working, I mean guns that actually fired rounds, blank or otherwise. We only used quarter loads with fine grain powder and flash cotton, enough to make some noise and startle a few audience members, but safe enough to fire at close range. At least that's what Alex told me. And since weapons handling was part of his livelihood, I thought I could trust him. Previously I'd just had the actors fire a good foot to the side of their target, the examples of Jon-Erik Hexum and Brandon Lee making me err well on the side of caution.

Unable to locate my gun anywhere it should've been, I started prowling along the tables where we'd moved papers and books to clear room for our stuff. "I wish people would just keep their hands off the props when they're set in place," I grumbled, inadvertently sending a pile of library books tumbling to the ground as I poked around. "And I swear, if one of the catering staff touched anything, I'll—" I stopped when I saw the barrel of a revolver poking out under a stack of papers in one of the cubicles. "How the hell did it get over here?" I picked it up and noticed the other revolver there as well. I put one of the guns back on the props table for Alex's scene as the Weasel.

Any answer that might have been forthcoming was cut off by the entrance of one of the caterer's assistants, a petite redhead with cornflower blue eyes, which she used to maximum effect whenever she looked at a member of the opposite sex. She started collecting the dinner dishes, looking flirtatiously at each male cast member as she took their empty plates. Daphne, Martha, Tasha and I were ignored, although she did remove our dishes.

As she reached the table nearest the door, the redhead suddenly burst forth into a flurry of speech. "You guys are an acting troupe, right? You do this stuff all the time, don't you?" Leaving no pause long enough for a reply, she babbled on, "I should send you my resume. I've done a lot of modeling, fashion shows and stuff like that, and I've been thinking I should get into acting and stuff, it'd be good for my portfolio. It's pretty easy, isn't it? I'd be good at it, because, really—" here she rolled her eyes in a world-weary manner, "—I'm acting every day of my life, really."

She stopped, like a talking toy whose pull string has run out. There was a moment of stunned silence until Chris said, "You might contact one Grant Havers. You two appear to have a lot in common."

Luckily Grant was in the men's room or we'd never have gotten rid of the girl. I opened the door for her in what could've been construed as a helpful gesture by those who didn't know me very well. "You can send a resume to us care of the library next week." She took the hint and left us in peace. Even better, the dessert, white chocolate mousse cake, was brought in by a less annoying member of the caterer's staff.

"This case had more holes in it than ten year old underwear," said Brad as he leaned back in a chair and ran his lines. "Why had Von Krump sent his plug uglies after me? It didn't seem like his style, but then Krauts never did have much sense in the style department. Still, I didn't think it was him. And if it wasn't Jimmy the Weasel or Stinky Dano who'd tried to put a hole in my favorite brain, that only left one person. One Ball Mahoney, sprung from the pen on account of graft in high places."

"That was a wonderful performance, Brad!" Franklin burst into the room and was now enthusiastically pumping Brad's hand up and down. This was his second appearance in our 'green room' to congratulate us since dinner had started; he'd been bubbling over with energy and excitement then as well. "You have taken the character of Club, peeled it open and boiled it down to the purest essence of Randell!"

Daphne and I grinned at each other behind Franklin's back. I don't think he realized this was a parody.

"I'm quite pleased with tonight!" he continued, oblivious to our amusement at his expense. "The Gala is completely sold out! The interest in Randell appears to be at a peak in Emerald Cove."

I couldn't resist it. "Franklin, don't you think that a large portion of the interest in tonight's event stems from all the publicity that Burke and Lucille's deaths have generated? It's got more to do with morbid curiosity than reverence for Shay Randell."

"Oh, I think you're being pessimistic, Connie." Franklin's expression was earnest and a little annoyed. "Granted, there are a few idle curiosity seekers among the audience—"

"Lookeeloos!" chorused Chris and Brad.

Franklin looked startled. "Uh, yes, if you will. But I think you'll find that this festival represents a major rediscovery of Randell by the mass populace. One that is long overdue, by my reckoning." He paused as the office door opened again. "And here's Andy! Well done, sir, well done!" Franklin grabbed Andy's hand and shook it vigorously.

"Thanks, Franklin." Andy looked as distracted as I'd ever seen him as he said, "Yeah, great job, you guys. Are you about ready to start Act II? They should be finishing up with dessert in about ten minutes."

"We'll be ready," Daphne assured him. He nodded and started to follow Franklin back out into the main library.

"Andy, is there anything wrong?"

"No, no, nothing …" He paused, waiting until Franklin had left the room and closed the door behind him. Andy looked after him with a small shake of his head. "That man will drive me to my grave yet."

"Seriously, Andy, what's up?"

He turned back to me. "Well, let's see. Detective O'Donohue is sitting at the ten thousand dollar table listening to Mrs. Romney—" That would be Marion Romney, wife of our most prominent city counselor "—explain how she thinks the murders are connected to a huge international drug smuggling operation, Lucille supposedly having been a key member of said ring—"

"O'Donohue is out there?" Daphne didn't look too happy with the news. I didn't blame her, considering the results of her discussion with Arthur Sloan and the likely displeasure of the detective-sergeant in question.

An even more unpleasant thought occurred to me. "Does that mean Honey is out there too?"

Andy shook his head. "No, O'Donohue assured me that Honey has been told to stay away from the library tonight."

"Why is O'Donohue here at all?" I asked. "We're nowhere near the cave. He couldn't possibly think there's going to be a problem here!"

Andy looked even gloomier. "He's here to help us all feel more secure. Or so he says."

"Pull the other one," Daphne snorted.

"Yeah, I know. Anyway, Honey might have been told to stay away, but I saw him cruising slowly by in his car when I went out to check on the valet parking. He doesn't look happy, kind of like the kid who wasn't invited to the party." Andy looked pretty unhappy himself. "Everyone connected to this festival seems to be going crazy. I got a couple of phone calls this afternoon, you would not believe how stupid they were. I mean, just on and on about the craziest things—"

Daphne gave him a quick hug and said, "Don't worry. In a few hours the whole thing will be over."

"I only wish it were that simple." Andy gave a heavy sigh. "But until the police figure out who the killer is, we're all going to be under suspicion. Let's face it, I couldn't stand either Burke or Lucille and I wasn't exactly quiet about my feelings."

"Neither was I," I said by way of comfort. "And I'd think that'd be more of a reason to think both of us are innocent."

Andy considered the idea. "Maybe you're right."

Grant came back into the room at that moment and gave Andy what I considered an unnecessarily cold look before turning an even frostier one on me. "I believe it's time to start the second act. They've cleared the dessert plates."

Mart hefted her saxophone. "I'll go start warming up the crowd."

I nodded. "You ready for your big scene, Andy?"

Andy brightened considerably. We'd given him a last minute cameo as an innocent bystander who gets plugged by the Weasel to show Club that he means business and Andy was thrilled to death—if you'll pardon the pun—to be included. "Should I stay dead until the end of the play?"

Ignoring Grant's derisive little laugh, I said, "As long as you can stand it. Try and set yourself up so that you die in front of the tables. That way you can watch the rest of the show."

The saxophone strains of Club's theme music drifted into the room as Mart took the floor. Immediately the actors gathered up their props and their characters. My stomach gave one nervous lurch as it always did before every act of every performance. We all made our way quietly into the small foyer that served as our backstage area. Alex gave me a quick reassuring smile when he caught my eye. If Grant noticed the exchange, he gave no sign, concentrating on adjusting his German officer's hat to the proper rakish angle. I had to admit Grant always gave 110 percent to his performances, both on and off stage.

The audience finished assembling in the lobby and I nodded to Brad. Pulling the collar of his worn trenchcoat up around his neck, Brad walked slowly to center stage, surveyed the crowd with a challenging stare and launched into the same speech he'd been rehearsing moments before.

I relaxed almost immediately. The alcohol had turned a receptive audience into a well-lubricated and appreciative crowd that roared with laughter at even our worst jokes. They laughed at the name One-Ball Mahoney, for chrissake!

Andy was standing to the right with several prominent celebrities. He looked a lot more cheerful and I felt a surge of altruistic pride that our show was helping to lighten his mood.

I caught sight of O'Donohue standing in back of the crowd. It looked like he was actually enjoying the show without the benefits of alcohol, unless it was just the relief of being free of Honey for a couple of hours that was making him smile. I watched as he laughed at Club's scene with O'Malley, the drunk Irish cop (that's right, no stereotype is too cliché for MFH). He caught me looking at him and gave a little 'thumbs up' gesture. I smiled back, more than a little relieved that he apparently wasn't holding the article in the Post against us.

It was time for Daphne's second appearance as Irene Malone, good girl gone bad as Club tries to get information out of her about her no-good boyfriend, Jimmy the Weasel. She's about to spill the beans when the Weasel appears just in time to slap her around and threaten Club. It was in this scene that we'd added Andy's 'death' to spice things up a bit. Audiences love it when one of their own, so to speak, gets pulled into the action. Lucille would've no doubt been appalled by Andy's participation. But not as appalled as she would've been had she known what part she would end up playing in our last walking tour.

Okay, enough of *that* line of thought. I concentrated on the show, my attention re-captured by Daphne's piercing squeal as she greeted The Weasel. Dogs were no doubt perking their ears up throughout Emerald Cove.

"So, you were gonna spill the beans, huh, dollface?"

"No, Jimmy, I wasn't! I swear it!"

The Weasel smacked Irene across the face, eliciting another squeal that could break glass.

"What's the matter, Weasel?" Club stepped forward. "You gotta beat up a woman to show how tough you are?"

And so on as Club and the Weasel exchanged macho threats, up to the point where the Weasel pulls out his revolver and tells Club that if he won't play ball …

" … people are gonna get hurt, see? Innocent people."

"You don't have the guts, Weasel."

Whereupon the Weasel fired into the audience, 'hitting' a pre-positioned Andy, who clutched his chest, uttered an "arrrgggh!" worthy of a Barrymore and staggered a few steps to drop 'dead' in front of a table. I noticed he made sure he could still see most of the action. I also noticed our corpse shaking with laughter as Club checked his pulse. Definitely no fear of rigor mortis setting in any time soon.

Grant tapped me on my shoulder and whispered, "Do you have the other revolver?" He looked worried. Trust Grant to *not* trust me to do my job.

Annoyed, I whispered back, "Of course I do!" I turned away from him before he could say anything else to piss me off and snuck a quick look in my evening bag just to be safe. Yup, my .38 was tucked away, handle up so I could grab it easily.

Daphne and Alex hurried back into the hallway and I gave them a thumbs up. Jah, folks, it vas now time for Lila Vilmer to make her appearance. And as with all dames in our play, Club gave me an introduction.

"She came at me in sections, with more curves than Lombard Street—"

I defy anyone but Cyd Charise to live up to that description.

"—I wouldn't trust her as far as I could throw her, but there was something about her."

I sat down across from Club, making sure my cleavage was displayed to the best of its advantage. At least according to Club's narrative. And so the scene continued, Lila Vilmer promising Club the location of the Peruvian Pigeon (it's loaded with snow!) in return for money until he exposes her true identity as a two-bit stripper, who stole the pigeon for Von Krump, who promised her a job at the Follies Berger (hey, if you want logic, don't hire us). At that point, Grant made his entrance as Von Krump, looking quite dashing in his uniform. I'm sure more than one heart skipped a beat in our audience. Mine, however, was not one of them.

Grant strode over to me, taking me by one arm.

"Haf you missed me, my strudel?"

"Get your hands offa me!"

"Still charming as ever. But perhaps I can be persuaded to take you back. There is a certain charm to your unrefined manner."

Oh, the irony of art imitating life. There was more than a little vehemence in my reply.

"I wouldn't go back to you if you were the last man on earth, ya Kraut creep!"

Grant's eyes spoke volumes and his grip on my arm hurt as he shot back, "You may not have a choice, liebchen."

Von Krump's attention switched to Club at that point, as his thugs beat the crap out of the stalwart detective to find out the location of the pigeon. Grant is supposed to shove me into a chair and leave me there, but for some reason he chose to keep a hold of me throughout most of the scene. I tried moving away, but he jerked me back against him. This was getting really irritating. I couldn't believe that Grant would act so unprofessional. In a few minutes I was supposed to shoot Von Krump in the shoulder so Club could get away. How the hell was I supposed to do that if Grant wouldn't let go of me? Rather than make a scene during the scene, I waited.

"Just when I thought I was on my way to the slabhouse," said Club as the two thugs worked their way up and down his face and torso with their fists, "Zelda made like a canary and started to sing."

"Stop it, already! He doesn't have it!"

"Enough! Very vell, my *lederhosen. Sprechen sie. Sprechen sie!*"

"The bird was sent to Carl's office."

The scene continued, Grant's fingers still digging into my arms. This was the outside of enough. Deciding that Vilmer aka Zelda the Zipper could get away with it, I deliberately stepped backwards with my heel onto Grant's foot, eliciting both a yelp of pain and my release as his grip involuntarily loosened. He shot me an outraged glance as the audience laughed. Hah. Never mess with a gal in heels. Hmmm. Not a bad line. Maybe we should add it to the script. Never mind, I thought as Damien Duran's death flashed into my head.

I moved behind Club as Von Krump made a grab for me. All of this was part of established blocking and I gave a mental sigh of relief as I pulled out my revolver and pointed it at Von Krump so Club could make his getaway. Von Krump glared at us as he spat out the words:

> *You may get away this time, Club, but you haven't seen the last of me! I vill return. I vill be back and vhen I find you, you will vish you had never been born!*

Club takes this opportunity to escape, but not, of course, without making another patriotic speech.

> *I'll be waiting for you, Von Krump. Because it's men like me who stand between the freedom and decency of the Stars and Stripes, and the death and destruction that lurk beneath the shadow of the Swastika! I'll be waiting. And I'll be ready. You can bank your balls on that!*

As Club turned to leave, Von Krump made a sudden lunge towards him. I fired my revolver, my arm jerking back with the recoil as Von Krump was hit in the left shoulder.

Grant spun around and clutched the shoulder, face white with shock as blood spurted out from between his fingers. Even as I admired his acting and the bloodpack, I realized there was something wrong. A recoil is caused by the inertia of the bullet being pushed out of the barrel. I shouldn't have felt anything from the quarter load blank with flash cotton.

The bullet fired from my revolver had not been a blank.

Chapter Eighteen

Even as my mind was rejecting the possibility that I'd really shot him, I automatically grabbed Grant's arm, both as part of the blocking and to support him. His face was white and his knees began to buckle. My brain was split into two sections, one hysterically screaming, "Oh, shit, he's bleeding!" and all sorts of other useless things, while the other half was calm and almost disassociated from the whole situation. Luckily it was the latter half of my mind that took control and told me to get Grant off stage before anyone else realized that he'd been shot with a real bullet.

"Give me a hand vit your boss," I said to the thugs, Chris and Shaun. "I vill take you to our little chateau in Düsseldorf, mein poopsie, vere you vill get better …"

I babbled on in character all the way through the hallway past the other actors to the back office, where Grant immediately collapsed onto a chair, hand still clutching his shoulder.

"Get O'Donohue in here!" I turned to Shaun, who was staring at Grant's bloody shoulder with incomprehension. "Try to do it quietly, if you can. It's nearly time for the second break, thank God, so you might be able to get him without anyone noticing."

Shaun nodded and left the room. I turned to Chris and snapped, "Help me get his coat off. Carefully!"

Grant was unusually silent as Chris and I slowly peeled off his trench coat. His face was still pale and sweat was pouring off his forehead. I assumed it was shock. I knew you were supposed to keep shock victims warm, but right now it seemed more important to find out just how much damage had been done by the bullet. We managed to get the trench off without Grant doing more than giving a sharp hissing intake of breath as the coat passed over the wound.

"Wow." Even Chris was impressed as we stared at the mess that was once a white shirt. There was so much blood … I didn't know where to start, if the bullet had passed through the flesh or was still in his shoulder. I caught myself before I started hyperventilating. Now was not the time for me to lose control.

"Chris ..." My voice came out a high squeak so I tried again. "Chris, please get some paper towels."

"Wet or dry?"

"Both."

Chris saluted and went to get the towels. He was calm in times of crisis. His attitude helped, because I was close to losing it, my control slipping every time I looked at Grant's bloody shoulder.

Grant sat with his eyes shut and teeth clenched as I tried to figure out where the bullet had entered without actually touching anything.

"Connie," he finally said in a hoarse whisper.

"Yes?" I replied, trying not to burst into tears.

"I think you should hold something against it to stop the bleeding. I'm feeling sick."

"Oh God, Grant, I'm sorry!" I immediately grabbed the nearest piece of cloth at hand, his trench coat, and pressed a sleeve against his shoulder.

"What happened, Connie?" His tone was neutral, but the accusation was there nonetheless.

I focused on the shoulder, not wanting to look at his face. "I ... I don't know."

"I thought you always checked the weapons for safety."

"I did! I mean, I usually do, but Alex took care of it this time, and—"

"I see."

I looked at him then, shocked as I read the silent accusation in his eyes. "Grant, it was an accident. There must have been a full load instead of a quarter mixed in the blanks, but ..." He just stared at me. "Grant, I swear to you it was a mistake. I know we fought, but I'd never ... I wouldn't ..." I shook my head as words failed me, and burst into tears as the realization that I could've killed him hit me like a right cross to the jaw.

"Shhhh ... ." Grant stroked my hair with his uninjured arm as I cried into the unused portion of the coat, still trying to maintain a steady pressure on his wound. "Shhhh ... it's all right, darling. It wasn't your fault ..." I felt his lips on the top of my head.

It was this tender scene that Chris walked in on. He carried loads of paper towels and was followed by the rest of the actors, including Alex. A disturbing mixture of anger and jealousy flickered over Alex's face, but was quickly replaced by concern as his eyes took in the blood. Before he could react any further, Daphne pushed her way forward and exclaimed in frankly horrified tones, "What happened?"

Before I could respond, Shaun and Andy came in with O'Donohue, who quickly took charge of the situation. He posted Andy by the door with, "Make sure no one else comes in here." Then he came over to where Grant and I were and knelt down by the chair. "Ms. Garrett, are you all right?" he asked me gently.

"Y ... yes," I replied, my tears having diminished to a few watery sniffles. "It's Grant. I shot him." Shit. There went the waterworks again. Chris handed me a couple of paper towels. I could hear the sound of the band starting up again.

"It's just a flesh wound," Grant told O'Donohue. "And it was an accident. It's not Connie's fault."

"Yeah," Daphne interjected. "I mean, we don't use real bullets. They're all supposed to be blanks."

"You *did* load all blanks, didn't you, Alex?" Grant's tone wasn't exactly accusatory, but it wasn't friendly either.

Alex's expression was downright hostile, but before he could reply, O'Donohue verbally stepped between them with "We'll get to that in a bit. Now let's have a look here ..." He removed the trench coat from Grant's shoulder and handed it to me. I hung on to the as though it was a lifeline as O'Donohue removed a section of Grant's shirt with the help of a pair of scissors. "Hand over a couple of those wet towels, please." He held out his hand without looking, like a surgeon at the operating table. Chris, like any good nurse, promptly deposited a wad of dripping towels into the detective's outstretched hand. O'Donohue did a double take as water ran down his arm. Chris shrugged. I'd told him wet, after all.

O'Donohue wrung out the paper as best he could and carefully mopped away some of the excess blood, continuously wiping up the fresh flow as he examined the wound. After a minute, he said, "Dry towels, please." Chris obliged. O'Donohue pressed the towels against the wound and looked at me. "Can you hold these here for now?"

I nodded and slipped my hand under O'Donohue's as he let go of the towels. Grant reached up and gently touched my face as I knelt by his side. God, I hope he didn't think this meant we were back together. I mean, if you accidentally shoot a guy, does it mean you're obligated to date him?

"Someone get some brandy from the bar," said O'Donohue. "It'll help the shock."

"I'll get it." Mart set down her saxophone and hurried out the door as O'Donohue continued, "The bullet only grazed the shoulder. It's not too deep, so barring infection there's nothing to worry about."

"Oh thank God ..." I heaved a soggy sigh of relief.

"But I still want him to go to the emergency room and have it cleaned out."

Grant started to protest, but O'Donohue cut him off. "With the risk of infection, you don't want to leave the wound untended." His voice took on a vaguely sardonic inflection as he added, "Even if it *is* only a flesh wound."

Guilt circuit on overdrive, I immediately said, "I'll drive him there."

"You can't, Connie!"

I turned to Daphne and demanded, "Why not?"

Alex answered for her, voice and face expressionless. "You're in the last act."

"Shit." I'd completely forgotten about the rest of the show.

"So am I," said Grant, his color slightly better than a few minutes ago. "And it's too late for an understudy to learn my lines."

As much as I hated to say it ..."He's right. We need him for the last act."

"And you know what they say—" Don't say it, I thought. But I knew he would. Even another bullet in the shoulder wouldn't have stopped him. "—the show must go on."

O'Donohue shook his head. "You guys are all nuts."

"No ..." Grant paused. "Actors."

I swear, he'd still be on stage in the middle of Armageddon. And I'm not talking about the crappy movie with Bruce Willis.

Andy, who had been listening from his post by the door, stepped forward and said, "There's a first aid kit somewhere around here."

O'Donohue sighed. "Okay. See if you can find it and we'll clean this up best we can here. But after the show, I want you at the ER. And the rest of you will need to stay here and answer some questions."

Grant nodded, stoically noble in his pain. Yup, now that the shock was wearing off, I could tell he was enjoying his role as wounded hero. Which was fine by me, because it helped turn me from Connie, hysterical female back into Connie, competent director.

A thought occurred to me. "What about the bullet?" Everyone looked at me. "I mean, if it *was* a bullet and not a full load blank. If the bullet didn't lodge in Grant's shoulder, it has to have continued on its trajectory and hit something else."

Daphne shrugged. "Well, I think it's safe to assume no one else was hit or we'd have heard about it by now."

"I didn't hear anything break," Brad said thoughtfully. "What about you guys?"

Chris and Shaun shook their heads 'no.'

"I doubt you'd notice under the circumstances unless a window had shattered or the bullet ricocheted off something metal," said O'Donohue. "We'll wait until the Gala is over to conduct the investigation."

Andy handed him a first aid kit. "I appreciate that, Detective. All of us do. We've spent so much time preparing for this night, I'm not sure what would happen if we had to cut it short."

O'Donohue sighed. "This particular crime scene is already so contaminated, I don't suppose it'll hurt. I'm assuming there aren't any more guns fired in your play?"

Both Daphne and I nodded.

"Which reminds me. The gun you fired, Ms. Garrett. Where is it?"

I pulled the revolver out of my black velvet bag and handed it over. He took it with his handkerchief and I gave a small humorless laugh. "There's not an actor in our troupe that hasn't handled that thing, not to mention the library staff and anyone else who's been in this room tonight."

"Ah." He popped open the chamber and ejected the bullets into his hand, examining them closely. Alex watched intently over his shoulder. "Well, these are all blanks."

I heaved another sigh of relief. "Then the one must've just been a full load."

"They were all quarter custom loads with flash cotton," Alex snapped. "I loaded them myself and I've got a damned good safety record."

I almost took a step back away from the anger in his eyes. "Alex—" I stopped, not sure of what to say. Unfortunately, Grant was not at a similar loss for words.

"There's always a first time for everything, including mistakes."

Alex's lips thinned, but he kept himself under control. Turning to O'Donohue, he said tightly, "I've got a Class One license for handling firearms. I'll be happy to show it to you."

O'Donohue nodded. "We'll deal with that later. For now just to be on the safe side, do you have any other guns?"

Grateful to have something else to think about, I did a quick mental tally of our hardware. "We have three guns that actually fire blanks. The others are just cap guns and plastic toys, like Chris's Tommy gun."

Chris gave his gun a demonstrative crank, the resulting sound like marbles in a tin can. O'Donohue grinned. "That's not a problem. Let me see the other blank guns.'

Brad immediately withdrew his .38 from his trenchcoat pocket and placed it on the table. Alex set his revolver down with just a little bit of a slam, not meeting my eyes. Shit.

O'Donohue checked the two guns. "Blanks," he said, and handed the guns back to their owners as Mart, bless her, returned with an entire bottle of very good brandy. "It's just about time for curtain," she said, pouring the brandy into paper cups and passed it out to all of the cast members, including Andy. O'Donohue shook his head when offered some, concentrating on cleaning up Grant's wound.

Alex downed his brandy in one gulp, crumpled up the cup and tossed it in the trash. Grant sipped his at a more leisurely pace, his color much improved. I didn't know what to say to either of them at that moment. Shooting Grant seemed to have improved my working relationship with him, but it wasn't helping things between Alex and me. He was furious that I thought he might have made an error when loading the blanks, and truth be told, I didn't blame him. Not a very good sign of faith on my part. And yet ... how had it happened if Alex hadn't made a mistake? What else was I supposed to think? What gave him the right to be pissed off at me for a logical assumption?

My rapid switch from remorse to anger reminded me of a slogan I'd read on a T-Shirt. 'Warning: I can go from sweetheart to bitch in 5 seconds flat.' Too true. And I didn't know which, if either, emotion was reasonable in the current circumstances.

I walked away from everyone else and nibbled nervously on leftover mousse cake, breaking off a piece of white chocolate trim as I tried not to pursue that particular line of thought any further for the moment. I wondered if I'd ever be able to do a show in the future without compulsively checking the chamber of my gun over and over again. Or if I'd even be able to pull the trigger. This festival had turned into a nightmare.

Brad came up, put an arm around my shoulder and squeezed. "It'll be all right, Connie. It's almost over and Grant'll be healed up in no time. Just our luck."

I smiled shakily. "Thanks, Brad. I'm just glad I don't have any more scenes with a gun."

O'Donohue straightened up and closed the first aid kit. "Okay, I'm finished. I'd better get back out in the audience."

I came back over and looked at his work The shoulder was now neatly bandaged, all excess blood wiped away. "How do you feel?" I asked.

"Not bad, all things considered." Grant smiled up at me and gave my hand a brief squeeze. "I'll need another shirt, though." O'Donohue had removed the ruined one, which now lay in a crumpled bloody heap on the table. My stomach gave a queasy turn and I wished I hadn't eaten that mousse cake.

"I'll get it." I went over to the costume table and found a clean white shirt, one of many that we'd purchased at thrift stores. As I helped Grant slip the shirt on, the band stopped playing and Mart went out into the library with her saxophone. Brad adjusted his fedora, grabbed his unlit cigarette and followed her. Grant stood up, wincing only slightly as he put on his Frenchman jacket and beret. With one last lingering touch on my arm, he too left the room. That left Daphne, Shaun, Chris, Tasha, and Alex, who should have had a storm-warning posted because of the cloud over his head.

Suddenly I realized I was supposed to be on-stage in five minutes. "Oh my god, I've got to change costumes!" Modesty cast to the wind, I hurriedly shimmied out of my Vilmer velvets and into the dowdy skirt and jacket I wore as Betty, Club's faithful secretary and Girl Friday. A brief glance assured me that our Peruvian Pigeon—a replica of the Maltese Falcon that we'd bought from our local mystery bookstore—was where it was supposed to be so I could locate it for the last scene.

I'd deal with Alex later. At the risk of sounding like Grant, right now I had a show to worry about.

Chapter Nineteen

Our final bow was met with thunderous applause by the pleasantly inebriated crowd. The third act had gone without a hitch: no late entrances, no missed cues, and no bullet wounds to screw up the works. Megan Fitzpatrick (aka Tasha) was unmasked as the real villain of the piece, and Carl Club had won yet another fight against corruption in the big city. Even better, all the flyers and business cards we'd placed on the desk were gone.

Trying to get back to the office after the show proved difficult as all of the actors were continually waylaid by guests wanting to give their congratulations. I usually love this part. Both Daphne and I tend to operate on pure adrenaline through most of our performances, so it takes awhile for the rush to wear off once the show is over. Schmoozing with friends and audience members is the perfect way to come down gently, so to speak. This time, however, all I could think of now was finding out exactly what had been in that gun.

Grant was as charming as ever to all admirers, no doubt keeping on his best face for that casting director, if they'd showed. And if he was in pain, he didn't show it. Ouch. Except when a well-intentioned gentleman slapped him on the shoulder.

I looked for Alex. He was surrounded by people, mostly women. He was giving every indication of enjoying the attention and not once did he even glance in my direction. I was amazed at how much it hurt considering I'd only known him for what? Three days? I was more than a little angry at his behavior. Wasn't it also a little early for the 'too good to be true' illusions to be shattered? I guess some of that old stuntman ego lurked in him after all. Damn.

I navigated my way through the crowd towards Daphne, who was talking to an unobtrusive-looking man in his sixties, obviously wealthy. Time served with Grant had taught me enough to recognize quality clothing when I saw it and this gentleman's suit had to have been tailored to fit him.

He shook Daphne's hand and walked away into the crowd right before

I reached her. Daphne saw me coming. "Connie, we've got more work! That man I was talking to? He *loved* the show! And he actually mentioned the writing specifically! And knew that *we* wrote it!"

I was pleased. Far too often the writing was either shoved in the background behind our flamboyant cast or it was assumed that one of the men, usually Brad, was the writer. It was nice to get credit *and* praise for our work all in one compliment.

Daphne wasn't through. "The best part, though, is that he says he wants to hire us for some other events. He said he'll contact us next week."

"What's his name?"

Daphne looked chagrined. "You know, I didn't even think to ask. You know how it is after a show. Oh well, he said he'd call."

"Let's start packing up our gear."

Daphne nodded and we made our way to the office. Before we had time to do more than walk in the door, Andy burst into the room, his mood noticeably lighter. He was carrying two bottles of Veuve Cliquot champagne. "You were great!" he said sincerely, giving both of us huge bear hugs. "Tonight went better than I'd hoped and a lot of that was because of Murder for Hire. I just spoke to Jason Downs and he was very impressed with the show, especially the writing. *Very* impressed! He sent this—" He held up the bottles of champagne "—for the cast with his compliments.

"Jason Downs?" Daphne exclaimed. "Is he still here?"

"Why, sure! But weren't you just talking to him, Daphne?"

We looked at each other and dashed to the door, scanning the crowd. Mr. Downs was nowhere in sight.

"Do you remember what he looks like?" I asked.

Daphne shook her head. "Rats."

We both started laughing, the kind of laughter that stems from nervous energy rapidly fading into exhaustion. Ah well, at least we knew he really existed.

Andy popped the cork on one of the bottles. As if by magic, the cast started trickling back into the office and Andy filled glasses for all of us, including himself. He raised his glass. "To the cast and creators of Murder For Hire!"

We all clinked glasses, one of those silly everyone having to touch everyone else's glass routines. All I have to say is that it's a good thing we were using plastic flutes because the force behind Alex and Grant's toast would've certainly shattered glass. On the other hand, Alex barely touched my flute with his, and once again downed the contents as if doing shots. Andy immediately refilled the glass. I couldn't resist. I moved next to him and said, "You want some salt and a slice of lime with that?"

Alex looked down at me. Okay, he glared down at me. But I thought I saw a glimmer of a smile somewhere deep behind the anger in his eyes. Just a glimmer, though. Not enough to break through the barrier that'd been slammed up between us.

Andy toasted us again. "You all enjoy yourselves. I'd better go mingle." As he left, O'Donohue came into the room. "I just wanted to let you all know that as soon as the crowd clears out, I'll need Ms. Garrett and whoever else was in the scene to help re-create the positions you were in when the gun was fired." He looked at Grant. "Mr. Havers, are you up to this?"

Grant nodded. It was amazing how he managed to convey just a hint of the wounded man bravely staying behind to help his fellow soldiers without actually *doing* anything. And it was amazing that I'd think such a bitchy thought considering he really *was* injured and that I'd been the one to inflict said injury. I was beginning to suspect that I just wasn't a very nice person. I drank some more champagne, wishing I were home in bed.

"Is it okay if we get our stuff together?" I asked O'Donohue. "I'd like to leave as soon as we're finished."

O'Donohue considered my request. "That shouldn't be a problem. Although I'd like you to leave the boxes of blanks so I can check them out. In the meantime, I'm going to ask the catering staff some questions. I'll see you out front in about fifteen minutes." He left, shutting the door behind him.

Against my better judgment I let Brad refill my glass with champagne. My head was starting to ache again and I knew I might have to take another migraine pill, but somehow at the moment I just didn't care. Downing the champagne in several gulps, I made myself stand up and started methodically gathering up costumes and props, dumping everything unceremoniously into our bags to be sorted out later. Everyone else, with the exception of Grant, helped, but for once he had a good excuse to be sitting down while the rest of us worked.

Alex handed me Grant's trenchcoat without a word. I winced at the sight of the shredded shoulder, tacky with drying blood, and stuffed it in one of the bags. I'd decide whether to toss it out or keep it later.

Grant had his eyes closed, as tired as I'd ever seen him. Guilt hit me anew. "Grant, do you want me to drive you to the ER when we're finished?"

He shook his head. "No, I'll drive myself."

I was surprised. I would've thought he'd play this particular wild card for all it was worth. "Are you sure? I mean, with the blood loss, you probably shouldn't be driving, especially since you've had brandy and champagne—"

"It's only a few blocks, Connie, and if they think I should have some-one else drive home, I'll call Max or Sarah. Since I'm staying at their home, it makes more sense." He looked at me with what I swore was genuine concern. "Besides, you're in worse shape than I am after this last week. You need to go home and get some sleep."

He did have a point, and I was too tired to argue, no matter how guilty I felt. "Just call me and let me know when you get there, okay?"

"I promise." He reached out and took my hand. "You did a wonderful job tonight." Before I could take my hand back, he'd brought it to his lips and kissed it. I restrained an impulse to wipe my hand on my dress, and smiled weakly, turning back to my work. I deliberately ignored everything and everyone except for the objects in front of me.

By the time we finished gathering up our mess, O'Donohue was ready for us in the library. With the exception of Franklin, all of the guests were gone. Unfortunately Honey had stopped cruising the mean streets of Em-erald Cove and was now at his partner's side, pen and notebook poised for action. I supposed it was a good thing he wasn't as enamored of his gun.

Andy stood off to one side sipping his glass of champagne and looking very pleased with himself, as well he should after all the work he'd done and the shit he'd had to put up with. Franklin was at the front desk, pour-ing himself a liberal amount of Chopin vodka into a plastic tumbler. He must've snagged the bottle before the catering crew had packed it up. Judg-ing from the exaggerated care with which he poured, he must've already put away a few shots. At least he had good taste in vodka.

As I tried to remember exactly where I'd ended up in the Vilmer/Von Krump scene, I noticed Franklin stroll over to Andy and put an arm around his shoulders as he said something I couldn't hear. Andy nodded and the two of them went back towards the offices. Andy paused for a moment. "Will you need me for anything else, Detective?"

O'Donohue thought it over and replied, "No, I don't think so. If I do, I'll let you know."

"Then I'll say good night to everyone now and close up when you're finished." He gave Daphne and me one last smile. "Thanks again, girls! And the rest of you too!" With that, he and Franklin vanished around the corner.

Tasha tugged on Brad's arm. "Honey, I'm gonna wait in the car." She yawned as she turned to O'Donohue and added, "If that's okay."

Honey looked as though he was going to put his worthless two cents in, but O'Donohue beat him to the punch. "That's fine. In fact—" this to Mart "—you can leave too, if you'd like." To Alex, he said almost apolo-getically, "I'd prefer that you stay around until we figure out exactly what hit Mr. Havers."

Alex didn't look pleased, but he didn't argue.

O'Donohue turned back to his 'actors.' I took my position, hand raised as if firing a gun. "I was here when I fired the shot."

O'Donohue nodded. "And where was Mr. Havers?"

"About where Detective Honey is standing."

Honey jumped as if goosed and moved hastily out of the way. What, did he think another stray bullet was going to be fired his direction?

Grant moved into his place, Chris and Shaun right behind him. Shaun studied their location very intently and said in his weighty manner, "I think … Grant was slightly to the … right, more in front of that book case. Right, Chris?"

"Right."

Grant adjusted his position accordingly. Chris and Shaun moved again so that they were in back and slightly to either side of Grant.

"Go ahead and aim," O'Donohue instructed me.

I did so, doing my best to recreate my exact motion. "Does this look right, Brad?" After all, he'd been right behind me when I'd fired.

"Looks good to me."

O'Donohue eyeballed the position and turned. He was now facing Grant and the bookshelf, which would've been hidden from the audience by the entry hall wall. He glanced at Chris, who was standing only inches away from Grant's wounded shoulder. "You're lucky. Bullet or blank, it missed you by inches."

Chris looked unperturbed and said, "I'm a Marine" as if no bullet would dare touch a member of the few and the proud. Or was that the Navy?

O'Donohue nodded gravely as if this made perfect sense and went over for a closer inspection of the shelf. After a brief examination, he pulled out a book. "This would explain why we didn't hear any impact. The bullet—" Omigod, it *was* a bullet! "—lodged in the wood, the sound muffled by the books." He held the book out, spine forward. The hole was obvious, straight through the 'D' in Dashiell. I'd shot *The Maltese Falcon*.

"Talk about cheap symbolism," Brad said solemnly.

I didn't know whether to laugh or cry. I guess I'd been holding on to the thought that it'd just been a mistake in the load of the blank, something with a reasonable explanation. But this? There was no way that someone like Alex—or myself, for that matter—would not have noticed the difference.

Alex was stricken, his face blanched of all color. "Jesus, how could that have happened?" He looked at me. "Connie, I swear to you that I double-checked everything when I loaded those guns."

I opened my mouth with absolutely no idea of what I was going to say, so it was a good thing that O'Donohue beat me out of the gate with, "I'll need to ask you some more questions and go through all of the ammo boxes. It's probably better if we do this down at the station." There was a collective gasp, excluding Honey, of course. Honey might as well have said, "Ahah! We've caught you red-handed!" for all the subtlety of his expression. Grant was also silent, but his thoughts were harder to read.

O'Donohue was aware of the perturbation that his words had caused and added, "I'm hoping that your expertise can help us get to the bottom of this particular mystery, Mr. Barnett. You're not being accused of anything at this time." The words 'at this time' hung in the air.

At that moment, we heard the sound of raised voices, followed by a door slamming. Seconds later Franklin emerged from the office area, a frown on his face and a slight weave to his walk. I hoped he wasn't driving anywhere in the near future.

O'Donohue had the same thought. "Do you need a ride home, Mr. Grace?"

Franklin shook his head. "I live down the street, so I walk." He spoke with the exaggerated enunciation of someone trying to convince themselves that they're sober. "Now if you'll excuse me …" After one unsuccessful attempt to manipulate the handles, which resulted in his walking into the closed doors, Franklin left the library with as much dignity as he could muster.

"Are we finished?" I was so tired and overwrought, I could barely stand up straight.

O'Donohue nodded. "For the time being." His words were punctuated by Honey flipping his notebook closed. "We'll see you all out. Do you mind riding with us, Mr. Barnett? We can bring you back to the library when we're finished."

I somehow got the feeling that this was not a request. Alex nodded reluctantly; I'm sure he had the same feeling.

Grant excused himself for a moment for a visit to 'the facilities', as he put it, while Daphne, Shaun, Chris and I gathered up all the bags so we could load them into my car.

As we went out the doors, I glanced back at Alex, who stayed inside with O'Donohue and Honey. He looked terrible, almost as bad as Grant had when I'd shot him. I wanted to say something to reassure him, but didn't have a clue what that something should be, especially when he wouldn't look at me. I followed Daphne outside, as miserable as I've ever been. The weather reflected my mood: cold, windy, and gloomy. The sky was thick with thunderheads, small drops of rain spitting down from above as we hurried across the parking lot to my car.

I popped the trunk and tossed in my armload of stuff, letting everyone else do the same. Daphne eyed me with some concern. Normally I insist on packing up the trunk myself, fitting things in like a puzzle so nothing gets crushed. Tonight I was just too damned tired. Still, old habits die hard, so I did a cursory check through the bags to make sure.

"Did you pack the Pigeon?" I asked Daphne. "I'm not seeing it in here."

She shook her head. "I remember seeing it on the props table, but I didn't pack it. Are you sure it's not in there?"

I dug through all the bags again. "We must've left it in the library. Let's just pick it up tomorrow, okay? I don't want to go back in there tonight."

Brad came up and gave us each a hug. "You two gonna be okay?"

"We'll be fine," Daphne reassured him.

"I'm gonna take off then. Tasha's snoring in the back seat, so I'd better get her home."

Chris, Shaun and Mart said their good-byes just as Grant came outside, looking pleased with himself, yet walking almost as carefully as Franklin had when he'd left. He was shortly followed by the two detectives and Alex, who was giving Grant a look that should've accomplished what the bullet had failed to do. I didn't want to know what poisonous little interchange had just occurred between the two.

After a brief hesitation, I walked over to Grant as he was deactivating his car alarm. "Are you sure you're okay to drive?"

"The police are going to follow me over to the hospital just to be on the safe side." He pressed another button on his key chain and there was a quiet 'kathunk' as the locks popped up. "I'll call you, Connie. Don't worry about it." Leaning down, Grant kissed me on the cheek and then got in his car.

One down, one to go. Taking a deep breath, I then approached Alex, who was getting into the back of the detectives' car. At least it wasn't the kind with the grilled partition between front and back seat. That would've just been too hard to take.

Honey looked as though he wanted to shoo me away from their car, but a warning glance from O'Donohue was all it took to stop him.

"Alex?" He straightened up at the sound of my voice and turned, his expression somewhere between neutrality and hostility. "Look, I ..." I stopped, once again at a loss for words. What the hell was wrong with me? I tried again. "Alex, I don't think you made a mistake."

"Could've fooled me."

I glared at him, good intentions buried under an avalanche of frustration at his sullen reply. "You know, I shot someone and I don't know how it happened! Put yourself in my shoes for a moment and ask yourself how *you'd* feel! Because you're not being fair!" I turned away and stalked off across the parking lot. I was halfway to my car when I heard, "Connie."

I stopped, not turning around, and snapped, "What?"

There was a long pause, finally ended with a short "Never mind." His words were punctuated by the slam of the car door.

Daphne gave me a sympathetic look as I walked back to my car. A few angry tears snaked down my face, despite my best efforts to hold them back till Alex was gone. I could pretend it was just the rain … if he ever talked to me again.

As if in response to my gloomy thoughts, the rain went from lightly spattering to actual rain drops. I tried not to watch as the detective's car drove out of the parking lot, but my attention was caught by another vehicle pulling in; a florist's truck.

"They're a little late for the Gala," said Daphne.

The florist's truck pulled up and parked right behind my car, blocking us in. A skinny kid in his late teens tumbled out of the driver's side, nerves clearly frazzled. He had an elaborate floral arrangement clutched to his chest, and started spouting apologies and explanations before his feet hit the ground. "Jeez, I'm sorry, I know I'm really late, my boss is gonna kill me, I had flat tire and spun out on the road … jeez, I'm sorry …"

I had a feeling my patience would run out of steam before he did. I cut him off in another round of 'jeez, I'm sorry, I'm really late,' with an abrupt, "Who's it for?"

The kid stopped mid-jeez, and squinted at the little white envelope stuck in one of those pitchfork shaped card holders. "Um … C. Carrot?"

"Carrot?"

"Sorry, the ink is running. Here." He held the card out. Daphne and I took a look at it.

I couldn't blame him; my last name *did* look like it was spelled 'Carrot.'

"It's for her," said Daphne.

"Great! Can you just sign here?" He handed me the flowers, and pulled a clipboard and pen from the front seat of the truck. He started to pass those to me as well, but Daphne intercepted them, scribbled a signature, and handed them back. "Thanks! I'm really sorry I was late—"

"Not a problem," I said, just wanting him to leave so we could get the hell out of there. "But you're blocking our car."

"Jeez, I'm sorry about that …" He was still apologizing as he drove away.

Daphne and I got in the car. I set the flowers down on the seat between us, opened the little white envelope, and read the card.

"For Connie, a swell dame if ever there was one. Here's to the future. Love and anticipation, Alex."

I handed Daphne the card, put my head down on the steering wheel, and cried.

Chapter Twenty

Daphne and I sat on big plaid pillows in front of the fire, wrapped in throws of clashing tartans. We resembled a couple of color-blind Scotsmen. We each had the inevitable mug of cocoa, with a full thermos standing by for refills. Daphne stared morosely out the window at the rain-slicked streets, the dim glow of the streetlights barely discernible through the storm. The light shower that'd started when we'd left the library had increased to a steady downpour, made worse by harsh gusts of wind that periodically rattled the window frames.

I cradled my half-empty mug and wondered if things could get any worse. I was still waiting for a phone call from Grant, worrying that his wound had been worse than O'Donohue had diagnosed. "What if Grant develops gangrene or something?" I said aloud. "What if he has to have his arm amputated?"

"You've seen *Gone With the Wind* too many times," said my level-headed partner.

"Well, he should've called by now."

"Connie, he's probably still in the waiting room," Daphne said reasonably. "It's only been an hour since we got home and you know how long it can take in the emergency room."

"Then they shouldn't call it that," I muttered darkly. "They should call it the 'hey, don't worry if you bleed to death' room if it's gonna take them so friggin' long to do something!"

Daphne wisely refrained from comment. She was right and I knew it, but I kept worrying anyway. It was better than trying to reroute my train of thought whenever it chugged up the tracks to Alex. I'd put the flowers in a dark corner so I wouldn't look at them; every time I saw them, I wanted to cry. And my eyes were still red and swollen from my mini breakdown in the library parking lot.

Daphne refilled our mugs from the thermos. "Connie—" Daphne paused for a moment, and then said, "Do you think Alex made a mistake?"

"I just don't know what to think," I said. "For someone who knows his job, that's a hard mistake to make."

"Do you think ... could he have done it on purpose?"

I shook my head emphatically, but my voice was less assured as I replied, "I just can't believe that. Why would he?"

"Well, jealousy is one of the classic motives for murder."

I gave a snort of laughter. "We've only known each other for three days."

"You two have gotten awfully close in three days."

"Yeah, but that's hardly time to develop the kind of grand passion that leads to murder. And Grant and I broke up."

"Did you tell Alex?"

"Of course I—" I stopped mid-sentence. Had I told Alex that Grant and I had officially called it quits last night? I replayed last night's events. "No, I didn't have time," I admitted reluctantly. "I was going to tell him after the show." Daphne just looked at me, so I hastily added, "But that still doesn't mean he tried to kill Grant. Besides, I think it's gotta be the same person that murdered Lucille and Burke. I mean, what are the odds that there are two killers running around Emerald Cove?"

Daphne sipped her cocoa thoughtfully. "Didn't you say that Alex had met Lucille before in Los Angeles?"

"He worked for her husband," I said slowly. "But that doesn't mean that they ever met or that ..." My words trailed off as I recalled the brief exchange between Alex and Lucille at the showing of *Down These Mean Streets* the other night. A vision of Lucille's red-taloned fingers running up and down Alex's arm flashed into my mind, along with the words "You do look familiar" and something to do with the virility of stuntmen ...

"What?" said Daphne, reading my worried expression.

I told her what I'd remembered, adding hastily, "But she also said something about being surprised she hadn't gotten to know him better. Not exactly basis for murder, right?"

"No-o-o, I guess not ..." Daphne looked doubtful. "But what if she wanted to get to know him better?"

"He'd say 'no.'"

"What if she wouldn't take 'no' for an answer?"

"You think she tried to rip his clothes off and have her wicked way with him?" I laughed. "Hell, I bet even Mavis would beat her in a wrestling match. Most of Lucille's weight was in her boobs." I know, I know, speaking ill of the dead isn't nice. And yet ... somehow I just didn't feel guilty.

"What if she tried to blackmail him?"

"That's just silly. He's a stuntman, not a politician."

"Maybe someone got hurt on one of his films and it was his fault, but no one saw it but Lucille."

I rolled my eyes, exasperated. "'I Saw What You Did Last B-Movie?' I don't think so. Besides, what about Burke? Or did he want to sleep with Alex too?"

There was a pause as we looked at each other, both said "Eeeeuwww!" and started laughing. Daphne and I never have been able to sustain any kind of disagreement longer than five minutes.

I took another swig of cocoa. "Seriously, Daph, you don't really think Alex killed anyone, do you?"

Daphne considered this, then shook her head 'no.' "Nah. Although I really couldn't blame him if he *did* try to knock off Grant after the way the jerk's been acting. Er ... sorry," she added, seeing my suddenly guilt-stricken expression.

"That's okay," I said. It wasn't her fault that Grant was an asshole, or that I'd shot him. "I just don't want to think about Grant or Alex or murder any more."

I looked around for a distraction and eyed the stacks of bags sitting in the entryway hall waiting to be unpacked. Nah. Too much effort. My gaze then fell upon the dining room table where we'd stacked scripts, contracts, reviews and other miscellaneous paperwork that needed to be filed. The cats had obviously been playing 'skid on the papers' in our absence, a game that involved a running start into a full-scale leap on top of whatever lay on the table and then skidding all the way across to then leap onto the nearest piece of furniture. Fun to watch, but hell on organization.

Heaving a sigh, I got to my feet and began gathering the mess into a pile, which I then brought over to the couch along with several small plastic file boxes. Might as well do something useful to take my mind off things until Grant called, because I sure as hell wasn't going to be able to get any sleep until he did.

Daphne set her cocoa down and joined me as I started sorting through the mess of paperwork we'd managed to accumulate during the course of the Randell Festival.

"I used to think it would be fun to be involved in a real-life mystery," said Daphne as she flipped open one of the file boxes. "But now I'm tempted to dump all this mystery entertainment and write something else. Like another gothic or a nice romance or something. Hey, Connie, why don't we write some of those bodice ripper things? At least no one would die during one of our performances."

"With our luck, we'd unleash a madman who'd go around ripping the bodices of all the women in Emerald Cove." I picked up another folder and began examining its contents.

Daphne laughed. "God, Mavis would love that, wouldn't she?"

I started to reply and then stopped as I picked up a packet of yellowed vellum stationary folded in half and tied together with a scarlet velvet ribbon. "Daphne, are these yours?"

"What?"

I held out the packet. "It looks like the mark of Guido."

Daphne took the papers and undid the velvet ribbon, shaking her head as she said, "Guido never wrote his poetry down. He said that his Muse wouldn't flow through him if he tried to commit his art to paper."

"Guido had more than a muse flowing through him," I said nastily. "What are they?"

Daphne unfolded the papers and looked at the first one. "Oh my God …" .

"What? What?!"

"These are the letters that Shay Randell wrote to Lucille."

"You're kidding!" I looked at the folder in my hands. It was the one Andy had given us when he'd returned our publicity photos the other day in his office. He must've accidentally gathered up the letters with the photos and reviews he'd put in the folder. "What does it say?"

Daphne scanned the letter and looked at me, her expression stricken. "I can't read this out loud."

"What? Why not?"

She merely shook her head and handed the stack of vellum to me. Itook one at random and read it aloud in its entirety:

> *May 14th, 1965*
>
> *My dearest Lucy, you alone know my true soul. My deepest torments, my highest plateaus of joy, are known only to you. Do you remember, sweet Lucy, the site of our first amorous encounter? The place where we shared that passionate and yet so spiritual union. Then afterwards we counted the stars in the sky above the sea and you told me how you always thought that the stars must be the physical embodiment of all lovers' ecstasy.*
>
> *Until tonight, my lovely Lucille, when we will add yet another star to the heavenly display.*
>
> *Yours forever, Shay.*

"Nineteen sixty-five?" I did some quick mental calculation. Damn, Lucille's plastic surgeon was better than I'd given him credit for.

Daphne, on the other hand, was in no frame of mind to appreciate the artistry of Lucille's surgeon. "That is so dis*gusting!*" she burst out. "How could Shay Randell, master of the snappy double-entendre and terse, back-alley prose, write crap like that? Where are the one liners, the barbed innuendoes, the smoking roscoes? What about the punches to the gut, the kicks to the groin? And where, for God's sake, are the glee globes?!"

"Well, he sure as hell wasn't writing about the Lucille that we knew."

"Are all the letters like that?" Daphne sounded downright pathetic.

A quick inspection showed that they were. No glee globes or roscoes; just a bunch of insipid purple prose.

"I wonder why Franklin was so bent out of shape about these?" I folded the letters back up and retied the velvet ribbon. "No deep dark secrets here."

"What do you mean?" Daphne exclaimed, taking me by surprise with the vehemence of her tone. "You've read this shit! It's a disgrace for a writer of Randell's stature to write mush like this, even in personal letters!"

"Daphne," I said patiently, using the same tone nurses use to patients in mental wards, "These are love letters. Hard-boiled prose is not romantic. To most people," I hastily amended as she opened her mouth to retort. "I admit that these are pretty awful, but you can't hold someone's love letters against them." She looked pretty unconvinced, so I forged ahead with, "Even the most hard-headed person is apt to become a little sentimental, or even insipid, when they're in love."

"A *little* insipid? Oh please!"

"Okay, a lot insipid. But I still think you're over-reacting." But I might as well have been talking to Renfield.

"Why on earth would he write goo like that?" Daphne was on a roll. "Why? That's what I can't understand. He was capable of so much more! A great writer like that shouldn't sink to the depths of Barbara Cartland, it's just not right!"

I rolled my eyes again. "Cut it out, Daphne, you sound just like Franklin!"

And a little light bulb flashed over my head.

Daphne glared at me. "So? What if I do? I kind of like Franklin! I mean, he's a little fanatical, but so what?"

I stared at her solemnly. "Daphne, if you're upset at the fall of your idol, just imagine how Franklin would feel."

"Well, he'd be furious, but ..." Daphne trailed off as she caught my meaning. "You're not serious, are you?"

"Other than the fact that Lucille was a bitch, no one's been able to figure out a reason anyone would want to murder her beyond the fact that she was irritating. But what about these letters?"

"But ... but Franklin wouldn't do anything like that ..." She paused. "Would he?"

"Neither of us know anything about Franklin other than the fact that he's a total Randellphile and reacts very strongly whenever the reputation of his hero is impugned. He also drinks heavily; we saw that this evening." Daphne nodded slowly. I continued. "Remember those threatening phone calls Lucille complained about?"

"The ones that we were sure were just a ploy for attention?"

"Right! Well, I bet she was serious. I think Franklin was calling her and demanding those letters! Andy told us that Franklin had been bothering him about the letters as well."

"And he did mention a phone call he'd gotten earlier this evening ..."

"And he used the term 'crazy', remember?"

Still obviously reluctant to cast Franklin in the role of murderer, Daphne said, "What about Burke? Where does he fit into all of this?"

"If he was as close to Lucille as we suspected, who's to say she didn't tell him about the letters? Or that he didn't say something to Franklin during one of their conversations that just pissed Franklin off? Hell, if the guy's as loony as it seems, it could've been anything! The only thing that doesn't make any sense is why he'd have been wearing heels when he killed Damien Duran." Daphne's eyebrows flew up at that, but I was on a roll. "And I'll tell you something else. I bet that it was Franklin who put the live ammo in my revolver!"

Daphne didn't bother to ask me why, which was a good thing, because I didn't have a logical answer for that particular conclusion, just a lot of half-formed (or half-assed) thoughts floating around in my head. One of them started crystallizing before the others and I ran with it. "If Andy was running true to form this afternoon, he'll still have that conversation on the machine in its entirety."

"And this means what, precisely?"

"It's proof!" I jumped to my feet. "I'm going to pay a quick visit to the library and listen to Andy's message machine."

Daphne was positively horrified. "Connie, you can't just go down there now!"

"Why not?" I stared at her defiantly. "After all, Andy gave me the keys, so it's not as if I'm breaking and entering or anything like that."

"Can't you just call O'Donohue and talk to him about this?"

"Are you kidding? I'm not saying a word to the police until I'm sure I'm right. Sloan would be sure to find out and I can just see the headlines 'Girl Sleuth Blows It Big Time!' No thanks."

Unconvinced, Daphne said, "You could get into real trouble, Connie. It's not worth it just to prove to Grant that he's wrong."

"It's not about that any more," I said. "All of us are suspects. O'Donohue could be making the same kind of speculations about us that you made about Alex. And asshole or not, Grant didn't deserve to be shot." My voice rose as I gathered steam. "I could have killed him, Daphne. I mean, he could be dead right now, not just injured. And even if it wasn't exactly my fault, I still would be the one who pulled the trigger. I have to live with that, and it pisses me off! I want to find out who did it and I want to be there when the cops cart him off in handcuffs!"

There was a moment's silence and then Daphne nodded. "I'm going with you."

I shook my head. "You can't. Someone needs to be here when Grant calls." Something else suddenly occurred to me. "And you have to call Andy! If I'm right about all this, he's got to be warned!"

I ran upstairs to change out of my thermal pajamas into jeans, sweater and boots, and then dashed back down to the living room where Daphne was looking for the Festival contact sheet that had Andy's phone number. I took my keys off their hook where I'd actually remembered to hang them. It was a good night for this particular personal best.

Daphne followed me to the door, the contact list clutched in her hand. "Are you sure about this?"

I nodded. "I'll just grab the tape and come straight home, okay?"

"Do you have your cell phone?"

"It's in the glove compartment." I slipped on my leather flight jacket and added, "If I'm not home in an hour, then you can call O'Donohue."

"Just be careful."

"Don't worry. Just don't tell Mavis! If she finds out I'm playing Girl Detective, I might as well move back to Los Angeles!"

With that I was out the door.

Chapter Twenty-One

When I pulled the car up in front of the library, the wind was blowing the rain across my windshield in lashing gusts that made visibility next to zilch. As far as I could tell, no one else was out and about in the neighborhood, but then who the hell else would be crazy enough to be outside, at midnight, no less, in weather as foul as this? I felt like every idiot gothic heroine that ever explored those forbidden chambers or went out onto the moors against every dictate of common sense and intelligence. It was rather embarrassing being living proof that clichés exist for a reason.

Oh well. After all, the library was not exactly my idea of a scary or foreboding place, even during a thunderstorm.

As that thought drifted complacently across my mind, lightning flashed, illuminating the front of the library, the parking lot and the turbulent ocean beyond. A crash of thunder followed far too quickly for comfort and I was forced to admit that the library looked anything but welcoming. I wondered if the police had cleaned up the blood on the office floor, and then was very sorry that I'd thought of it.

"Let's get this over with," I said out loud, my voice annoyingly weak. Nancy Drew's voice wouldn't be weak. Oh no, no quaver in the vocal chords for *that* teenage wonder woman with her annoying expertise in everything a person could think of doing, not to mention that damnable ever-changing hair color.

I mentally shook myself. Sitting in the car and mulling over Nancy Drew's hair color would get me precisely nowhere. As a procrastination tactic, it was pathetic. Switching off the car lights, I retrieved my cell phone from the glove compartment, shoved it in my jacket pocket, and braced myself for the onslaught of rain that would greet me when I opened the door. Sure enough, I was soaked to the skin before I could even slam the damned thing shut. The rain plastered my hair to my head in wet tendrils. which were then pried loose by the fierce wind and tossed in front of my eyes. I ran for the porch and skidded across the tiled verandah, nearly falling on my ass. I managed to catch myself on the door-handle before losing my balance completely.

I fumbled with my key ring, my fingers numbed by the bone-chilling wind. Even though the porch was roofed, the rain still hit me in enthusiastic gusts. Daphne was right: I was going to get a cold.

After several botched attempts, I managed to insert the library key in the lock, pushing the door open with a shove. I slipped inside and shut the door behind me, turning the inside lock just in case.

I stood and dripped on the welcome mat for a moment, not wanting to leave any conspicuous puddles of rain water on the floor if the police should happen to come back that evening. I stripped off my wet gloves and stuck them in a pocket of my bomber jacket. I wasn't worried about finger prints. Mine were already plastered all over the library, along with those of dozens of guests, actors, employees, etc.

The library was dark, the only illumination provided by the occasional flash of lighting. I thought about turning on one of the library fluorescents, but there was an off chance that someone in the neighborhood might notice and phone the police. I could just imagine the shit hitting the fan if O'Donohue and Honey caught me here. Honey would have me convicted in a matter of minutes. Asshole.

If I weren't so tense, I would've appreciated the authentic *film noir* atmosphere that nature was providing. The shadows that were cast during those intervals turned the familiar layout of the library into something alien and creepy. I pulled out my mini-maglight, switching it on to provide a thin beam of light that was only marginally better than nothing.

I made my way carefully to Andy's private office. Now that I was inside with the door safely locked behind me, I felt remarkably calm for someone who was technically guilty of trespassing. The library was still, except for the sound of my footfall and the elements raging outside. The driving patter of the rain on the roof was rather soothing and I began to relax and enjoy myself. After all, I was living an adventure with all of the prerequisite ingredients. Well, most of them. I had neither a romantic hero or a dashing villain to spice things up, but considering what the villain of this piece had already done, I was grateful for the exclusion.

The door to Andy's office was locked, a drawback I hadn't expected. It had an old-fashioned lock on it so I stood a good chance of being able to pick the lock. Hey, all those Nancy Drew books had to have been good for something and in my case, they provided me with the inspiration needed to learn how to wield a mean bobby pin. All I needed was a tool.

I ran my fingers through my hair to see if there was a stray bobby pin left over from my forties 'do. No such luck. I then went through the pockets of my jacket with the aid of my maglight light. I found my keys, a stray Hershey's Kiss, a packet of Kleenex, my gloves, and a small Swiss Army knife. I ate the Kiss and flicked open the knife. One of the blades was thin enough to fit into the lock, sliding in with room to spare. I fiddled with it for a moment and was quickly rewarded with a 'click' as the tumblers fell into place. Just call me Ms. Drew. I pushed the door open, went inside and shut it partially behind me.

Andy's office was in its usual state of mess, boxes of flyers and T-shirts from the Festival scattered all over the floor. The desk was covered with books and papers. I was sure the answering machine was somewhere underneath the layers.

I debated if it would be safe to switch on the little desk lamp. The sliding door that led out to the side porch was curtained, besides which I didn't think anyone could see over the brick wall. The window in Andy's office faced the ocean, so I took a quick peek out to see if anyone was crazy enough to take a late night stroll on the beach. As far as I could see, it was deserted. Even through the rain I could see the breakers roaring in, the ocean white-capped and turbulent. The rip-tides must have been something.

I took off my wet jacket and draped it over a chair. I confronted the task at hand. I switched on the lamp, quickly locating the answering machine under a pile of paper. Sure enough, the 'call' light was blinking. I hit the rewind and waited till it was finished. It took a while and I hoped this meant that Andy had indeed inadvertently recorded his conversations, specifically the one that had to be from Franklin.

I settled back in Andy's chair, hit 'play' and listened.

The first few calls were just miscellaneous messages, most of them to do with the Randell Festival. Every now and again Andy would pick up mid-message and carry on a conversation without bothering to hit the 'off' button. I fidgeted impatiently as I had to listen to assorted people ramble on, most of them using ten words where one would do. Why can't the English teach their children how to be succinct?

The words washed over me. Didn't Andy ever erase messages? I wished I had another Hershey's Kiss. I seriously considered brewing a pot of coffee, but then remembered that the coffee maker was in the staff office.

Another message began. This one caught my attention, not because it offered any clue to the murders, but because the caller was the last person I'd expect to call Andy. It was Alex, leaving a brief message about meeting Andy before the show to discuss things. My eyebrows shot up with surprise as Alex's voice was one that I would never have expected to hear. And while his brevity was commendable, couldn't he have been more specific? What things? Could Daphne's speculations about blackmail have a basis in fact after all? I was really beginning to loathe mysteries.

The next caller was just as much as a surprise as Alex. This time it was Grant, sounding typically condescending as he began to leave a message 'regarding the cast bios, specifically his.' And that he hoped Andy would have 'the delicacy and good taste' to leave the review previously discussed *out* of Grant's bio when writing the article for the local paper. He would see Andy that evening at the show where they could 'discuss the matter further.'

'Click'.

Boy, if *I* were Andy, I'd stick the article in just on general principal. Why couldn't Grant see how irritating he was? Or was he so sure of his own superiority that he didn't care who he alienated? My guess was option number two.

I glanced down at the desk. The words 'Cast Bios' inked across a folder, caught my eye. I couldn't resist. Keeping an ear out for Franklin's voice, I opened the folder and sifted through the contents. I skipped through mine and Daphne's bios, having seen them earlier. Andy had made it sound as though we were doing this in between Broadway engagements and film commitments.

Ah, there it was. Grant Havers, Actor. I skimmed the bio. It was short and basic, giving a list of the productions Grant had done as well as a summation of his training. While it wasn't the glowing write-up he'd given to Daphne and me, there didn't seem to be anything that Grant would object to …

Oops … here it was. "It seems that Mr. Havers has certainly come a long way since his first starring role as the Captain of the swim team in the unlaudable film, *Boys Will Be Boys*." This was followed by photocopy of a review of the mentioned film, the kind that was rated by the star-system. You know, one star through four stars, with a large blot meaning BOMB. It looked like the review had been taken from a book along the lines of *The Golden Turkey Awards* and had won the honor of BOMB.

The review came with a fuzzy black and white photo depicting a group of handsome beef-cake type guys in Speedos, grinning boyishly at the camera and at each other. I looked closely, not seeing Grant's name under any of them. I looked again, stopping this time at 'Brand Hardell'. Sure enough, there he was. Younger, but definitely Grant. I read the review, which was short, succinct and brutal:

> Boys Will Be Boys *is an inane film concerning the exploits of a boys' swim team and their adventures in Europe. The movie stops short of porn but goes way beyond the boundaries of good taste and good filmmaking. Thinly veiled homo-erotic overtones and crass sexual situations as the swim team tours Europe.*

Ouch. No wonder Grant didn't want this mentioned, considering his new macho image.

I folded up the review and stuck it in my jeans pocket. I had to show this to Daphne. Some things were just too good not to be shared. I'd just slip it back on Monday so Andy could finish the article.

A new message started. I sat up straight as I recognized Franklin's voice. This was it.

Although it was obvious that Franklin had been drinking, the call started out innocuously enough. But it quickly became equally obvious that on the subject of Shay Randell, Franklin's elevator did not go all the way to the roof.

Franklin started with a mild critique of Andy's speech of the previous night and what he termed a 'rather blasphemous attitude' towards Randell.

> Andy: (non-apologetically) Well, I'm sorry you feel that way, Franklin, but I think my attitude was geared towards truth, not blasphemy.
> Franklin: (heated) You called Randell an alcoholic!
> Andy: (patiently) He *was* an alcoholic, Franklin. You know that, I know that, it's common knowledge.
> Franklin: (slurring his words) What's wrong with a little drink? Most of the great writers drank!
> Andy: (pause) Franklin, have you been drinking?
> Franklin: (truculently) What's wrong with that?
> Andy: (choosing words carefully) Nothing, Franklin. It's just that maybe we should have this conversation when you're sober. Maybe tonight after the show, hmmm?
> Franklin: (shouting) Don't you patronize me, dammit!
> Andy: (heaving a huge sigh) I've got to go, Franklin. We'll talk about this later.
> Franklin: Just a minute! You still haven't given me an answer on those letters. I want them handed over, Andy, I won't stand for them being made public! They're a disgrace to Randell's good name.
> Andy: (losing patience) Randell doesn't *have* a good name, Franklin. And I'm not giving you the letters, so just drop it, okay? I'm going, now.

At which point Franklin began ranting, unspecified threats spilling from his usually good-tempered lips in a torrent that had to be heard to be believed. A final 'click' ended the conversation as Andy hung up mid-rant.

Wow. I remembered Franklin's mild, good-natured behavior towards Andy at the Ball. Either he was an excellent actor or just plain crazy. After hearing this conversation, I'd opt for the latter. It was too bad. I liked Franklin, all neurosis aside. But if he was fanatical enough to murder in order to protect his hero's good name, it was time for the police to step in.

I stopped the tape and popped it out. I tried tucking the tape in my jeans pocket, but they weren't having any of it. I stuck it in my bomber jacket instead, vowing to knock off those morning cinnamon rolls.

Picking up my jacket, I stood up to leave, reached to switch off the lamp … and froze. My jacket slipped from suddenly nerveless fingers onto the floor.

A slowly spreading pool of dark liquid stained the floor by one of the bookshelves flanking the desk. Sticking out from behind the shelf was a hand, fingers splayed in the pool of what could only be blood. I choked back the bile that rose in my throat and forced myself to go take a closer look at what lay behind the bookcase.

Although he was lying face down, I knew it was Andy. Blood was oozing from a large wound on the top of his head. His hair was matted and the skull looked … pulpy. Lying next to his battered head was our missing Peruvian Pigeon, the base of which was now covered in blood, along with bits of skin and hair. I lost the battle with my rising gorge, and only just managed to turn in time to heave up my dinner into a metal trashcan.

Once I regained some semblance of control over my stomach, I put my fingers the side of Andy's neck and felt for a pulse. It was there, faint but discernible. Franklin must have bashed Andy over the head with the statue while we'd been tracing the path of the bullet. I didn't know much about head injuries, but I *did* know that if Andy was going to make it, he needed medical care as soon as possible. Enough of this Nancy Drew shit. I had to call the police.

Stumbling to my feet, I picked up the receiver to dial 9-1-1. As I pressed the first '9', both the lights and the dial tone went out.

This was not good.

I grabbed my jacket and got my cell, fingers leaden and clumsy as I hit the 'on' key and dialed 9-1-1. Several agonizingly long seconds passed as I waited for the call to ring through. Nothing. I hit 'end call' and tried again. My phone gave a loud 'beep' and there was just enough time to see that the battery icon was blinking before my cell phone died.

Shit.

Over the pounding rain I heard the sound of the front door opening and then a 'click' as it was re-locked. My first thought was that it had to be O'Donohue or Honey because a: who else would be here this time of night and b: they'd have a key. I cringed when I realized what trouble I'd be in when they found me. On the other hand, it saved me the trouble of calling the police.

Then another, far more frightening idea occurred to me. What if the other midnight visitor was Franklin coming back to make sure he'd accomplished what he'd set out to do? After all, why would the police re-lock the door from the inside?

I crept to the office door and started to shut it as quickly and quietly as I could.

"Connie." As soon as I heard my name spoken in that hoarse, insinuating whisper, I knew it wasn't O'Donohue or a library staffer who'd joined me in the darkened library.

"Connie ... Come out."

My blood turned to ice as he/she spoke again, the voice hollow and inhuman. Whoever it was knew that I was here, possibly because they'd seen my car. Which would mean that the intruder knew me well enough to have figured out why I was here. If it was Franklin, as I suspected, I was in far more trouble than a dressing-down or trip downtown with O'Donohue. I was in danger of ending up like Lucille.

I shut the door silently, only to hear a clattering noise as my knife, which I'd left hanging in the doorknob, fell to the floor. I cursed under my breath as I heard a low chuckle from the main library. Footsteps came towards Andy's office.

I fumbled with the lock, turning it into place just as the intruder stopped outside the door. I took a step backwards, then two more as the knob was slowly turned back and forth. There was a scrape as he/she picked up my knife and inserted it into the lock. "Open the door, Connie. I can pick the lock just as easily as you did ..."

I backed up, giving a gasp as my back slammed into the edge of the desk. There was another snigger, a dry, papery sound which unnerved me completely.

"Afraid of the dark?" The hoarse whisper again, something about it confirming my gut feeling that my tormentor was male. "Don't worry, I'll be with you soon."

Whoever was out there—and I was sure it was Franklin—had to be using the eerie whisper to maximize my fear. I had no doubts that he was going to kill me, so why bother to disguise his voice unless he enjoyed the game? This thought helped to loosen some of the paralyzing terror because it pissed me off. Two people were dead because of this maniac, three if Andy didn't recover. And I'd be damned before I'd sit and wait to be the next victim, cowering like a damsel in distress while he added me to the list.

There was a rattle as he began using my make-shift lock pick. I had to act fast, because it would only be a matter of minutes before the door was opened. Shoving a chair under the door-knob, I looked around for something to use as a weapon. If I could even briefly incapacitate him, I could get out the front door.

My heart sank as I realized that my options for weapons were limited to books and one small desk lamp. There was Andy's chair, but it was so large and awkward that I'd probably only succeed in throwing out my back if I did manage to heft it. Then I remembered the Peruvian Pigeon.

This all raced through my mind in a matter of seconds. I reached down and grasped the statue used to bludgeon Andy. My fingers touched blood and something that made my stomach churn again. The Pigeon slipped from my suddenly nerveless fingers and hit the floor as I fought a sudden wave of dizziness. I grabbed hold of corner of the desk and concentrated on my breathing until the faintness passed.

"What are you doing, Connie? I hope you're waiting for me ..."

Call me a wimp, but I just couldn't bring myself to pick up the Pigeon again. I immediately set about executing the only other option I could think of. Grabbing my maglight from the desk, I moved to the side door, unlocked and opened it. I slipped outside, grateful that the side patio was covered. My gratitude dissolved when I saw that the tall metal gate between the patio and the street was padlocked shut.

I cursed under my breath, weighing my options as I glanced over my shoulder to make sure the office door was still barred. The gate was taller than me by several feet and topped by wrought iron spikes. I remembered all the reasons I'd gotten out of stunt work.

Down at the other end of the patio were the stairs to the beach. In low tide this wouldn't be a problem, but with the storm raging I was likely to run into trouble. There was no way off of the beach for at least a quarter of a mile in either direction because of cliffs on both sides. The nearest stairwell was to the left beyond Davy Jones' Cave, past rocks, more cliffs, and tide pools. Crossing the area in front of the Cave was likely to be difficult if not impossible. And a worse scenario applied to the stairwell down the beach in the opposite direction. To gain access to that one, I'd have to skirt the edge of Surfer's Cove, impossible to do at high tide in the best of weather.

I turned back to the gate with its daunting metal spikes. Fear is a marvelous incentive. I tucked my maglight in one of my boots. Taking a deep breath, I made a leap for it. Grabbing one of the spikes at its base, I tried to heave myself up, but the soles of my boots could find no purchase on the rain-slick metal. I slid back down, landing with an ignominious 'thump' on my behind that would've gotten me laughed out of any stunt association.

The sound of wood scraping across tiled floors galvanized me. I leapt to my feet and risked a glance inside Andy's office. The chair was sliding slowly away from the inner door as my tormentor shoved from the other side. Why the hell hadn't I grabbed the Pigeon?

I had no choice. I slammed the sliding door shut and ran down the rain-slicked stairs to the beach, intending to try and cross the tide pools in front of Davy Jones Cave. Keeping my footing with great difficulty, I reached the bottom of the stairs and paused on the strip of sidewalk between the library and a cement wall, which separated the buildings from the beach. I could just barely hear the sliding door being re-opened.

I stumbled up over the wall, immediately buffeted by the wind and rain as I lost what small protection the shelter of the walls had given. My sweater was immediately soaked through to the skin and I realized that I'd left my bomber jacket, along with the tape, in Andy's office. Good move, Garrett. Not only would I die of pneumonia, but I'd left the evidence behind. But there was no way in hell that I was going back for it.

I prayed that the lightning would hold off long enough for me to reach the Cave under cover of the rain and darkness. I could barely see in front of me as I moved down the beach near the edge of water, going for the hard-packed sand, thinking to myself, 'Why didn't you just try and bash him with the chair, you wimp?' To which I answered, 'Because you'd be a dead woman with a bad back.'

I risked a glance back over my shoulder but couldn't discern anything through the storm. I couldn't even make out the silhouette of the library, which gave me some confidence that my pursuer wouldn't be able to tell which direction I went.

The waves were crashing on shore with an amazing volume, like the roar of a dozen freight trains. Rain poured off my face and hair, dripping into my eyes and mouth. Hard to believe I'd ever thought walking on a beach during a rain storm was romantic.

My eyes had adjusted to the darkness enough to discern that the strip of beach that usually lay between the caves and the ocean was completely covered by the pounding surf. The only way to the other side was to go under the natural archway that we'd incorporated into our performance. The same archway under which Lucille's body had been found.

I pulled out my maglight from my boot. The thin beam barely made a dent in the darkness, but it was enough to show that water now frothed around that archway at an unknown depth. I stared at it in dismay, thinking of the last bad storms we'd had in Emerald Cove. Several young boys had been swept off some rocks they'd climbed, despite signs posted stating the danger. The one survivor had said that they'd wanted to 'watch the waves' and that it just hadn't occurred to them that the sea would be stronger than *they* were. I had no such illusions. The thought of wading into that swirling, turbulent water which could hide any number of jagged rocks was petrifying. I couldn't do it. Anything was preferable to that.

And then I thought of Lucille's water-logged, bloated corpse and Andy's smashed head.

Taking a deep breath, I plunged in, immersed up to my knees in frigid water. I waded in under the arch, using the mag to try to pick a safe course through the rocks. The pull of the tide and the wash of the waves constantly knocked me off balance.

The water level rose to waist-deep as I passed through the arch. The undertow became more insistent as the rock wall on my right gave way to open ocean, blocked only by a few rocky islands barely poking above the water. The tide pools were completely covered by the foaming water. There was no way I could get through to the stairwell on the other side. It would mean going around a cliff face that had only a tiny strip of rocky beach during high tide. And even through the storm I could tell the waves were crashing head-high against the rocks. If I made the attempt, I'd be crushed against the cliffs or swept out to sea.

I stood where I was for a moment, trying to keep my balance in the turbulent water while I quickly racked my brains for some other means of escape. I knew that the platform and stairs that led to the Gnome's Den lay somewhere to my left. Best case scenario, the door at the top of the stairs was unlocked (*Hah! Wishful thinking, Pollyanna*, I told myself even as the optimistic thought crossed my mind), or had a lock that I could pick, giving me access to the store and perhaps a working phone. At the very least, I could hide up there, wait out the storm and hope that the murderer had chosen to go the other direction down the beach. Worst case scenario, I could get lost in one of the other holes and arches that led to dead-ends honeycombed throughout the cliff. I'd heard of people drowning in holes that were deeper than they appeared.

A particularly large wave threw me against a ledge under the shelter of the overhanging cave entrance. It knocked my maglight right out of my hand and into the water. Cursing vociferously, I made one brief attempt to fish for it, but gave up when the undertow did its best to pick me off of my feet and wash me out to sea. I grabbed for the ledge and was surprised and gratified to feel wood under my fingers. I'd been washed right up to the platform, the far side of which stuck out further in the water, and was now holding on to one of the wooden posts set into the rock ledge.

Grasping the post with both hands, I heaved myself up onto the wet rock, slithering on my stomach until I was completely clear of the water. I lay there for a minute panting with exhaustion, one foot hanging over the edge of the platform. This kind of exercise I didn't need.

Although the sound of the wind and rain was somewhat muffled, the pounding of the surf was amplified by the cave walls, echoing with an eerie hollow booming that made me think of zombies pounding at the confines of their coffins, trying to get out.

Next I'd be seeing drowned corpses floating in front of me, swollen fingers wrapping themselves around the wooden posts as they tried to drag themselves out of the water and join me on the platform … I quickly pulled my foot all the way on to the platform and sat up, cursing the results of a vivid imagination combined with a life-long diet of horror films.

Lightning crackled outside, briefly illuminating the cave and the water. I gasped as I saw a tall figure silhouetted against the archway. I immediately flattened against the rock, hoping against hope that he hadn't seen me.

"Connie …"

The sound of my name barely carrying above the surf did it. I scrambled to my feet, slipping on the wet rock as I ran to the wooden stairs. I started to climb, one hand on the rail as my boots kept sliding on the damp, mossy wood. My sodden clothing weighed heavily on my limbs, making my climb up the endless stairs right out of a nightmare where I could only run in slow motion.

Up here the light was non-existent. I couldn't even see the rail under my hand. Claustrophobia started pressing in on me as I went further up into the damp tunnel. The rain and surf were barely audible.

I found the door with a 'thud' as I ran straight into it, banging my right knee painfully against the heavy wood. I groped for a handle or door knob, my panic and claustrophobia increasing with each passing second. Finally my fingers closed over a cold metal bar. I twisted it and shoved on the door with all of my strength. It didn't budge. And without my maglight, there was no way I could see to pick the lock, assuming there was one. For all I knew, the door could be barred or padlocked from the inside. And I no longer had my knife.

"God *damn* it! Shit!" I slammed my fist against the door in frustration, only succeeding in hurting my hand.

Then, over the muffled roar of the waves, I heard a voice. I listened carefully.

"Connie …" Once again, I heard the sound of my name being called in that insinuating whisper. My scalp crawled as I pressed backwards against the door as if the damp wood could conceal me. I was trapped, cornered, no place to go except back down the stairs where a murderer was waiting.

Except he wasn't waiting. There was the squeak of shoe against rock and then the slow, steady tread of footsteps ascending the stairs. The steps paused. "Connie … I have a knife. Listen!" A horrible grating sound followed, presumably a razor sharp blade being scraped against the rock wall. "I might not use the knife, though. Why don't you come down and find out?" He paused. "No? All right, I'll come to you." The footsteps resumed.

I tried to hold back the panic that threatened to send me bolting down the stairs in blind terror. I was astounded that Franklin's normally mild voice could sound so menacing. I never would have figured him capable of the subtlety and finesse of this terrifyingly cruel game he was playing.

I moved to the side of the staircase and reached blindly over the railing. My hand touched damp rock, but there seemed to be a gap between the stairs and the wall. I dropped to my knees and reached down below the stairs, discovering a space of at least two feet between the edge of the stairs and the floor. Without further thought, I slipped under the rail and let myself down onto the slanting rock floor as quietly as possible. I was acting out of pure instinct, an animal going to ground to elude its hunter. If I could slip past him, I could retrace my path to the library. Sitting down, I slid forward on my behind, staying as low to the ground as possible.

He spoke again. "Still waiting for me, Connie? So romantic, don't you think?"

I realized that he was only a few feet away, around a bend in the wall. I pressed myself closer to the stairs and wedged myself underneath them as far as possible. I tried not to think of the spiders and other creatures that were probably nesting comfortably on the underside of wood.

I lay still as footsteps rounded the bend, passing over me and continuing upwards. I waited until I thought he'd reached the top and then wriggled back out from under the stairs, sliding down as fast as possible. There was no time for stealth. My pursuer had reached the top to discover my absence and was now descending the stairs, although not with the speed I gained by sliding down the water-slicked rock.

"Connie, you're only making this more difficult for yourself." There was an undercurrent of annoyance in his voice. Good. I planned on making this as difficult as possible.

The light increased slightly as I neared the bottom of the staircase and the sound of the surf increased in volume as it echoed through the cave. I could see the platform, the water roiling about it in a frightening fashion. I hoped I could still make it out through the archway.

The drop-off was so sudden that I barely had time to cry out in shock as the ground vanished beneath my legs and my body slid off into space. I hit the water, the underside of my right thigh bashing against a submerged rock with a force that jarred my entire body and sent a wave of nausea straight through me. The leg immediately went numb.

A wave smashed over me, sending me back against the wall, scraping my hands and the back of my head against the rock. I struggled to stand up, sputtering as another wave threatened to submerge me. Catching hold of a rock, I pulled myself upright, ignoring the pain of my bleeding hands.

My leg was another matter. The slightest pressure on it was agony, cutting through the initial numbness like a butcher knife. If it wasn't broken, it was certainly bruised all the way to the bone. It almost gave way beneath me so I tried to switch all my weight to the left leg. I let the pull of the tide help me as I half-limped, half-swam towards the archway.

The water level had risen chest high and another wave roared in before I could reach the archway. I was knocked off balance as my injured leg *did* collapse. I was buffeted into more submerged rocks, swept to the left like a piece of cork. If I was carried past the other edge of the platform, it was certain I'd be battered to death against the cliffs, saving Franklin the trouble of killing me.

I struggled against the current as another wave pushed me backwards. I hit a large expanse of rock and clutched at it with desperate fingers as I felt myself being sucked back out by the fierce undertow. My fingers grasped rough concrete. I was at the platform, but I couldn't get any real purchase on the surface. I could feel my grip slipping as my hands started to slide off the piling. Then my wrists were seized in a strong grip and I was pulled unceremoniously up onto the platform. Outcroppings of rock scraped my body along the way and I gave a yelp of pain as my injured leg was jarred by the edge of a concrete piling. But the pain was nothing compared to my terror.

My 'rescuer' yanked me to my feet and shoved me away from the encroaching waves. Holding my wrists painfully behind my back, he pushed me towards the stairs. I staggered as my leg gave way and would have fallen if he hadn't been holding me up. Then with a sudden movement, he released me with a shove and I sprawled onto the stairs, barking my shins painfully against the edge. My hands picked up splinters and my injured leg flamed with pain. I lay there for a moment, paralyzed by fear.

"Connie ..." No whisper this time. Just a familiar tone that turned my name into a caress. It wasn't Franklin. Shock hit me with a force equivalent to a kick in the gut.

I turned slowly onto my back, not daring to believe my ears. A well-timed flash of lightning illuminated the face of the murderer. "Grant ..." I whispered. A crash of thunder punctuated his name. Never tell me that nature doesn't have a sick sense of humor.

Chapter Twenty-Two

Grant sat down next to me on the stairs, resting one hand on my body in a familiar fashion. My sweater, ripped and tattered in several places, had pulled up out of my jeans so his hand lay against the bare flesh of my stomach. My skin gave an involuntary ripple of revulsion as I was hit with the realization that I'd shared my bed and my body with a murderer.

I held myself still, not trusting myself to speak. But then Grant had never been shy about filling a conversational void.

"Surprised to see me, my love?" That voice, so rich and sensual. An undercurrent of amusement ran through his words, causing a sliver of anger to penetrate my fear. Any lingering doubts I had as to his guilt dissolved in that instant. But maybe if I played it right, I could talk my way out of this.

Trying to inject a note of relief in my voice, I replied, "If I'd known it was you, I wouldn't have left the library."

"No?" Still that amused tone as he idly ran one finger across bare skin.

"Of ... of course not." Not my best reading, but not bad under the circumstances.

"Why did you run away then? We could've had a lovely little tryst if you'd stayed." I willed myself to hold still when his hand wandered further up my torso. The edge of the stairs pressed painfully into my back and the pain in my leg made it hard to concentrate.

"I thought you were Franklin." This, at least, had the ring of truth to it.

His hand stopped its upward progress. "Franklin?" Grant sounded genuinely surprised.

"Yes. I'm ... I'm pretty sure he's the one who killed Lucille and Burke, and who tried to kill Andy." He didn't say anything, so I continued, "Jesus, Grant, do you think I'd have risked the water if I'd known it was you? I would've drowned, or been smashed to pieces if you hadn't pulled me out. As it is, I think I might have broken my leg. You picked a hell of a time to play a sick joke." I finished on a note of righteous indignation and waited.

Grant was unusually silent for a moment. I started to breath a little easier. "Why did you take the review, Connie?"

"The ..." His non-sequitorial question caught me by surprise. "What are you talking about?"

"The review, Connie." His voice was very gentle, as was his hand as it traced the line of my face from cheek to throat. There was nothing reassuring in his manner. "If you thought it was Franklin, why did you take the review?"

"You mean *Boys Will Be Boys*? I ..."

My words were cut off along with my breath as Grant's hand closed around my neck just under the jawline. "Ah, I thought so ..." He easily resisted my attempts to pry his fingers from my throat, not bothering to use his other hand, which had resumed its leisurely exploration of my upper body. "I almost believed you, Connie. You're actually a better actress than I've given you credit for."

The fingers around my throat tightened imperceptibly as I tried in vain to pull them away. My head felt swollen, the lack of air sending dots of light flashing in front of my eyes. My chest was on fire for want of oxygen, the need for air overriding even the pain in my leg.

"You couldn't possibly have thought it was Franklin ... No, not my Connie. You're far too intelligent ... One of the things I love about you." Just as the last of my air began to fade, Grant loosened his grip on my throat, turning the gesture into a caress as I took in great, ragged breaths of the chill air. "Or is it possible that I'm over-estimating you, sweetheart?"

I concentrated on breathing.

"You really haven't figured it out, have you?" Grant sounded genuinely amused. "Well, so much for your infamous deductive skills. Come on, now, Connie, use your brain! I would've thought the review would clue you in since you've been part of the Industry for so long."

I stared at him blankly. What was it about the damned review?

Grant shook his head. "Connie, Connie ... Let me explain it to you." His patronizing tone was enough to make my hackles rise. Even as a murderer, Grant was incredibly annoying. "You've seen the review. So you know that I made an ... unwise career decision back in the days when I didn't have an agent to guide me. I never thought it would matter, though. That kind of trash usually goes straight to video, if it's released at all. I thought it was locked away in some film vault. It never even made it on to the USA Network, for Christ's Sake, so I thought I was safe. But some damned writer, probably one of a hundred people who actually saw the movie, had to include it in his damned book."

"Jesus, Grant," I said hoarsely, staring at him in disbelief, "It was only a movie! What difference could it possibly make?"

"You of all people should realize what casting directors and producers are like in Hollywood. It's all image, Connie. And what kind of image would it be for the star of O'Mallet to have been in a low-budget, soft-core porn film that would only attract the kind of audience who subscribe to *International Male?*"

"But you used a pseudonym," I said, still grappling with the concept that Grant had killed over a review. "The odds of anyone reading that review, let alone recognizing you, before the casting director makes the decision are incredibly slim! And after you've been cast, surely it wouldn't matter!"

"The review by itself? No. But I'd already been recognized, you see."

I thought back to the party at Jason Down's house. Lucille cornering Grant, the trapped look on his face, which he struggled manfully to turn into flattering interest in what she was saying ..."Lucille?"

Grant gave me an approving pat on the shoulder. "Very good, Darling! Maybe you'll get a detective's star after all. Lucille was the wife of the late Gerald Fife, owner and executive producer of Plateau Pictures. Fife was responsible for a glut of exploitation films done at minimal budgets. One of them was *Boys Will Be Boys.* Lucille recognized me and informed me that it would be her pleasure to re-release the film, as well as show both film and review to the casting director of *O'Mallet.* Unless ..." He paused briefly before continuing distastefully, "Well, you've heard of the casting couch."

"So you *killed* her?" I was incredulous.

"With great pleasure. Aside from finding her utterly repulsive, how could I ever trust that she'd keep her promise? That kind of woman has no morals."

I would've laughed, but a commentary on Grant's hypocrisy hardly seemed prudent. My throat still felt like I'd drunk a swig of Drano. Besides, Grant showed no signs of turning the conversation over to me. "I'd asked her to meet me in between shows, at the Cave. Once I'd held her head under water for a few minutes and finished the job with seaweed, it was an easy matter to stash the body under the platform until the next show and rig it so it would appear instead of the dummy."

"But you didn't have time, you were talking to your agent ... He verified your story!"

"Darling, I'm a hot commodity. Do you think a decent Hollywood agent would think twice about lying in order to protect an investment?"

I couldn't argue with that. Another question rose to mind. "What about Burke?"

"All of a sudden you're interested in my motivation, hmmm?" Grant gave a short laugh, devoid of any real humor. I cringed as his hand tightened briefly on my throat again. "I don't like being dressed down in front of a bunch of amateurs, Connie. But—" His grip loosened. "—that's in the past. Back to Burke. Aside from the potential that Lucille just might tell him about the film, it seemed like a good idea to keep the police from digging too deeply in Lucille's business. I thought that adding Burke to the deceased roster might throw them off. It was easy. I overheard him tell Franklin that he was going down to the Cave, so I followed him. He'd been drinking, so it was no trouble to give him a quick bash on the head, strangle him and arrange the body. No great loss, don't you agree?"

"Why didn't you just make it look like an accidental death? Why the seaweed?" I was struggling to understand the mind of someone I thought I knew so well. There was more to Grant than I'd given him credit for, but all of it was twisted.

"Connie," Grant chided, "Don't you have any sense of real drama?" He chuckled. I hated him with a passion. "Besides—" Grant paused again, choosing his words carefully. "—I enjoyed it, Connie. In its own way, murder is as much an art form as acting or writing. One still has to make *choices*."

I couldn't speak.

"And as for Andy, well, you saw the review on his desk. And heard the phone conversation. He didn't really need to die, just be put out of action for a while. Either way would've suited me. I just needed enough time to take the article. I doubt that Andy could put two and two together and come up with anything that made sense. I'd planned on Alex shooting him during the play. But you, my love, picked up the wrong gun. Ah well, the best laid plans ... so after Franklin left, I went back and used your little statue when Andy had his back turned.." He smiled.

"Jesus, Grant ..." I felt sick, not to mention used and utterly stupid. But I still had one unanswered question. "Did you kill Damien Duran?"

"Who?" Grant stared at me blankly for a few seconds. "You mean that geriatric board member who drowned? Why would I bother with someone as insignificant as that?"

I was almost relieved. The thought of Grant in high heels was enough to send me over the edge. "I ... I don't know. I just thought—"

"The problem, my love, is that you *didn't* think. I can't believe you thought it was Franklin." Grant sounded offended. I didn't want him offended, not with his hand still on my throat.

"I ... I thought it had to be him. After all, he had the most access to Andy's keys and—"

Grant laughed. "I didn't steal Andy's keys, Darling. Yours were much easier to copy and replace, considering how careless you are. What surprised me was that they were actually hanging on the hook when I came over the other night. I should thank you for making it that much easier."

No, I thought, you should thank Daphne.

"After all," he continued, "Franklin hardly has the talent or the imagination to have terrified you as thoroughly as I have. Confess, Connie, you *are* terrified, aren't you?"

I was silent.

"*Aren't* you!" Grant's voice rose in instant fury. Reaching into his pocket, he pulled something out as the hand on my neck entwined itself in my hair, yanking my head back. I didn't have time to feel relief at having his other hand off my body because he pressed what could only be a knife blade against my throat.

Oh God, I'm dead, I thought. Out loud I gasped, "Yes! Y ... yes, I am!" My breath came in short, shallow gasps as I waited for the knife to bite deeper into my flesh. Amazingly, he withdrew it, chuckling with satisfaction.

"So, how do you like me as a psychotic killer, Connie?" Grant's tone was conversational, all traces of fury gone. "Pretty effective performance, wouldn't you say?"

"Is that what this is?" I asked, my voice cracking as outrage warred with fear. "A performance?"

"Well, that's not *all* it is ... Not by any means. But I do take pride in my craft. You should be proud of me too." He toyed with the knife blade, running the edge gently down my neck to one shoulder. I didn't move, afraid that anything I said or did would send that blade stabbing into my flesh.

However, when Grant used the knife to casually rip away a section of my sweater, I couldn't help but flinch backwards, stopped by the hard wood of the stairs. "Don't move, sweetheart," Grant cautioned as he disposed of most of the sweater. "I don't want to hurt you." When he cut through my bra strap, I whimpered, hating the helpless sound I made. Snick. There went the other strap.

Jesus ...

His other hand found my right breast and he caught his breath. "Why, Connie, you must be ... cold ..."

"You ... bastard ..."

Grant laughed, never stopping the movement of his hand on my breast as he whispered, "But Connie, you always loved it when I did this ..." I shuddered in revulsion. "See?" Grant mistook my reaction for pleasure. "Let's get rid of those jeans ... I know how much you hate wet denim."

The knife moved down my bare stomach to my jeans. Grant inserted the tip under the waistband, preparing to cut the water-logged material from my body.

I couldn't take it any more. "Jesus, Grant, stop it!" My voice had a ring of true hysteria as I grabbed at the hand holding the knife.

"Why, Connie, what's the matter?" The bastard actually sounded genuinely surprised. "I thought you liked role-playing ..." He slapped my hand aside and tore through the waistband.

"No!!" I grabbed for the knife-hand again. Abandoning my breast, Grant caught my hand this time, very gently pinning it by my side.

"Connie ... what are you afraid of? This?" He held the knife in front of me. I cowered back against the stairs. "Darling," he said in perfectly reasonable tones, "Do you really think I'd cut you with this? You know how hard wet denim is to take off."

"Please don't ..." I hated myself for begging, but I couldn't stand Grant's hands on my body any more.

"Do you want me to get rid of this?" He touched me lightly on the side of my face with the blade.

"P ... please stop it ..." I shut my eyes.

Suddenly I was free. The cold steel no longer touched me and Grant no longer held me down. My eyes flew open as Grant stood and took several steps away from me. I struggled to sit up as he said, "I'm hurt, Connie. Do you really think I'd use a knife on you?" He tossed the knife away where it fell with a clatter on the platform. I stared after it, then back at Grant as he held his hands out to me in a placating gesture. Did he really intend to let me go? "Really, Connie, I should think you've known me long enough to trust me at my word. After all, we *are* lovers." He took a step towards me. I pulled myself up a step. "I don't want to use a knife on you, Darling," he continued softly, coming forward again. I whimpered again and continued to back slowly up the stairs. "Do you know why?" Lightning flashed again as I shook my head. He smiled just before we were cast back into the gloom, and what I saw in that smile was enough to send me to my hands and knees, ignoring all the pain as I made a desperate scramble up the stairs.

Grant leapt forward and grabbed me by an ankle. I tried to kick with my other leg, but he was too strong. He pulled me back down the stairs, chuckling every time the jarring contact of each stair caused me to gasp as white-hot pain shot through my injured thigh. Grant was enjoying my fear and agony, feeding off of it as though it were applause for his performance. In a sick way, I suppose it was.

I was pulled all the way to the bottom where Grant turned me roughly onto my back. He then leaned over me, his arms on either side of my body, trapping me there. "You see, sweetheart," he said conversationally, "if I stabbed you, it would spoil the continuity—the flow, as it were—of the previous deaths. No, they need to find you with seaweed wrapped tightly around your neck, your lovely body clasped in the cold embrace of the sea. Just like the others."

Yesterday I would have burst into laughter at Grant's florid speech, but under the circumstances his words were chillingly effective.

"And you see, Darling," he continued, leaning forward and placing a gentle kiss on my forehead, "You're the only one I can really take my time with. And because of our relationship, it'll be that much more special." He kissed me again, on the mouth this time. Nauseous with fear and revulsion, I jerked my head to the side to avoid his lips, striking out with my fists in an attempt to shove him away. He grabbed my wrists with one hand and my chin with other, forcing his mouth on mine again in a kiss that was meant to hurt. I retaliated by viciously biting his lower lip, causing him to jerk away with a yelp of pain.

The satisfaction was short-lived. His open hand slammed across my face, cutting my lower lip on a tooth and knocking my head against the edge of the stairs. Grant grabbed my throat and said tightly, "Don't do that again, Connie. You don't want me to lose my temper. Do you understand me?"

I managed to croak out a hoarse "Y ... yes."

Satisfied, he let go of my throat. "You're a very exciting woman, Connie. A pain in the ass as a director, far too opinionated for your own good and a little too independent. But very exciting. I'm going to miss you." He reached down and began working the buttons on my jeans. "Damn it, I wish you'd just let me use the knife! These things are plastered to your legs, it's going to hurt like hell to pull them off, you know ..."

He was right. It did hurt like hell, especially since he jerked them down far more roughly than necessary. I gritted my teeth, not wanting to give him any more satisfaction by crying out. The downward progress was halted by my boots, so Grant moved off me to remove them. I could only lie there, my legs hopelessly trapped in wet denim. "This really isn't what I'd hoped for us," he informed me, tossing one boot aside and working on the other one. "But it's better than watching you waste your time on a mediocre stuntman. Ah, there we go." The other boot came off, cast aside with the first. He renewed his efforts on my jeans. "You know, it was almost worth getting shot to see the suspicion fall on Alex. After all—" He gently patted his left shoulder. "—it *is* only a flesh wound."

As Grant started laughing, I suddenly understood the term 'righteous wrath' because the feeling swept over me like a hurricane. The colossal ego of the man infuriated me. I knew that although part of his sexual excitement was caused by my fear and the power he had over me, another part of him truly believed that I'd enjoy it. And the bottom line? Only an actor would commit murder because of a review.

My legs were momentarily freed as the jeans finally came off, Grant leaning back and slightly up with the momentum of the pull. It was the only chance I'd get and I took it. "You bastard!" I kicked up wildly with my good leg and connected hard with what I hoped was his groin. As he doubled over towards me, I followed up by slamming my forehead against his face, knocking him backwards.

Lightning flashed, showing me that the water was now several inches deep on the platform. I saw a glint in the water that might be the discarded knife. I crawled past Grant's prone figure as he lay groaning on the rock. Every movement was agony, but immobility meant death. Water hit me in the face as I neared the edge of the platform and scrabbled with numb fingers for the knife. Soon the platform would become dangerous. The force and depth of the waves would easily sweep us off.

The clouds broke apart for a moment, long enough for a stray shaft of moonlight to show me what I was seeking. It had settled into a depression in the rock and was now under several inches of water. Just a few more feet ...

A wave swept over me as the moon went back behind the clouds and my fingertips reached for the knife.

Something grabbed my ankle and pulled. My fingers slid ineffectually over the butt of the knife hilt and I screamed as Grant yanked again, shifting his grip higher on my leg directly where I'd slammed it on the rock. He tightened his fingers and laughed when I screamed again. I thrashed and kicked, wild with fear and pain. His grip broke for a second and I lunged for the knife again, but an incoming wave knocked me backwards directly into Grant's waiting arms.

I fought him, filled with a berserker rage, biting, clawing, hitting. Several of my blows connected and I had the satisfaction of seeing my nails rake furrows down his neck as he jerked his head aside at the last minute. The lightning obligingly illuminated the Cave at that moment. It showed the unbelievable fury that distorted Grant's face, making him truly ugly for those few seconds.

As thunder cracked, Grant hauled off and hit me in the face with a closed fist. I didn't quite lose consciousness but I was dazed enough to make it easy for him to force me to the ground, one of my hands trapped painfully beneath the combined weight of our bodies. I had nothing but a g-string to protect my skin from the abrasive rock and the chill water. I could almost hear Daphne's voice, "If you'd wear real underwear, Connie, this wouldn't happen." If I was channeling her, I could've used more useful advice.

Grant pinned my other hand to my side, grabbed my hair and brought his face close to mine. Ignoring the waves that swept over us, he said quietly, "Do you know what it's like to die by strangulation, Darling? I'm told it's very painful, especially if it's done slowly, bit by bit. You'll take that last desperate gulp of air just as my hands tighten around your neck … but that will be used up very quickly as you panic, your chest tightening as your lungs start to strain for oxygen. It's like having a fire lit inside of you. And I intend to bring you to that point over and over again, until you beg me to finish it. Just to end the agony of not knowing if that time will be the last … or not. But don't worry. I still love you … so I'll make sure that your suffering is tempered by pleasure." Almost conversationally he added, "I've heard that sex and suffocation go well together."

I choked as a wave washed over us, covering my head for a few seconds. Something slimy draped over my face, adding to my panic as I fought for breath, spitting salt water out of my mouth only to have it replaced by more. Grant hauled my head above water by my hair, a strand of seaweed trailing off to one side.

"Drowning is not what I have in mind for you, don't worry. And now that the ocean has obligingly provided me with a tool …"

Grant let go of my hair and wrapped the seaweed around my neck with one hand. Water foamed about us as he said with pleasure, "I've wanted to try this ever since we watched *Rising Sun.*"

"You're sick!" I choked.

"I prefer to think of myself as open to new experiences."

The moon came out as Grant took hold of the seaweed and pulled it taut, reaching for the drawstring on his sweats at the same time. In doing so, however, he freed my hand. I used it, clawing at his face. He dropped the seaweed in order to protect his eyes. Seizing the advantage, I swung a fist, catching him square on the jaw. I twisted beneath him and managed to get my other arm free as well. Off-balance as he was, I was able to throw him off and roll away to the side.

I could no longer see the knife, but I made a lunge for the area where I knew it had been. A wave crashed over us, its retreat to the ocean threatening to take me with it, but I found the depression and felt the smooth wood of the knife hilt. My hand closed around it and I brought the blade up and out just as Grant seized me by my poor abused hair and hauled me back. I slashed him across the shoulder, ripping his sweat shirt. He let go of me as I made another swipe, barely missing his face this time. He recoiled at that but then feinted in, dodging a thrust aimed at his chest. He grabbed me by the wrist and twisted my arm sharply, jerking it to one side. The knife went flying off of the platform into the water.

Grant hit me again, open-handed this time, knocking me back against a cement piling. Another blow sent me to my knees and a third took me flat on my back, stunned. Once again Grant straddled me, pulling the seaweed into a taut noose around my neck. And once again he fumbled with his sweat pants, his breathing heavy from a combination of exertion and excitement.

I'd always bought into the myth of my own invulnerability, sure that I could handle anyone or anything with the skills I'd learned. But I didn't have the strength to stop Grant from doing whatever he wanted to me. My best efforts hadn't been enough and there would be no last-minute rescue. For the first time in my life, I truly believed that I was going to die, and in a bad movie moment, no less. I shut my eyes as he reached for me.

His fingers were hooked over the elastic of my g-string when someone yelled my name from the archway. Grant froze.

Even over the storm I recognized the voice. It was O'Donohue. And then I heard Alex call my name as well. What do you know, the cavalry had arrived after all.

As the urgency of the situation became apparent, all thoughts of re-enacting a scene from *Rising Sun* vanished from Grant's mind. Pulling his sweatpants back up, he grabbed me, forcing me to the edge of the platform under cover of the pilings and the dark. I screamed Alex's name as I struggled, guessing what Grant now had in mind.

Another monstrous wave rolled in, obscuring Grant's movements as he shoved me as hard as he could. I went off the platform and into the water. grabbing for the wooden post as I fell in. Somehow I managed to catch hold of it and I clung for dear life.

What happened next was so ludicrous that I found it hard to believe even while it was happening.

Grant seized one of my hands and pretended to pull forward, all the while trying to pry my fingers loose with his other hand. During this, he yelled, "Hang on, Connie! I've got you! Don't give up!" He started smashing my fingers with his fist. I could feel my grip give way under his blows but I still hung on grimly, even as I realized with a doomed certainty that my rescuers wouldn't be able to reach us in time, if indeed they could make it through the water at all.

"O'Donohue, she's slipping!" Under the cover of darkness, Grant struck at my head. My vision blurred and my grip began to loosen. The combination of Grant's blows and the battering push and pull of the water was weakening the last of my resistance.

"Connie, hang on!" Alex's voice, closer this time.

"Don't worry, Sergeant," yelled Grant. "I've got her!"

I opened my eyes as a shaft of moonlight showed Grant's face clearly. It was unbearable that my last sight would be his smugly triumphant expression. He'd walk out of this scot-free, having tried his best to save me.

As he drew his arm back for the final blow that would send me out to sea, lightning flashed and a wall of water crashed over my head, enveloping Grant as well. Already overbalanced, Grant was swept off his feet and into the wood rail by the receding water. Weakened by the storm's battering, the rail cracked as Grant slammed into it. Both the section of railing and Grant pitched into the sea.

Nature had one last laugh by giving me enough light to see the look on Grant's face as he fell head first into the water. His final expression was total disbelief that this could happen to him. He hit his head with a sickening crack on a submerged rock. I turned my head and watched him being pulled out through the cave into the open sea, even as my grip finally gave out.

I didn't even try to fight as the undertow started to take me after Grant, but once again I was stopped by a hand on my wrist pulling me back up towards the platform. Other hands reached down to pull me out of the water.

I looked up and saw O'Donohue and Alex at my side, Honey above me as all three men got me up on the platform, supporting me as they carried me over to the stairs.

I looked at all three of my rescuers as O'Donohue asked, "Connie, are you all right?" Even Honey looked concerned, bless his ferrety little face.

What could I reply to that? I could give them a list of aches and possible fractures, not to mention the damage done to my self-confidence. But all that came out was, "Cold ..."

Alex immediately stripped off his soaking wet shirt and draped it around me, doing more for my modesty than my body temperature.

"Damn it, Connie," he said in a voice fraught with a dozen different emotions, "Don't *ever* pull a stunt like this again!"

As if swimming mostly naked in a raging storm while battling with an ex-boyfriend-turned-murderer was something I did every day.

"Not to worry ... Thanks, Alex. Thanks, O'Donohue. Thanks, Honey."

And with that, I passed out.

Chapter Twenty-Three

It was Monday morning and I was stretched out on the couch in front of the fireplace, my right leg elevated by pillows to avoid any contact with what turned out to be a really bad bone bruise. I'd spent all of Sunday in the hospital being treated for lacerations, bruises, a mild concussion, and my injured leg. I was lucky. According to the doctor at the hospital, I'd sustained as close to a hairline fracture as one could get without actually breaking the bone. So I was spared the discomfort and inconvenience of a cast, but would be using crutches and then a cane until my leg could support my weight on its own. Another reason to cut back on those cinnamon rolls in the morning.

I looked pretty bad, a black eye and a large bruise across one cheek being but two of my battle scars. I looked as though I'd gone a round or two with Mike Tyson. I was still a little woozy from the pain killers they'd given me at the hospital, but I'd recovered enough to hold court in the living room, sustained by the crackling fire and a cup of cocoa laced with Kahlua, Daphne's latest taste sensation.

Having Alex by my side didn't hurt either. He'd driven me home from the hospital this morning, a huge bunch of autumn-colored flowers and an unopened bottle of Laphroig waiting for me when I arrived. Daphne arranged the flowers in vases throughout the house and the Laphroig was stashed away for later this evening, provided I wasn't still popping pain pills.

The entire cast of MFH was over and I'd told the story of my harrowing adventures several times, with Alex's help. If O'Donohue and Honey hadn't dropped Alex back off at the library precisely when they did, I'd have ended up the same as Lucille and Burke and been found in the cave, seaweed wrapped around my neck. The only difference is that I would've been found without any clothes on, and while I've never considered myself a particularly modest person, that somehow made it even more horrible when I realized how close I'd come to dying.

"How did you figure out Connie was at the library?" Tasha asked Alex, blue eyes wide as she sipped her cocoa.

"Yeah," said Shaun. "Or where she went?"

"Elementary, my dear Watson," replied Alex. "Connie's car was in the parking lot, the door to Andy's office was wide open, and so was the side door. Connie's jacket was lying on the chair, so it didn't take too much to figure out she'd gone down to the beach. And since the Cave had already figured so prominently in the case, it just made sense. At least to O'Donohue. So Honey went the overland route to the Gnome's Den while O'Donohue and I took the beach."

"Did anyone actually suspect Grant?" asked Brad.

"Well, I suspected him of being an asshole." This was from Chris, stretched out on the rug in front of the fireplace, a plate of freshly baked snickerdoodles at his side.

I smiled in spite of myself and then said with total honesty, "Not me. I had Franklin pegged."

Franklin looked up from his contemplation of one of Daphne's Nick Diamond novels, an expression of mild surprise on his face. "Really? Why?"

I choose my words carefully. "Well, it's just that ... you sort of tend to get kinda bent out of shape whenever anyone criticizes Randell, and those letters to Lucille were pretty awful, so ..." I petered out, at a loss for words.

Franklin pondered this for a moment. "I guess I do overreact a little. Especially when I drink. But you really thought I was the killer?"

I know I looked embarrassed, but I owed the man the truth. "Well ... yes."

Franklin positively beamed. "That's *great!*"

Whatever floats your boat, I guess.

It was kind of weird having Franklin in the house considering that less than twenty-four hours ago he was our number one suspect, but he'd heard about my narrow escape and had stopped by to see how I was. I was touched that he'd made the effort. Even better, Franklin had visited Andy at the hospital yesterday and brought the good news that Andy was not only still alive, but that his condition was no longer critical. The wound had looked much worse than it was and he was expected to eventually make a full recovery.

I think that today Franklin had planned on delivering his news and the box of chocolates he brought for me and then leaving, but he'd discovered Daphne's collection of pulp detective fiction and had taken up residence in our living room, a stack of books at his side. Daphne was seated next to him and the two seemed to be having quite the time comparing opinions. This worried me. Maybe Franklin didn't cry over sunsets, but he did drink heavily and I wasn't sure I was up to his level of fanaticism on any sort of regular basis. Still, who was I to make judgments on the romantic choices of my pal and partner, all things considered?

The doorbell rang. Daphne reluctantly got up from her seat next to Franklin and went to answer it. I reflected that one silver lining to my injuries was that they exempted me from phone/door duty for several weeks at the very least.

Our latest visitors were O'Donohue and Honey, the former bearing a large box from Le Chocolate Shoppe, the latter wearing a distinctly uncomfortable expression. I wondered if it was because he'd seen me without clothes on. Or if indeed, it was because I was the first woman he'd seen nearly naked before. If I'd had one more pain pill, I think I would've asked him.

As it was, I greeted them both with effusive thanks, telling everyone that if it hadn't been for their quick thinking, I'd be dead. Honey puffed up with pride and kept his mouth shut, so I knew that for once I'd said the right thing. O'Donohue smiled and handed me the box of chocolates. I immediately ripped off the wrapping and opened it.

A half pound each of Bordeaux's and bittersweet truffles, and a pound of mixed. I raised my eyebrows. "You guys really *do* take detailed notes, don't you?"

O'Donohue smiled at me. "You never know when it'll come in handy. Although why you deserve these after doing something as idiotic as going to the library by yourself ..." I looked up at him, in the middle of devouring a truffle. Shaking his head, he abandoned his lecture. "Never mind."

As I set the box of chocolates on the table, something unpleasant occurred to me. "Did ... did you find Grant ... Grant's body?"

O'Donohue shook his head. "Not a trace of it. But that's not surprising, considering the storm. We may never find him if he was carried out to sea."

I shut my eyes and shuddered as it once again hit me that I'd been sleeping with a psycho. Alex looked at me in concern. "Does your leg hurt? Do you need another pain pill?"

I shook my head. "I'll be okay," I lied. I knew it would bother me for a long time, the fact that my judgment could be so out of whack that I'd once considered the possibility of spending the rest of my life with the same man who tried to kill me. Talk about a 10 on the embarrassment scale.

On the other hand, I'd been right about Alex. His phone call to Andy had been nothing more ominous than wanting to find out the best time to have flowers delivered. As for the hard feelings, once he'd had time to cool down and get over his initial shock at one of the bullets being real, he realized that I wasn't so much doubting him as trying to find an acceptable explanation for why I'd shot Grant. And he'd also realized that it wasn't fair to expect me to take his professional competency on faith when we'd only just met. In other words, his ego wasn't as important as I was, and that's all it took for me to let go of my injured pride.

Okay, it didn't hurt that the man was partially responsible for saving my life, but I would've forgiven him anyway. Even without the flowers and Laphroig.

O'Donohue was looking at me in some sympathy. "Connie, I know how you must be feeling, but it will pass. Believe me, time really does heal all wounds, no matter how cliché that might sound."

"Detective O'Donohue is quite right," Franklin chimed in solemnly. "As Mick O'Mallet would say, 'all troubles pass through quickly, like a bad burrito.'"

Both O'Donohue and I looked at him for a brief moment. Then I broke into a smile and said, "Thank you, Franklin. That helps put everything in perspective."

He nodded and went back to his book.

"By the way, Connie," O'Donohue said, "you were right about the heel mark."

"So Grant really didn't kill Damien Duran."

O'Donohue shook his head. "Nope. We took another look at the mark on Duran's body and it matched up perfectly to a pair of 4 inch stilettos owned by Ms. Lucille Monroe."

Daphne and I exchanged looks. I'd been right about Lucille after all. But who would have ever thought that one small, local festival could have spawned *two* egomaniacal, psychotic killers?

"Jeez," Daphne finally said. "I guess she really *did* take the Gala more seriously than we thought."

"Evidently," said O'Donohue.

Brad looked thoughtful. "I wonder whether she would have tried to kill you, Connie, if Grant hadn't killed her first."

I shuddered as the image of Grant strangling Lucille played in my mind, segueing into those last horrific moments I'd had with him.

O'Donohue quickly changed the subject. "Just for the record, I talked to your friend Sloan this morning."

"Not exactly our friend," Daphne amended.

"Um, and just for the record, so did I." I had the good grace to look embarrassed as I added, "I'd better warn you, when I spoke to him, I was pretty high on those pain pills."

O'Donohue groaned. "I'm sure we can expect an interesting article in tomorrow's issue of the *Post*."

"'*Cutie in Crime Nearly Slain by Beau Gone Bad?*'" I suggested, trying to get into the spirit of things.

"If we're lucky."

I sighed. "I still can't believe it was Grant."

"Well," sniffed Honey. "I had my suspicions."

We all ignored him.

Mavis joined the group, having popped in the back door—gee, what were the odds?—without knocking. "Hi, everyone!" She paused when she saw the two detectives, no doubt lamenting the fact that she hadn't changed out of stretch pants and oversized sweater into her red velour robe. Her chagrin was mitigated by a warm hug and a 'Mavis! You look radiant!' from Brad. She immediately brightened and handed me a bottle of wine, a box of pastries from a local patisserie, along with an assurance that she'd never liked Grant, and if I needed anything for the pain, she'd be able to 'fix me up in no time.'

"She means aspirin," Daphne said hastily as Honey raised an eyebrow and shot Mavis a suspicious glare. All we needed was to have the police think that our landlady was the drug czar of Emerald Cove.

Mavis had let the cats in with her entrance and I was soon cradling a purring Renfield in my arms. And a possessive one; Alex had his arm around me and Renfield promptly bit his hand. I hoped this didn't bode ill for the future.

Sam and J.D. decided to settle on Franklin, who looked momentarily surprised but made no effort to displace them even though their furry bulks obscured the book he was reading. He started petting them rather absently as Daphne looked at him with a speculative expression that made me think that for better or for worse, this could be the beginning of a beautiful friendship.

Mavis settled down in a chair across from me and said, "I've got some exciting news for you, girls! I've got a new tenant moving in to the guest house!"

Daphne and I looked at each other. This couldn't be good. "He's not a banjo player, is he, Mavis?"

"Oh no, nothing like that. This young man does historical recreation at Renaissance Faires!"

That didn't sound too bad.

"He's a Celt," continued Mavis, pronouncing the 'C' like an 'S'.

I was confused. "He's a basketball player?"

Mavis giggled. "Oh, I'm always getting that wrong. I mean, a Celt!" She used the hard 'C' this time. "He explained it very thoroughly. He's part of a Scottish clan! You know, like in *Braveheart!*" Mavis beamed at us as though this were the most exciting news in the world.

I was getting a bad feeling about this. Evidently so was Daphne, who asked, "What exactly does he do in his ... clan?"

"Why, he's the bagpiper!"

I shut my eyes. When I finally opened them, I said calmly, "Alex, would you please open the Laphroig?"

THE END

ABOUT THE AUTHOR

Dana Fredsti is an ex-B movie actress with a background in theatrical sword-fighting. She's spent the past seven-plus years volunteering at the Exotic Feline Breeding Facility/Feline Conservation Center (www.cathouse-fcc.org) in Rosamond, California. Dana's had a full-grown leopard sit on her feet, been kissed by tigers, held baby jaguars and had her thumb sucked by an ocelot with nursing issues.

She's addicted to bad movies and any book or film, good or bad, which includes zombies. Her other hobbies include surfing (badly), collecting beach glass (obsessively), and wine tasting (happily).

Along with her best friend Maureen, Dana was co-producer/writer/director for a mystery-oriented theatrical troupe based in San Diego. While no actual murders occurred during their performances, there were times when the actors and clients made the idea very tempting.

She's published numerous articles, essays and shorts, including stories in *Cat Fantastic IV,* an anthology series edited by Andre Norton (Daw, 1997), *Danger City* (Contemporary Press, 2005), and *Mondo Zombie* (Cemetery Dance, 2006). Her essays can be seen in *Morbid Curiosity,* Issues 2-7. She's also had several low-budget screenplays produced and currently has another script under option. Dana was also co-writer/associate producer on *Urban Rescuers,* a documentary on feral cats and TNR (Trap/Neuter/Return), which won Best Documentary at the 2003 Valley Film Festival in Los Angeles.

Printed in the United States
94760LV00005B/49-57/A